Opposites Attract

Ethan wasn't refined. He didn't open car doors or automatically guide her elbow when walking. But, when she talked, she felt he really listened. When he talked, she felt he spoke the truth. And when he looked at her, he really looked. He saw her – the good, the bad, the everything. Alexis had told him things about her life that she barely admitted to her best friend and he was still here, kissing her as if her past didn't matter. As he touched her, she felt as if he was accepting who she was, faults and all. She tried to catch her breath, but her heart was racing fast and her body was tight with longing.

Alexis refused to touch herself. She was already heated to the point of urgency and seeing her half-naked body, her dishevelled hair, was arousal enough. She wiggled her hips, finally deciding to push the bottoms off as well. There was no point in wasting time with undressing.

Opposites
Attract

Michelle M Pillow

In real life, always practise safe sex.

First published in 2005 by
Cheek
Thames Wharf Studios
Rainville Road
London W6 9HA

Copyright © Michelle M. Pillow, 2005

The right of Michelle M. Pillow to be identified as the Author of
the Work has been asserted by her in accordance with the Copyright,
Designs and Patents Act 1988.

Design by Smith & Gilmour, London
Printed and bound by Mackays of Chatham PLC

ISBN 0 352 34011 8

Chapter One

Upper East Side, Manhattan, New York City, New York.

This was a bad idea. No, it was a horrible idea. Driving cross-country from New York to San Francisco, California had to be a mistake. There really wasn't anything in the middle of the United States worth seeing, was there? Some wheat, maybe a cow or two? Isn't that why everyone took airplanes over it? And wasn't there a desert thrown in there somewhere? Didn't people die in deserts every day? Isn't that how they got their names, because they were deserted?

Alexis Grant shivered at the idea. Seated at a sidewalk café she looked into her roommate's expectant, hopeful face and she knew Susan wasn't kidding. Her friend wanted to do it. She wanted to get into a car and see all America had to offer. Only problem was, they didn't have a car. Well, Alexis had one, but it was a limo and it belonged to her mother, and she doubted the woman would let her take it cross-country.

Susan Chapel was Alexis's best friend. They'd met in college – all right, Susan went to college, Alexis went to college parties. Still, they met on campus, hit it off and after Susan graduated with a degree in literature they moved in together. Susan went on to be a teacher at a very prestigious private school while Alexis went on to attend bigger and better parties. They'd been roommates ever since.

'Oh, did I show you my new jeans?' Alexis asked as a distraction, moving her plate to the side to show Susan the pair of low-riders she had on through the glass table-top. 'They're Diesel, right? I usually don't like this designer, but I just had to have them. They fit too perfect.

I'm so glad I lost that extra five pounds. Talk about getting overweight.'

'I say gain the five back, you're skin and bones,' Susan said, winking playfully. The woman regularly had a smile on her face and Alexis loved the fact that she always tried to say something nice about everyone – no matter who they were. Though shy in social situations, Susan was a real sweetie. That's where Alexis's outgoing nature came in handy. They were a perfect fit.

'Ah, thanks, sweetie.' Alexis smiled. She angled her hips in the chair so Susan could see her jeans from the other side. 'They're cute, right?'

'They look exactly like the pair I got at the second-hand store for fifteen dollars. Please tell me you didn't pay full price.' Susan took a sip of coffee. 'You so don't need to spend a hundred dollars on one pair of jeans.'

'A hundred and thirty-nine, and ew! These are not like second-hand.' Alexis frowned. 'How can you buy used clothing? How do you know the person who owned them before you wasn't a prostitute? You might get some sexually transmitted disease just by putting them on.'

'It's not like I'm wearing vinyl hot pants,' Susan grumbled. 'And they're clean.'

'Ew! I'd never talk to you again if you wore hot pants.' Alexis giggled.

'You're such a diva. Anyway, Lexy, would you listen? Ted knows this guy, whose cousin's dad's best friend has this son, who's going to drive to California.' Susan smiled. Alexis wondered if the idea might just go away on its own – like if she stared at Susan with a blank look on her face for long enough. 'Anyway, the guy has room and said we could go along if we pay for part of the trip. It sounds perfect. I want to travel and you want to take pictures of stuff. This would make the perfect portfolio. I think we should do it. Every American should at least see their own country, right?'

'Uh, no. Why would I want to see the country? Every American should see Europe, but not the icky parts, just the nice ones like Rome and Paris. If you want to see

America, then just look around you at New York City. There's a reason why we get so many tourists. People come here to see America, not the desert. Everything that's great about our country is right here. We have Times Square, the Statue of Liberty, Ellis Island.'

'Do you even know what Ellis Island is?' Susan asked.

'Sure, people came over from Europe on boats and that's where they went first.' Alexis grinned. 'See, my point exactly. It's where all the tourists went to. They liked it so much that they became immigrants and just stayed.'

'Your sense of history is truly frightening.' Susan shook her head.

'Whatever.' Alexis motioned her hand in annoyance at the comment. 'Who cares about history? It's so yesterday.'

Susan looked slightly shocked, for a moment not realising Alexis's flippant joke.

'Well, get you!' she laughed. 'Why did you minor in history anyway?'

'Um, you were saying,' Susan answered instead.

'We have Broadway, the wonderful view from here in Manhattan of the bridge.'

'Brooklyn Bridge,' Susan supplied needlessly.

'Yes, thank you. We have Yankee Stadium, Chinatown, Central Park, the Village, Empire State Building, museums and –'

'Crime, poverty,' Susan inserted.

'Fifth Avenue for the best shopping. Though, did you notice that a lot of retailers are moving off of Fifth?' Alexis shrugged. 'Anyway, we have the best shopping.'

'Crime and poverty. Darcy Mayors said she was almost mugged last week by gang members.'

Alexis frowned, turning her eyes down to her plate. She leaned forward and said quietly, 'I don't want to talk about stuff like that.'

'Just because you don't talk about the bad, doesn't mean it didn't happen,' Susan said. 'You should try turning on the news sometimes. It might broaden your view of the world.'

'Why? So I can become an addict like you and watch it

every time I'm near a television? No thanks, sweetie. I figure you'll just tell me what I need to know.' Alexis leaned over and took a bite of her salad, stabbing a tomato with her fork as she looked around at the tall buildings. She loved everything about Manhattan – the smells, the look, the sound. She liked the traffic and people rude enough to mind their own business. She liked clubs that stayed open past midnight. She liked concrete and steel and buildings that didn't house farm animals, not that she could exactly remember seeing farm animals up close. Animals belonged in the zoo, where they were safely tucked inside a cage.

'Anyway, you live here so you know what we have. I rest my case. We've seen the best of America.' Alexis took another bite. She loved the sidewalk eateries of Manhattan. When the weather was nice, like this fine spring afternoon, it was as close to heaven as she was likely to get. The breeze was a little cool, carrying with it the smells of the garden next to the Southwestern Grill, and she was so glad she wore her new black cashmere sweater. She bought it to go with the jeans. How could she not? They looked too cute together.

'You're telling me a cross-country trip doesn't interest you in the least?' Susan persisted.

Alexis rolled her eyes. She was sure pointing out how grand New York was would've changed Susan's mind. Maybe she needed to take a different approach. 'Do we even know who this guy is? Or do we just take Ted's dad's uncle's cousin's nephew's word that he's not a psychopathic killer or a junkie or a ... parolee?'

'Ted's friend's cousin's dad's best friend's *son*,' Susan corrected.

'Thank you, schoolmistress Susan,' Alexis drawled sarcastically.

'Sorry, taking work home with me again. Now, I believe you were saying something about being an overly judgemental, paranoid –'

'Oh!' Alexis laughed, knowing Susan only teased. 'And

you are too easy-going for your own good. It wouldn't hurt you to be more suspicious of people.'

'My easy-goingness goes well with your many eccentricities.' Susan winked.

'I come from money, so I'm pretty sure that entitles me to a few eccentricities.' Alexis laughed, as she lanced another tomato.

'Like not being able to hold down a steady job?' Susan took a sip of her lemon water. 'Care to tell me what happened this morning with Mr Turner?'

'Uh, you know, same thing.' Alexis shrugged delicately.

'So basically you told him you didn't feel like getting out of bed before noon because you went to another nightclub opening to make an appearance.'

'Yeah, basically. As if I'd really miss an invitation to Bella's opening? That would be like committing social suicide.' Alexis made a face, unashamed. 'Don't worry about it. Employment is overrated. Besides, if I had to work, we wouldn't be sitting here enjoying this fine spring day at our favourite little sidewalk café. Which, I might add, is another wonderful thing about our city.'

'Alexis?' Susan asked, leaning forwards. 'You're avoiding, aren't you?'

'Avoiding what?' Alexis took another bite of salad, angling her arm so her diamond tennis bracelet wouldn't fall into her low-carb dressing.

'Do you want to go to California?' Susan sat back in her chair. 'You're always talking about moving there.'

'I talk about a lot of things that I don't really mean. Besides, honestly, why would you want to move anywhere? New York is the centre of the universe. Aliens could land and this is where they'd come to hang out.'

'Aliens?' Susan chuckled. 'Your defence is that New York now might attract aliens? Does our television talk to you? Are you hearing voices in your head?'

'Shut up, you know what I mean.' Alexis waved her fork lightly to dismiss the alien comment. 'Why do you want to move? We have a great apartment –'

'In your mother's hotel,' Susan interjected.

'Ah, my mother's five-star, Upper East Side hotel,' Alexis said. 'We have room service. We never cook.'

'Which your mother pays for.'

'Maids.'

'Your mother's.'

'Hey, why you getting down on my mother all of a sudden?' Alexis asked, frowning. This worried her. She couldn't lose Susan. She was the only person Alexis could stand being around for long periods of time. 'Are you saying you're unhappy?'

'No, it's just . . .' Susan frowned. 'Ted thinks that maybe it's time we did things on our own.'

'Oh, Ted thinks?' Alexis dropped her fork, losing her appetite.

'Well, your mother's not always going to be there to support us.'

'Oh, she doesn't support you.' Alexis reached to pat Susan's hand. 'You pay your own way, sweetie.'

'Fine.' Susan looked away. 'You won't be able to live off your mother forever.'

'I see.' Alexis hardened her expression. 'I don't think my life is any of Ted's business. I can't help it that he's jealous. I can't help that I was born with money. Does he think my life's a bed of roses? It's hard being rich. People think it's easy because I have money, but they're wrong. I'm always being looked at and I have it twice as bad because I'm pretty. I have to deal with jealousy all the time. In fact, just this morning, some scrubby little nobody, with that black gothic whatever make-up, was staring at me as I –'

'No, Alexis,' Susan tried to interrupt. 'I –'

Alexis's cell phone rang, cutting Susan off. Alexis held up her finger and reached down into her pink rabbit-fur handbag for her phone. Flipping it open, she said cheerfully, '*Buon giorno.*'

Alexis felt the blood rush from her face, as her mother's butler spoke in a rush from the other end. His stiff accent made the words all the more surreal. 'Mrs Grant . . .

arrested ... embezzlement ... agents...' She felt dizzy, sure she didn't hear him right.

'Wait,' Alexis said, stopping him mid-sentence. 'What do you mean my mother has –' she lowered her tone, covering the mouthpiece '– been arrested?'

'Alexis?' Susan asked. 'Lexy, what's wrong?'

Alexis's eyes widened. She felt as if she were drowning. Everything moved in slow motion. She blinked, looking at the waiter, who was suddenly at their table. She focused on his black vest and matching apron. The red rose on the breast pocket caught her eye and she stared at it. The waiter waved his hand in front of her face, drawing her attention back up.

'Miss? Miss?' She saw the waiter's lips moving, but couldn't hear his voice.

'All right, I'm coming home.' Alexis blinked rapidly, looking around. She felt faint, like she was falling. She heard Susan scream, before everything went black.

'Alexis?' Susan jumped up from the table, as the waiter caught her friend. She ran to the cell phone, picking it up. 'Hello? Who is this? What did you say?'

Susan listened, but no one was there.

'Miss,' the waiter said.

Looking at the man, she said, 'Get me some water. Now!'

'But, your cheque...?'

Susan ignored him, fanning Alexis's face in worry. Someone handed her a wet napkin and she pressed it to her friend's flushed cheeks. 'Alexis? Honey, wake up. Wake up. What happened? Who was that?'

Alexis blinked, coming back to consciousness. Susan felt as if a weight was lifted off of her. She'd been so worried. Alexis's mouth moved and Susan leaned down just in time to hear her whisper, 'Call a cab. We have to get home. They're taking everything.'

One month later...

The trial wasn't even close to being over, but Alexis's

life of privilege was. Men in cheap suits raided her apartment, laying claim to everything that wasn't tied down, treating her like she was the daughter of some Mafia kingpin. Everything was gone – the money, the servants, the hotel stocks, jewellery. Even the furniture had been seized by the government – at least the furniture that didn't belong to the hotel.

'Do you have any drugs in the apartment we should know about?' they'd asked her. 'Do you have any guns, knives, or other weaponry? Are you aware that your mother is under arrest for embezzling funds? Has she ever handed you strange packages and asked you to store them?'

What was she supposed to say to that? Alexis chuckled darkly, remembering how she'd replied. 'Yeah, my mother gave me a square-cut diamond and not a princess cut for my thirteenth birthday. It came in a box from the wrong jeweller. That was strange. She usually got the jewellery part right.' The agent looked like he wanted to slap her. Alexis didn't care. Didn't they have real criminals they could've been out arresting?

'Alexis?' Susan yelled, sounding oddly excited for such a horrible day. They were being kicked out on the streets like hobos and her friend was yelling in her happy voice. 'Alexis, are you here? Come on, I've got some great news.'

Alexis plucked a tissue from the box next to her on the floor. They were cheap tissues. She couldn't afford the lotion kind any more. She could barely afford a free drink of water. What was she going to do?

She didn't feel like talking to Susan, so she stayed hidden in her corner, sitting on the floor of her former home. The hotel manager had agreed to let her stay a few weeks to have time to pack. He was a nice man, one Alexis wished she had paid more attention to. But now her two weeks were up and she had to go. Susan convinced her to sell some of her clothing. She did, getting maybe a quarter of what she paid for it. Still, it wasn't a whole lot of money after she paid the bills her mother no longer could cover. Not paying wasn't a choice. News like that would've spread through her social circle, destroying her reputation. Alexis might be debt free, but she could barely afford a week at the Flea Bite Inn.

Susan said that Ted offered his place. The last thing Alexis wanted was to live with Susan's boyfriend. But where else was she to go? What was she going to do? He'd probably gloat that he was right when he'd said Alexis couldn't live off her mother for ever. How in the world had he known? Was it so obvious to everyone else that her mother was a criminal? Alexis had known the woman her whole life and didn't know she was a criminal.

She glanced around the living room. The penthouse boasted enormous windows that gave a panoramic view of the city in every direction. There was a concrete fireplace wall. The hotel provided big-screen televisions in both the master and secondary bedrooms and a flat screen in the living room, all of which included surround sound and DVD players. They even had a television in the bathroom and kitchen area.

The suite had hard-wood floors, vintage chandeliers and a sound system on the terrace. In the bathroom there was a two-person steam shower and a separate cast-iron, claw-foot bathtub. In the bedrooms they had king-size beds with feather white comforters and six full-length pillows.

The furniture was all custom-made. Alexis had chosen the mohair fabric sofa with the red fabric pillows and matching chair. She insisted the hotel decorator buy the Monaco hand-painted end tables and matching plant stand. She was the one who said hang neutral beige curtains to offset the red of the furniture. She picked the hand-woven rugs and Tiffany lamps. This was her home and now it was going to be rented to strangers.

'There you are, Lexy,' Susan said, coming around the corner. 'What are you doing on the floor?'

'Why are you so chipper?' Alexis grumbled, blowing her nose.

'I was just over at Ted's.'

'What, so you get laid?' Alexis frowned.

'Well, uh, yeah,' Susan said, looking slightly embarrassed.

'Lucky. I couldn't get laid if I paid a man,' Alexis said. She hadn't got laid once since her life had crumbled. It would just be her luck if her body had already rusted shut. A month without sex? If anyone asked her, that was the real crime in this whole situation. Did she even need to recall the fact that the agents had taken her 'toys' as well? Yeah, like she was going to have the lawyers get her vibrators back for her. The newspapers had been bad enough without adding that fuel to the fire.

'Lexy,' Susan said, her voice mildly scolding.

'I don't understand how my mother's bad decisions can affect me so much. Just because an ill-gotten fortune paid for my life doesn't mean my life has to be put into the newspapers. Have you looked at today's headlines? The tabloids are interviewing ex-boyfriends I never knew I had. Apparently, I've had sex in some fetish club with a whole group of them. They would never have dared to say that about me before. Now, there is no fortune, there is no life, no respect. My life is over. I'd be better off dead.' Alexis sniffed, feeling very fatalistic.

'Forget the papers. Didn't we say we weren't going to read them? I've even stopped watching the news, so you shouldn't start listening to it now.' Susan stroked back Alexis's hair. 'What's really going on, Lexy? Did you see your mother and her lawyer today?'

'He can't do much else for us,' Alexis said. 'He said it's better for my mother in the long run, if we just let the government have the rest of my things since I can't produce receipts for them. Who the hell keeps receipts for everything?'

Alexis took a deep breath, trying not to cry. Thanks to her mother's lawyer, Alexis managed to get some of her belongings back – clothing, her camera, Susan's stuff. But almost everything else had technically belonged to the hotel.

'We don't have a home. We don't have a car. Crissakes,

I can't even hold down a job. I barely have an education, unless a mail-order diploma from the Photography Institute and a fluency in Italian counts as a worthwhile education.' Alexis started crying anew, weeping into her hands.

'We have each other,' Susan said, sternly. 'And don't you forget it. Now, I want no more talk of dying. You're a fighter, Lexy. Now, what happened today with your mom? Did she look well?'

'It was awful, Susan.' Alexis sniffed, grabbing another tissue. She dried her eyes. 'I had to look at her through a pane of hard plastic. She was always so elegant and now she's been reduced to a cheap orange jumpsuit. I'm sorry, but that colour was all wrong for her. It drained her face of all life and she always had her hair perfectly upswept, you know. Now it's in an ugly bun. They didn't let her have make-up, so she looks all old and tired. I barely recognised the woman.'

'Well, Lexy, maybe make-up isn't what is important to her right now,' Susan said. 'What did she say?'

'You're on your own, kid. Find yourself a rich first husband.' Alexis swallowed, near tears as she thought about it. 'How am I supposed to find a rich husband in Manhattan? The whole city knows about Francine Grant's arrest. No decent family will touch me with a ten-foot pole.'

Susan opened her mouth, but nothing came out.

'Then to make matters worse, when I went out last night to the clubs to relax and forget, the doorman wouldn't let me directly in. He told me to wait in line like a damned poser. Alexis Samantha Wellington Grant is not a line-waiting poser. It isn't fair. I've done nothing to deserve this. I'm a good person. Well, in my heart I am. I never talk shop owners down on their prices. I always tip the wait staff – the ones who've done a good job anyway. I gave all of last year's designer clothing to charity auctions.'

'You're right, nobody deserves what you're going through,' Susan said.

'Oh, and three years ago, remember I hosted and

planned that event to benefit a local children's hospital. What was the name of that hospital again? St Hope? St Kids? Well, the event was fabulous. We raised several thousand dollars for the poor sick children and I wore the most beautiful black and gold lace, imported Victoria Royal gown.' Alexis cried harder. 'But there isn't going to be any more imported Victoria Royal gowns. No more Vera Wang or Helen Wang. No more DKNY. No Via Spiga or Versace. No more shopping in Italy. There isn't going to be any more designer anything. My life is over, Susan. I'm a nobody. I'm nothing.'

'Oh, OK,' Susan said, her voice so soft Alexis could barely hear it. 'Just calm down. We're not homeless. We're going to be just fine. That's what I came to tell you. I have a plan.'

'A plan to get our home back?' Alexis asked, hopeful.

Susan glanced around. 'No, that would require a miracle. We can't afford this lifestyle any more but, don't worry, I have a great plan. A perfect plan.'

'What?' Alexis was almost afraid to ask, but she was getting desperate.

'Remember I was telling you about that guy, Ethan James, who's going to California?'

'You mean the cousin's uncle's sister's brother guy?' Alexis sniffed, blowing her nose again. Her skin felt chapped and she reached next to the box of tissues for her La Prairie day lotion. She dabbed it under her nose. She wouldn't be buying any more of that for a while.

'Yeah, him. Well, he hasn't left yet. In fact, Ted said he met him and that he's still willing to take on passengers.' Susan smiled. 'You said you wanted to get out of here and get a fresh start. Well, let's do it. Let's go to California. It's summer and school isn't in session so it's not like I'll lose my job if I leave. Ted has said he wants to come. He has his laptop so I can check my email if they need me for any reason. It's perfect, Lexy. It's just what we need.'

Alexis baulked. Her nose was stuffy and it made her voice sound a little funny. 'No.'

'What? Why?' Susan sat back on her knees and grabbed

Alexis's hands. She squeezed lightly. Then, feeling the used tissue wadded in Alexis's palm, she grimaced and let go. Susan wiped her hand on her faded blue jeans.

'There's one small problem,' Alexis said, throwing the tissue away, only to grab another. 'The guy wants someone to help pay for the trip. I can't even afford a cab ride across the city, let alone a ride across the whole United States.'

'Ted doesn't think it'll be a problem,' Susan said. Alexis was really getting tired of what Ted thought. If Susan hadn't seemed so happy with him in the past, she would've tried to break them up. 'He says that Ethan's going to be working his way across. We can too. We'll find work. It'll be an adventure and Ted says that people are friendlier in the Midwest. They'd be willing to help a stranger out and give us jobs to do.'

Alexis studied Susan carefully, not relishing the idea of holding up a sign that said, 'Will work for food.' She started to protest, but her friend had a look of hope and excitement that she'd never seen in her. It sparkled in her blue eyes and shone like a beacon from her face. In light of her own uncertainties, Susan's enthusiasm was a great influence.

'What kind of job?' Alexis asked. She dabbed at her eyes. They were puffy and sore. 'I won't clean toilets.'

'Deal. I promise I'll clean any and all toilets we come across.' Susan stood up, reaching down to pull Alexis to her feet. 'Come on, Lexy, let's say goodbye to this place. Our futures might be a little simpler for a while, but when we get to California things will get better.'

'Promise?' Alexis faced Susan, needing someone to take charge, to tell her that everything was going to be all right.

'Promise.' Susan tilted her head to the front door. 'I've got doormen waiting to take our bags down. Ted is downstairs with a cab. We'll spend the night at his place and then tomorrow the four of us are off to California. Oh, this is going to be so much fun, Lexy. I promise you'll have a good time.'

Chapter Two

Ethan moaned, quickening his thrusts as he plunged into the blonde beauty beneath him. Ah, she felt damn good. Sex had to be one of the best inventions ever given to man. He was really going to miss New York City for this very reason. Not to worry, a man in his profession could easily get more sex buddies and they'd all be just as pretty as Sandy here. There was just something about a tattoo artist that drove the women wild. He was like a rock star without the music.

Sandy panted, spreading her legs wider, screaming, 'Fuck me! Fuck me!'

Ethan frowned, automatically leaning over to kiss her to keep her quiet. He'd told her before to stop doing that. He had neighbours. Then, remembering that he was leaving the next morning and this was his send-off present from her, he grinned. He stopped thrusting and flipped over on his couch, taking her with him.

Sandy was a stripper by profession and had the sexy body that went with the job description. Ethan reached for her fake breasts. They were enormous in his palms, a little stiff, but really fun to look at. She rode him harder as he tweaked her nipples.

Sandy screamed like a porn star. Ethan grinned. He knew she was screaming for effect more than from a natural physical reaction. He didn't care. It made him feel like a king all the same.

'Say my name, baby,' Sandy demanded, tossing back her head and swinging her dyed blonde locks back and forth as she wriggled around on his body. 'Tell me how you want it.'

Ethan took her hips and arched himself deep into her. 'Give it to me, Sandy. Ah, yeah. Just like that.'

Sandy tensed, looking down at him. She stopped moving. A pout on her face, she said, 'My name's Cindy.'

'That's what I said,' Ethan lied. 'Of course I know your name. Now, give it to me, Cindy. Ride me, baby. Ride me, just like a naughty little cowgirl.'

'Cowgirl?' Her frown deepened and she looked confused. Ethan wanted to growl in frustration. He bumped his hips, trying to get her to ride him to release. Damn, but he was close! 'You said you wanted me to be your princess.'

'And now I want you to be my dirty little cowgirl,' Ethan said. He pushed up, knowing he needed to take over the pacing again before he exploded in agony. If she kept stopping, he'd have to work twice as hard to get her to climax. 'Get doggie style for me. I want to ride my nasty little cowgirl.'

Cindy instantly flipped over. Ethan came up from behind her and slipped deep into her wet body. He thrust like a madman, reaching around to play with the swollen nub he found hidden in her soft curls. He could've finished if he wanted to nearly ten minutes ago, but it was a matter of male pride that he got the woman to climax. 'Mm, ride me, cowboy. Break this dirty little cowgirl in good. Yippee-ky-yi-yaaa!'

Ethan was glad she was turned around, because he had to suppress a laugh as she attempted her cowgirl screams. He felt his body nearing the end. He was close. He was coming ... coming ...

'Yee-ha! Ride 'em cowboy.'

He pumped harder, losing all amusement at her continued yells as he grabbed her hips. He held back, tensing as her body caught up to his. The moment she began to clamp and spasm, he let loose of his control, coming heavily into the condom he wore.

'Ah,' he grunted, going rigid as his hips jerked on reflex. Cindy fell forwards on the couch, panting and whimpering. Ethan fell back, lying on the opposite side.

'What time is it?' Cindy asked, breathless. A light sheen of sweat beaded her flushed features as she flipped over onto her back.

Ethan glanced around his barren two-room apartment. Basically there was his living room that doubled as a bedroom and tripled as a kitchen, and a bathroom. Everything but the couch and his alarm clock was packed up. Whatever couldn't fit into his suitcases had been sold for cash. Seeing the clock, he answered, 'About midnight.'

'Ah, shit!' Cindy cried, jumping up. 'I'm late for work again. Sal's going to be so mad at me. I'll be lucky if he doesn't fire me for sure this time.'

'You're his best dancer. He won't dare fire you.' Ethan watched her get dressed, finding it a particularly interesting show. He put his hands behind his head, not bothering to hide his nudity. Why should he? He worked hard for his muscled physique and liked showing it off. The small apartment reeked of sex, giving him a sense of satisfaction. Cindy fitted her tight body and large breasts into a barely there slip of a sequinned dress.

Hurrying over to him, as she put on her impossibly high heels, she leaned over and quickly kissed his cheek. 'Drive safe, stud. I'll look you up if I'm ever in San Fran!'

Ethan just smiled. He didn't move until he heard the door open and shut. Then, reaching down, he felt around in the dim light for his cell phone. Without bothering to sit up, he hit a button and began scrolling through his list of phone numbers. 'Let's see ... Rachel, Janet, Mandy, Tracy, Lindsey, April, Ginger ... Mm, Ginger, hello.'

He grinned and hit the button. Ginger was a freak who especially liked to be taken in the behind. Ethan chuckled. After his and Sandy's ... er, Cindy's session, he needed to take a shower anyway. Might as well kill two birds with one stone. The phone rang, and Ginger picked up with a breathy, 'Hello.'

'Hey, baby, it's Ethan. It's my last night in town and I was lying here all alone thinking about you.' He used the persuasive tone all women loved. 'Yeah, I'm going to California tomorrow to tattoo on movie stars. Want to come over? I really would like to see you. Ten minutes? Perfect. I need to take a shower, but I'll leave the front door unlocked. Yeah, baby, I'll see you in a few minutes. Oh, yeah, sure we'll watch a movie or something. Good idea.' Ethan glanced around. He didn't have a television anymore. He'd sold it for the trip. 'Yeah, me too, can't wait. Sure, I still got the piercings. I'm counting the minutes. Bye, baby.'

Susan shut the French door between Ted's bedroom and living room. Seeing Ted lying across his bed in black silk boxers, she sighed and made a face of relief. Alexis was finally asleep. Susan felt bad for her friend, knowing she needed her right now. Thank goodness Ted was such an understanding boyfriend. She knew Alexis wasn't the easiest person to put up with. Alexis was dramatic, demanding and a borderline diva. But she was also Susan's best friend and Ted respected that, even if he didn't understand it at times.

Ted wiggled his eyebrows and reached over to pat the bed next to him. Damn, but he was one of the sexiest men she'd ever seen. He had dark hair that flopped down over one eye and always looked as if he'd just woken up in a pleasurable mood. He wasn't too muscled, but was definitely toned. His broad chest had a small sprinkling of hair in the middle. It matched the dark treasure trail leading beneath his navel to his crotch. But Susan's favourite feature was his brown eyes. They were the kindest she'd ever seen on another human. It's what first made her ask him out six months ago. Even though she hadn't said it to Ted, or anyone else for that matter, it'd been love at first sight.

Susan grinned at his invitation and untied her black silk robe. It glided to the floor, revealing the metallic cross-lace corset she wore underneath. The underwire cups pressed her breasts up, giving her a decent amount of cleavage. The silver thong panties matched perfectly. Ted liked getting her pretty lingerie and she liked wearing it for him.

'Come here, gorgeous,' Ted said, his voice dipping.

Susan crawled up onto the bed. 'We have to be quiet. Alexis is sleeping.'

'Uh,' he pouted, giving her the 'I don't wanna' look.

'Sorry, marathon man,' Susan giggled.

'But it's going to be such a long drive. Who knows when we'll get another chance?' Ted said, reaching to pull her on top of him.

Her body settled into his familiar one. She instantly nestled her legs between his thighs, leaning over to kiss his mouth. He was aroused, the hard length of his cock pressed against her stomach, as his hands roamed down over her corset to grab her butt and squeeze. Susan pulled back with a half laugh, half groan. 'Oh, we'll get a chance.'

'Promise?' He grinned, looking so sexy her thighs tightened.

'Mm, yeah, I promise.'

'Can we still have quiet sex right now anyway?' he asked, again squeezing her butt and pulling her tighter to his body. The motion drew her cheeks apart in a way that drove her to distraction. Ted knew it too.

Susan leaned over and began kissing his neck. 'Mm, I don't know.'

'Well, how about a hand job?' he asked. Susan knew he was teasing. 'Can I get at least that much?'

'Sure, I'll go get you a box of tissue and some alone time,' she teased back. Ted growled, flipping her over onto her back. Susan giggled. 'Shh, you'll wake Alexis up.'

'You made sure to pack sexy underwear, right?' Ted leaned over to kiss the top of her breasts, stopping to flick his tongue down into her cleavage.

'Maybe,' Susan answered.

'Can we have sex in every state along the way?' He drew his hand up, cupping her chest as his legs settled between her thighs. Burying his face in her cleavage, he pushed her breasts up to smother his face, stifling a groan.

'Maybe,' she giggled.

'Damn, you smell good.' He took a deep breath from

between her breasts and let loose a throaty groan of appreciation.

'I taste better.' Susan parted her thighs.

'Oh, yeah?'

'Mm-hmm.'

Ted eagerly took the invitation and kissed his way down her body. He stopped at her chest, pulling her nipples out over the top. Susan moaned, wiggling her hips against him. He sucked her nipples between his teeth, giving each ample attention before moving on. Kissing between the cross-laces of her corset, he made his way down the centre of her body. His tongue dipped into her navel, swirling it. She arched her back in pleasure. Hooking her panties, he pulled them down over her hips.

'Mm, you shaved. I like it,' Ted said.

Susan glanced down. He was positioning himself between her thighs. Looking up at her, he moved to lick along her clean-shaven folds, drawing his tongue down her slit. Focusing on his efforts, he twirled the tip over the sensitive bud he found hidden.

'Ah!' Susan sighed breathily, trying to stay quiet. She thrashed on the bed, reaching to pinch her nipples. Ted sucked her clit between his teeth, flicking his tongue back and forth. A thick finger slipped inside her pussy, working slowly in and out of her opening, rubbing her sweet spot. She clamped her thighs down hard on his head, holding him to her as she rocked her hips to his mouth. 'Ah, Ted, ooh. That feels so good.'

Her stomach tightened and she bit her lip to keep from moaning too loudly. He kept his finger moving inside her as he pulled himself up between her thighs. Sliding his hand under the pillow, he grabbed a condom and tore the package open with his teeth. One handed, he slid the condom over his erection. Then, removing his hand, he replaced his finger with his cock, thrusting into her ready body.

She loved being with Ted. He knew just how to stroke her, how to make her feel beautiful and loved. When he looked at her, it was as if she was the only woman in the world.

Susan lifted her leg over his shoulder, opening herself up to him. Ted groaned, working back and forth, going deeper with each pass. He braced his weight on his hands, moving in such a way that his body rocked along her sensitive bud. Each push sent wonderfully erotic sensations through her. She freely touched his chest and arms, amazed each time they came together by how wonderful he could make her feel. No matter how often they had sex, she never got tired of it. He knew all the right places to touch, the right pressure to use.

Susan moved her hips in circles against him, hitting her clit even harder. Her orgasm hit her like a wave, rolling over her body until she could barely breathe. Her sex clamped down on him hard. Ted buried himself to the hilt, jerking above her as he came.

'Ah, baby, you feel so good,' Ted whispered next to her ear, stopping to kiss her lobe. 'I'll never get tired of doing that.'

'You better not,' Susan said. 'Or I'll just have to get kinky on you.'

'Mm, kinky, you say.' Ted leaned up and grinned. 'Well, maybe I am a little tired of it.'

'Oh, you!' Susan hit his arm, giggling as he kissed her.

Alexis lay on Ted's brown leather couch. She was wide awake. Ted's apartment was nice, true to the industrial, unpretentious style of the Meatpacking District. Not so nice as her former penthouse, but elegant with classical lines. Ted was a polo shirt, khaki pants kind of guy. It went well with Susan's dressy casual style.

Ted was by no means a rich man, but he did rather well for himself. His bookshelves were filled with books he'd actually read. A couple of photographs hung on the wall – one of a sidewalk, another of a sidewalk café in Paris. Susan had bought them for him from a street vendor.

By the occasional soft noise coming from Ted's bedroom it was easy to guess what he and Susan were doing. It's not that she wanted Ted for herself, but she couldn't help but be jealous of her friend. It felt like an eternity since she'd been laid. Well, a little over a month. After her mother's arrest hit the news, every one of her lovers had quit returning her calls.

She'd only had two half-offers in the last month. One was the pizza boy who'd offered to buy her pizza for her when her credit card was declined. She'd been desperate, for both attention and food, but she'd never be that desperate. The second offer was from one of her lovers who had wanted her to use the back entrance to his home so he wouldn't be seen with her. Yeah, like she'd lost all self-pride.

Feeling the ache in her loins, she sighed. OK, so she was pretty close to losing all self-pride. It seemed like everyone was getting laid but her.

Maybe pizza boy was free?

Argh. What was she thinking?

Alexis turned into the couch cushion and pulled the pillow over her head. There, now she couldn't hear them. How long could Ted and Susan have sex anyway? Didn't they remember they had to get up early tomorrow to go to California? Shouldn't they be sleeping instead?

Alexis sighed, wallowing in her misery. California. It was a good idea. It had to be. There she could get a fresh start. She wasn't so foolish to believe they wouldn't have heard of the now infamous Francine Grant there, but they might not know Alexis Grant. Maybe she'd even reinvent herself like a movie star. She'd have to work on finding a new name.

Closing her eyes, she tried to go to sleep. Ted's light moan penetrated her sound barrier. She grimaced. Yep, everyone was probably getting laid tonight but her.

Ethan honked his horn twice as he waited for his travelling companions. He wondered if they'd even hear the horn over the loud construction in the background. A couple of the men hadn't moved since he'd pulled up, leaning against their work truck as they made loud cat-calls to a leggy blonde. Ethan couldn't help but laugh. It seemed everywhere he went construction workers were all the same. No woman was safe when it came to their shameless flirtations. Though, as the woman walked by him, he could understand their attraction to her. A woman didn't dress in a short skirt and high heels unless she wanted to be noticed. He smiled and couldn't help but think that in this neighbourhood it was hard telling if the blonde was really a woman.

Turning his attention back up the side of the brick building, he hoped they didn't try to bring too much luggage. He'd told Ted to pack light. His 1965 Lincoln Continental might be a big car, but there was only so much room in his trunk after tattoo equipment and his luggage. He wasn't going to throw any of it out. How else was he going to pay his way across?

By taking companions with him they should make fairly good time, not that he had anywhere he had to be by a certain day. Going there was an adventure in and of itself. He could easily go on his own, but it would be nice to have someone help with the driving and someone to talk to when the highway seemed to stretch a little too long.

Leaning against his hood, he sighed. The Meatpacking District used to be one of his favourite sections of the city. The district's brick streets and awnings had a gritty, raw feel to them as if straight out of a 1970s gang movie and, being one of the last market districts in New York, it was bound to have a little of that working-class charm you couldn't find in Chelsea. But as of late the Chelsea crowd was slowly taking it over with fancy restaurants and overpriced galleries. They nestled right next to the few remaining meat businesses, most of whose low-rise build- ings still reflected the turn of the century style in which they were built. It was morning but the area was already busy. Even with the upscale changes, this was still defi-nitely one of the more distinctive places in the city.

Ethan yawned. He was tired. OK, so maybe spending his last night in New York banging every sexy skirt wasn't the most responsible plan he'd ever come up with. But damned if he wasn't feeling relaxed today. Ginger had been a minx. Just like he planned, she'd hopped straight in the shower with him and he'd had her pinned against the stall wall before barely getting out a 'Hi, how are ya?'

Ethan knew two women were coming with them on the trip, Ted's girlfriend and her friend to be precise. Ethan didn't really feel like catering to two females, but what could he do? He really didn't feel like footing the bill for everything either. He'd already determined that there would be no sexual encounters with his travelling companions – at least not until they were in California. There was no reason to complicate the trip and the last thing he wanted was some girl hanging on him, thinking they were boyfriend and girlfriend. Ethan shivered. No thank you. But Ted seemed pretty cool. Hopefully the chicks would be too.

'What. Is. That?'

And, then again, maybe not.

Ethan frowned at the haughty voice. Tilting his head down to look over the top edge of his sunglasses, he grimaced. The woman was eyeing his car with a look of complete and utter disdain. With just one glance he knew the type. Rich. Spoiled. Aggravating. They were planning a road trip and here she stood in a silk floral dress – no doubt by some designer he never heard of. Didn't she get the concept of comfort? They weren't going to a fashion show.

Ethan sighed. She was pretty, but pretty in a way that was so fake it made him sick. Well, not so sick that he wouldn't be willing to sleep with her should she offer it up. Her dark hair was perfect. Her dress was perfect. Her strappy little high-heeled shoes were perfect. And her make-up and sunglasses and tiny purse? Yep, all perfect.

Ethan hated the look of her kind of perfection. He supposed it came from being an artist. He found perfection in non-perfection. This woman looked delicate, like a doll someone had kept on a shelf her entire life. Her hands were lifted up by her shoulders, as if she could contract some kind of disease just from looking at his car.

Please, not her, he thought, not saying a word. *Let her walk on by.*

Alexis looked at the horrible car. At least it was black, which was about the only good thing she could say about it. OK, it might have been a little naive of her, but when Susan said they were taking a car, she assumed the vehicle was made within the last five years. This giant monstrosity was hardly a safe mode of transportation. She had one word for it.

Ew.

Pulling the sunglasses from her face, she turned to study the man next to the car. This clearly was a mistake. For heaven's sake, he couldn't be her ride. His light-brown hair was short, spiky and tipped with the most ungodly shade of bright red – as was his goatee. He was also covered with tattoos – from his wrists to where his arms disappeared under his raggedy old T-shirt. Even the side of his neck had some sort of fire growing over it like fungus.

'Mr James?' she managed, her voice tight.

The man nodded. Was it just her, or was there something very gangster about the way he tilted his jaw up at her? All right, he probably learned the attitude in prison. Alexis took a step back. If she could just edge to the building before he got any ideas, she'd run back to Ted's apartment and bolt the door. If he didn't leave, well, they'd just call the police.

'Oh, wow,' Susan yelled, coming from the stairwell. Alexis tried to grab her friend's arm as she passed, but missed. 'Cool wheels.'

Ethan pushed up from the car, grinning at Susan. Her stomach tightened at the look and a shameful tingling erupted inside her. She suppressed it, refusing to let her lack of sex make itself obvious to this nasty tattoo artist. Alexis watched, her mouth open, waiting for her chance to rescue her friend so they could escape.

'Thanks,' Ethan said. His voice was low and primitive, and his accent was only lightly influenced by New York. If she had her guess, he was born elsewhere. Alexis shivered. OK, so he had a nice voice. So did some serial killers, she imagined.

'I did most the work myself,' said Ethan. 'It's not finished yet.'

'What is it?' Susan asked, giggling. 'Sorry, I know nothing about cars, but I love looking at them. This one has such character.'

'Yeah, that's what I thought when I first saw her. It's a 1965 Lincoln Continental.' Ethan smiled. 'It's a work of art, or at least will be when I get done with it. There's a shop in California that I heard about that specialises in custom –'

'It's old,' Alexis said, her tone condescending. She wrinkled her nose in disgust. 'Surely, this thing is not safe.'

Susan paled, frowning at her. Alexis shrugged. What was the big deal? It was the truth. 1965 was old, especially for a car.

Ethan looked at Susan. 'Is your friend OK? She does know I can hear her right?'

'I'm Susan.' Susan grinned, holding out her hand. 'Ted's girlfriend. Thanks so much for letting us tag along. This is going to be so much fun.'

'Hey, glad to have the company,' Ethan said. 'I didn't really feel like driving it by myself.'

'I see you met Al –'

'Sam,' Alexis interrupted. She gave Susan a meaningful look. Susan frowned, even as she shrugged. 'My name is Samantha Wellington.'

'O-K,' Ethan drawled, looking her over. She couldn't see his eyes through the sunglasses he wore, but she knew he was looking. All men did. He was probably contemplating where in the US he was going to hide her body after he finished doing unnatural things to it. Alexis felt a jolt of desire. OK, the fact that she was becoming aroused by a nasty tattoo man only meant she'd been too long without a vibrator.

'Um, Susan, can I talk to you for a minute?' Alexis waved her friend over.

'You two got bags?' Ethan asked. 'I want to hit the road.'

'Hey, yeah, they're up here,' Ted said from the stairwell, carrying down his luggage. 'Want to give me a hand?'

Alexis waited until Ethan passed her before saying to Susan, 'Are you insane? We can't go on a road trip with him. He's been in prison.'

Susan frowned.

'Did you see the tattoos?' Alexis persisted.

'Not everyone who has tattoos has been to prison, Alex –'

'Sam. I decided last night I'm changing my name to Samantha Wellington. Sam for short.'

'What is going on with you?' Susan asked. 'Is this some sort of mental breakdown? Sweetie, I know you've been under a lot of stress, but this is a vacation. You're supposed to relax. OK? Promise me you'll mellow out and take it easy on Ethan. I know how you can get.'

'Hey, look, thanks and all, but I'm not riding in a car with him. He's probably running guns or dope or something.' Alexis lowered her voice to a whisper. 'I've heard about this. I'm not going to be a patsy for some ... *criminal.*'

'I can still hear you,' Ethan said behind her back, sounding amused.

Alexis turned to glare at him, only to stop when she saw he was carrying her luggage. Popping his trunk with a button on his keychain, he tossed her first bag in. She gasped, fearing he was going to launch her camera next. Screaming, she ran to pull the camera bag away from him.

'Hey,' Ethan growled, as she scratched him in the process. 'What's wrong with you, lady? Are you mental?'

'Don't call me mental,' Alexis spat. 'I'll carry this myself.'

'That's all you had to say, doll.' Ethan shook his head and moved to help Ted pack the other suitcases so they'd fit.

'I'm not a doll,' Alexis said. She saw a grey plastic box in the trunk and shivered. He probably kept the weapons he used to murder people inside it.

Ethan gave her a quick once-over. 'Uh-huh.'

'Ugh.' Alexis rolled her eyes at him. Grabbing Susan by the arm, Alexis pulled her friend away from the car. 'I'm not going and neither are you.'

Susan sighed. 'You have to go. You have no place to live, no money, no –'

Alexis glared. Under her breath, she hissed, 'Fine.'

Susan smiled, though it was strained. Alexis knew she was trying her friend's patience, but could Susan really blame her? They knew nothing about this man.

'You want to pat me down for drugs or are we ready to go?' Ethan asked, smirking. Alexis frowned. Oh, this man was too much.

'I'm ready.' Susan grinned and threw her arms wide, yelling, 'Goodbye, Manhattan!'

Ted laughed, opening the car door for her. With a gallant sweep of his arm, he ushered Susan into the back seat only to climb in behind her. The heavy weight of the door caused it to fall shut. Alexis walked over and tapped her foot as she waited for Ethan to open the passenger door for her. She gave him an expectant look. He glanced at her, the door and then back to her. Without saying a word, he climbed into the driver's seat and left her standing on the sidewalk.

'Good to know he lacks for manners as well,' she mumbled, pulling her door open herself, careful not to ruin her manicure on the handle. Sitting on the black leather seat, she turned her eyes to the window and didn't say a word. Ethan started the car and she was amazed that it sounded quiet. She braced herself, waiting for the engine to backfire like she'd seen in movies. The car slipped into gear without so much as a choke.

Susan giggled in the back seat at something Ted said and Alexis could hear them kissing. She closed her eyes. This was going to be a long trip.

Chapter Three

Ethan glanced over at the passenger seat. 'Sam', as she wanted to be called, stared out the window. Her body looked to be wound so tight, it was like she thought she'd get a sexually transmitted disease just from sitting on his seats.

He looked over his car and didn't see what the big deal was. His car was a beautiful machine – one he'd put way too much money into. Though, to be fair, he'd done most of the work to it himself. The silver and black dashboard was a true work of art, as were the silver-plated foot pedals. It had clean, formal lines and a beautiful black leather interior with white accents. The suicide doors were factory, but he'd put on a new grille and custom wheels. It had power brakes, power steering and power windows. The V8 engine could purr like a kitten or roar like a lion.

He glanced at the woman again. She was so close to the door she looked ready to bail if he so much as tried to touch her. He had no desire to touch her. Well, that wasn't exactly true. The wind had blown her skirt up slightly as she belittled him and his life of crime to her friend and he'd seen two very delicious thighs. Hey, he was a man. Just like he could get a woody looking at some actress on TV, so could he get hard looking at the little ice princess next to him. She was slender, too slender. No doubt she was on some kind of diet. Her kind always was.

Ethan didn't mind a little meat on his women. In fact, he much preferred them to be softer. That's how women were made to be. How in the evolution of culture they ever got to the point that it was considered sexy to be thin as a rail with bones poking out, he had no idea. Give him a softer woman any day. Someone who was ten pounds overweight – just the right size to be damned sexy in a dress and still have a nice soft feel to hold on to while he slept with them. Like Susan in the back seat. She was a nice size and cute too. Besides, she liked his car. That was always a plus in his book.

Glancing in his rear-view mirror, he reminded himself that Susan was taken. Too bad. Just thinking about sex had made him hard. He shifted uncomfortably on his seat. He would've thought he got enough action the night before.

He glanced over at 'Sam'. Hell, he knew who she was. Alexis Grant. He read the papers. Of course, Miss High and Mighty would never believe he could read – what, with being in prison and all. He frowned. Had she actually said that? And in front of him? What a bitch.

'So, Ethan,' Susan said, leaning up to rest on the edge of the front seat. New York City was slowly disappearing into the distance. It had taken a few hours to get off the island of Manhattan. Thankfully, traffic hadn't been too bad. 'What do you do?'

'I'm an unemployed tattoo artist,' Ethan said. Alexis snorted. He chose to ignore her.

'Is that why you're going out to California?' Ted asked.

'Yeah, going to open my own shop.' He got nervous and excited every time he thought about it. 'I met up with a piercer last year at the Las Vegas convention. Thought I might look him up and see if he wanted in on it.'

'What kind of business plan is that?' Alexis demanded, turning her dark eyes to him.

'I got a plan,' Ethan said. He gripped the wheel tighter and felt the tension working its way up his arms.

'What? Look up some stranger you met at a convention and maybe open a shop?' She shook her head. Mumbling, she said, 'That's not a plan. That's stupidity.'

Susan quietly pulled away, sinking into the back seat. An uncomfortable silence followed. Alexis didn't seem to notice. Ethan shook his head. This woman was really too much. He hadn't been in prison before, but he might just be after this trip – for throwing the she-bitch out of a moving vehicle.

'You know, doll, I've never been in prison so you can ease up on the fear,' Ethan snapped.

'I was arrested once,' Susan said, her voice cheery. 'In college.'

Ethan chuckled. It was obvious Susan was trying to lighten the mood.

'You did?' Ted asked. 'For what?'

'Um,' Susan sounded guilty. 'Jaywalking ticket I forgot to pay.'

Ted laughed. 'My little rebel.'

'I got you beat,' Ethan said.

'I bet you do,' Alexis said under her breath. He did his best to ignore her.

'I've only been arrested one time and that was for drunken misconduct when I was sixteen. I'd been caught peeing in public at our town's annual Thanksgiving Day Parade.'

'You did not,' Susan said.

'It was a dare. I hit one of those stupid floats,' Ethan said. He didn't think it was such a big deal. It hardly qualified him for America's Most Wanted. Besides, he was still kind of proud he was able to hit the moving target from the kerb. 'My family still plays the news footage every year at Thanksgiving. It's a new James family tradition.'

Susan and Ted laughed. Alexis said, 'How quaint.'

'Listen, doll, I don't know what your problem is, but you better stop taking it out on me or I'll pull this damned car over and let you walk your scrawny ass back to New York. That is if they'd even let you back in.' Ethan forced his hands to relax as he dropped one to his lap. There was no way he was going to let Alexis know she was getting to him. Her kind was like piranhas. They liked attacking the weaker fish.

'You can't threaten me,' Alexis gasped. The look of stunned amazement on her face was priceless. Ethan would've traded his favourite tattoo machine for a picture of it. He'd hang it in his new shop, right on top of a dart board. 'How dare you speak to me that way?'

'It's my car,' he said dryly. Her mouth opened, but no sound came out. She snapped it shut and glared out the car window. Directing his question towards the back seat, he asked, 'So, what's your guys' plan?'

'I work online as an internet stockbroker,' Ted said. 'So basically, I can do that anywhere.'

'What about you?' he asked, glancing over his shoulder at Susan.

'Oh, you know, get apartment, get jobs,' Susan said. He looked at her reflection in the mirror. She was staring at the back of Alexis's head. Ted met Ethan's eye and gave an apologetic glance to the woman in the front.

Ethan shrugged it off. He was irritated, but he wasn't going to let it bother him. Maybe they'd just got off on the wrong foot. Glancing across the seat at Alexis, he stiffened. And, then again, maybe not.

Several hours and a gas station on the New York–Pennsylvania border later, Alexis still stung from Ethan's remarks about her butt. In fact, she was so self-conscious about it that she'd made her way to the gas station bathroom to check it out. It looked the same to her, but maybe it really was scrawny. She resolved to start doing leg lifts immediately.

The bathroom was disgusting. Toilet paper stuck to the dirty tiled floor. Used paper towels were piled so high on the trashcan they fell over the side. Alexis didn't dare look, but some kind of water leak came from underneath a stall door. Really, what had she expected? This bathroom had to be symbolic of the whole trip, perhaps of her whole new life.

Alexis took a deep breath and then another. Tears welled in her eyes. Her life had become a dirty bathroom. It would explain why, for brief instances during the drive, she thought Ethan looked almost cute.

'Hey, Al – ah, Sam?' Susan called, knocking on the door. 'You all right in there?'

Alexis sniffed, looking around for a tissue. She didn't dare touch anything. Dabbing her wet eyes with her fingers, she took a deep breath. 'Come in.'

'The door's locked,' Susan called.

Alexis rolled her eyes and unlocked it. Susan looked around. 'Why's the door locked? There are like five toilet stalls in here.'

'I needed some private time,' Alexis said.

'Oh, your period didn't start today, did it?' Susan asked, instantly sympathetic. 'Do you need something? I might have some pads out in the car. That would explain why you're so irritable today.'

'No, my period didn't start.' Alexis sighed. 'Thank God, I could not deal with that right now.'

'Then what are you doing in here?' Susan glanced around.

'I told you.' Alexis turned to the mirror, moving back and forth as she looked at the way the straight skirt pulled against her as she moved. Her butt didn't look too bad so long as the skirt was moving around it. The dress was by designer Helen Wang. It was one of her favourites. The charcoal flower print on lilac silk chiffon was a gorgeous combination. The dress was sophisticated, yet light and fun with its ruffled bodice and spaghetti straps. Luckily, when the agents took everything, the dress had been at the dry-cleaners, or they would've taken it along with everything else. It really must have been divine intervention that she finally remembered to pay one of the hotel maids to take her dirty laundry. 'I needed some private time. I've been cooped up in that car with Mr Insufferable for so long I was going crazy.'

'Ah, it's only been a few hours and he's hardly said a word to you,' Susan said, frowning. 'I think he's pleasant. You should be a little nicer to him.'

'Me? Nicer to him?' Alexis balked. 'Did you hear the way he talked to me? He's already threatened to do me bodily harm.'

'What? He threatened to hurt you?' Susan asked, finally looking appalled. 'When? What happened?'

'You were there,' Alexis said, shaking her head. 'Remember, he threatened to throw me out of the car.'

'Lexy –'

'No, it's Sam,' Alexis corrected.

'Fine, *Sam*, I wanted to threaten to throw you out. You insulted the man's car, called him a criminal and assumed he'd been to prison because he has tattoos.' Susan took a deep breath. 'I think you might have deserved that one.'

Alexis had never seen her friend so worked up. She bit her lip. 'He said I had a scrawny ass.'

Susan blinked several times before laughing softly at that. 'What does he know? He's a man. He probably just meant you're skinny. I've been telling you that for ever now. You should gain some weight.'

Alexis sniffed. Smiling gratefully, she said, 'Thanks, sweetie, you always know what to say to make me feel better. All right, I'll try to be good. I promise.'

'Thank you,' Susan said. 'Now, come on, the guys are ready to go.'

Alexis followed Susan out of the bathroom and through the crowded aisle of the gas station. Ted was paying for a couple of drinks at the counter. The sales clerk, a middle-aged man in a red vest, barely even looked up as he counted back change. Ted in turn ignored the clerk. He glanced at Alexis. 'You want anything?'

'No, I'm good. Thanks.' Alexis forced a smile, thinking, *See, I can be good.*

Alexis walked to the car. Ethan leaned against the hood, his arms crossed over his chest, his head thrown back as the light breeze tried to whip his spiky red-tipped hair. His T-shirt moulded his torso, blowing up slightly at the stomach. What in the world possessed a man to get that many tattoos on him? She didn't understand it at all. It wasn't as if he was ugly to begin with. Sure, a little band of barbed wire if you were going for the rebel look or that black tribal stuff, but a whole arm? Two arms full of bright colours? And who knew what else.

Her eyes dipped over his stomach and thighs. OK, why

was she suddenly curious to actually see what else for herself? Telling herself to say something nice to him, she said, 'You'd look better without the red goatee.'

Ethan tilted his head down, looking over the top edge of his sunglasses. Slowly, he pulled them off his face. Blue, his eyes were blue with just a hint of green. She was surprised to find they were very pretty. Slowly, he looked her over and she felt her body heating at the way in which he seemed to take in her every curve. Breathless, she waited for him to speak. 'You'd look better if your body could actually fill out that dress.'

Alexis gasped, too stunned to retort. She didn't move as he slipped his glasses back on and walked around the car to get in.

'Let's go,' Susan said. Ted opened the door for her. 'I'm ready to roll.'

Alexis opened her own door, sliding into the passenger seat. Without looking at Ethan, she lifted her chin and said, 'I need you to stop somewhere.'

He turned to her. 'We are stopped somewhere.'

'This place won't work,' Alexis insisted. 'I need you to stop some place else.'

'For what?' He was gritting his teeth now. She could actually see it.

'I need to use the restroom, if you must know.' Alexis pressed her lips tightly together and gripped her little handbag.

'Didn't you use the bathroom inside?' Susan asked.

'No, ew!' Alexis turned around in her seat. 'Did you see that place? Gross.'

'It's a bathroom,' Ethan said, his voice rising in exasperation.

'It's a gross restroom and I have to go. Just pull over some place else,' Alexis said.

'Listen, doll, I am not stopping every five miles so you can inspect bathrooms to see if they're good enough to pee in. Either you get out of this car and go to the bathroom right now, or the only place I'm pulling over will be the side of the busy interstate where everyone can see you. Your choice.' Ethan motioned his hand towards the gas station. 'Decide fast.'

'Oh!' Alexis gnashed her teeth and got out of the car, storming back inside. The man was really too much.

Ethan watched Alexis leave for the bathroom before taking a deep breath. All day it had been something with her. The music wasn't right. The car was too hot. The car was too cold. The roads were too bumpy. He drove too slow, too fast, too straight. The bathrooms were too icky for her delicate, pampered bottom. Turning to Susan and Ted, he asked, 'Is she for real?'

Ted couldn't meet his eyes. He turned to gaze out the window.

'She spent nearly a half-hour in that bathroom and she didn't even use it?' Ethan continued. 'Is she doing this because I tried to kick her out of the car? Because I really can't think of anything else.'

Ted chuckled. 'My guess? It's because you made a comment about her ass being scrawny.'

Susan looked embarrassed. 'I'm sorry, Ethan. She's going through a hard time right now in her personal life. I've never seen her act this horribly before. She's just under a lot of stress.'

'You always do that,' Ted said softly. He sighed, shaking his head. 'You don't have to make excuses for her. Her attitude today has been horrible. I'm embarrassed we even invited her at this point. This trip was supposed to be a fun adventure. She's done everything she could think of to make sure we're all as miserable as she is.'

'I know,' Susan said, her voice harder than usual. Ethan saw Susan stiffen, getting a little defensive at Ted's words. Alexis really didn't deserve such a loyal friend. Under her breath, she asked, 'Can we not talk about this now?'

Ethan turned in his seat to look straight ahead. He took a deep breath, doing his best to be calm, to just let everything that had to do with Alexis Grant roll off his back. 'Listen, I'm trying hard to take into account that her mother just got arrested. I know that stress can make people act in ways they don't usually behave, but this? This really is too much.'

'I know.' Susan leaned forwards and placed a light hand on his shoulder. 'I'll have a talk with her. I promise. It's just she's not used to living like a real person. She's grown up in hotels with maids and room service and limo drivers that she has gotten to boss around since the age of five. I'm so sorry –'

'Don't apologise for her. She's a grown woman and not your responsibility.' Ethan saw Miss High and Mighty coming from inside. He started the car before she got back in.

Sliding into the seat next to him, she crossed her arms over her chest and didn't say a word. That suited Ethan just fine. It seemed the only time they could get along was when they didn't talk at all.

'Can I see the map?' Alexis asked, turning around to look at Susan. Pennsylvania was a pretty state full of mountains and trees, with apparently no place to pull over to eat along the interstate. Alexis wasn't hungry, but she was ready to take another break away from Ethan. 'Where are we?'

'We're not almost there yet, if that's what you're wondering,' Ethan said.

'I wasn't,' Alexis snapped at him, making a face and rolling her eyes. They'd been driving pretty much non-stop all day. Though it was beautiful, the state seemed to go on for ever.

'I think we should be almost out of Pennsylvania,' Susan said, handing the map she'd printed off the internet to Alexis. 'Close to the Ohio border. We just passed a sign that said Youngstown.'

'It doesn't seem like we've gotten very far,' Alexis said, eyeing the map. She looked out the car window, watching the rolling green hills in the distance. Pennsylvania wasn't a bad state. She'd been through the area before.

She'd actually stayed at a bed and breakfast once with her mother when she was little. It was one of the rare times they had vacationed together. Well, her mother was taking a working vacation with her current lover at the time. She ended up buying the bed and breakfast and tearing it down when the man dumped her. Anyway, the place had been beautiful, close to a quaint little covered bridge and a quiet stream.

Alexis took a deep breath, drawing her thoughts back into the car. The landscape around them looked the same as it did back then, but it didn't hold the same childish fascination and pleasure. 'Why did we come this way anyway? Isn't there a shorter route?'

'I've been this way a thousand times and I didn't want to have to follow a map,' Ethan said. 'Takes away from the spontaneity of the trip.'

Great, Alexis thought, *a man too good to use directions. He'll get us lost for sure.*

Pretending to study her manicure, Alexis asked, 'Still, shouldn't we be further than this by now?'

'We would be if someone didn't take an hour each time we stopped,' Ethan grumbled.

'Well maybe if your piece of junk car didn't toss me around so much, I wouldn't need to take such a long break to recover,' Alexis returned, mimicking his tone.

'And maybe if you weren't such a spoiled little prin-cess –' Ethan began.

'Hey, you guys want to stop somewhere for the night? It's starting to get late anyway,' Ted said, ending the impending fight. 'Cleveland is only about an hour's drive and I saw some signs for hotels. It's been a long first day and we should maybe stop to relax, eat and perhaps go over a game plan for the trip?'

'Sounds good to me,' Ethan said, lightening his tone as he spoke to Ted.

'Fine,' Alexis said, only too happy to get out of the car. 'We should have some sort of itinerary. If we stick to it we could get to California in a few days.'

'A few days? This isn't an airplane, doll.' Ethan laughed.

'Airplanes only take a few hours, *doll*,' she said.

'Whatever,' Ethan dismissed. 'I am not driving with an itinerary. That takes away from the adventure. I say we go with the flow, whether we get there in two days or fifty.' Ethan glanced at her, his look challenging. Was he just trying to think of ways to upset her? 'Do what we feel like doing.'

'Great idea,' Susan said happily. 'We don't have to be there any time soon. We're free as the wind.'

'Cool,' Ted added. 'My accounts are pretty much automatic and I can check on them anywhere, so long as I can plug my computer into a phone line every once and a while.'

'I feel like having an itinerary,' Alexis said between clenched teeth.

'Then it's settled,' Ethan said. 'No itinerary. If there's anywhere you feel like detouring to, we'll take a vote. Majority rules.'

'Agreed,' Ted said.

'Agreed,' Susan said.

'Whatever,' Alexis grumbled. She was clearly outvoted in this. She rested her head back and closed her eyes, keeping her arms crossed over her chest as she leaned towards the door and away from Ethan. The man just bugged her, any way she looked at it, especially because she was attracted to him. To make everything worse, it now seemed their cross-country trip just turned into a cross-country never-ending nightmare.

Chapter Four

Ethan took a deep breath. This wasn't going to work. He'd be better off cutting his losses and taking Alexis back to New York City. The first day of driving had been horrible. Pennsylvania was a long state to travel through to begin with, then add to that the fact there had been no place to really pull over to escape Alexis's attitude, he never thought the day would end. When Ted asked to pull over in Cleveland for the night, he couldn't have been more relieved. They didn't make very good time, but that didn't matter. He hadn't lied when he said he had nowhere to be.

'I'm not sharing a room with that psychopath,' he heard Alexis say from where she whispered with Susan. Did the woman have a hearing problem? Did she not realise her whispering wasn't actually quiet?

The hotel clerk looked at him and smiled. She was young, pretty and was definitely checking him out. Her hair was feathered at the sides in a sort of 70s retro and she wore a brightly knitted sweater under her dark-blue work vest. Her eyes dipped and her voice probed, as she asked, 'You and the gal-pal in a fight, eh?'

'She is not my girlfriend,' Ethan said, recoiling in horror at the very idea. 'She's just some pain in the ass.'

The clerk giggled, tossing her blonde hair over her shoulder. She blinked her big blue eyes at him as she bit her lip. She wore too much green eye-shadow and her cheeks were a bright shade of pink. Ethan didn't care. He liked seeing people express their individual style, especially when it was a little off from norm.

'So, just the one night?' the clerk asked.

Ethan nodded. His attention was again caught by Susan

and Alexis talking in the corner of the lobby. The hotel wasn't a bad one, but surely nothing the rich Alexis was used to. To his surprise, she didn't complain about the location, even when they stepped into the tiny blue and red lobby with its broken television set and old mismatched couches.

When Susan suggested they get two rooms instead of three, he should've said no. Ethan didn't know why he agreed to split the cost of the room with Alexis. All day in the car with her had been a real chore. Did he really want to be around her all night as well?

Maybe it was the look on Alexis's face as Susan said the words. Ethan chuckled to himself. She looked horrified by the idea. So horrified, in fact, he'd come to the conclusion that whatever pain he suffered in her presence for the night would be well worth watching her suffer alongside him.

'Listen, the trip is young,' he heard Susan say. 'You don't have a lot of money. Sharing a room is the best solution for that.'

Ethan already guessed the woman was broke. She hadn't eaten a thing all day. Maybe she should try selling her three hundred dollar designer dress. It only made sense. Many boutiques in New York would've given her a good price for it.

'But, we don't know him,' Alexis said. 'What if he tries to rape me?'

Ethan rolled his eyes. Yeah, like he'd cast his line into that fishing hole. He'd have more fun trying to hump an iceberg on the *Titanic*.

'You and Ted get your own room,' Alexis said, sounding panicked. Ethan hid his grin. Oh, yeah, she was already suffering. Usually he wouldn't take pride in a woman abhorring him, but with Alexis he was willing to make an exception. 'I don't want to share with him.'

'Ted is paying for our room tonight,' Susan answered.

'Must be nice to have a man paying for everything,' Alexis snapped. 'What happened to wanting to make it on your own?'

Susan actually looked guilty at that. Ethan watched them, not even pretending he couldn't hear them. Since they were speaking loud enough to be heard, who was he not to listen to the conversation?

Ted walked in the door. He'd been on his cell phone with one of his colleagues from work. 'All set?'

'Ah, not quite.' Ethan pointed at Alexis and Susan.

Susan said, 'No, go ahead, we're ready.'

Ted came up next to him. Under his breath, he said, 'You sure you want to spend the night in the same room as that barracuda?'

The clerk giggled. Ted smiled. Ethan shrugged. 'Yeah, we'll try it out for a night and see if we can't play nice. Susan was right about saving money where we can. If by some miracle the sleeping arrangements work, it's the wisest choice. That is, if I can keep myself from raping her before the night's over.'

'She didn't say that, did she?' Ted asked, appalled. Ethan chuckled and nodded his head. He liked Ted. They'd gotten along almost instantly. 'Man, she's such a drama queen.'

'You guys travelling far?' the blonde clerk asked. Ethan again smiled at her. She was young, twenty perhaps. When she moved her whole body bounced with energy.

'California,' Ethan said, easing his voice so it dripped honey. She responded just as he knew she would. Her eyes cast down and her lips puckered ever so slightly.

'Man, I wish I could go to California.' Her sweet voice was almost a pout. Ethan swallowed. Maybe he should get his own room, then again, maybe he could get them a free room.

'Yeah, I'm a tattoo artist,' Ethan said. 'I'm going there to open my own shop. You know, tattoo on movie stars.'

The blonde's eyes rounded. 'Really? I so want a tattoo.'

'Do you?' he asked. Yeah, he really was the rock star without the music. Everywhere he went doors just seemed to open with those simple words: *I'm a tattoo artist.*

'Uh huh.' She leaned forwards. 'Do you have your stuff?'

'Yeah.' Ethan leaned in.

'You, ah, want to trade for the room?' She leaned closer, glancing around. 'My boss is gone tonight. So long as you're out of here by eight tomorrow morning.'

'Very cool,' Ethan said. 'What you want?'

'A butterfly on my hip. About this big.' She rounded her fingers to the size of a quarter.

Ethan grinned. Two free rooms for a tattoo that would take him about ten minutes to do. Yeah, he'd definitely gotten into the right profession.

'Are you finished flirting or should we just camp out here?' Alexis asked.

Ethan closed his eyes. To the clerk, he asked, 'How much do the rooms usually run?'

"Forty dollars with the coupon from the phone book,' the blonde said, handing him two sets of keys.

'Great, thanks,' he said before turning to Alexis. 'You owe me twenty bucks.'

The clerk giggled.

Cleveland was definitely not her city. So what if Susan said it was known for rock 'n' roll and Lake Erie? She didn't care. She didn't want to be there. And it wasn't like she had the extra money to go to any of the museums, or the zoo, or to theme parks, or shopping, or anywhere cool. No, all she got was a cheap hotel room so far away from the water it was like Lake Erie wasn't even there.

She wasn't expecting much by the looks of the lobby, but she was expecting more than this. The room was flooded with pastels. She'd seen rooms like this before – in movies about poor people. What was this place? A one-star hotel? A no-star? Well, what did she expect for twenty dollars? At least it looked clean enough.

There was a round table with a complimentary notepad and pencil on it. A small television set sat in the middle of a long brown dresser. The only piece of artwork was of a Southwestern influence and hung in a mauve plastic frame. It matched the mauve floral pattern of the bedspread. Alexis stared at the queen-size bed in horror. The hotel room only had the one bed. It looked stiff, if the bedspread was any indication. She sighed. It would probably be too much to ask that Ethan be gentleman enough to sleep on the stained mauve carpet.

'Hey, move, this is heavy,' Ethan said from behind her. 'The room's not going to bite you, doll.'

Alexis sat her camera bag on the table, getting out of his way. She ignored him as she took out the small battery charger and plugged it into the wall. The red light on it blinked, showing the battery was low. She'd probably have to leave it plugged in all night.

'What is that anyway?' Ethan asked.

'Camera,' Alexis said, her tone flat. Did the man not know what a camera was?

'Uh, yeah, I see that. What kind?'

'Do you know your cameras?' Alexis asked.

'I'm an artist,' was his answer. 'I've seen a few.'

'Oh, do you sculpt? Paint?' She turned, frowning as he watched him plug in a laptop. Then, some machine she'd never seen before. It was a big square with a digital panel and dials.

'I tattoo.' He glanced at her. The dim room was lit by a lamp on the dresser, but the light still managed to pick up the colour of his eyes. She had to look away first. There was no way she would allow herself to think any part of this man was cute.

'I thought you said you were an artist.' Alexis frowned in confusion.

Ethan shook his head in obvious exasperation. 'Tattooing is an art form.'

'Art is found in museums,' Alexis argued. 'Drawing silly little pictures on people is not art. Little children do that to each other in school.'

'Ever hear of the tattoo museum in Amsterdam? Or the ones here in the US? The one in Oxford?' he asked, chuckling to himself.

'No,' she said carefully. 'Still, art is old, you know. The forms have been around for a long time. When did tattooing start? The 1950s, with biker gangs and sailors?'

'Um, try about thirty eight thousand BC,' he said. 'It's a lot older than some of your so-called art mediums.'

'You're kidding.' Alexis stepped closer to him. She looked at his little eclectric box with renewed interest. 'They didn't have electricity back then.'

'Not all tattoos are done with electricity.' Ethan laughed and she had the feeling it was at her expense. Even so, he had an almost adorable charm when he smiled.

'How do you know that?' she asked.

'I read.'

She looked up. Ethan was close, maybe a little too close and she smelled the faint trace of cologne. She'd caught whiffs of it in the car, but now it started to curl around her senses. Glancing down, she reasoned that his skin would feel the same in the dark as a non-tattooed man. She'd already hit rock bottom. Could she really get any lower? The strange attraction she'd been trying to deny since first seeing Ethan leapt in her stomach. If they were to find a little mutual release – release she obviously needed – who would ever find out? It's not like Susan would ever believe it happened. Refusing to back down, she curiously waited to see if he'd make a move to touch her. 'What's that box thing?'

'Power supply. I'm going to give the hotel clerk some ink tonight.'

'Is that safe?'

Ethan stepped closer. His arms crossed over his chest and he said quietly, 'Are we actually having a conversation that doesn't include fighting?'

Alexis blinked, surprised. He was right. How could she have even for one second considered sleeping with the insufferable man? Stiffening at the sardonic look on his face, she said, 'You know, it's people like you who spread disease.'

'Oh, here we go.' He turned his back on her. 'Save the speech, doll, I don't want to hear it – not from an uninformed, judgemental priss like you.'

'Ah! You are the rudest...' She took a deep breath. 'Where are my bags?'

'In the trunk of the car where you left them. Need the keys to go get it?' He pulled the key ring out of his pocket and held it up. 'Just push the little button twice. The trunk has electric locks.'

Alexis couldn't believe it. She'd seen Ted carrying up Susan's belongings for her. Now Ted was a gentleman. Was it too much to ask for the same courtsey from Ethan?

She snatched the keys, stomping from the room. His laughter followed her out the door. Damn him, the barbaric jerk.

'Hey, what ya doing out here?' Susan asked, coming out of her room. She glanced down at Alexis's bag on the ground. 'Did something happen? Did Ethan kick you out already?'

The evening was a little cool. From her spot she could hear cars travelling over the nearby interstate. The sky was dark and the streetlights shone down on the abandoned parking lot. They were on the second storey, along the back of the hotel. Beneath her, she saw the red dot of a cigarette as an overweight man smoked. His white T-shirt was stained with sweat beneath the underarms. Alexis knew, because he'd offered to help her with her bags. She was still creeped out by it.

Alexis glanced at the bag by her feet and then to the room she shared with Ethan. 'No. He didn't kick me out.'

'Did you lose your room key?' Susan insisted.

'No.'

'Well, it's not like this parking lot is a great view,' Susan said. 'Are you pouting?'

'I think Ethan's in there having sex. I didn't want to walk in on it.' Alexis couldn't meet Susan's eyes.

'What? You're kidding,' Susan said, whispering. The curtains were drawn and she looked at them sideways, trying to see in.

Alexis shook her head, giggling slightly at Susan's look. 'No. I heard buzzing. I think they're using toys.'

'Oh, my gawd. Gross.' Susan wrinkled her nose. 'Come on, let's listen.'

'Ew, no,' Alexis said, unable to help herself as she crept to the door.

Susan leaned her ear to the wood. 'Shh, listen.'

Was it wrong of her to be jealous of Ethan right now? How come Mr Bad Ass got some action and she, a perfectly normal woman, couldn't even find a decent pity lay. Pouting slightly, Alexis said, 'It's bad enough I have to go in there afterwards.'

'I don't hear anything,' Susan said. Alexis leaned next to her. The buzzing started again and Susan had to hold her hand over her mouth to keep from laughing.

'Oh, gawd. That hurts,' a woman's voice cried. 'Stop. Stop. It hurts. Are you sure it's not too big?'

Too big? OK, even though she hated the man, that comment was intriguing. Alexis widened her eyes as the buzzing stopped. 'Maybe he's not doing it right.'

'Maybe the toy's broken,' Susan added. 'I never heard one that sounded like that.'

'What are you two doing?' Ted whispered from right behind Susan.

Susan gasped, jumping as she spun around. She gave Alexis a dirty look. 'Ah, nothing.'

'What's going on in there?' Ted asked.

'Nothing.' Susan playfully stepped in his way when he tried to move towards the door.

'Nothing, eh?' Ted looked at Alexis.

Alexis giggled. 'Ethan's got himself a little friend.'

Ted frowned.

'He's, you know,' Susan said.

'He's bumping uglies,' Alexis answered.

'Gross, Lexy, that's vulgar,' Susan scolded, even as she nodded at Ted.

'What? It's true. I highly doubt any *lovemaking* is going on.' Alexis chuckled. 'Please say I can sleep on your floor tonight, Ted. I'll owe you for ever if you let me.'

'How do you know he's in there with someone?' Ted asked. 'Did he say?'

'Nope, heard it. Went to the car to get my bag and came back to . . .' Alexis waved a hand towards the door.

'You mean he didn't carry your bag up for you?' Susan asked, frowning slightly.

Alexis shook her head in denial.

'Hey, did you hear that?' Susan turned to Ted. 'He didn't carry up Lexy's bag.'

'Well, he's not her servant or her boyfriend,' Ted defended.

'Well, I guess that's true,' Susan said.

Alexis frowned. Well, so much for Susan's support. 'He's not a gentleman, that's for sure.'

Susan giggled as a loud moan sounded and then a high-pitched screech. She waved Ted to the door. 'They're using toys. Come on, listen.'

Ted leaned his ear to the door. Alexis and Susan did the same. The buzzing sounded, turning on and off several times. The woman moaned, making strange noises. Ted aughed and knocked on the door.

'Come in,' Ethan yelled.

'No!' Susan and Alexis cried softly at the same time.

'Relax, detectives,' Ted mused. 'He's giving the hotel clerk a tattoo in exchange for free rooms. The man is definitely a charmer. I was impressed. If he keeps it up, maybe the whole trip will be virtually free.'

Ted stepped in, smiling as he was proven right. Ethan had moved the round table next to the bed and was in the process of throwing away some of his mess. He pulled a long sheet of paper off the bedspread. It had the wrinkled imprint of the clerk on it.

'It's so neat.' The blonde clerk was looking at her hip in the mirror, grinning. Alexis sat her bag on the dresser, glancing down to see a bright blue and yellow butterfly on the woman's hip. She hated to admit it, but it was kind of cute. The girl definitely had the stomach for it. The woman turned and showed her hip to everyone. 'Isn't it groovy? I mean, really to die for?'

'Yeah, it's the bee's knees,' Alexis drawled sarcastically. Ethan glared at her. The poor clerk didn't even realise she was being made fun of.

'Thank you, Ethan,' the clerk said.

Alexis watched as Ethan took apart his machine, throwing a white tube and some other stuff in the trash along with little red ink cups. Then, when he'd finished cleaning up the area, he threw his gloves in the trash as well.

'How about a free movie as a tip?' the clerk asked.

'Cool,' Ethan said. 'Thanks.'

'This is awesome,' the clerk said. 'OK, I have to get back to work. I'm like the only one here tonight. I so have to call Janet. She'll never believe I did this. Oh, for the movie, just give me ten minutes and then punch in the code for the one you want. It should come on.'

Ethan thanked her again. Alexis waited until the girl was gone, before asking, 'You going to charge me for the movie, too?'

Ethan grinned, but he didn't look happy. 'Depends. You going to watch the movie?'

Alexis huffed in outrage. 'I can't believe you're charging me twenty dollars when you got the room for free. Half of nothing is nothing.'

'Ooh, yeah, let's go, honey,' Ted said. 'This is going to get ugly.'

Susan shut the door as Ted led her out of the room.

'Yeah, so? You didn't do the work. I did. It's called trade,' Ethan said. 'Otherwise, we'd have given money to the hotel, the hotel would've paid her after taking a cut and she would've paid me for the tattoo. This way, we cut out the middle man. Everyone wins.'

'Everyone but me,' Alexis said.

'Not everything is about you, doll. How are you possibly hurt?' he asked, moving to the bathroom. She heard him washing his hands. When he came back, he was drying them on a towel. 'You were going to pay twenty for the room anyway. You're not out anything.'

'Fine, you cheap bastard.' Alexis nodded stiffly. 'You want your money? I'll give you your money.'

Alexis went to her camera bag, which was now on the floor, and dug into the side pocket. Her hands shook as she pulled out a twenty-dollar bill. She threw it at him.

'Wait,' he said as she turned to open her suitcase. She

pulled out a nightgown and watched him from the corner of her eye. He lifted his hand to give the money back to her.

'No, it's yours,' said Alexis. 'You're right. I don't want it.' Alexis gripped her nightgown and stormed past him. 'I'm taking a shower. And don't try to charge me for the water – I already paid.'

Ethan sighed, feeling like a jerk as Alexis slammed the bathroom door. He'd meant to aggravate her and only ended up feeling like a low-life piece of scum. Moments later, he heard the shower turning on. Crossing over to her camera bag, he unzipped the pouch and slipped the money back inside.

'At least this way I know I'm not a jerk,' he said under his breath. He slowly packed up his equipment, found his keys by her suitcase and carried his tattooing gear down to the car. She was still in the shower when he got back. Lying on the bed, he threaded his fingers behind his head.

For a moment, earlier when they'd stopped arguing long enough to talk about art, it wasn't so bad. What had it been? All of three seconds?

Ethan sighed. He'd dealt with narrow-minded opinions like hers before about his chosen profession and wasn't surprised she'd been programmed to think that way. To people like her, all tattoo artists were dirty, uneducated, untalented hacks.

However, what people like Alexis didn't seem to realise, or want to realise, was that he'd gone to art school at the same time he'd been apprenticing for tattooing. He'd paid his dues. He'd worked full time as the grunt in a tattoo shop. It was an old tradition, the tattoo apprenticeship. It was a rite of passage into the business. He had to answer phones, sweep floor, layout the artwork, take out trash, pick up food and deal with the attitudes of the artists above him.

Anything the boss wanted him to do, he did. He'd put in his time and he worked hard and not once had he complained. Everyone did it. It was how the business worked. But did people like her realise it? Could they appreciate his hard work and dedication to his craft? No. They thought he just woke up one morning and said, *Hey, how can I not work today and rip people off? I know, I'll become a tattoo artist. That takes no talent.*

'Why do you even care what she thinks, Ethan?' he muttered to himself. He heard the shower turn off. Maybe he could make an effort to be nicer to her.

Alexis stood in the shower crying. What was wrong with her? She always felt like crying nowadays. But, then again, why shouldn't she cry? Life wasn't fair. It was hard and she felt sorry for herself. Her stomach growled, but it was like she'd been too paranoid to buy food when they stopped. She'd found herself tallying her money in her head, worried about every last penny, wondering if she counted it right. She'd never worried about money before and now she was too scared to spend a dime on a piece of candy – not that she'd ever buy candy. It was way too fattening.

Alexis forgot to bring her body wash, shampoo and conditioner with her into the shower and was forced to use the little complimentary bottles the hotel provided. They didn't smell bad, but they weren't what she was accustomed to. Afterwards, her skin was too dry and a little itchy.

The warm water felt good and she let it hit her body. Looking towards the bathroom door, she frowned. She didn't understand men like Ethan at all. It wasn't just the tattoos. It was everything about him. He wasn't nice to her, not that she exactly deserved his kindness. Still, a gentleman would have politely ignored her irritation and bad mood, waiting patiently until she was in a better frame of mind. Ethan just kept pushing and talking and returning insults until she couldn't see straight. Then, he charged her to stay in a room he'd gotten for free. It sucked too, because it was either pay him twenty or give the girl at the desk forty for her own room.

Alexis got out of the shower and dried off. Looking at

her skimpy nightie, she frowned. She'd been so irritated with Ethan that she hadn't paid any attention to the clothes she grabbed. It was a sheer mesh chemise that only fell to the tops of her thighs. The little slit up the side showed even higher. The embroidered flower top hid her nipples with artfully placed roses, but other than that the bodice was see-through. The skirt was a little better, but in the right light she saw her thong panties just fine.

Pushing open the door, she stuck her head out. The television was on and she could see the flipping channels even as she didn't see him. 'Um, you out there?'

'Yeah,' Ethan answered.

'Can you leave?' she asked.

'Hey, I'm not going anywhere,' Ethan said, sounding irritated. 'This is my room too.'

Alexis shut the door and looked at herself in the mirror. She so did not fit these horrible surroundings. The nightie probably cost more than all the furnishings in the room combined. Well, Ethan didn't seem interested in her anyway so what did it matter if he saw her dressed like this? Opening the bathroom door, she stepped out. Her heart fluttered nervously, but she forced herself to walk across the hotel room. She passed the television and heard Ethan gasp.

'Damn,' he whispered, as if he couldn't help himself.

'Excuse me?' Alexis turned to him, frowning. He looked way too sexy sprawled out on the bed. His bare feet were close to her and he adjusted his legs slightly, letting one knee fall to the side. Strong legs led to delectable hips and a narrow waist. The way his T-shirt fell to the side revealed the small trail of hair on his lower stomach.

Ethan cleared his throat. 'What? Oh, the . . . ah . . . Green Bay Packers lost.'

'Isn't that a football team?' Alexis asked, confused. 'And isn't the Superbowl in February?'

'Uh, yeah, it's a post-season game,' Ethan said.

Alexis was still confused. Post-games? Did they have post-games? Ah, what did she know about football anyway?

Ethan sat up and quickly changed the subject. 'Why don't you get dressed? We'll go get something to eat.'

Alexis averted her eyes. 'No, I'm fine.'

'Unless you snuck something in the bathroom, you haven't eaten all day,' Ethan said. 'Come on, get dressed.'

He noticed? Alexis blinked in surprise, oddly touched. 'Yeah, I ate. I'm good.'

'Really?' he challenged. 'When?'

'This morning. Ted bought bagels.' Alexis crossed to the bed, refusing to look at him.

'You know, most people eat at least three meals a day,' Ethan said, his tone wry.

'I'm not hungry. What are you? The food police?' Alexis pulled back the covers and crawled next to him. Tugging at the blankets, she felt him get up off the bed. She wasn't tired, but she wasn't sure what else to do.

'You're going to bed already? It's early.'

'I'm tired.' Alexis could feel him studying her. She pulled the covers over her head to hide. She didn't want him looking at her.

'Want me to bring you back something?' he insisted.

'No.' Alexis heard the door open and close. Slowly, she peeked out. Sitting up, she grabbed the remote. Her stomach growled and she had a small headache. Flipping through the channels, she settled on an old melodrama to take her mind off her problems. It didn't work. The couple was rich and lived in a house that only reminded her of everything she'd lost.

Tossing the remote aside, she stared at the door. For the first time in what felt like a long time, she didn't think too much about her financial problems. However, finding herself attracted to an arrogant tattoo man was definitely a problem all its own.

Chapter Five

Alexis opened her eyes and the first thing she saw was doughnuts on the round table. Blinking, she sat up. She didn't remember falling asleep the night before. In fact, she didn't remember Ethan coming back to the room the night before. She wondered where he slept. A small chill worked over her body, but she pushed it aside. Looking to his side of the bed, she saw that his pillow looked slept on. So he did spend the night by her, or at least part of it.

Hearing the shower running, she tired to ignore the doughnuts and quickly got dressed before Ethan came out. The dress she wore the day before hadn't been the most comfortable outfit for travelling so she decided on a V-neck, green-apple-coloured mesh shirt with an empire seam beneath the breasts. The shirt was two layers with a built-in lighter green camisole underneath.

Her Joie jeans were made of vintage denim with little buttoned pockets in front and a button fly. They rode low, showing off just a peek of midriff when she walked, but not her panties. She hated when girls showed off their underwear. It seemed trashy. The black leather boots weren't her top pick to go with the outfit, but she didn't really have a choice. It wasn't like she had her entire shoe collection with her any more to pick from.

Taking a deep breath, she tried not to dwell in self-pity. Alexis Grant as a fighter. It was about time she remembered that.

Ethan closed his eyes, letting the cool water of the shower hit his skin. He'd gone out the night before with Susan and Ted and they'd ended up drinking beer until about one in the morning. They'd gotten along rather well when

Alexis wasn't there to dampen the mood with her negative thinking. Then why in the world did he spend most of the night wishing she was there to liven things up?

Ethan shook his head. Liven things up? Yeah, he had issues. He so needed help. Only a fool would wish Alexis to be with them.

To make matters worse, he'd struck out for female companionship at the bar and grill they'd gone to, not that he'd been trying hard to find some. Alexis was asleep when they got back. The soft glow of the television illuminated her soft skin. Groaning, he remembered how her poor excuse for a nightgown had been pulled ever so slightly to the side exposing the curve of a small, ripe breast. To a drunken Ethan, that had been torture. He'd lain awake, staring at her nipple, thinking of all the ways he'd like to bring it to erection. The damn thing had taunted him until he was erect himself.

Masturbating next to her in bed seemed a little uncouth so he did the next best thing he could think of. He tried to 'walk it off'. He'd been the first on at the doughnut store that morning. The cool air did him some good because he'd finally managed to calm his raging hormones to a manageable level.

When he got back to the room, Alexis was still asleep. Only this time, instead of a breast, her backside was exposed and he got an all too good look at her thong panties. Just thinking of her smooth butt, outlined by the soft morning light coming through the narrow slit in the floral curtains made his gut clench.

Ethan stifled a groan and fisted his erection from underneath, letting the water help his hand glide over the length. He was mindful of the piercings he had along the top of his shaft as he stroked. The four little barbells made a frenum ladder up his penis. Women loved the piercings, as it gave a French tickler effect.

Remembering her thong underwear, he clung to the image, using it as he caressed himself. Ethan stifled a groan. He'd thought about kissing her nipple for so long his mouth actually ached to have it between his lips.

He wondered what her cream would taste like, if he were to part her thighs and kiss her most intimately. Each woman was different. Some were sour, some sweet, some tangy and some just the perfect combination of all three. When she'd stepped out of the shower wearing nothing but her little nightie, he'd nearly lurched off the bed in attack mode. He had to make some lame excuse about football just to cover his response. The way the television light had illuminated her from behind had been torture. It silhouetted her body, showing the space between her narrow thighs, the outline of her slender waist. She was a lot skinnier than he liked, but still, she'd looked damn good in that nightgown.

The image of her silhouetted body replaced the one of her butt in a thong. He stroked harder, squeezing his turgid flesh almost painfully. He shouldn't be masturbating to Alexis. If he were thinking clearly, he'd know he didn't like her, couldn't possibly want her. Obviously, he wasn't thinking clearly. Just remembering her defiance turned him on more.

Reaching down, he cupped his balls, rolling them lightly in his palm. That felt good. Oh, he was close. If he just let go, he'd be there. He held back, savouring the anticipation of release, liking the image of Alexis's body in his head. Just a little longer, he wanted to hold it off just a little longer.

A knock sounded on the bathroom door. 'Hello?'

Hearing her voice, his body instantly jerked. He came hard on the shower wall. His mouth opened, frozen as he concentrated on not grunting his release. The knock sounded again, a little more insistent.

'Um, sorry to bother you, but I really need to use the bathroom,' Alexis called, 'and you've been in there a while.'

'One moment,' he said, his voice hoarse. He tried to slow his heartbeat by taking deep breaths. His body protested as he shut off the water, wanting to bask in the afterglow of release.

Nearly stumbling, he grabbed a towel and wrapped it

around his waist. In his haste, he threw the door open a little too quickly and dropped the towel. He wasn't sure which of them was more shocked. Her eyes rounded and she gasped.

'Ah, shit, one second. Sorry. All yours.' Ethan hurried out of the bathroom as Alexis hurried in. Once the door shut, he started laughing. He'd just acted like a teenager caught masturbating by the girl he had a crush on. What did it matter? It wasn't like she knew what he was doing. It wouldn't matter if she did. He was an adult.

Still chuckling at himself, he grabbed the first pair of blue jeans he found and slipped them on. Then sniffing an old T-shirt out of habit, he was glad to find it smelled clean. He pulled it over his head, hoping day two of the westward adventure would be better than the first.

Ohio had been hilly as they'd neared Cleveland. But somehow, as they drove away from the city, the land became suddenly flat. As the car rolled down the interstate, Alexis saw peeks of Lake Erie's shoreline through the trees. The water was almost a dark-green colour, but still very beautiful.

'Look, we can go to a corn festival,' Susan said cheerfully, pointing at a sign. 'They have bluegrass.'

No one answered her.

Alexis sat in the back seat and didn't say a word. When she'd gotten out of the bathroom that morning, Ethan insisted she eat the doughnut. Out of principle she tried to protest, until he said it was part of the free continental breakfast that came with the room.

Everyone was getting along fairly well. It was probably because she didn't really speak to Ethan and he'd barely said two words to her since getting in the car. However, Ethan, Ted and Susan seemed to have a lot to talk about. Apparently, they had a great time the night before. Alexis really couldn't be mad about it. She'd been asked.

Ethan was tired so Ted said he'd drive. Alexis was only mildly horrified by the fact their driving directions consisted of the words 'just drive westward-ish'. Apparently, Ethan really didn't own a road map.

Susan was cuddled up next to Ted in the front seat. Barry White, Al Green and Miles Davis whiled away the morning hours, filling the silence with their beautiful music. The compilation CD belonged to Ted and Alexis was a little surprised when Ethan didn't protest. Weren't men like him supposed to listen to punk rock or nu metal?

Alexis glanced over across the seat. Taking a deep breath and then another, she squirmed, uncomfortable and suddenly very hot. Moisture dampened her panties and she parted her legs, hoping to cool herself without anyone noticing. The image of Ethan in a bath towel wouldn't leave her, especially the part when he dropped the towel while opening the bathroom door. It would seem Mr Tattoo was also Mr Well Endowed.

Muscles rippled over his form, from his hard stomach to his big shoulders. Both arms were covered with colourful tattoos, as well as part of his chest, but his stomach was left bare. She wondered why. His nipples were pierced with two horseshoe-shaped rings in them. She could see the faint outline of the rings beneath his T-shirt. She shook her head, taking another deep breath.

Was the car suddenly too hot? She lightly fanned the front of her shirt.

Strangely, his tattoos didn't seem to distract from his amazing physique. If anything, they added a bad-boy appeal. And, was she mistaken, or had something silver glinted on his semi-erect shaft? Alexis felt heat rushing to her features. Should she even be thinking about Ethan's penis?

OK, as future boyfriend material Ethan didn't stand a chance. But as a fantasy to file away for a later day? Why not? Alexis suddenly realised one of Ethan's incredibly blue eyes was open. She'd been caught staring – at his crotch. Biting the corner of her lip, she said the first thing that came to her mind. 'You really would look better without the red goatee.'

His brow arched slightly. Then, closing his eye, he said, 'And you would look better if you gained fifteen pounds.'

Somehow, when he said it, she couldn't take it as a compliment. Alexis glanced down, feeling suddenly very self-conscious. She hugged her arms around her waist. Sulking, she turned to stare out the window. Some adventure this was – endless roadside upon endless roadside and a travelling companion she wanted to toss out of the car.

'Guess what?' Susan said, moving around to look at the back seat. Alexis turned her attention from the miles of grass and farmland to her friend. Susan held up the free notepad from the hotel. Talking to both Ted and Alexis, she said, 'I did a search last night on the internet about the Great Lakes and we're really close to Detroit.'

Alexis glanced at Ethan. He was still asleep.

'I thought maybe Ethan would like to see some of the car museums they have there,' Susan said. 'You know, since he's really into his car.'

The last thing Alexis wanted to do was detour for a car museum. She was about to say something when Ted vetoed the idea for her.

'Ah, no, babe, I think we'd have to backtrack a little to get to Detroit,' Ted said, yawning. 'Mm, I don't know about you two, but I'm ready for a break. I'm going to pull in up here and find some place to eat.'

'Sounds good, honey,' Susan said absently, reaching to pat his shoulder. She lovingly smoothed out the sleeve of his polo shirt before looking back at Alexis. 'Well, then, how about we subtly work our way north and go to Lake Michigan?'

'Why?' Alexis frowned.

'Because they're the Great Lakes,' Susan said. 'And because I've never seen Lake Michigan.'

'We just saw Lake Erie,' Alexis said.

'But, I haven't seen Lake Michigan,' Susan insisted. 'It's an altogether different lake.'

'You want to detour just to see some more water?' Alexis asked.

'No, I want to detour because it will be fun.' Susan sighed. 'And because I haven't seen you take your camera out of its bag once.'

'Hey, how about this diner?' Ted asked with an uncomfortable laugh. Susan and Alexis both leaned to look out the window.

'Sure,' Susan said.

'Fine with me,' Alexis added.

Ted merged lanes and started slowing down. 'Ah, great, it's right by a gas station too. Perfect.'

'How are you going to build a portfolio if you don't take pictures?' Susan asked, picking up with Alexis where she'd left off.

'I haven't been inspired,' Alexis said quietly. Her photography was a private thing and she really didn't feel like discussing it with Ethan next to her, whether he was asleep or not. She glanced at him. He looked asleep. Still, he was a self-proclaimed artist and she really didn't want anyone judging her work. She couldn't take another blow to her ego right now. Her photography was the only thing she'd ever taken some sort of pride in, besides shopping. To have someone tell her she wasn't any good would hurt too badly and she had no doubt Ethan wouldn't pull his punches if her photographs were terrible. 'And I forgot to charge the battery.'

'Liar,' Ethan mumbled, not opening his eyes. Alexis made a weak noise of embarrassment. Susan frowned slightly at her in question. 'Mm, Ted, why don't we go to Lake Michigan? I've never been there. I'd like to mark it off my map.'

'Fine by me,' Ted said.

Susan looked at Alexis a while longer, before saying with forced enthusiasm, 'Yeah, cool.'

'Mark it off your map?' Alexis questioned. Her voice was sharper than usual in her irritation at being called a liar. So what if she'd lied? She had her reasons.

'Never mind,' Ethan said, still not looking at her. He angled his body towards the door, giving her his back. 'A girl like you wouldn't get it.'

Ted pulled up to the small roadside diner. There was nothing special about the red and white checkers along the top edge, or the boring inside décor. It had the same red curtains, vinyl booths and black and white photographs that all roadside diners seemed to have. Alexis was loath to spend money. What had happened to her? She was wearing a three hundred dollar Cynthia Rowley shirt and wondering if five dollars for a hamburger was too much. She'd ordered the small dinner salad and knew her stomach would be gnawing at her after an hour.

'You know,' the waitress said, sticking a pencil in her hair. She nodded at Alexis. 'You look just like that woman on the news.'

Alexis didn't move, didn't make eye contact. She sipped her water. 'You don't say.'

'Can I get a hamburger?' Ted asked. 'Medium well. Fries. No onions.'

'Sure thing.' The waitress grabbed her pencil and studied Alexis. 'What is that woman's name?'

'I'll have the same,' Susan said, her voice a little rushed.

'Sure thing, sugar.' The waitress wrote the order down and said, 'What was her name? I know I know it. It was just on the television. Frankie? Frannie?'

'I'll have the same only with onions,' Ethan said. He sounded sleepy. 'And you're thinking of Audrey Hepburn, the old actress.'

'Huh, that must be it,' the waitress said, seeming pleased the mystery was solved.

Alexis turned to Ethan in surprise. He thought she looked like the beautiful, classical film star? The waitress left.

'What?' Ethan asked when Alexis stared at him. 'You do around the chin.'

Susan hid a smile behind her hand.

'You're still too skinny,' Ethan said, almost defensively.

'And you'd still look better without the red goatee,'

Alexis answered, though her words lacked her previous conviction. There was no way Ethan could know just how much he'd helped her out with the waitress. The last thing she wanted was everyone pointing and staring at the convict's daughter.

Susan excused herself for the bathroom. Ted and Ethan talked sports, while Ethan made a rose out of a paper napkin. He tossed it absently on the table by Alexis. She blinked, wondering if it was for her. He didn't look at her, so she doubted it.

'I got it,' Susan said, coming back to the table. 'How about we go to Door County in the upper peninsula of northern Wisconsin? I was just talking to this woman from Chicago and she said that her family has a summer home up there. It's supposed to be really pretty this time of year. Since we are going to see Lake Michigan anyway.'

'Why not?' Ethan asked. 'I need to mark Wisconsin off my map.'

The waitress came back with their food. As they ate, it was decided by majority vote that they'd drive all the way along the coast to go to Door County. Alexis didn't vote and the others didn't ask her opinion. She was pretty sure they just assumed she'd say no.

A girl like you wouldn't get it.

Alexis took a deep breath, turning on the mattress as she curled to the very edge of the bed to escape Ethan's heat. Just feeling that much of him was doing wicked things to her body. It was like she was in a constant state of arousal and couldn't do anything about it. Right now wasn't any better.

A girl like you wouldn't get it.

She couldn't sleep. It had been almost two days since he said that to her and she couldn't get it out of her head. To top it off, she was horny and depressed – a horrible combination.

They weren't making very good time travel-wise, but none of them seemed to care. It was strange not having an agenda – no dinner parties she had to attend for her mother, no new clubs she had to make a social appearance at. Is this how most people lived? Without the pressure of social life? Somehow, she doubted it. This laid-back attitude had to be the other end of the scale. Most people probably fell in the middle.

The second day they'd driven straight through Ohio and much of Indiana, stopping to spend the night in a hotel much like the first. Ethan pulled his same routine, charging her twenty dollars for a room he'd gotten for free. The next morning, she awoke with a coffee and fast-food breakfast sandwich awaiting her. The sandwich was gross, the coffee worse and Alexis was sure it was one of the nicest things anyone had ever given her. She knew he'd paid for it, but he didn't say anything except 'continental breakfast'. There was no way the cheap hotel provided its guests with free fast food.

Day three Susan drove. She took a scenic tour through Indiana, which Alexis assumed meant they'd gotten lost. The day had been pleasant with a warm, inviting breeze outside. They'd driven with the windows rolled down.

A girl like you wouldn't get it.

Alexis sat up in the bed. The hotel they were at was in Wisconsin. The landscape only subtly changed over the course of the trip, but she'd been too distracted to really notice it.

She was having a hard time sleeping next to Ethan anyway. Damn him for dropping the towel. She had to be confused. It was the only way she could explain her sudden fascination with tattoos or, in particular, the ones on Ethan's body. Every chance she got, she tried to study the intricate lines on his arms. The artwork was a hotch-potch of different designs connected with swirled water patterns on one arm, fire on the other. There was subtle shading to some of the pieces that she found quite remarkable. He'd caught her staring a few times and frowned at her, but said nothing.

The red light on her camera battery charger caught her attention. Slowly, she crept across the hotel room and grabbed her camera. Attaching a lens, she then loaded the battery and tiptoed across the floor. She contemplated her actions for about a second before stepping on top of the dresser to get a better angle. Lifting the camera, she focused on Ethan. He was sleeping on his stomach, only wearing flannel pyjama pants. She was able to get a fairly good amount of his back and arms in the frame. Now she'd be able to stare at the picture and not the man.

As she took the picture, the flash lit up the room. Ethan moaned, shifting slightly on the bed. Alexis held still, quietly waiting to see if he'd wake up. When he didn't move, she quickly placed her camera back in its bag and crawled into bed.

Ethan moaned as she snuggled beneath the covers. She felt his weight shift as he moved. His leg brushed the back of her naked calf and he moaned again, this time louder. Alexis stiffened, holding still as she waited to see what would happen. Her leg tingled where he touched her.

She felt him turn behind her moments before a hand glided over her hip. The pink and tan leopard print chemise only fell to mid-thigh and the warmth of his fingers easily met her skin through the mesh. The nightgown pulled up as he caressed to expose her matching thong panties.

Alexis didn't make a sound. He was probably just sleeping and she really didn't want to wake him up. Ethan moved his hand down, bringing the mesh against her flesh in a long caress as he worked aimlessly over her hip. He cupped her naked butt, squeezing the cheek lightly. It felt good to be touched after what seemed like an eternity. OK, a little over a month was hardly an eternity, but it had been a really hard month.

'Mm, come here,' he said sleepily. With a strong tug, he slid her back, until his body curled around hers. She felt the heat of his erection between the cheeks of her ass, as his legs pressed into her thighs. His pyjama pants were soft, but offered little in the way of a barrier. He slid a hand intimately over her stomach, pulling her firmly against his cock. 'You smell good.'

Alexis felt a shiver of pleasure at his compliment. He sounded drowsy and she wondered if he was even awake. His body was warm and his chest rose and fell in even breaths. When he didn't move, merely held her, she wiggled her butt slightly against his erection under the pretence of being asleep.

Her movements caused his hand to stir once more. His erection rubbed against her, as his fingers glided up to cup her breast. Warm breath fanned over her throat as his face burrowed into her hair. His lips met her neck, causing a small gasp of surprise to escape her as goosebumps rose along her body. Her neck had always been so sensitive. Ethan chuckled; again the sound was sleepy.

He gently rocked his hips into her butt, pushing his shaft firmly against her. Her stomach tensed. Cream gathered between her thighs, dampening her panties. She wanted him, wanted him to touch her, kiss her, make love to her. He was warm and hard and he smelled really good.

Ethan stirred restlessly against her. One of his arms was trapped near her head as she used it for a pillow. He kissed her neck, working his way to an ear. He massaged her breasts, running his fingers lightly over her nipples through the thin nightgown. Alexis spread her thighs, slipping her leg over his, opening her body up to his exploring hands. He took the invitation, instantly working down to her hips.

Groaning, his hand slipped over her panties. 'Mm, oh yeah, nice. You're so warm and wet.'

'Ah.' Alexis arched her back. The man really knew how to work magic with his fingers. He stroked lightly at first, just brushing over her panties along her folds, teasing her slit until she squirmed for more.

Alexis arched, angling her hips. Ethan took the hint, dipping his hand beneath the thin layer of mesh. She relished the intimate contact of his finger against her wet pussy. He found the small pearl hidden in her folds. Reaching behind her back, she pulled at the waistband to his pyjama pants. He made light noises of pleasure, leaving her body long enough to free himself. When he again touched her, his hard penis worked along her butt cheeks. Her thong pulled, rubbing inside the cleft. The smooth length of his cock felt so much better than soft flannel.

Alexis knew she should push him away, pretend to wake up and feign outrage at his boldness. Ethan wasn't her type. He was all wrong. He had tattoos for crissakes. Society would freak if she were to...

Were to what? It wasn't like he was asking her to marry him. It wasn't like they'd be seen together socially. He merely had his hand down her panties. They were in the middle of Nowhere, Wisconsin. No one who mattered would know. Not even Ted and Susan would believe anything sparked between her and Ethan. This could be her dirty little secret.

Suddenly, he slipped a finger up into her body and she forgot everything but the pleasure of being touched. He pulled her to him. As his hand rocked up into her, her butt rocked along his erection. Alexis reached behind to pull him closer. Her fingers dug into his firm hip, practically clawing him with her longer nails. Ethan groaned in obvious pleasure.

Alexis's body jerked as the beginning tremors of her orgasm washed over her. Oh, she needed it. She'd been in an almost constant state of half-arousal since they first met. Her hips strained, rolling in small circles. Ethan knew just how to touch, how to work his calloused finger over her clit, sticking another inside her to put pressure on the sweet spot. Her ass clenched his erection as she wiggled against him. Reaching for a breast, she tweaked her own nipple.

'Ah. Oh. Damn.' Ethan began to actually thrust in earnest. 'Damn, baby. I'm not even inside you and I'm about to come. It's never happened like this.'

Alexis bit her lip to keep from answering. If she were to pretend later she was taken advantage of, she couldn't give herself away. No doubt Ethan would gloat that she'd needed him to get off.

Mm, but truth was, she did. Her fingers felt nowhere

near as nice as his did running up inside her. His fingers were thicker, longer, warmer. She could tell he'd done this before, many times. He knew just where to push as he continued to hit the sweet spot hidden in her passage, using just the right pressure and the right pace.

'Keep riding my hand, ah, keep moving just like that. Mm, yeah. Little faster,' he urged. He kept his hips pressed tight to her body as she obeyed.

His thumb stroked her sensitive bud, as if he'd timed her body's response somehow. She came, making soft, involuntary noises in the back of her throat. A low grunt joined hers. Ethan trembled slightly and she felt liquid warmth spreading over her back as he came.

The sensation brought her mind crashing to reality. She gasped loudly. What had she just done? And with Ethan James?

'Mm, Cindy,' he whispered, nuzzling her neck. His hand withdrew from her panties, skating up her stomach towards her breasts.

Alexis felt as if she'd been slapped. Cindy? Cindy? No he did not!

'What the . . .? Pierre?' Alexis whispered, containing her anger as she forced confusion to her voice. She blocked his roaming hand with her arm. 'Pierre, what are . . .?'

'Pierre?' Ethan's voice snapped, loud. He pushed back from her and seconds later the lamp flicked on. When she turned to look at him, his pyjama pants were pulled back up his waist. 'What the hell? Who's Pierre?'

'Ew,' Alexis cried, forcing disgust to replace the confusion. Did he actually call her Cindy? That jerk. 'Ethan? Gross. What did you do to me?'

'Gross?' he repeated, as if he'd never heard the word in his life.

'What's on my back?' she asked, knowing full and well what it was. 'Oh my . . . did you . . . relieve yourself on me? Are you like some dog that dry humps a person when they're sleeping?'

'Wait a minute.' Ethan lifted a finger. 'Did you actually just call me a dog?'

'If the leash fits,' she quipped. She made a great show of getting out of the bed and examining her back in the mirror. 'Ew. You are so paying to wash this.'

'Hey, you enjoyed it too,' Ethan said, pointing at her to emphasise his words. 'Don't try to deny it.'

'I thought I was with Pierre,' Alexis lied. 'I was dreaming of my summer in the south of France.'

'Uh-huh.'

'Hey, listen, Ethan, I'm flattered and all.' Her tone belied her words. 'But we're not getting together on this trip, got it? You're not my type.'

'Boy, you really know how to crush a guy.' Sarcasm dripped from his tone. 'Please, doll, I don't want you. I have a newsflash for you. You are not my type.'

'What? Rich and educated not your type?' Alexis charged. She put her fists on her waist, facing him down. Tilting her head, she gave him her most arrogant look.

'According to the papers, you're not rich any more.' Ethan returned her look with one of his own.

She dropped her arms from her side. She felt weak. Her voice a whisper, she asked, 'What do you mean by that?'

'Come on, I know who you are, Alexis Grant. Your picture has been in the papers. Oh, but that's right, I'm just the scum of the earth. It's amazing I can even read the newspaper, let alone remember what it says.' Ethan snorted in disgust. 'Did you actually think changing your name to Sam was going to fool me?'

Alexis didn't move. Actually, she had. Refusing to answer his question, she said softly, 'I'm going to take a shower. I need to wash your stench off me.'

Chapter Six

Alexis frowned as she looked across the parking lot. The grey Impala looked somewhat familiar. Well, it was probably that she'd seen many of them since leaving New York. Then, seeing an overweight guy with a cigarette watching her from inside the car, she stiffened.

'It's your turn to drive and to pay for gas.'

Alexis spun on her boot heels, instantly forgetting the man in the car. She didn't move to catch the keys Ethan tried to toss at her. They landed on the ground with a clank. He frowned. Until that moment, they hadn't spoken. She was determined to forget what had happened and, by the look on his face, Ethan wanted to do the same.

His red-tipped hair was damp from his shower and she noticed that he'd trimmed the red from his goatee. Having the colour gone was actually a big change. He looked almost normal.

Ethan watched her expectantly, his blue-green eyes brilliant in the morning light. She couldn't remember the name of the town they were in, but they were close to Lake Michigan and the air had a crisp chill to it. Alexis shivered. He glanced down to his keys, drawing her attention back to the present.

'Oh, ah,' Susan said, hurrying to pick up the keys. 'Actually, I want to drive again.'

'I think we should split duties,' Ethan said through clenched teeth. 'There will be plenty of miles for everyone.'

'No, really, I love driving.' Susan nodded her head emphatically. 'I want to.'

'You hate driving,' Ted said. Susan's eyes widened and she shot him a stern look. He hesitated for a moment and looked embarrassed. His words very unconvincing, he added, 'Uh, never mind. I'm thinking of someone else.'

Susan took a deep breath. 'Sam?'

Alexis closed her eyes as Ethan chuckled. The sound was mocking.

'You know what, I'll drive.' Ethan swiped his keys off the ground. He pointed at Alexis as he walked around the car. 'But you're still paying for gas. It's time you learned that everything isn't handed to you on a silver platter.'

Alexis didn't answer. Susan touched her arm, drawing her attention. 'What's going on?'

'Nothing.' Alexis shook her head. Then, reminded of her humiliation, she said quietly, 'Go ahead and call me Alexis. He knows. He knew all along.'

'Is that why he's looking at you all funny? Did something happen?' Susan persisted.

'No, nothing happened.' Alexis reached for the door.

Once she was in the car, Ethan merely snorted as he started the car.

Alexis placed her arm along the window, watching the quaint little houses with their picket-fence yards as Ethan drove down the quiet street.

'This town's pretty,' Susan said. Alexis knew her friend was trying to lighten the mood in the car. 'I'd love to live near water like this.'

The road turned, winding slowly. She saw glimpses of water through the houses and trees. The road curved to the left and soon they were driving close to Lake Michigan's shore. A family walked along the small beach. Two small children ran ahead of their parents. They were bundled in bright pink jackets. Alexis fingered the strap of her camera bag. It was next to her on the seat.

'You want me to slow down?' Ethan asked.

Alexis blinked in surprise, turning to see who he was talking to.

'If you want to take pictures I can slow down and you can hang out the window,' he offered.

'Why? So you can run me into a pole?' she asked, looking away from him.

Ethan sighed, loud and long. 'Not everything is said to be mean, Alexis.'

Ethan clutched the steering wheel, doing his best not to think of the morning's events. He'd known what he was doing, maybe not from the first moment, but he'd known who was in his bed. It didn't help that her soft, feminine smell wrapped around him in sleep. And did she have to wear such sexy nightgowns? Come on, what was a guy to think? She paraded around in those skimpy little numbers, feeding fuel to his already flaming libido.

He had woken up, aroused from dreaming about Alexis. He wasn't sure how it had gotten there, but his hand was on her hip, rubbing her flesh like it had a mind of its own. Her skin was smooth, like she'd just shaved her legs. He'd forced himself to stop, to see how she'd react. She'd pressed her tight little butt up next to his cock and wiggled.

Ethan shifted in his seat. He grew hard just thinking about it. Watching Alexis out of the corner of his eye, he sighed. He wasn't sure what made him think about it, but her style today matched his car. She had a very Audrey Hepburn quality with her black long-sleeve shirt and dark eyeliner. Her denim jeans were dark and tight. Her hair was pulled back into a puffy, stringy bun-looking thing. It had a messy elegance to it with the dark wisps falling around her features. He had to give it to her credit. She knew how to put together a good package.

Susan giggled in the back seat. She did that a lot. He heard Ted whisper, but couldn't make out the words.

The water was beautiful, if not a little grey. The sun streaked across the glassy surface. He saw Alexis finger her camera bag again, playing with the latch. She hardly ever let it out of her sight and she caressed it when she wasn't paying attention, but then she refused to take a single picture. It made no sense.

I'm a fool, he thought, seconds before opening himself up for another of her attacks. 'I want pictures from this trip for my shop. We've already missed several states. If you lean out the window and take some pictures that I can upload to my computer, then every time I get a free room, you get a free room.'

Her big eyes turned to him and he pretended to study the road. He waited for her answer, almost tense. Slowly, she pulled her camera out and slipped on a lens. She sat for a second before rolling down the window. Cool air whipped inside the car, but no one complained.

Ethan saw Susan move to smile at him in the rear-view mirror. She winked, mouthing, 'Thank you.'

He nodded once.

'Do you, ah, want anything in particular?' Alexis asked.

'How many pictures does that thing hold?' Ethan dared to look at her. Her expression was softer than he'd ever seen it and her eyes looked almost scared.

'Several hundred. I have a couple of memory sticks,' she answered.

'Then just shoot everything.' It took all his control not to smile at her.

The coastal road changed, taking them through a small forest. The white bark of the birch trees made a beautiful contrast to the darker shadows behind them. Hours passed fairly quickly. Small wooden signs along the road boasted crafts and seafood.

They'd been driving for some time when Ted chuckled, 'There's another bar.'

'I know, what is that? Fifteen along this road?' Susan laughed. The bars were actually small trailers with signs in front. They were set up in little inlets along the road. It was the strangest thing.

'We need to stop for gas,' Ethan said. 'We should be getting close to a town.'

'Ah, good, I'd like to stretch my legs a little,' Alexis said.

I'd like to stretch your legs. Ethan's eyes darted involuntarily to her long legs at the comment. He stiffened, forcing himself to stare at the road. All day thoughts like that had been popping into his head. It would seem the morning's events only whetted his appetite for more. Yeah, he needed to get laid and fast.

Sturgeon Bay, Wisconsin was picture perfect – so much so that it actually looked like a living postcard. Alexis did as Ethan suggested and took pictures of everything. The great thing about digital was that she could weed through the photographs later and delete the ones she didn't want. The streets were clean and many of the houses looked late nineteenth century with tri-coloured wood siding and manicured lawns. Alexis wasn't sure what to think of it. The place was almost too perfect – and too quiet, too clean, too middle America – and she found herself missing the busy, dirty streets of the city. Even the people were dressed a decade behind the times, their floral print dresses and denim hardly the latest New York trends. Though, to be fair, it wasn't their fault New York was the heart and soul of the United States. They were more of the . . .

Alexis bit her lip, wondering what part the dairy state could qualify as. Bones, maybe?

Trees seemed to grow everywhere, the long white birch trunks shadowing the side streets. There was a collection of quaint little shops boasting cheap vacation T-shirts and cherry-decorated knick-knacks. A large drawbridge in the centre of town lifted over the dark waters of Lake Michigan to let yachts pass under. Seeing it rise up over the glistening surface was amazing, the steel beams a testament to man's ingenuity.

'I've always wanted to go on a yacht,' Susan said, pointing at the large white boat. 'Can you imagine that only one family lives on that thing?'

'You mean one prince,' Alexis said, chuckling.

'What? Your family didn't have a yacht?' Ethan asked.

It took her a while to answer, as she tried to decide if he was just being curious or mean. 'No, my mother hated boats.'

They stopped at a little corner gas station. Alexis watched from just outside the car as Ethan talked to the cashier. The girl giggled, tossing her short brown hair. Ethan grinned, a truly stunning look as he flirted with her. Alexis felt jealousy unfurl in her gut. She knew she had no claim on him, didn't really want him for herself, but did he have to be so blatant? It wasn't as if that morning meant anything, but did he have to hit on the very next woman he came across?

'You look like you're about to spit nails,' Susan said, leaning up against the hood. 'Care to share?'

'It's nothing,' Alexis said.

'You know, I don't really like this depressed, closed-up version of yourself you got going on.' Susan threaded her arm through Alexis's, shivering in the chilled breeze.

'Ethan might have come onto me this morning,' Alexis said. It didn't feel right not telling Susan things, but she wasn't about to confess how he'd literally come onto her. 'Just a little.'

'What he do? Ask you on a date?' Susan cuddled closer, laying her head on Alexis's shoulder. 'Brrr, it's chilly here. I thought it'd be warmer today.'

'I think it's because we're close to the water,' Alexis answered.

'So, do tell,' Susan prodded. 'What he do? Do you like him? What did you say?'

Seeing Ethan coming from inside followed by Ted, Alexis said, 'Later.'

'OK, but I want to know everything.' Susan moved from Alexis to Ted, hugging him around his waist as he tried to open the car door. The couple looked comfortable together. Alexis glanced at Ethan. His eyes trained on her for a brief moment. He was wearing a navy-blue technician's panel jacket with the small logo for Adam's Heating and Air embroidered on the front. On the back was the screen-printed emblem of a skull surrounded by spider webs with the words, 'Tornado Tattoo'.

'Man, you wouldn't believe this guy,' Ted said, laughing, as they got into the car. He nodded his head at Ethan. 'Everywhere we go it's been the same. He smiles. The girls whimper. He says he does tattoos and they offer him stuff. Man, I'm beginning to think I got into the wrong business.'

'Hey, you better not think about trying to seduce other girls to get what you want,' Susan said, slugging his arm.

'Yeah, being cool does have its perks,' Ethan said, starting the car.

'What did you get this time?' Susan asked.

'Actually, we'll get to see a yacht later,' Ted said.

'We get to go sailing on a yacht?' Susan gasped in excitement. Alexis couldn't help but smile.

'Ah, well, not exactly.' Ted chuckled. 'We kind of got jobs cleaning yachts and sailboats. That girl's uncle owns a shipyard and he's hooking us up. Since it's spring, everyone's getting their boats out. They're understaffed and overworked.'

Alexis's expression fell. They got her a job cleaning boats?

'Pays pretty well I guess,' Ethan said. 'Tressa says they're desperate for help this week.'

Tressa? Alexis frowned, turning to get another glimpse of the gas-station cashier. She was watching them out of her window. The woman would so be named something like Tressa. Ethan reached into his back pocket, pulling out a piece of paper.

'What's that?' Alexis asked. 'Her phone number?'

'No.' Ethan smirked. 'Directions to a house we can rent pretty cheap. It'll only cost us thirty bucks a piece for three days.'

'Three days?' Alexis asked. 'We're going to be here that long?'

'Why not?' Susan asked. Alexis could tell her friend liked the idea. 'It's a beautiful location. I saw a sign back there for fresh cheese. You know, Wisconsin is the dairy state. We have to try the cheese.'

'I want to try some of that cherry wine,' Ted said. 'Sounds interesting.'

'I think I saw a billboard for vineyards,' Ethan said. 'And I got a map of the peninsula.'

'You actually bought a map?' Alexis asked, unable to help herself.

'Only of the peninsula,' Ethan said, winking at her. 'Don't worry, doll, I can still get us lost in the Midwest.'

Her stomach fluttered nervously at the playfulness of his tone. OK, why was she flirting with Ethan?

The directions led them through a long grove of trees, taking them to the outskirts of town. Ethan slowed down, looking for street numbers. 'Ah, here it is.' He turned into a long driveway. A new, modern ranch-style house was on one side of the drive. An older dwelling was on the other.

'Which do you think is for rent?' Susan asked.

'That one.' Ethan pointed to the older one. It was blue-grey. The paint was chipped off the sides and it was smaller compared to the other nineteenth-century houses in town. 'Tressa said they'll have a washer and dryer inside we can use, a fridge, stove, whatever. The weekenders cancelled and lost their deposit, so we get it half-price.'

'Perfect,' Susan said. 'I could stand to do some laundry.'

'Mm, I could stand for you to do my laundry, too,' Ted said.

'Me too,' Alexis quickly said, scrunching up her nose and making a silly face.

'Well, as long as you're offering,' Ethan said, laughing as Susan baulked in horror.

'Nice try, guys,' she said dryly. 'But, I'm not doing anyone's laundry but my own.'

They got out of the car. A woman came out of the ranch house and smiled, waving. She was elderly, with hair as white as snow and thick glasses that hung from a gold chain. She wore a pink smock with cherry patterns over her clothes that buttoned down the front. By the fine dust it looked as if she'd been baking.

'Are you Tressa's friends?' the woman asked. She walked in an unusually spry way for her obvious age.

'Hi,' Ethan said. 'I'm Ethan James. This is Ted, his wife, Susan. And this lovely woman over here is my fiancée, Alexis. Tressa mentioned you had a place to rent?'

Alexis froze. What? She was his what? She might be a

little out of it, but she was pretty sure she'd remember getting engaged.

'She all right?' the woman asked, nodding at Alexis. 'Are you all right, dear?'

'Oh, yeah, sure. She's a little travel sick, that's all.' Ethan walked around the car to her. He put his arm around her shoulders and squeezed. 'Aren't you, honey? She'll be fine once she lies down.'

'Oh, poor thing,' the woman said. Reaching into her smock, she pulled out a set of keys. 'We had a cancellation for the weekend, so it'll be a hundred and twenty dollars up front. Firewood is in back. Feel free to light a bonfire in the fire pit. Row boat's on the dock. Life jackets are in the shed. No loud music after ten o'clock, but you can stay out as late as you want.'

'Sounds perfect. Thank you,' Ethan said. She unlocked the side door and handed him the keys. Ted pulled out his wallet and gave the woman sixty dollars for him and Susan. Alexis reached into her camera bag and handed the woman thirty. She blinked in surprise, looking from Ethan to Alexis and then back again. Ethan handed her thirty as well. She took their money and left.

'It looks like my grandma's house,' Susan said, laughing. 'Look at all this stuff. It has to be from the fifties.'

From the side door they could walk straight into the kitchen, down the basement steps, or into a small bedroom. The home was completely furnished. In the kitchen, an old floral vinyl tablecloth matched the pale-yellow chairs. A corded, rotary dial phone hung on the wall. The cupboards were stocked with a hotchpotch of dinnerware – from green glass bowls to pottery-spun coffee mugs to shot glasses. The refrigerator was empty and there was no food in the house.

Beyond the kitchen was a living room. Old photographs hung on the wall next to giant plastic butterflies. The burnt-orange couch had doilies over the arms and the avocado chairs matched the avocado carpet. The carpet was faded where the light shone in the large bay window.

Alexis stepped closer to the window, setting her camera down on a chair. The back yard overlooked the bay. She could just make out the faint outline of a lighthouse across the water. 'Wow.'

'Great view,' Susan agreed. Then, with a mischievous glint in her eyes, she said, 'So, um, Ethan, remind me again. When exactly did you and Lexy here get engaged?'

'Tressa told her grandma that on the phone,' Ted answered. 'She said the woman would hassle us less if we were serious couples on vacation and not just drifters.'

Alexis didn't say a word. She felt Ethan's eyes on her and wondered at it.

'Mm, well, I kind of like the idea of playing house for a few days.' Susan wiggled her eyebrows suggestively. 'I saw some stairs. Want to see if that leads to another bedroom?'

Ted groaned. 'Yeah, let's go check that out.'

'I think they just claimed the upstairs,' Ethan said.

'I'm going to go get my stuff,' Alexis answered. 'Can I have the keys to the trunk?'

'I'll come with you.' Ethan led the way back outside. He popped the trunk.

'There are three bedrooms!' Susan called, waving from a second-storey window.

'Great!' Ethan yelled back. To Alexis, he said, 'You should be happy. You get your own room.'

'Do you have to tattoo the girl now?' she asked, wondering again at the jealousy.

'Actually, no, she said her parents would kill her.' Ethan laughed as if at his own private joke. 'I figured if everyone wants to, we could go out tonight. I might be able to scrounge up some business that way.'

'Did you really get us jobs cleaning yachts?' Alexis asked, her tone a little sharper than she'd have liked. She wrinkled her nose in distaste. 'I think I'll have to pass.'

'What?' His tone mocked her. 'Afraid to get your hands dirty?'

'No. I just don't feel like being someone's maid.'

'Tell me then, Ms Grant, how exactly do you plan on making any extra cash on this trip?' Ethan asked.

'I'll...'

'Yes?'

'I'll think of something. It won't be cleaning yachts.'

'You know what your problem is? I mean, don't get me wrong, you got a lot of them, doll. But one of your main problems is that you're just too ... prissy.'

Alexis gasped. 'I am not prissy.'

'Yes, doll, you are. You're like a little ornament someone stuck up on a mantlepiece for twenty years.' Ethan slung a bag over his shoulder before reaching to grab a second one. 'I'll bet you've never actually been dirty a day in your life.'

Alexis grabbed her bags and followed him inside. His words stung. 'What does getting dirty have to do with anything?'

Ethan stopped, turning on his heels so fast she almost ran into his chest. Looking down at her, he grinned. 'Ah, trust me, some of the best activities in life come with getting dirty.'

'You're a pig.'

'Yeah, probably, but the ladies must like it because I do get laid a lot.'

Unable to stop the words, she said, 'What? I'm not the first sleeping woman you've attacked with a dry hump?'

Ethan frowned. 'I can't figure something out. Are you mad that I made you come? Or are you mad that I'm never going to do it again? Or is it you're mad at yourself for liking these scummy tattoo artist's hands on your little debutante body?'

Alexis felt the blood drain from her features. 'I did not like it.'

'Methinks you protest too much,' Ethan mocked, walking to the side bedroom. He tossed his bags on the bed.

'Now listen here, Sir Stupid.' Alexis followed him. 'I am not protesting.'

'I'll take this room. Wouldn't want any of my late-night guests keeping you all awake.'

'Well, maybe it'll be my late-night guests that keep you awake,' Alexis said.

'Doll, the men you sleep with probably can't stay up past ten.'

'What is that supposed to mean?' She put her hands on her hips.

'It means, that you wouldn't be able to handle anything more than a stuffy, uptight, anal retentive, briefcase-carrying snob who has more interest in pleasing himself and his greed than the woman in bed with him. The kind of man who wouldn't be capable of showing you a knock-down, drag-out good time in the sack because he's too worried about what everyone else thinks. Just. Like. You.' As he said the last word, he shut the bedroom door in her face.

'That's not true,' Alexis yelled, stomping away from him. She marched into the bathroom and threw her bags on the floor. She knew that Ted and Susan were probably having sex upstairs and the last thing she wanted was to have to listen to them.

Bright-pink tile lined the walls. There was a cluttered décor to the house that she didn't like. Knick-knacks were everywhere, stuffed onto every little nook and cranny, from figurines to decorative tins cans to little toy soldiers. The bathroom was no different. The pink towels were edged with lace and embroidered with large roses. The yellow shower curtain matched the kitchen more than it did the bathroom.

Alexis studied herself in the mirror, surrounded by the pink gaudiness. What was she doing here? How had her life come to this? And why in the world was thinking of Ethan having sex with other women driving her mad?

Suddenly, Alexis smiled. So, he thought the only type of man she could get was anal retentive. He thought she didn't know how to have a good time. She turned to dig through her bags. Pulling out a slip of a dress, she grinned. She'd show him she knew how to have a good time. Then, when he was begging her to sleep with him, she'd deny him. Oh, yeah. Tonight was going to be fun.

* * *

'Mm, nice.' Susan eyed Ted from her place on the bed. Stretching her arms above her head, she smiled. The bedroom was filled with lace and doilies. The old wooden dresser had to be an antique, as was the vase on top of it. The bed creaked as she moved. It was old as well.

Ted threw off his polo shirt, revealing his muscled chest. Then, slowly, he undid his fly, one slow button at a time. Susan wiggled with anticipation, her body ready for him. She wore a pink stretched lace cami and matching thong. A thin ribbon formed a bow between her breasts. She toyed with the ribbon, wrapping it around her index finger.

'I forgot to tell you something,' she said, suddenly remembering Alexis's words. 'Alexis said Ethan might have come onto her.'

'You're kidding, right?' Ted laughed, as he pushed his pants off his legs. Standing in his red boxers, he grinned and crawled onto the bed. Susan pointed her foot at him. He kissed it, lightly working his way up her ankle and calf. Between kisses, he said, 'Ethan can barely stand her.'

'Mm, yeah, she'd probably just misread something he's done. He's not really the type of man she's used to.' Susan sighed, jerking slightly as Ted's lips reached her knee. His tongue flicked, sending goosebumps over her body. She loved it when he kissed the tender flesh on the inside of her knee. 'I hate to admit it, but I think it's funny how he handles her. And it was so sweet how he got her to take pictures. I know she's been dying to get that camera out of her case. She's always scared people are going to hate her work.'

'Mm,' Ted answered.

'Are you listening to me?'

'No, I'm trying not to,' Ted said. Susan gasped. He groaned, grabbed her leg and pulled it to the side. He began licking and nibbling her inner thigh. 'I really don't want to think about Alexis right now, honey. You keep saying her name and Little Ted is likely to lose his hard on.'

'So, you're saying it would only take –' Susan gasped as

Ted grabbed her thighs and jerked them further apart. In the same fluid motion, he pulled her sex to his mouth, boldly licking her through her lace panties. 'Ah!'

'Mm, that's better,' Ted said as she worked her body against his mouth. 'You always taste so good.'

Susan forgot all about her friend as Ted kissed her. She liked watching his head between her thighs. When he grabbed her panties and worked them off her hips, she couldn't help but squirm. Her hands clawed at her cami, pulling it down off her breasts.

'Turn over, I want to watch,' Ted said. He got off the bed and pulled off his boxers. Then, as Susan got on her hands and knees, he slid a condom over his cock. His hand instantly went to her butt, caressing it.

Susan felt him come up behind her, felt the heat of his body along her sex. She loved that first touch of his body to hers as he readied himself to enter, the slight, involuntary tensing inside her pussy as she awaited his thrust. She relished the first moment of anticipation and longing, the uncertainty of the moment. Would he take her hard? Soft? Fast? Deep?

'You're gorgeous, you know it,' Ted said, his voice soft. He was always saying things like that to her.

His body worked against her, as he took her with slow, shallow thrusts, the kind that drove her to the point of madness. She tried to push back, wanting more, but he held her away, knowing how to stir her passions. His finger slipped around to find the pearl buried in her moist folds. He stroked her clit, thrusting deeper at the same time until he filled her completely.

'You're so sexy. I've been thinking about having my way with you all day.' Ted thrust again, working his hips in little circles as he stayed deep. 'Mm, I love you, Susan.'

'I love you,' she said, her words breathy as she neared her climax. Ted pushed her swollen clit, massaging it harder the closer she got. Her breasts ached to be touched and she moved one hand to grab them, pulling at her nipples. Ted kept the stimulation going, the jolts of his movements thrusting her along his warm hand. Her cream made his fingers glide over her sex. When she came, the climax washed over her in a tender, slow wave.

Ted kept moving, even as her climax slowed, until finally his body jerked his release. Groaning softly, he fell on the bed next to her. Running his hand over her butt, he gave it a playful squeeze. 'I wonder if this town has a lingerie shop. I'd love to get you some black leather.'

Susan giggled and looked around the bedroom. 'I don't think this is a black leather kind of place.'

'Mm, too bad.' He pulled her into his arms. 'I guess I'll just have to settle with covering you in cherry wine.'

Chapter Seven

Smoke filled the small bar as they made their way to a corner booth. The locals looked at her like she was nuts. Could she really blame them? She looked better suited to a trendy New York club than in a bar filled with fanatical football fans in their green T-shirts and beer-company banners.

Alexis definitely felt overdressed for the occasion. In fact, she was so overdressed she was scared of sitting in her white halter dress for fear of staining it. The cotton pique material was embroidered with little blue and yellow daisies. The deep V-neckline dipped low between her breasts, so low she couldn't wear a bra with it. Several times she caught men staring at her chest. She just took it for granted in New York that everyone dressed like her. Here, they seemed a little more conservative – at least from what she could tell from the women. Even the females wore the state's green and yellow football colours proudly.

Now, Ethan fitted right in. He wasn't wearing sport-team paraphernalia, but a faded grey T-shirt and old blue jeans. He walked confident and relaxed. To her shame, she actually caught herself checking out his butt.

Alexis eyed the booth before sliding in. She looked expectantly for a waitress. There wasn't one. Then, frowning, she lifted her arm to wave the bartender over. Ethan grabbed her hand, laughing. His warm palm closed around her wrist, drawing her fingers to the table. 'I'll get the drinks.'

'I'll come with you.' Ted winked at Susan.

'I'll have a Manhattan,' Alexis said as the men walked away.

'You look nice, Lexy,' Susan said.

'I'm overdressed.' Alexis glanced down, feeling out of place. When Ethan said they were going out, she never imagined it would be to a place like this. She'd seen the town. It was pretty. Surely they had something a little swankier.

'You're beautiful.' Susan grinned, slipping next to her in the booth. 'Don't worry about it. Now quick, because I've been dying to know, tell me what's going on between you and Ethan.'

'He's a jerk. I can't stand him,' Alexis promptly answered. 'He's insufferable. Mean.'

'I think he's nice,' Susan said.

'He told me the only guy I could get was an unaware jerk with a briefcase who wouldn't know how to have fun if it bit him.'

'Well, it does kind of sound like the guys you usually date.' Susan shook her head when Alexis started to protest. 'Quit avoiding the topic. How'd he come onto you?'

'He started fondling me in the bed. Nothing came of it. I threw him off me and told him to leave me alone.' Alexis averted her gaze. It wasn't necessarily the whole truth, but close enough. 'He called me Cindy and said he was sleeping when it happened.'

'So you're not attracted to him?' Susan asked.

'Nope, not in the least,' Alexis answered.

'Then, you wouldn't care if he went home with someone else tonight?'

'Not at all. I welcome him to try.'

'Oh, good, cos it doesn't appear like he's got to try. By the looks of it, he's already scored.'

Alexis instantly turned to look at Ethan. Jealous anger reared its ugly head. She didn't want him, but she didn't want the two hussies at the bar to have him either. How was he going to suffer in his desire for her if he was with someone else?

The blonde, a tall skinny number, was already touching his arm, laughing dramatically at whatever he said. Alexis had spent many hours in the car with the man. He was not that funny. The redhead, a smaller woman with large breasts, cornered him from the other side. Ted excused himself, carrying two beers. He set one before Susan, as he slid into the seat. Alexis frowned. Ethan was still preoccupied at the bar and she had no drink.

'Here, take mine,' Ted offered.

'No, I ordered a Manhattan.' Alexis watched Ethan, willing the two women to leave him be.

Ted chuckled. 'You're going to get a beer.'

After several minutes, Ethan finally joined them. The redhead went to a jukebox and played a country song as her blonde friend went to the bathroom. Ethan glanced at where Susan sat with Alexis. Without having to be asked, she moved to sit by Ted. Ethan began to sit, sliding a beer in front of Alexis.

'Excuse me,' Alexis said tartly. 'I have to powder my nose.'

Ethan reversed directions, getting back out of the booth. As Alexis walked away, she heard Ethan, Ted and Susan laughing.

She stepped into the small bathroom, setting her purse on the one sink. The faucet leaked, but she ignored it. There were two stalls and Alexis pretended to fix her make-up as she waited for the blonde to come out of one.

The toilet flushed and, after a few moments, the blonde stepped out. Alexis met her eyes through the mirror. For a moment, the woman looked like a deer caught in headlights right before impact. Alexis smiled and the woman took a hesitant step forwards.

'Hi,' Alexis said, dotting lip gloss on her finger.

'Hi,' the woman answered, hesitating slightly as she moved to wash her hands. She had the same accent everyone around this part of the US seemed to – Belgian with a Canadian flare. Everything seemed to be pronounced with a long 'o' sound. In the harsh light of the bathroom she didn't look as pretty. Her blonde hair was more the work of bleach than of nature. Her make-up was too dark and her clothes too tight.

'You live here?' Alexis asked.

'Oh-yah.'

'It's very pretty.'

'Uh-huh,' the blonde hesitated, her mouth working for a moment. 'Is that your boyfriend out there? He said he was single.'

Bingo! thought Alexis. That's what she was waiting for.

Alexis forced a laugh. 'Who, Ethan? Gosh, no. I mean, he's charming when you first get to know him, but . . .'

'But what?' the woman prompted.

Alexis made a face and glanced over her shoulder to the door as if they'd be overheard. 'Can you keep a secret?'

The woman nodded eagerly. 'Oh-yah, I'm real trustworthy.'

'Well, I mean he's cute, right? Any woman would die to have him. But, I just can't get over the fact that he's . . . you know . . . diseased –' Alexis pointed meaningfully down to the floor '– down there. I heard him telling Ted that it actually leaks green stuff when he pees. I mean he says it's not contagious and that the burning isn't so bad once he got used to it, but I don't know.'

The blonde paled.

Alexis smiled. Women were so easy to manipulate, especially when they were a little drunk. Backtracking a little so she didn't seem like a jealous loser, she said, 'Oh, but he's really nice. If you like him, you should totally go out with him. He'll treat you like a lady.'

'Oh, no, I mean, I would, but I have a boyfriend,' the blonde said. 'In fact, I have to go meet him in a few minutes.'

'Oh.' Alexis let a small pout form on her lips. 'Well, do me a favour. Don't go running straight out of here. Wait a few minutes before you leave. Ethan is so sensitive. The last time a woman didn't seem to take interest he cried for days.'

The woman's face fell slightly and she nodded. 'I won't, but I do need to get going.'

'Oh, well, OK, it was great to meet you. You have a lovely town,' Alexis said.

'Yeah, thanks.' The blonde left the restroom. Alexis waited a few minutes before walking back out into the bar. Ethan stood up as she neared the booth. Sliding in, she nearly laughed to see the blonde and her friend leaving.

'How much do I owe you for the beer?' she asked, forcing a smile.

'What?' Ethan turned from where he watched the two friends leave. 'Oh, you can buy the next round.'

'Suits me.' Alexis turned to Susan and Ted. For some reason she was suddenly feeling very festive. 'So, how bad do you think cleaning yachts is going to be?'

'You'll do it?' Susan asked in surprise.

Ethan turned to her, looking equally as shocked.

Alexis shrugged. 'Why not? This trip is supposed to be fun. I'm having fun, aren't you? And I always wanted to see the inside of a yacht.'

Ethan didn't get it at all. Eight girls all lined up, ready for action, and then bam. Nothing. It was like he'd suddenly developed leprosy. And, to make matters worse, he wasn't able to drum up any solid tattoo business. There were a lot of drunken maybes, but no definites. They'd even gone to different bars. Every place it was the same. He'd start being charming. It looked like it worked. He'd leave, letting the anticipation simmer. But then, instead of them coming to him, they actually left without so much as another look.

Ethan shook his head and gripped the steering wheel tight as he drove them home. Hearing Alexis hum softly, he turned to study her. She looked damned fine tonight, but she always looked good. However, tonight it was more than her outfit, it was her whole demeanour. She was smiling more, a bright smile that lit up her whole face. It was like she was happy, relaxed. Maybe it was the alcohol. She had five beers and to a skinny girl that could be a lot. Ethan had no idea why he kept track of how much she drank, but he had.

She'd gotten more than her share of attention that was for sure. She was asked to dance twice. He wondered at the satisfaction he felt each time she refused.

'I like this town,' Alexis said, leaning her head to the side.

Ethan chuckled. 'You look like you like everything right now.'

'What's that supposed to mean?' she demanded, sitting straighter.

'Ah, do we have to do this tonight? It's late. I'm tired.' Ethan shot her a sidelong glance. He had had a few beers himself and needed to concentrate on the road. He wasn't even close to drunk, but he didn't want to risk driving recklessly with other people in his car. 'Can't we call a truce until tomorrow morning?'

'Fine.' Alexis yawned. 'But don't think this means I like you, because I don't.'

She just couldn't leave it alone, could she? Ethan rolled his eyes. 'Fine. I don't really like you either.'

'Good.' This time her voice was a sleepy mumble. 'I actually think I loathe you.'

'I loathe you too.' His voice was low. Ted and Susan looked to be asleep in the back seat.

'I hate your tattoos,' Alexis said, her voice softer with each word.

'You're too skinny,' Ethan whispered. He glanced at her.

Alexis's head lay against his seat. She was turned to the side, facing him. For a brief moment, her eyes opened to look at him. She blinked several times. 'Do you really think I'm ugly?'

'I never said you were ugly.' Ethan wondered at the sadness in her voice. Where was the confident she-demon who'd tormented him for days? 'I just think you should stop starving yourself for no reason.'

'Then do you think I'm pretty?' she asked, not looking at him again. He forced his attention back to the road.

Yes, Ethan thought, *I think you're gorgeous.*

He didn't answer her. His body stirred to life, all too

ready to remember her softness from the night before. She didn't seem to notice as her breath deepened. She was asleep.

Alexis opened her eyes. Her vision swam a little, but not bad. Her body felt delicate from drinking the night before, but nothing she couldn't handle with a shower and some strong black coffee.

Slowly, she became more aware of her surroundings. A pink and yellow macramé wall-hanging came into focus in front of her. A warm body curled behind hers in bed and she felt the unmistakable push of an erection to her back. Alexis tensed. It took several seconds for her to remember where she was.

Doing a quick assessment of her body, she realised she was still in her dress. That was good. Her panties were on. Even better. Ethan's smell was unmistakable and she knew it was him. She closed her eyes, automatically snuggling back into his protective warmth. Mm, perfect.

What? Her eyes popped open in shock at her own thoughts. *No, no, not perfect. Not perfect at all.*

Alexis started breathing hard. What should she do? Outrage. She should feign outrage.

Yeah, yeah, outrage.

'Not again,' she said sharply, jerking her body from Ethan's. The movement jarred her head and she instantly felt nauseous. Covering her eyes with her hands, she moaned, 'Oh.'

'What...?' Ethan said in sleepy confusion. 'What are you doing down here?'

'What am I...?' Alexis lowered her tone. 'That's a good question, Ethan. What am I doing down here? I mean, besides the obvious?'

Alexis gave a scornful look down his naked body. Gasping, she couldn't help but stare at his erection. There were piercings on it. Her mouth worked, but no sound came out. Ethan grimaced and covered his waist.

'What is it about me sleeping that makes you think I want you to dry hump my back?' she asked.

'Hold on one second,' he said, sitting up. 'I was not dry humping your anything.'

'Really?' Alexis glanced down at his waist, secretly hoping for another peek. Piercings? She wondered what they were for. 'Then how did you explain that?'

'Morning wood,' he said, unashamed. 'I'm a guy. It happens. Now, what I want to know is how did you get into my bed?'

'Well, I think that's obvious. I fell asleep in the car and you put me in here.' Alexis made a move for the door. The last thing she wanted was to get caught in Ethan's room when she had one of her own. How in the world would she explain that to Susan?

'No, I distinctly remember carrying you to the couch.' Ethan stood up, gripping the covers around his waist.

She shivered. The room suddenly seemed too small for the both of them. Ethan looked really cute in nothing but pink bedcovers.

'I don't want to hear it.' Alexis stormed out, marching straight to the bathroom to take a shower. It didn't take her long to strip out of her clothes and jump into the warm stream of water. Closing her eyes, she groaned. What in the world did he need those piercings for?

'*Mary Margaret, Sammy's Pride, Rachel's Promise.*' Susan stopped walking along the docks where she was reading the names of boats. She glanced at Alexis. 'Why do men always name their vehicles after women?'

'It's a compliment,' Ted assured her, kissing her head.

'Having a boat named after you is a compliment?' Susan asked, unconvinced.

'I think it depends on the boat.' Alexis pointed across the water to a beaten-up sailboat with chipped paint.

'Hey, don't knock it. The guy's probably fixing it up himself. There is some pride in that, you know,' Ethan said.

'Please,' Alexis said. 'Quit being so sensitive. We're not talking about your precious car.'

'I'm only saying –' Ethan turned to her.

Alexis held up her hand, cutting him off. 'Can you just not talk to me? Ever.'

'What did I do to – ?' Ethan reached to touch her arm.

Alexis pulled away from him, walking faster along the dock.

Susan caught up to her. 'Wow, what was that all about?'

'Nothing,' Alexis said.

'Lexy?' Susan insisted, nudging her playfully in the side. 'Don't make me tickle it out of you.'

'Really, it's nothing. We just don't like each other. You can't make two people like each other when they don't.' Alexis glanced over the water. She'd much rather spend the day out sailing than inside a yacht cleaning. Still, she'd said she would do it and do it she would. She needed the money. 'By the way, just wanted to remind you that you promised to clean any and all toilets on this trip. I'm holding you to that.'

'Ew, I was hoping you forgot.' Susan made a face, laughing. 'Now, come on, please tell me what's going on. It's like this trip started and you don't talk to me any more. Are you mad at me for making you come?'

'You didn't hold me at gunpoint.' Alexis stopped walking. Noticing that there were no longer footsteps behind them, she turned. Ethan and Ted were talking to a man with a beard. The men were far enough away that they wouldn't be able to overhear their conversation. 'I was mad at first, but not any more and never really at you. You were right. There is nothing for me in New York. Let's face it. I don't have the best employment record. I've never held a job longer than two weeks, so I've already burned whatever bridges I had. No one in their right mind would give me a recommendation. I have no actual higher education and any place decent isn't going to hire Francine Grant's daughter for anything more than a sideshow novelty. So, the way I look at it, I can either stay in New York and get a job as a hostess in some one-star restaurant or I can go to California.'

'And get a job in a two-star restaurant?' Susan teased, grinning.

'Exactly,' Alexis said. Leaning her head back, she took a deep breath. 'How did it come to this, Susan? I was so defined by my station in life. Now I'm no one. I have no money, no connections, no social status, no education –'

'Hey, stop that.' Susan pulled her arm, drawing her attention back. 'Stop the pity party. You have me and together we can handle anything, remember? You have to stop feeling sorry for yourself. Look around you. You're actually free. You're young, pretty and so what if you haven't been to college? You're smart. Alexis Samantha Wellington Grant will always land firmly on her feet.'

Alexis smiled. She hugged her sweater around her body. She really hated to clean ships in her designer clothes. Only problem was, she didn't have any non-designer clothes. Hearing footsteps, Alexis turned. A cute man in white slacks and a bright-blue jacket made his way along the docks. His blond-tipped hair blew around his head. Alexis instantly smiled at him.

'Hi,' he said, nodding as he made a move to walk past. He had a bright smile and though he wasn't drop-dead handsome, he wasn't bad to look at.

'Oh, sir, excuse me,' Alexis said. She affected her most helpless look.

The man stopped, turning. She could tell he came from money. He had that look to him, the look of breeding and sophistication. Besides, he was wearing what had to be at least a two hundred dollar track jacket. If Alexis knew anything, she knew her clothes. This one's cut was too precise and elegant to be from a shopping mall. Growing up rich had taught her a few things. Spotting others with money was one of them.

'Can I help you?' he asked, still grinning. Alexis liked his straight, white teeth. This was a man who took care of himself, or at least had good doctors to do it for him.

'We're a little lost,' Alexis said, without thinking. 'Have you seen a sailboat called ... ah ...' She glanced quickly at Susan. Susan didn't move. '... *Teresa's Mischief*?'

'No,' he said, 'I don't think I have.'

'Mm, darn.' Alexis pouted, pushing out her lower lip.

'These docks can be a little confusing,' the man said. 'I'm Brice.'

'Lexy,' Alexis said, holding out her hand for him to take. He held it briefly, looking her in the eye.

'I'd be happy to help you find it,' Brice said. 'My yacht is just down the dock. It's being cleaned this morning, but maybe if we can't find your sailboat then you and your friend, of course,' he stopped to smile at Susan, 'might want to come out with me this afternoon –'

'Hey, you guys ready?' Ethan called. 'We're all set.'

Brice blinked several times and took a step back as he looked at Ethan. 'Oh, I'm sorry, I didn't know you were here with someone. Still, I'd be honoured if you'd all join me.'

'Oh, we're not with him,' Alexis said quickly. She glanced desperately at Ethan, hoping he'd go away. If she played her hand right, she'd be able to squeeze a decent meal out of this guy and a night in someplace classy.

'Alexis, Susan, come on,' Ethan yelled. 'These ships aren't going to clean themselves!'

Alexis wanted to die.

'Well, it looks like you're busy. Another time, perhaps,' Brice said, starting a fast retreat the way he'd come. 'It was nice to meet you.'

Alexis glared at Ethan as she made her way over to him. Pushing his arm, she said, 'You're a real jerk, you know it.'

'What?' Ethan glanced at Susan. 'What did I do now?'

'I'll tell you what you did. You just ruined my chance at getting a decent meal in a nice place.' Alexis pushed his arm again when he tried to get too near. 'I had him practically eating out of my palm before you had to open your mouth. He'd already invited us out on his yacht.'

'You were going to whore yourself out for a meal and a boat ride.' Ethan frowned. Was it just her, or did he look disappointed?

'Did you just call me a whore?' Alexis asked. She looked to Susan for confirmation.

'If the hooker boots fit,' he mumbled.

'Ah, let it drop, Lexy,' Susan said. 'We couldn't have gone out this afternoon anyway. We have boats to clean.'

Alexis growled, pushing past Ethan to join Ted by the docks. He was helping the bearded man carrying buckets and cleaning supplies.

'Where did Mr Trenton go?' the bearded man asked, more to himself.

Susan asked, 'Guy in the blue jacket?'

'Oh-yah, that's him. One of the richest men in the county,' the bearded man answered. 'He owns three boats. Says he's fixing them up to sell them. It's kind of a hobby with him. You're cleaning two of them today so make sure you do a real fine job. He's very particular.'

Susan pointed down the docks. 'I think he headed back that way.'

Alexis turned to glare at Ethan. Under her breath, she said, 'Really, one of the richest you say.'

'Sure.' The man cleared his throat. 'OK now, you have the list. I'll be back in three hours to see what you've got done.'

Ethan did his best to avoid Alexis most of the day. Scrubbing boats wasn't exactly his idea of a good time either, but he wasn't scared of a little hard work. Besides, it would be a great story to tell one day. How many people could say they once scrubbed yachts in Wisconsin?

The boats had an elegant, streamlined beauty. Ethan rubbed down the railing along the sides. The docks were quiet, except for the sound of the boats drifting lightly into the wood planks they were tethered to.

He'd known exactly what he'd been doing when he ruined Alexis's chances with Mr Trenton. At the time, he'd been disgusted that she'd throw herself at the man like that, just because he looked rich. OK, so he was rich, but that didn't excuse her behaviour. Besides, how could he not embarrass her after her little stinging comments that morning about him not being able to control himself as he dry humped her leg? And then she'd treated him as if he wasn't worthy of even talking to her.

'Hey, easy, or you're going to rub right through the metal,' Ted said, laughing. 'I think it's polished.'

'What?' Ethan blinked, realising he was gripping the metal rail hard. He let go.

'I tell you what,' Ted said, stretching his arms. 'When they said we'd be cleaning yachts, I pictured those big cruise-like ships you always see on television commercials for the Caribbean. I'm glad they only turned out to be these motor yachts and sailboats.'

'I know. I was a little worried about that myself,' Ethan chuckled in agreement. 'How do you think the girls are doing on the inside? They about ready to move on to the next one?'

'I'll check.' Ted disappeared into the cabin door. Ethan glanced around. It looked clean, cleaner than it was before they climbed on. Ted came back up carrying buckets. 'All done.'

'Ugh, how many left?' Susan asked, swiping her forehead.

'Five down, three to go,' Ethan answered.

'Only five?' Susan laughed. 'Don't tell me how much we're going to make until after we're done. I doubt any amount of money is going to be motivating enough.'

Ethan hopped down onto the dock. Ted passed him the buckets and then got down to help Susan. She kissed him lightly before hauling her bucket to the next sailboat.

Ethan glanced up at Alexis. The woman looked miserable, but to her credit he hadn't heard her complain once.

'Here,' Ethan said, offering her a hand. She glared at him, moving along to the other side of the boat to climb down by herself. Ethan grabbed his bucket and followed Susan and Ted.

Once they were loaded on the sixth ship, Susan and Alexis automatically went inside the cabin to get started. Ethan grabbed a rag and began working on the deck.

'Oh my!' Susan yelled. 'Ted!'

Ted disappeared into the cabin. Seconds later, his head popped out of the cabin. 'Hey, Ethan, come here, you have to see this!'

Ethan followed him into the cabin. A row of grey carpeted stairs wound down into a living room. The place was gorgeous with dark mahogany walls and shelves, a matching table with leather chairs and a fully stocked bar.

'Back here,' Ted said, waving his hand. Ethan followed him to the back room. A strange smell drifted through the door.

'What is that?' Ethan asked. He stepped into the bedroom. The place was practically destroyed. The king-size bed was messed up. Used condoms were stuck to the floor, the nightstand and he even saw one hanging over the side of the trash bin.

'This is so gross,' Susan said. 'There is a vibrator on the floor over here.'

'I'm not cleaning this. I'd rather starve,' Alexis said.

'What is that smell?' Ted asked. He kicked the bedspread over, revealing vomit. He jumped back. 'Oh. Nasty.'

'That's foul,' Susan said, running for the door. She bumped into Ethan on the way out.

'I'm not touching any of this,' Alexis said, right behind Susan. Ethan shut the door once they were all out.

'What kind of gross bastard would leave a mess like that?' Susan asked, shivering violently.

'Ew, ever hear of a trash can? I wouldn't be caught dead with someone like this. It's just sick,' Alexis added.

Ethan glanced around. Seeing a picture, he grinned. 'Why, Lexy, look. It's your good friend, Mr Trenton.'

He pointed at the photograph of Mr Trenton shaking someone's hand, watching as Alexis turned. The horrified look on her pale face only caused his grin to widen.

'Oh, gawd, I think I'm going to be sick.' Alexis ran up the stairs, covering her mouth with her hands. Susan was right behind her.

When they were alone, Ted said, 'You know, seeing that

look on Alexis's face is almost worth having to clean that mess up. I get so tired of girls thinking money equals decency.'

Ethan laughed. 'I know exactly what you mean.'

Chapter Eight

'I can't believe we did all that work and only made a hundred dollars a piece,' Susan said, suppressing a yawn.

Alexis stared into the flames from her place on a log. The guys had built a bonfire in the back yard. The bay stretched out before them. Moonlight and street lamps reflected on the calm glassy surface. It was quiet on the shore. No boats were out on the water that they could see. Susan cuddled with Ted on a wooden-bench swing. Ethan came from the house carrying a bottle and four glasses.

'What do you have there?' Ted asked.

'Ah, compliments of Mr Trenton,' Ethan said, holding up a bottle of fine brandy.

'Did you steal that?' Susan asked.

'I like to think of it more as a well-deserved tip,' Ethan said.

'You should've taken more.' Susan shivered. 'That was just plain nasty.'

Alexis wrinkled her nose in disgust. Luckily, none of the other boats had been as bad as Brice Trenton's. She shivered. And to think she'd actually wanted to go home with the guy just for a nice place to sleep. She looked over the old house. It was looking better and better each second.

'He was nasty, wasn't he?' Alexis laughed as Ethan handed her some brandy.

'To Mr Nasty,' Ted said, holding up his glass.

'To Mr Nasty,' the others repeated, toasting.

Alexis took a sip, coughing as the heady liquor burnt its way down her throat. Standing, she yawned. 'I think I'll go to bed.'

Handing her glass to Ethan, she caught his eyes briefly before walking up to the house. Once alone inside, she took a deep breath. What was happening to her? She didn't know who she was any more. Nothing felt normal. Being on those rich boats, she didn't feel as if she belonged on them, not as she once had. Maybe it was because she was cleaning them.

Reaching into her pocket, she pulled out the hundred dollar bill. It felt good, knowing she'd earned it with her own two hands – hands that were chapped and sore because of it. To be honest, she was all but useless as a maid. Susan had had to show her how to do everything.

Alexis looked out the window, watching the firelight silhouettes of her travelling companions. She hated to admit it, but she felt more at home with them than she ever had growing up. Susan had been there for her, but not like this. Before Alexis had always just paid for everything – they'd lived in her mother's hotel, eaten her mother's food. She couldn't explain it, but in the course of her mother's arrest and the pending trial, she and Susan had become closer than ever before.

Alexis glanced towards the stairs. She heard a loud shout of laugher from outside. She was tired, but she had the strangest urge to go back out and join the others. Grabbing her camera, she went back to the bonfire. They all turned to her in surprise.

Alexis shrugged. 'Changed my mind.'

'A woman's right,' Susan said, giggling as she raised her glass.

Ethan looked up at her. He'd taken her place on the log. Holding up her glass, he handed it to her. 'Here.'

'Thanks,' Alexis said. He moved over and she sat down by him. A silent truce seemed to go up between them. Holding her glass with both hands, she studied the way the dark liquor reflected the firelight.

'Mm, take a picture of us, Lexy,' Susan said, hugging herself to Ted. 'I want to remember this moment for ever. It's perfect.'

Alexis set down her glass and pulled out her camera. Taking a couple of shots, she asked Ethan, 'You want one?'

'Sure.' He smiled, a full bright smile. The orange fire-light reflected off his features. He really was handsome, in a laid-back sort of way. Alexis's hands shook, but she managed to take a couple of pictures of him. Studying them on the back panel of her camera, she was happy to see they came out decent.

'Hey, I have an idea,' Ethan said, standing. 'Why don't we take that row boat out on the water? There's bound to be some great shots out there.'

'Great idea,' Ted said. 'I'll bet it's beautiful out on the water.'

'And cold,' Susan added, yawning.

'Oh, come on, we'll grab blankets. It'll be great.' Ted pushed her up, forcing her to sit.

'Lexy?' Susan asked.

'Sure, I'm game,' Alexis answered.

'OK,' Susan said. Ted jogged for the house to get blankets and Susan called, 'Grab some food. I'm starving.'

'We don't have any food. No one went to the store,' Ted called back.

'Oh, yeah.' Susan giggled. 'Do you think if I look pathetic enough, I could get him to go to the store for us?'

'Probably,' Ethan said.

'Mm, he is a sweetie, isn't he?' Susan stretched. 'I can't believe you guys are getting me back onto another boat.'

'At least we don't have to clean it.' Alexis followed Ethan and Susan down to the little deck to the row boat. It was small. The paint on it was chipped and it was nowhere near as nice as the boats they'd spent all day cleaning.

'True enough,' Susan said, 'true enough.'

Ted came back and moments later they were on the water. Susan fell asleep in Ted's arms. Alexis took pictures of the water, the bonfire, Susan and Ted. She wanted to take a picture of Ethan rowing the boat, but couldn't force herself to turn the camera in his direction. She didn't know why she was nervous. Maybe it was because she didn't know where she stood with him. Sometimes he liked her, others he didn't. Sometimes he was nice, others not so nice. He complimented and criticised. Smiled and frowned. And he took up more time in her head than nearly every boyfriend she'd ever had.

'Here, want me to take one of you?' Ethan asked. He brought the oars up and just let the boat drift.

'Naw, that's –'

'Come on, you need a picture of yourself. How else are you going to remember today?' he asked.

'I don't want to remember today.' Alexis gave a derisive laugh, but handed him the camera anyway. 'In fact, there are several things I'd like to forget about today. I don't know how you guys cleaned that mess up. I still gag every time I think about it.'

'When I was apprenticing I had to clean up puke a few times. People would get nervous before their piercings and then, after it was done and they realised it wasn't so bad, their adrenaline would come crashing down. Some fainted. Some threw up.'

'So you pierce as well?' Ted asked.

'No, when you apprentice, you kind of get stuck doing all the grunt work of the shop – answering the phones, cleaning, giving care instructions, making needles, stuff like that. Sick customers were just the down side.' Ethan held up the camera. 'Say cheese.'

'Cheese.' Alexis gave him an impish grin. The flash went off and he handed the camera back to her.

'Will those come out? It's so dark out,' Ted said.

'They should. I've opened up the aperture and . . .' Alexis shrugged, not wanting to get into it and risk sounding like an idiot. 'Yeah, they should.'

'You know, I thought you'd set up some tattoos while we were here,' Ted said. 'Seems a lot easier than scrubbing boats for cash.'

'I thought so, too,' Ethan answered. 'I tried. I was hoping to get a tattoo party started, but the few people I had lined up just sort of ran out on me. It was the strangest thing. Too bad, I'd have liked to have made some extra cash.'

Alexis gave a guilty look over the water.

'Susan mentioned she wanted to help lay out designs,' Ethan said. 'I've been to some parties where if you get going you can make several thousand in one night.'

'Several thousand?' Alexis almost choked on her own spit.

'What, doll? Thought a man like me couldn't make that kind of money?' Ethan picked up the oars and began rowing them towards shore.

'Why do you have to take offence to everything I say?' Alexis asked.

'Why does everything you say have to sound offensive?' Ethan returned.

Alexis bit her lip and didn't answer. They got to shore rather quickly. No one said a word. So much for Ethan and her silent truce.

That night, Alexis slept alone. She missed Ethan's heat as she snuggled under the covers. The house made strange noises and she suddenly realised how quiet the outside was. She was used to the sound of the busy city. It was almost frightening. She slept with the light on.

The next morning she didn't feel at all rested. Ted had coffee and cinnamon rolls waiting in the kitchen. Before she got up, everyone had voted to drive up along the peninsula since they only had one night left in Door County.

The drive turned out to be pleasant. Alexis forgot her troubles as she took pictures of everything – cherry and apple orchards, bright-red barns in green fields, birch trees lined up along the road, horses, cows, tourists and locals. They passed through scenic villages where the streets seemed packed with tourists. The store fronts had great hand-carved wood signs and decorative latticework. They even saw goats grazing on top of a roof covered in grass.

'You have to take a picture of that,' Ethan said. 'I want to hang it in my shop.'

They stopped in shops along the way. Some had

antiques, others crafts, some sold cherry wine and fresh Wisconsin cheese. Alexis loved the shopping, but was hesitant to buy anything. Every time she picked something up she remembered cleaning the boats and would set it back down.

'Here, I've got us all something,' Ethan said, tossing a bag through the opened car window onto Alexis's lap.

'Cool, what is it?' Susan asked.

Alexis dug into the bag. She held up a grey T-shirt that read 'Door County, Wisconsin'. 'T-shirts?'

'I don't think Lexy's ever owned a T-shirt in her life.' Susan laughed.

'Then I'd say it was about time.' Ethan winked at Susan and Alexis wished the look had been for her.

'Ten bucks says she never wears it,' Ted said.

'You're on,' Susan called his bet. 'You hear that Lexy? There's five bucks in it for you if you wear that thing for a whole day.'

'In public,' Ted added.

Ethan just laughed.

'Don't let me down,' Susan said.

Alexis eyed the T-shirt. 'Huh. Five bucks?'

'Come on, Lexy.' Ted's voice was teasing. 'You know you can't be seen in that thing. Think of the embarrassment.'

'Ethan, can I borrow your jacket?' Alexis asked.

He slowly shrugged out of his jacket and handed it to her. Alexis slid down in the car seat, working her arms out of her designer shirt. The jacket was warm and smelled like him. She managed to get her shirt over her head while staying under the jacket.

'Uh, you need any help in there?' Ethan asked, laughing as she tossed her shirt out from underneath.

Alexis peeked over the top and shot him a rueful look.

'Can't blame a guy for trying.' He winked. Alexis felt her insides flutter. She wondered how long their good mood towards each other would last this time.

Alexis disappeared under the jacket and put the T-shirt on. It was loose around her body, but comfortable. Sitting up, she handed Ethan his jacket. 'Ah, there.'

'Lexy, you're killing me,' Ted said.

'Hey, sorry.' Alexis grinned. 'But I want the five dollars.'

It was a brilliant day. They drove north to the very edge of the Door County peninsula. The shore had white pebbles along the beach and the water had been a crisp blue. Susan wanted to take a ferry to Canada but she was outvoted, so instead they'd walked along the shore with their shoes off picking up small shells that littered the beach. Ethan couldn't help but watch Alexis as she took pictures. Her hair whipped around her face, and when the sunlight hit her just right, she was more stunning than any woman he'd ever met – like a 1950s film star.

A cold breeze swept up from the water, but the walk was worth it. Alexis took photographs of Susan getting a piggyback ride on Ted and then one of them kissing by the water when they didn't know they were being watched.

'Thinking of working for a tabloid?' Ethan asked, kicking at the sand.

Alexis frowned. 'What?'

'Sorry, bad joke. I just meant you taking pictures of them when they're not looking.'

Her frown deepened. Ethan wanted to kick himself.

'I didn't mean anything bad, just that … You know what, never mind. Forget I said anything.'

'I'm hungry,' Susan yelled, jogging for them. 'Let's go find some food.'

Alexis pulled her camera strap securely on her shoulder and walked off, refusing to look at him. As the two women walked towards the car, Ted joined him. 'She mad again?'

'Who knows,' he grumbled. 'When's she not mad?'

'Good point.' Ted laughed. 'Ready?'

Looking at Alexis, he sighed. 'Yeah, let's go.'

They drove in silence, each gazing out of the opened windows at the passing landscape. A black cow mooed alongside the road as Ethan stopped the car near a fence and he chuckled when Alexis nearly jumped out of her skin.

'Hurry, go,' she ordered, panicked.

'It's just a cow,' Susan said. 'Relax.'

'I don't care. It looks hungry.' Alexis slid on her seat, coming closer to Ethan's side.

'They're not –' Ethan couldn't get the words out.

'I saw the running of the bulls,' Alexis said. 'You can't tell me they're not mean.'

Ethan didn't try to argue, but the heifer was hardly a vicious bull. The car was again silent as they drove the rest of the way back and it was late afternoon by the time they got back to the rental house. They did their laundry, showered and packed up what they could into the car. Ethan bought a pizza from a local eatery and they all sat around the small kitchen table for dinner.

Ethan smiled to see Alexis was still wearing the grey T-shirt. He didn't know why he bought it for her. The T-shirt only served to hide the curves of her body, not that she didn't manage to make it look good.

Taking a bite of pizza, Ted said, 'Damn, this is good. This has to be the best pizza I've ever had.'

'Mm, fresh cheese,' Susan added. 'I love the cheese.'

'You're addicted to cheese,' Alexis said, laughing.

Ethan laughed as well. It was true. Susan had already eaten two bags of cheese curds and a half-bag of fresh mozzarella string cheese.

A knock sounded on the door. 'Ethan? Can we come in? It's Tressa.'

'Sure,' Ethan called back. Tressa came in with a group of friends.

'Hey,' Tressa said, smiling. 'You still inking?'

'Sure am. You bring me some victims?' Ethan smiled. Tressa was a cute little brunette with a round face. She wasn't stunningly gorgeous, but she had a happy laugh and an easy smile. She had the most adorable Belgian-influenced accent like most people seemed to carry in this part of the States.

'This is JT, Jason, Cheryl, Marcy,' Tressa said, pointing around the group as she spoke. 'And that quiet guy in the back is Pug.'

'Cool. Hey, guys, just give me a second to clean up this mess and get my stuff out of the car, then we'll get started.'

Alexis watched Ethan work. Pug, a large man with a round, baby-soft face, carried in cheap beer by the armful. She noticed that Ethan didn't drink and even encouraged those wanting tattoos not to drink until after he was done.

Pug asked for a bulldog. Ethan pulled out his laptop and within seconds was printing the outline of a bulldog. JT and Jason both wanted the same black tribal armbands. They brought the design with them. It looked like the picture had been torn out of a magazine and carried around in a wallet for years. Marcy asked for a ladybug on the top of her foot. Ethan had it drawn before she'd even finished explaining. Cheryl asked for a butterfly landing on a rose or a dove carrying a fig leaf. Since she was undecided, Ethan let her roam the files in his laptop for ideas.

Tressa, however, got nothing. She smiled, flirting and laughing outrageously with Ethan. Alexis tensed every time the woman opened her mouth.

'Could someone hand me that new pack of paper towels?' Ethan asked, as he set up his work area on the kitchen table. Alexis jumped forwards before Tressa could. She handed them to Ethan. He blinked in surprise, but nodded. 'Thanks.'

'You need anything else?' Alexis asked.

'No, thanks, I'm good.' Ethan turned back to Pug. Alexis watched him put the layout he'd made of the bulldog on the man's arm by carefully pressing a piece of paper to Pug's skin. He slowly pulled it off. The purple outline of the bulldog was left. Then, tearing a needle out of a sterile pack, he began adjusting his controls on the power supply, listening to it buzz as he stepped on the foot pedal. 'All right, you ready?'

'I'm so going to laugh at you if you cry,' JT joked.

'Don't be a baby, Pug,' Tressa said.

'Or we'll tell everyone,' Marcy added.

'Can we take pictures?' Cheryl asked.

'Oh, we forgot the camera.' Tressa pouted.

The buzzing of Ethan's needle filled the kitchen. Susan and Ted disappeared into the living room to play cards. Alexis felt a little like an outsider as she watched Ethan work from the doorway. Still, she was fascinated with the whole process. She'd never actually seen anyone get a tattoo. She'd seen the hotel clerk with the butterfly on her hip right after, but that was the closest she'd ever gotten.

The bulldog only took about half an hour to complete. Ethan stopped, cleaned up his area and then reset it from scratch. Next, he started on JT's armband.

'Hey, is it cheaper if we share the same ink and stuff?' JT asked at one point. 'Marcy's my girlfriend so I know where she's been.'

Marcy blushed.

'Oh yeah, she's been with me,' Pug said. 'Last night.'

'Dreams don't count, Pug,' Marcy said, laughing.

Alexis was amazed as Ethan actually tensed. His smile fell slightly. Very evenly, he said, 'I won't do that.' His flat tone ended that conversation quickly.

Ethan worked at a steady pace, joking as he went along. Once he had Alexis get him a glass of water. She smiled triumphantly at Tressa. The woman didn't seem to notice, so the victory was lost. The more Tressa drank, the bolder she got with her flirting. Several times the woman reached over to touch Ethan's thigh. To Alexis's dismay, Ethan didn't shake the woman off.

After JT, Ethan did Jason's armband. JT and Pug razzed him about it good-naturedly. Jason kept turning pale, forcing Ethan to stop several times and give him a break.

Unable to endure Tressa's blatant flirting with Ethan, Alexis joined Ted and Susan in the living room. They were playing rummy. Susan sat on the couch. Ted lay on his side on the floor.

'Want in?' Susan asked, motioning to the deck of cards. Alexis noticed a little pad and pencil from one of the hotels they'd stayed at. Susan had been taking all the freebies from the rooms – miniature soap, conditioner and shampoo, lotions, even tissues. Alexis thought it was funny.

'No thanks,' Alexis said, sitting on the couch.

'How's it looking in the kitchen?' Susan asked, curious. 'Does it look painful?'

'Susan wants a tattoo on her butt,' Ted teased.

'I didn't say that,' Susan said.

'You didn't have to.' Ted winked. 'I read your mind.'

'If you can read minds then why are you losing?' Susan asked. 'I think you just read your own mind.'

'Yeah, I just like to see your butt.' Ted turned to Alexis and added, 'Ethan seems busy.'

'That Tressa woman is in there practically throwing herself at him. It's gross,' Alexis said, sighing heavily.

Susan smirked, sharing a private look with Ted.

'What?' Alexis demanded.

'Oh, nothing.' Susan's voice raised a few pitches.

'I don't care that she is,' Alexis said.

'Uh-huh.' Ted drew a playing card.

'We know,' Susan added, drawing when Ted discarded.

'He can sleep with Tressa.' Alexis sat up, trying to look them both in the eye. They kept staring down at the cards. 'I really don't care who he sleeps with.'

'Yep,' Ted said.

'Yuh-huh,' Susan added.

'You two are impossible. I'm going outside to take pictures of the water.' Alexis stood.

'OK,' Ted said.

'Have fun,' Susan added.

When Alexis walked out of the room, she heard them laughing behind her back. What did they know anyway?

'Can I have your keys?' Alexis asked Ethan in the kitchen.

'Yeah, give me a second.' He put the finishing touches on the ladybug before taking off his gloves and fishing his car keys from his jeans pocket. He handed them to her.

Alexis didn't say a word as she went outside. She'd put her camera bag in the car so she wouldn't forget it in the morning. Taking it from the front seat, she shut the door.

'He's an amazing artist, eh?'

Alexis looked over at Tressa. She pulled a couple of beers from a beat-up brown pickup.

'Ethan,' Tressa said when Alexis didn't answer her. 'He's good, eh? It must be cool getting to travel across country like you are. I wish I could go.'

'It's all right,' Alexis said, shrugging.

'I'd kill to go,' Tressa said. 'So, are you and Ethan, you know, together?'

'No.' The word came out automatically.

'Oh, so, you're not together?'

Was the girl deaf? Alexis frowned. 'No. We aren't.'

'Then, he's free,' Tressa persisted.

'Of course he's free. I mean ...' Alexis shrugged.

'What do you mean, "of course"?'

'Well, he ... never mind.' Alexis hid her grin as she turned to go inside. 'I shouldn't say anything. It's his business.'

'Ah, come on,' Tressa wheedled. 'I'll give you a beer if you tell me.'

Alexis didn't really want the beer, but she nodded anyway. 'Will your grandma care that you're here?'

'No, she's asleep by now. That's why we came over so late. I wanted to make sure she didn't see Pug's car. She doesn't care for him.'

Alexis popped the can open and took a sip. Whatever kind it was, the beer tasted awful. She pretended to swallow. To Tressa, she said, 'If you like him, you should go for it. He's really sweet.'

Ethan stretched his arms above his head. He didn't actually think he'd end up making any money this weekend. Truthfully, he was giving the tattoos away cheap, but something was better than nothing.

'If you like him, you should go for it. He's really sweet.'

Ethan stopped. Was Alexis talking about him? He

willed the people in the kitchen to be quiet so he could hear. He edged closer to the back door.

'I mean, he hasn't hooked up with anyone here yet,' Alexis said. 'Well, um, not today.'

Ethan frowned.

'Not today?' Tressa asked. 'Does he hook up a lot?'

Ethan tried to get closer. Tressa was cute and was definitely into him. He wasn't sure if the flirting would go anywhere or if he'd allow it to go anywhere if it did. She was a nice woman, but she seemed a little on the needy side. The last thing he wanted was a woman demanding he check in with her from the road after one night. Or worse, hopping in his car to go with him.

'Well, you know.' Alexis laughed. Ethan grimaced at the telling sound. What was she doing? 'OK, you seem nice and I don't want to see you getting hurt. Ethan's a dog, D-O-G dog. I mean, he'll tell these girls he'll call and then doesn't. He acts all sweet, but then we have to hear him make fun of them in the car the next day. I'm too self-conscious to sleep with him myself, especially since hearing him go on and on about my jiggling belly fat.'

Ethan gripped the doorframe. It took all his willpower not to go charging outside.

'You aren't fat,' Tressa said. Ethan closed his eyes. The girl sounded a bit outraged. He didn't blame her. By the picture Alexis was painting of him, he didn't like himself very much either.

'Oh, thanks, sweetie,' Alexis said. 'Don't say anything, OK. I mean, Ethan's one of those guys who's great on a friend level, but as a lover? He's kind of shallow.'

'Oh yah, Pug's like that,' Tressa said. 'It's cool. I'm not really into him anyway.'

Alexis chatted with Tressa for a while, about her home, about the bay, about the big fish sculptures they'd seen downtown. Then JT called for her, saying Cheryl was getting ready to get her tattoo. Apparently, Cheryl changed her mind and decided on a little ladybug as well.

Alexis made her way down to the water, only feeling mildly guilty for talking about Ethan behind his back. She didn't know what got into her. It was just the idea of him getting laid when she wasn't made her mad. She took a deep breath. OK. That wasn't the whole truth. But she didn't want to delve into the whole truth.

Alexis toyed with her camera, playing with the tele-photo lens. Sitting on the wooden-bench swing, she watched the moonlight rippling on water. It was peaceful here, beautiful. She glanced down at her T-shirt, tracing the letters printed on it with her fingernail.

A car started and Alexis watched as Tressa and her friends left. She had no idea how long she'd been sitting by the water. The door opened and she watched Ethan carry his stuff to the car. He did look kind of cute in the moonlight. She snapped his picture, careful not to use the flash. She was almost sad to be leaving Wisconsin.

Susan lay on her stomach, surfing the internet. 'What do you think about North Dakota?'

'I don't know.' Ted lay next to her on the bed, his feet by her elbows. Lightly, he traced his fingers over her calves. 'I think Ethan mentioned going down to Iowa City. There's a zine shop down there.'

'That could be cool,' Susan said. She looked up Iowa on the internet. 'What's a zine?'

'Um, magazine without the financial backing of large corporations,' Ted answered. 'Small press stuff. I guess Iowa City's known for it.'

'Ah, I see.' Susan nodded. 'We should be able to make Iowa City tomorrow. Can you believe it's already been a week since leaving New York?'

'Mm, it's gone fast,' Ted agreed.

'I wish we could travel for ever.' Susan sighed wistfully. 'I love it.'

'I'd imagine you'd get tired of it after a while. You know, start wanting your own home.'

'Maybe.' Susan clicked the mouse, cruising an Iowa website.

Ted laughed. 'What was with Alexis tonight? Was she jealous or what?'

'I know.' Susan sat up. Leaving the computer on, she turned to lay by Ted. 'Do you think it's possible she's got a crush on Ethan?'

'Man, I don't know. For everyone in the car's sake I hope not.' Ted shivered dramatically. 'Those two are already at each other's throat half the time. Just imagine if you added sex and romance to the mix.'

'Oh, you're right.' Susan kissed his cheek and moved back to the computer. 'I'll talk to her tomorrow and see what's up.'

'Good idea.' Ted moved to run his hand up her calf to her inner thigh. 'Um, but could you maybe turn that computer off and see what's up with me tonight?'

'Oh.' Susan giggled. 'Has something come up?'

She shut down the computer and closed the top. Turning, she crawled over his body. 'I love you.'

'Mm, what you wearing under there?' Ted asked, trying to see down her shirt.

'Granny panties and a sports bra,' Susan teased.

'Sexy.' Ted flipped Susan on her back and began kissing her neck. 'Very sexy.'

'Oh, you think so?' she asked, nearly squealing with pleasure as he discovered her pink lacy bra and matching panties.

Ted worshipped her body with his kisses, licking and nibbling a hot trail over her skin as he stripped her of her clothing. He swirled his tongue over a nipple, sucking it lightly between his teeth before moving to smother the same attention on the other one.

'Mm, you always get to play, I want my turn.' Susan forcefully pushed him on to his back. Ted groaned as she stripped him of his clothes. Then, taking his socks, she tied his arms to the headboard. 'Ah, much better.'

Susan sat astride his thighs as she teased his body. First, she ran a silk shirt over his skin, sweeping it over his flesh in light feathery caresses. Ted bucked as she brushed it up his inner thigh and over his erection.

'More,' he demanded.

'What do you say?' Susan asked, her tone scolding. She ran the silk up over her naked breasts, letting him watch as her nipples hardened.

'More, please, Mistress Susan,' Ted instantly amended.

'Ah, that's better.' Susan giggled, unable to help herself. She was never very good at staying in character. Ted never seemed to mind.

Dropping the silk over his face, she began the slow process of licking and kissing his body from his neck to his stomach. As she neared his arousal, his back arched off the bed.

'Susan, please,' he begged.

'What do you want?' Flicking her tongue over the tip of his cock, she asked, 'This?'

'Yes.'

'How about this?' she asked, moving her fingers to lightly caress his balls.

'Mm, yes, harder, please.'

'Ah, and how about this?' Susan sucked the end of his shaft between her lips, toying with the head.

'Ah, yes!' Ted bucked, trying to delve his shaft deeper into her mouth.

Susan teased him a while longer before giving him what they both wanted. She rolled her tongue down his shaft, sucking gently. Her hands kneaded his balls, massaging them in her palm. Ted's body strained beautifully against the ties as he worked his hips back and forth. She liked watching his muscles stretch and contract beneath his skin.

Susan sucked harder, knowing from experience that he was close. His body jerked. Then, right as he was about to come, she pulled down on his balls, stopping his ejaculation. Ted grunted in satisfaction as he felt the tremors of an orgasm but stayed hard and ready for more.

Susan was ready, but knew anticipation only made things that much sweeter. Leaving him tied to the bed, she stood and went to her bag. Kneeling where he couldn't see her, she pulled out a leather corset that zipped up the front and left her breasts bare.

'Susan?' Ted called.

She didn't answer as she slipped thigh-high pantyhose over her legs. She was so aroused, each brush of material against her skin made her jolt with anticipation. Last, she slipped on a pair of black crotchless panties. Slowly, she stood. Ted's breath caught.

'Mm, damn, honey, where'd you get that?' he asked.

'Bought it before we left, along with a few other special items.' She pursed her lips as she let him look his fill. 'You like?'

He nodded eagerly. 'What else you buy?'

'Mm, if you're a good boy on this trip, you might just get to see,' Susan assured him. It was erotic and empowering at the same time to see the look of complete lust on his face.

'I'll be good,' he promised.

'I know you will.' Susan crawled over his body. He stared at her breasts, licking his lips. His legs moved restlessly on the bed as she kneeled before him, slowly rubbing her body as he watched. She cupped her breasts, pinched the nipples, before moving lower to stroke between her thighs. Cream made her fingers glide over her sex. She leaned her head back and sighed with pleasure.

'Honey, please, you're making me crazy,' he said.

Susan eagerly crawled over him. She stroked his shaft a few times before lowering her body onto his. He filled her up completely. Rocking her hips, she gave him a great show as she touched herself. Ted groaned in approval. Staying upright, she rolled her hips in slow circles as she reached down to stroke the sensitive pearl hidden within her folds. Her body clenched his.

'Ah, yeah, honey, that's it. Oh, you're so beautiful,' Ted said, his words soft and breathless.

Susan climaxed moments before she felt his body release. Her heart beat fast in her chest, pounding in her ears. Falling limply on his body, she tried to catch her breath.

'Mm, you can have your way with me anytime,' Ted said.

Susan giggled. 'I know.'

'I'm easy, I know,' he agreed. 'Now, untie me so I can get a better look at this outfit.'

Chapter Nine

'Oh God, pull over,' Susan said, grabbing her stomach. She was in the back seat, her head on Ted's lap. Alexis noticed that Ethan didn't slow down this time. Susan had been moaning the same thing for the last several hours. 'I think I'm dying!'

Alexis turned around in the front seat. Susan looked miserable. 'Susan? Sweetie? Can I get you something?'

'I'm never eating cheese again,' Susan swore, clutching her stomach.

'How much did you have?' Alexis asked.

'All three bags,' Ted said. 'She ate the last of the mozzarella this morning.'

'No, I had four,' Susan said. 'I ate the last of the cheese curds last night.'

'When?' Ted asked, surprised.

'You were sleeping. I was hungry.' Susan moaned louder, her eyes watering in her misery.

'Oh, no, sweetie,' Alexis said, 'you can't eat like that with fresh cheese. It's not like what we get in the stores. I had the same thing happen in France.'

'I have cheese poisoning,' Susan said dramatically.

'No, you're just . . . bound up,' Alexis assured her.

Susan turned her back on Alexis and moaned pitifully. Alexis sat back down. There was nothing she could do for Susan. Seeing a road sign, she said, 'Hey, we're entering Illinois.'

Ethan snorted, not saying a word. Alexis watched him from the corner of her eye. He'd been in a horrific mood all morning. Turning her attention to the countryside, Alexis stared out the window. Ethan had turned the music off at Susan's request and they rode in silence.

'What about Chicago?' Alexis asked after several miles passed, hoping to cheer everyone back into the adventurous spirit. 'They have some great museums.'

'Too late. Already passed the turn-off,' Ethan said, his words hard.

'What? So we can go six hours out of our way to see upper Wisconsin, but not twenty minutes to see Chicago?' Alexis mumbled, more to herself than to anyone in the car.

'It's more than twenty minutes,' Ethan ground out. Alexis glanced at him. He was tightly gripping the steering wheel. That man was brewing for a fight.

'I just want to be in California already,' Susan said, her voice pitiful. 'Or any place with a hotel that I can curl up and die in.'

'Do you want me to stop before Iowa City?' Ethan asked.

Alexis grimaced. Sure, when he talked to Susan he could sound nice and concerned.

'No,' Susan said. 'Just keep going.'

The car again fell to silence. Illinois passed by rather quickly. Alexis was too preoccupied with Ethan's moodiness and Susan's misery to see much more than the blurring miles of green and brown countryside contrasted with the bright blue of the sky. White puffy clouds dotted the heavens, but their beauty was lost on them.

Ethan stopped for gas. Susan refused to get out of the car. Alexis bought her friend a bottle of water and some stomach medicine.

'Huh,' Alexis said, looking across the parking lot to where a man fuelled his car several stalls away. 'There's that grey car again. I think he's going the same way we are. Weird.'

'You going to get in?' Ethan asked, ignoring her observation.

Alexis watched the man by the grey car as he lit up a cigarette and paid with a credit card right at the pump. Across from him, a middle-aged woman pulled up in a minivan full of kids. Her slicky jogging suit swished as she got out and then all at once the other doors opened and children in soccer uniforms practically poured out. The man with the cigarette frowned at them as they screamed and ran towards the convenience store without stopping to look for traffic.

The woman saw him smoking and said, 'Hey, you can't smoke that here.'

'Yeah!' a snot-nosed kid at her side piped up, putting his hands on his hips. 'Cancer sticks are bad for you and will make the gas station blow up.'

The man's eyes flickered up to Alexis briefly but he didn't act like he recognised her. Then it hit her where she'd seen him. It was the overweight man with the sweaty armpit stains who had offered to carry her luggage that first night.

'Buzz off, lady,' the man grumbled. 'This is a free country and I'll do whatever the hell I want to.'

The woman gasped, grabbing her child as she ran without bothering to fill up her van. Ethan made a rude grunting noise and Alexis climbed in next to him. He started the car.

'You should've seen the way the clerk was looking at Ethan,' Ted told Susan.

'Yeah, I think she actually started praying when she saw my tattoos,' Ethan added. Susan groaned, obviously not in the mood to laugh and Ted reached over from the back to turn on the radio for her.

As they drove into Iowa, the landscape again flattened out. The hills weren't as steep as before.

'What are they growing?' Alexis asked, curious as she nodded at the bright-green fields stretching out beyond the interstate. 'Corn?'

Ethan just grunted.

'Probably,' Ted said politely. 'Kinda hard to say.'

By the time they reached Iowa City everyone was just ready to get out of the car. Ethan turned in near the downtown area and pulled over at one of the first hotels they saw from the road. He didn't even try to charm his way into a free room. Alexis stood beside him during check-in. The man was obviously checking Ethan out. She bet if he wanted, he could've gotten the free room. Ethan didn't seem to notice and, if he did, he didn't care.

'How much for a double?' Ethan asked the clerk, looking through him more than at him. His hands gripped so tight around his wallet that his knuckles were white.

Alexis frowned. Ethan had never asked for a double before. In fact, he'd just taken whatever free room the clerk gave him for trade. It was usually the single hidden in the back of the hotel.

'The only doubles we have are in smoking,' the clerk answered, clicking away on his computer.

'Ew,' Alexis said, her voice soft. 'Those always smell horrible, even when you don't smoke in them.'

Ethan looked at her as if contemplating taking the double just to annoy her. Alexis was actually surprised, when he said, 'Two singles by each other if you have it and on the first floor, near an outside door.'

'A man who knows what he wants,' the clerk joked. Ethan glanced at her, but didn't answer. The man clicked away on his computer. 'Hmm, looks like I have something by the pool.'

'That would be great,' Alexis said, trying to cover up for Ethan's rudeness.

'Here you go. Just head through those doors and it'll be on the other side of the pool or you can drive around to the south entrance. Check-out is by eleven. Enjoy your stay.' The clerk smiled, handing over the room cards. He needlessly straightened his black vest before sitting down.

'You unlock the rooms. I'll drive around and get the bags.' Ethan shoved the keys at her. He stormed out the door.

Alexis took a deep breath. She couldn't wait for today to be over. Glancing at the clerk, she said, 'Thank you.'

Alexis found their rooms easily enough by the indoor swimming pool. Ted carried Susan in and she went straight to bed. Ethan carried in all the bags. Alexis blinked in surprise to see him get hers. He'd never done that before. Alexis held open the door to their room for him. He didn't say a word as he stepped past and his look said she'd be better off not talking to him.

After being in the car with him all day, Alexis didn't feel like being around Ethan, especially since he was in such a foul mood. Without saying a word, she pulled out her swimsuit and went to the bathroom to change. The indoor swimming pool had a hot tub next to it and the thought of hot water was too inviting to pass up.

The two-piece swimsuit was the only one she had left. Before her life fell apart, she'd owned nearly fifteen of them. The coral, lime-green and ivory striped top tied once behind her neck and again behind her back. The neckline dipped low between her breasts forming a triangle. The bottoms matched the top tying low on each hip.

Pulling her hair up off her shoulders, she clipped it into a messy bun. As she stepped out of the bathroom holding a towel, she didn't bother to cover up. She swore she heard Ethan's breath catch slightly.

'Where you going?' he asked, his tone lighter than it had been all day.

'To perform brain surgery on a monkey,' Alexis said sarcastically, pulling open the door. She didn't bother looking at him. 'Then, I'm going to go save the world from supernatural evil, cure cancer and eat a house.'

'Alexis –'

Alexis shut the door before he could answer. She didn't really feel like talking to Mr Moody anyway.

The hotel swimming pool wasn't too busy. Nearby, on the other side of a black iron fence, teenagers played video games. Two middle-aged women in long bathrobes played next to them on the pool table.

Three businessmen in suits and ties sat around a white plastic table near the pool. One had his briefcase open and was taking out documents. He stopped mid-action when he saw her. The other two turned to see what he was staring at. Alexis smiled slightly, pretending not to notice. There was something about being stared at by complete strangers that always improved her confidence.

Walking to the wall, she turned the dial for the little

round hot tub. The water jets started and bubbles rolled in the steaming water. Alexis dipped her toe along the water's surface, spreading her arms for balance. She knew she was just posing for her audience's viewing pleasure, but she needed the ego boost.

She lowered herself into the water. Glancing at her hotel room, she saw the curtain shift over the inside window. Ethan was watching her. She sat in front of a jet, letting it massage her lower back. After hours of sitting in a car, it felt great.

'Hey, looks like we had the same idea.' Ted stepped into the water. He chuckled. 'I think I scared away your admirers.'

Alexis glanced over her shoulder. The businessmen were packing up.

'How's Susan?' Alexis asked, stretching her arms along the back of the hot tub.

'Sleeping.'

'Well, that's probably the best thing.'

'Yeah.' Ted glanced to Alexis's hotel room. 'Where's Ethan?'

'In there,' Alexis looked to the window. She was sure she saw the curtain shift again. 'Pouting or brooding or whatever it was he was doing today.'

'Yeah, I noticed.' Ted sighed. Leaning his head back, he closed his eyes. 'Susan's worried about you, you know.'

'She is? Why?' Alexis blinked in surprise.

'She thinks you're mad at her for taking you on this trip. She says you haven't been talking to her lately.'

'I told her not to be silly,' Alexis said. 'I'm not mad.'

'I don't think she believed you.' He suppressed a yawn. 'I'd consider it a favour if you'd reassure her again.'

'Sure, but it really isn't her. She's great. She's Susan.'

Ted laughed in understanding. 'Yeah. She is great, isn't she? Did she tell you I almost asked her to marry me?'

'You...? What? What do you mean almost?' Alexis asked, sitting up straight.

'I didn't get the words out, but she knew. You women can read us men like books. You pretend you can't sometimes to feed our egos, but you know what's going on in our heads, I'm sure of it.'

Alexis glanced to her hotel room. She knew for a fact that wasn't true. She didn't know what was going on with Ethan at all. 'What happened? Why didn't you?'

'Because she started talking about you. About how you were going through a hard time and needed her.' Ted gave Alexis a pointed look. 'I'm not trying to be mean. I understand. She loves you and I'm fine with that. But when I get married, I want my wife to think of me first. I know it sounds selfish but I think that's what marriage is about. She can't focus completely on us if she's always worried about you.'

'Ted...' What could Alexis say to that? Her first impulse was to yell and scream. She stayed calm. Ted wasn't a mean guy. He cared for Susan. Alexis knew that.

'No, like I said, I know. I'm not mad about it. I'm willing to wait until the right moment. I just thought you might like to know that I do love Susan enough to step aside until she's ready for me. My only hope is that someday you're ready enough to let her marry me. She cares what you think, Alexis. She won't say yes unless she thinks she has your blessing.'

'Ted...' Again, what could she say? She looked help-lessly at him and shrugged. An uncomfortable silence settled over them and Alexis couldn't meet his eyes. Ted leaned his head back and relaxed.

'I'm glad we had this talk, Alexis,' Ted said after several minutes had passed. He stood, smiling as he grabbed his towel from a chair. 'Goodnight. I'm going to bed.'

'Goodnight,' Alexis said. The water lost its appeal and she got out, wrapping herself in a towel.

She liked Ted, so it was hard to be mad at him, though his words stung. Was he right? Was she somehow holding Susan back from a life? Sure, Alexis had leaned on her friend quite a bit since her mother's arrest, but isn't that what friends did? Frowning, she realised the friendship had been a little one-sided lately. She'd been doing all the leaning and Susan the carrying.

Thinking back, she couldn't remember once in the last month when she'd asked Susan how she was doing, how her relationship with Ted was. Since the couple always looked so happy together, Alexis had just assumed everything was fine. Actually, it was more like she'd been too selfish with her own worries to even wonder if everything was fine.

Resolving to stop being so self-involved, Alexis went back to the hotel room. In her eagerness to leave Ethan, she'd forgotten her key card. She knocked on the door. When he didn't open right away, she knocked louder. Ethan pulled the door open. He was on the phone talking to someone named Jack. She grabbed nightclothes. Not feeling like wearing a silk nightie, she looked at Ethan's open bag. A pair of sweatpants lay over the top. Crossing over to his bag, she picked them up. Waiting until he turned to her, she wiggled them in the air. 'Can I borrow these?'

'Yeah, sure.' he nodded once, before saying into the phone, 'Oh, what? No, it was nobody important.'

Alexis gasped, frowning. Well, that wasn't very nice. Not wanting to listen to any more talk of people she didn't know, she ignored Ethan and took a quick shower.

The stretched black lace camisole top had a built-in bra and scalloped edges lined the bottom edge, falling just above her navel. A dark-blue ribbon weaved through the black lace and tied beneath her breasts forming a bow. Beneath the sweats, she wore a matching pair of all-lace boy shorts. The designer would probably have a fit if she knew Alexis was wearing the sexy outfit with a pair of men's sweatpants.

'Who cares what the designer thinks,' Alexis said, knowing that before her mother's arrest, she never would've said something like that. 'I want comfort.'

Ethan hung up the phone and lay down on the bed, flipping through channels. Alexis came out of the bathroom. Sitting cross-legged on the floor, she began rubbing lotion over her arms. His attention shifted from the television to her. 'What's that scent called?'

'It's a mix of cucumber and green tea,' Alexis said.

'You hungry?' he asked.

'A little.' She tilted her head back, rubbing lotion over her neck.

'Want takeout?' He shifted on the bed. The woman even made his sweatpants look good. He watched her fingers dip under the top edge of her camisole. He licked his lips, wishing she'd go just a little lower.

'Sure.'

'Want to spring for a movie?' he asked. His body stirred. Alexis finally looked at him. He quickly sat up, trying to hide the erection pressing against his flannel pyjama pants.

'OK,' Alexis answered.

'Something wrong?' Ethan frowned. He'd been so busy staring at her camisole, he didn't notice her sad expression.

'Why did you tell that Jack person I was nobody?'

'What are you talking about?' Ethan asked, confused.

'You were on the phone. I asked to borrow these pants and you said I was nobody.' Alexis pulled up a pant leg and rubbed lotion on her calf and foot.

'I don't remember. Jack's my brother. If he thought there was a girl in my room, he'd probably tell my mom. Since I don't bring girls home, she'd assume I was serious with someone and would call all my aunts. They'd start planning the wedding and it would explode from there.' Ethan laughed, knowing he wasn't really exaggerating. 'It seemed easier not saying anything.'

'Oh.' Alexis waved her hand in dismissal, but the action looked forced. 'Not that I care or anything. I was just curious. Is Jack a tattoo artist as well?'

'No, he's a graphic designer in Baltimore.'

'Is he your only brother?' Alexis rubbed lotion on the other calf.

'No, there are five of us.' Ethan watched her hands, partly mesmerised.

'Any sisters?'

'Nope, all boys.' Ethan grinned.

'All artists?'

'Um, more or less.' He reached for the hotel's courtesy folder on the nightstand and began flipping through the menus. Pretending like he didn't care either way, he asked, 'Why the sudden interest in my family?'

He held his breath, waiting for her answer. Out of the corner of his eye, he watched her put her lotion in her bag. Standing, she said, 'No reason.'

'Chinese?' he asked, looking at the menu and picking up the phone.

'What?'

'Do you want Chinese food?'

'Sure.'

Ethan called the order in. Alexis came over, reading the menu over his shoulder and pointing to what she wanted.

'I'm glad to see you eating finally,' Ethan said, hanging up the phone.

'Yeah, well.' She looked uncomfortable. He quickly changed the subject before she demanded he call back to cancel her food order.

'How about you? Any family?' As soon as the words were out he wanted to kick himself. He already knew the answer to that. The whole United States knew the answer to that. Her family life had been posted all over the news stations.

'You read the papers,' she said softly. 'It was all in there. Every last detail, even some that weren't true.'

'Want to talk about it?'

'No.'

'Want to borrow my phone card and call your mom?'

'Can't. They...' Her eyes teared up and she blinked rapidly, trying to hide it. She paced the room like a caged animal. 'They won't let me call her. I can only write her letters.'

'I'm sorry,' he said, and he meant it.

'Ah, it's not like she was really a good mother anyway, you know. It's not like she was ever around. When I was sixteen, she caught me sleeping with my boyfriend in her bed. Stupid, right? I knew she'd be home and on some level I wanted her to catch us. Do you know what she did? She laughed and said if I liked being in her room so much I could just have it since she was never home to use it. My mother caught me having sex and she gave me a new bedroom. She even had it redecorated.'

'Wow,' Ethan said, for lack of anything better.

'Oh, it gets better.' Alexis sat on the bed next to him. Suddenly, her face fell as she looked at him. 'You don't want to hear this. Why don't you order the movie? I don't care what it is so long as it's not tragic. Just pick something upbeat.'

Ethan sensed she needed someone to talk to. Maybe someone other than Susan, someone removed from the situation. 'I don't mind. If you want to talk, it's fine. I won't say anything.'

'Really?'

She looked so vulnerable in that moment. It nearly broke his heart to see it. Reaching his arm out, he said, 'Come here. Lay down next to me.'

She started to move only to hesitate, unsure.

'I promise, no funny stuff,' he swore, grinning. 'Come on. I'll be the perfect gentleman.'

'You sure you know how?' she asked wryly. He winked at her, grinning. She slowly nodded. 'OK.'

Ethan lay on his back. Alexis stretched out next to him, her head on his arm as she faced him. Her hand lifted above his chest, hesitating before moving to rest over his heart. Their bodies were stiff for a few moments, but slowly relaxed.

'Think we should time how long we can go without fighting?' he teased.

Alexis chuckled. 'What do you think our current record is? Five minutes?'

'Six,' he said. 'Think we can beat it?'

'I don't know. We're still awake.' She smiled, tilting her head back to look at him. 'You're not half bad some of the time, Ethan.'

'You're pretty OK yourself sometimes, too, Sam.'

She chuckled, burrowing closer to his side. 'Samantha Wellington is my middle name. I didn't really lie about it.'

'You have four names? Alexis Samantha Wellington Grant?'

She laughed harder. 'My mother said it should be a prerequisite for being born into money. It sounds more impressive. Either that or you tack on the titles, so and so the third, the fourth, Jr, Sr.'

'I like it when you laugh,' Ethan said, not knowing what prompted him to admit it. He'd been so angry with her all day, but now she was being so likeable. He smelled her lotion, the sweet blending of cucumbers with a hint of mint. Her body was soft next to his, comfortable.

'So, four brothers? Or did you say five?'

Ethan wondered at the change of subject and decided to keep compliments to himself for the time being. 'Mm, five total including me. Jack, the oldest. Then Rob, second oldest. Me. Hugh. And Jon, the baby.'

'What was that like? I can't imagine. The only children around in my house belonged to the maids. I wasn't allowed to play with them.' She kneaded her hand softly along the centre of his chest, smoothing and crumpling his T-shirt with her palm.

'Well, I was the middle child, so I didn't get beat up as much as the younger ones. Though, we did give our mother many grey hairs doing all the normal boy stuff.'

'Like what?'

'Well, let's see. We spray-painted skulls on the house for Christmas one year, set a shed in the back yard on fire, tied Jon naked to a tree and left him for a few hours.'

'What? Why?'

'He was the bait. We were trying to catch a cougar.' Ethan chuckled at the memory.

'Did you live in New York?'

'Nope, Kansas. Midwest born and bred. We're scattered all over the country now. My parents live in Kansas still, but are currently travelling the globe. Last I heard they were on their way to Slovenia.'

'And you wanted your little brother to get eaten by a wild cat?'

'No, he was just bait,' Ethan said. 'The plan was to fight the cougar with sticks once it got there.'

'That's not a very thought-out plan.'

'You weren't around boys too much growing up, were you?'

'What was the naked part for?' Alexis asked, leaning up to study his face.

'Little brother torment.' Ethan curled the arm under her head around so he hugged her lightly to his body. 'Jon ended up being the biggest one out of all of us. He'd kick our ass now if we tried it again. Actually, we're kind of waiting for him to take his revenge.'

'Really?' Alexis asked, her eyes round.

'No, not really.' Ethan chuckled.

'What about your parents, were they around?' Alexis draped her arm around his waist, holding him gently. Ethan heard the loneliness in her voice.

'Every day.'

As they continued to talk, their bodies relaxed more and more into each other. Ethan felt bad for Alexis. The poor woman had missed out on so much growing up. She had everything handed to her, every materialistic comfort known to man. She'd lived in a mansion, and not just one, as her family owned several. He'd lived in a modest middle-class home, sharing a bedroom with Jack and Rob until he was fifteen and then he'd shared with Hugh and Jon for another three years.

Alexis had tutors that travelled with them. Unfortunately, the tutors spent more time sleeping with her mother than actually schooling her. She'd spend her days shopping while Ethan had gone to public school in hand-me-down clothing.

Alexis spent holidays abroad, opening a mountain of Christmas presents alone or sometimes with a maid. His family got together every holiday, no matter what. Hearing her story really made him appreciate his family. Until Susan, Alexis had no real friend but he'd always had his brothers.

'Why do you suppose we always fight?' she asked softly, not meeting his eye.

'We're both hard-headed and come from different worlds.'

'Does this truce mean we're friends?' She drew her arm from his waist and laid it between her body and his side.

'I'd like it if we were. We have a lot of miles left to travel together. It'd be cool if we could get along at least half the time.' Ethan wanted to kiss her, but held back. He couldn't be sure she'd want him to. The last thing he wanted was to push her away and start another fight. It's the same reason why he didn't ask her about her little comments to Tressa.

Somehow, during their talk, he'd managed to keep his arousal from becoming fully erect. Her hand brushed over his chest, passing absently over a nipple. Hot desire washed over him, filling his loins. His breath caught and held. He looked at her. Her dark eyes stared at him and for a moment he felt lost. He wanted to make love to her, wanted to strip her of her sexy little camisole and kiss every inch of her body.

He glanced at her lips, wondering if his kiss would be welcomed. His instincts said yes. Every nerve pulled him towards her, urging him to roll over and pin her beneath him. But theirs was a very delicate truce and he didn't want to break it. Ethan decided to take her friendship and stick to the original plan not to get involved with his travelling companion. It would make things too awkward between them.

A knock on the door saved him from having to decide. Ethan untangled his limbs and answered the door. It was their food. He paid the delivery boy and set the bags on the table. The enchanted spell between them lessened, leaving behind an easiness that had not been there before.

'I was thinking,' Alexis said, biting into an egg roll.

'What's that?' Ethan reached over and stole a second egg roll from her plate. She made a slight face of annoyance but didn't stop him.

'Well, after the boat thing, I really don't want to work my way across as a maid. Don't get me wrong, I'll work, just not cleaning anything. Believe me when I say I'm not cut out for it.'

'What if that's the only job we can get?'

'Well, then I guess I have to do it.' Alexis shivered in disgust. 'But no more vomit and dirty condoms.'

'I agree. That was bad.'

'Anyway, you said you make a decent enough living with these party things, right?' Alexis set her egg roll down and gave him the most adorable wheedling look he'd ever seen.

'What?' he asked, almost scared.

'Well, what if I helped you somehow?'

'Huh? You want to be a tattoo artist now?' he asked, confused.

'No, nothing like that. What if I lined up some people for business and helped you do those design layouts? I can run the computer. And if you go through that care stuff, I'll type it out and give it to everyone.'

'It's already typed out.'

'Oh,' she looked a little disheartened. 'Then I could still trace the layout thing on that purple stuff. And get you water. And, um, you know, stuff like that.'

Ethan tried not to laugh, but it was hard.

'You hate the idea, don't you?' she asked.

Ethan studied her. He really didn't need any help and it would be more profitable in the long run if he'd just tell her no, but something in the way she looked at him made him say, 'OK. Sure. We'll try it out and see how it goes.'

'Really?' Alexis squirmed excitedly in her chair.

'Trial basis, mind you,' he said, wondering what he'd gotten himself into. He had no problem paying for things if he had the money. Greed had never been a big problem for him. 'And you can't get that look on your face when you talk about the art.'

'What look?'

'The one of disgust, like you just ate a sour pickle.' Ethan reached for a box and scooped some noodles onto his plate. 'You have to at least pretend you get the tattooing thing.'

'But I kind of don't get it,' she said. 'Why would you want to mark yourself up like that? It's so permanent.'

'Why do you dye your hair or put on make-up or wear designer clothing? It's a form of self-expression. It says who you are to the world. Sometimes tattoos show memories of the past, like when a loved one dies. Sometimes they represent who you are, where you've been. And sometimes, they're just something cool you do for fun.'

'You make it sound poetic.'

'Ah, well.' He shrugged, not wanting to get too preachy. 'It's what I do.'

'So, how about that movie?' she asked, wiping her hands on a paper napkin.

'You want action, funny, or funny-action?' Ethan stood, putting all the containers into the plastic bag. Tying the bundle up, he threw it in the trash.

'Action-funny.' Alexis grabbed her toothbrush and went to the sink next to the bathroom.

'I'm going to go get a soda from the machine, you want?' Ethan asked. 'I'll go pay the clerk and order the movie while I'm at it.'

'Sure, anything diet,' Alexis said.

'Got it,' he said, walking out of the room wearing only his pyjama pants.

Alexis finished brushing her teeth and went to sit on the bed. It had been an amazing evening. Ethan was actually very sweet. He was funny, kind and when he talked about his family she could tell they were close. She was almost jealous of him in that regard, which was strange. She'd been raised to believe that everyone was jealous of her because she was rich. Maybe there was more to the world than having money.

Ethan came back, set two drinks on the dresser and

toyed with the TV, setting it to the right channel. Alexis watched him in silence. For a moment, right before the food came, she'd been sure he was going to kiss her. She'd wanted him to, desperately. She'd wanted him to touch her, make love to her. She'd even settle for one of the tightly pressed dry-hump sessions she was always yelling at him for.

Ethan turned off the lights and crawled into the bed next to her. The room darkened and lightened with the glow from the television. He adjusted the pillows against the headboard. Then, without asking, he pulled her next to him, draping his arm around her shoulders. Alexis didn't really pay attention to the movie, as she enjoyed the feeling of being held.

Chapter Ten

Alexis slept by Ethan all night. The next morning, her body nearly stung with longing. She was so aroused she could barely stand it. Lying in his arms, she'd waited for him to make a move. Her breasts ached and just the idea of having sex with him had dampened her panties. She even wiggled against him, hoping he'd start touching her. He didn't.

Alexis ended up masturbating in the shower, touching herself, pinching her breasts, stroking her tender body to climax. She was left unfulfilled. It had definitely been too long since she'd been intimate with a man. After her shower, just one look at Ethan's butt in his loose-fit blue jeans brought all the longing back tenfold.

Susan said she felt much better, though she swore off all dairy products. No one felt like getting back into the car, so they took a short trip into downtown Iowa City. They parked, opting to walk the city streets. Alexis took her camera, aimlessly taking pictures of everything. She even managed to get brave enough to put Ethan in the shot several times.

Downtown was filled with a strange mixture of business people, artists, writers, college students and families. Children played in a water fountain, which sprayed straight up from the sidewalk in the middle of a cement square. It was a little warm and Ethan and Ted were only too happy to join the kids running through the water. The kids thought it was hilarious and Alexis was sure she'd never laughed so hard in her life. Afterwards, Ted had run up to Susan, getting her wet as he smothered her in kisses. Alexis looked at Ethan. For a moment, he looked as if he might do the same. Instead, he shook his red-tipped hair, sprinkling her orange cashmere sweater with droplets of water.

As Ethan and Ted air dried, they browsed a novelty toy store. Ethan bought two Chinese-influenced lunch pails and a postcard book of old cult classic movies. Ted bought Susan a wind-up cat made out of tin. Alexis refused to spend any of her yacht-cleaning money on toys.

Susan and Ted decided to check out a used bookstore while Ethan got directions to a zine shop. It was on the top level of an old building. Alexis went with Ethan, wanting to give Susan and Ted time alone – or that's what she told herself as she watched Ethan's tight butt as he climbed the narrow stairwell.

The wooden floors creaked and there was only a little stream of light coming from an outside window. The owner, a man in his mid-twenties, seemed to know a lot about a great number of things. He had short cropped hair, metal hoops in his ears and a large black swirl of tribal art tattooed on his right arm from wrist to shoulder.

'Hole ... teenage angst ... comic ...'

Alexis only caught part of Ethan's words. She didn't understand half of what they said as she flipped through the independent writings showcased on the walls. As she browsed, the two men continued to discuss politics, tattoos, comic books, punk music and underground publishing. She'd never felt so stupid in her life.

Comic books she understood. She didn't like them, but she understood them. The shop had several she'd never heard of. It wasn't too surprising. If Hollywood hadn't turned it into a movie, she didn't know what it was.

A lot of the zines were collections of poetry or political essays. Some of them were photocopied pages, whereas others were books built by hand, cut out and pasted with string binding. Many of them were quite artistic. She would never have imagined a place like this existed and it completely fascinated her.

Finally, after an hour of looking around, she settled on some homemade soap the store had displayed by the old cash register. There were little buried trinkets in the middle of the bars. Ethan bought the owner's self-published book and got it autographed.

'That guy's going places,' Ethan said about the owner, as they walked out of the building. Then, eyeing her bag, he asked, 'What did you get?'

'Oh, I bought some soap from his girlfriend. She makes it herself.' Alexis reached into the bag. 'See, isn't it cute?'

'Didn't see any zines you liked?' he asked, chuckling.

'Honestly, this might make me sound stupid, but I don't think I understood what they were written about,' Alexis answered. 'The words were all jumbled.'

Ethan laughed, slinging his arm playfully around her shoulders. 'That's OK. It's an acquired taste.'

'I, um,' Alexis began to reach back into her bag. 'Never mind.'

'What?' Ethan asked, hugging her closer as they walked. He craned his neck, trying to see into the bag.

'I bought you a present.' Alexis reached into the bag and handed him a black T-shirt with the zine shop's logo on it.

'Aw, cool, I didn't see these,' he said, taking the shirt. He set down his bags. Then, right in the middle of the busy sidewalk, he slipped out of the damp T-shirt he was wearing and stuffed it into a bag. Alexis's eyes devoured his trim stomach and chest. Silver horseshoe barbells hung from both nipples, causing them both to be erect points. She wondered if he wore them for sexual pleasure. She was almost disappointed when he pulled on the shirt she bought him. 'Perfect. Thank you. I love getting T-shirts when I go places. They remind me of where I've been.'

'Do you forget easily?' she teased, bumping into him with her hip. She wished he'd put his arm back around her. He didn't.

'There's supposed to be a great hot dog place a couple blocks this way,' Ethan said. 'Hungry?'

'Hot dogs?' Alexis asked.

'Mm, yeah.' Ethan nodded enthusiastically. 'Don't tell me you've never had a hot dog.'

Alexis didn't answer.

'Holy cow! I was just kidding, but you haven't, have you?' Ethan leaned his head back and laughed.

'It wasn't exactly on the chef's menu,' Alexis answered wryly, feeling a bit defensive.

'How can you possibly call yourself an American if you've never had a hot dog?' Ethan smiled and it lit up his entire face. Alexis noticed a group of young women walk by carrying book bags. They stared openly at Ethan. He naturally turned to smile at them. Alexis wanted to throw something at the girls, right after she smacked the flirtatious smile off Ethan's face.

'Well, have you ever had tandoori lamb or chicken della robbia?' Alexis asked.

'I'm almost scared to ask what's in it,' Ethan admitted. He led the way to another old building and again took the stairs to the top floor. 'You people eat raw fish eggs and stuff.'

'It's nothing more dangerous than the leftovers they stick into hot dogs, I assure you.' Alexis watched his butt as he climbed. She really needed to get her head on straight. Ethan was so everything she'd never wanted in a man. So why was she wanting him? It had to be a purely sexual thing. She wanted sex and he oozed sexual charm. Besides, she'd spent the night in his arms, his incredibly built, strong arms, and as she looked at him she was a little surprised to realise she wasn't noticing his tattoos as much.

Ethan ordered a hot dog smothered in sauerkraut, onions, relish, tomato and hot mustard. Alexis nearly gagged. Then, when she refused to open her mouth, he ordered her a plain. Seconds later the boy behind the counter was handing them their meals.

'I'll even pay,' Ethan said, handing the cashier some money. 'Ketchup?'

Alexis nodded weakly. 'Sure, why not.'

Ethan squirted ketchup on the hot dog and carried them to a small booth in the corner. When she didn't eat, he asked, 'You're not scared are you?'

'No, just wary.'

Ethan took a big bite, making small, almost sexual noises of appreciation as he chewed. Alexis took a small bite, resolving not to think about what was in it. It wasn't bad, a little salty, but she didn't see what the big deal was.

'Want to try mine?' Ethan held his unbitten end up to her. She watched a piece of sauerkraut and tomato fall off onto the table.

'Ah, no.' Alexis firmly shook her head. As she watched him take another bite, all desire she had to lean across the table and kiss him faded away. She was sure it wouldn't come back until he'd at least brushed his teeth.

Ethan nodded, pleased when she finished most of her meal. 'See, that wasn't so bad, was it?'

'Someday, I'm going to ask you the same thing. I'll take you to a nice restaurant and order for you and make you eat it,' Alexis said.

'Deal. It's a date,' Ethan answered. 'Only, no snails.'

Alexis wondered at the pleasure that curled inside her at the statement.

'Well, it's a friend date,' Ethan amended when she didn't answer.

Her pleasure lessened some. 'It's OK, I knew what you meant.'

Ethan watched Alexis out of the corner of his eye. She seemed like she was having fun, but she didn't really say as much. He was amazed that he actually got her to eat a hot dog. The look on her face as she bit into it had been priceless.

Susan and Ted had agreed to meet them that evening to go back to the hotel. It was already decided they'd spend another night in Iowa City before heading on. Ethan smiled. That meant he had Alexis all to himself the entire day. So far it had been good. He told himself he was just cementing their friendship. He also told himself he knew that was a lie. There was more between them. He just didn't want to look into it. Why ruin what they had going?

Taking a handful of mints as they walked out of the restaurant, he popped one in his mouth. The rest he shoved into his pocket for later. The boy at the counter didn't even look up. When he got outside, Alexis had her camera out. 'I'm glad to see you taking some pictures. Care if I look?'

She stiffened, instantly changing the subject. 'Didn't you say something about a museum?'

Ethan didn't press the issue. He could well understand being sensitive about art because he used to be the same way when he was younger and just starting out in the tattoo business. The wrong type of criticism could really hurt a budding artist's career.

Ethan took her to a museum the guy at the zine shop told him about. It had an extensive collection of taxidermy animals, including the model of a giant prehistoric creature. He thought it was cool. Alexis didn't seem too impressed. She kept saying, 'Poor little animals.' By the time they left the museum it was time to meet Susan and Ted by the sidewalk water fountain. They drove back to the hotel.

Alexis leaned her head back on the edge of the hot tub and smiled at Susan. Ted and Ethan had gone to get dinner. It was nice to have some alone time with her friend. 'This is the life.'

Susan made a choking noise. 'Excuse me? Did Alexis Grant just call sitting in a cheap hotel's hot tub "the life"?'

Alexis chuckled. 'Hard to believe, huh? I hardly believe it myself. But, it's almost like I've forgotten what it's like to be rich. Don't give me that look. This isn't so bad, you know.'

'This, ah, wouldn't have anything to do with Ethan, would it?' Susan asked carefully.

'No, why?' Alexis lied, refusing to look Susan in the face. It had a lot to do with Ethan. Today had been nearly perfect. Maybe being middle class wasn't as bad as her mother made it sound.

'Well, because you two seem to be getting, you know, cosy.'

'Cosy? Me and Ethan?' Alexis forced a laugh. 'Why? Because we're getting along? I'm sorry, did you want us to call off the truce and go back to fighting?'

'Well, no,' Susan said. 'I just don't think it would be a good idea for you to get involved with him. We have a lot of travelling to do and well . . .'

Alexis finally looked at Susan. 'Well?'

'He's not your type, Lexy.' Susan gave her a look of concern. 'I've known you a long time. And I know everything you've had going on in your life recently. You're confused. You'd have to be after all you've been through. It's a lot of changes in a short time. But, someday soon, you'll start feeling like your old self again. Ethan James doesn't fit into the picture of the old Lexy.'

'Are you saying I'm too shallow to date someone like Ethan?' Alexis wondered if she should be insulted. Then, knowing it was Susan who spoke, she didn't take offence.

'No, I would never say that. But, you are a different breed than he is. You like designer clothing and elegant houses. Ethan is the type of guy who'd be content living in a studio apartment over some restaurant.'

'He eats hot dogs and I eat caviar,' Alexis said softly, thinking of the day she'd spent with him. They really were different.

'Exactly!' Susan said, seemingly pleased that Alexis understood.

'And you don't think I could learn to like hot dogs?' Alexis dipped her fingers into the water, twirling them around.

'No, sweetie, not in the long term. I just don't want to see you getting all confused over a fling.' Susan edged closer, making her way around the edge of the hot tub so she could sit by Alexis.

'But I might have to,' Alexis said, tears welling in her eyes. 'The caviar's gone.'

'Oh, no, don't cry.' Susan gave her a hug. 'Is that why

you've been nice to Ethan? You think you can't get any-one else? Oh, Lexy, this thing with your mother will blow over. You'll find yourself some rich man with influence. You'll fall in love and have the fairy-tale life all us normal women dream of.'

'Do you know what us non-normal women dream of?' Alexis asked, sniffing.

'Oh, sweetie, I didn't mean to imply you weren't normal.'

'I know, I didn't take offence. I really wanted to know. Do you know what us non-normal women dream of?' Alexis pulled back, looking Susan in the eye so she'd know she was serious. 'We dream of the kind of happiness you and Ted have found together. I want you to know if ever you decide you're ready to get married and have kids and do all that stuff, I'm happy for you. Ted's a great guy and he cares for you a lot. I just wanted you to know that.'

Susan's eyes teared up. 'Really?'

'Of course, really,' Alexis said. Susan hugged her tighter.

'Now, I don't mean to be lewd, but this is kind of a turn-on,' Ted said. 'Is that what you two do when we're not around?'

Alexis pulled back, laughing. She wiped the tears from her face under the pretence of being hot. Susan did the same. They smiled at the men.

'Mm, smells good,' Susan said, eyeing the takeout bags.

'Fried chicken, mashed potatoes and brown gravy, corn, biscuits, coleslaw,' Ted said. 'Oh, and diet soda as requested.'

'Perfect. Give us a second and we'll be in.' Susan winked at him.

'Don't take too long or we'll eat without you,' Ted said.

Alexis watched Ethan as he carried in the food bags. He met her eyes, but didn't say a word.

When they were alone, Susan said, 'Now, about you and Ethan.'

'Oh, don't worry about that,' Alexis assured her, not

wanting her friend to worry. 'Nothing inappropriate has happened. We're getting along as friends. That's it. We both know nothing more would ever work. Besides, neither of us wants more.'

'Are you sure?' Susan asked. 'Because you said he came onto you.'

Alexis laughed. 'I think I was being a tad dramatic that day.'

Susan giggled. Dryly, she said, 'You? Dramatic? No way. I don't believe it.'

'So, no more worries?' Alexis asked.

'No worries, we're good.' Susan stood and stepped out of the hot tub. 'Now, let's eat. I'm starving.'

Alexis was right behind her.

Ethan closed his eyes. Images of Alexis in the hot tub danced in his head – the steam curling around her body, her chest flushed and wet from the hot water, the little striped bikini she wore. He got hard just thinking about it. Only in his head, he kept the fantasy going. In his head, he was with her, stripping the bikini off her wet breasts, licking her warm nipples.

'Ethan?'

Ethan jerked, coming back to reality. He looked at Alexis. They'd eaten dinner in Susan and Ted's room earlier and afterwards she'd gone swimming. He'd spied on her from the hotel window. What could he say? It had been a great show.

'Did you hear me?' Alexis asked. She was still wearing her bathing suit and he was hard pressed not to stare at her breasts. 'I said I have tattoos lined up for you.'

'What?' Ethan sat up, finally paying attention.

'Yeah, I ran into a married couple on their honeymoon. They want matching tattoos of champagne glasses or something on them. And then I ran into a girl who works in the laundry here at the hotel and she thinks she has like ten friends that might come down tonight. And then –'

'Wait, you lined all this up for tonight?' Ethan asked.

'Yeah, I was out recruiting for clients after my swim. Is that a problem?'

Ethan chuckled, not really in the mood to work. If he had his choice, he'd go back to the little hot-tub fantasy he had rolling in his head. People always talked big, but when it came down to getting the tattoo, they usually didn't show. 'No, it's fine.'

He leaned back, not really worried about it.

'Great, cos the married couple's waiting outside.'

Ethan watched. He was a little stunned as she showed in the newly-weds. They were young and had never been tattooed before.

When Alexis said she'd been out recruiting for clients, she hadn't been kidding. He didn't know how she did it, but there was a large group of Iowa City locals hanging out at the pool waiting for their ink. The laundry girl turned out to be a lesbian with seven roommates. Ethan could just guess the reason she was there as she stared at Alexis in her swimsuit. Alexis didn't seem to care as she helped people choose designs and laid them out. He couldn't blame the woman. Alexis was hot.

When the last person left, it was past midnight and he was exhausted. Alexis was still in her swimsuit with a towel wrapped around her waist. She shut the door, nearly jumping in excitement. She clapped her hands. 'Oh, did you see how good we did? I know we had to have made at least twenty-five hundred dollars tonight.'

Ethan grinned at her enthusiasm. It was indeed a very profitable night. 'What I want to know is where did you learn to handle people like that?'

'What can I say? I was raised to charm and get what I want out of people.'

'And where did you learn to lay tattoos out? I mean, really lay them out?'

'Well, I watched you do the layouts. It's just tracing,' Alexis said, tilting her head in confusion.

'No, I mean pick the designs out like that, determine

the sizes and areas.' Ethan stretched his arms over his head.

'Oh, that.' She waved her hand like it was no big deal. 'I just thought of it as clothing, or decorating a house. You look at the lines, study the area you have to work with and *voilà*. You hang a picture on the wall.'

Ethan forced himself off the bed and moved to grab a pair of boxers from his bag. He went into the bathroom.

'You know,' Alexis called through the door, 'when we started this trip, I never would've called what you do art. But I would've been wrong. You're a very talented artist, Ethan, and I'm impressed with how sterile and clean you are. You take your work very seriously.'

Ethan slowly changed into his boxers as he listened to her.

'Anyway, what I'm trying to say is, I think you'll do great opening a shop in California – plan or no plan.'

Ethan smiled softly at her words. He stepped out of the bathroom. 'Thank you.'

'Yeah, well.' Alexis waved her hand. 'It's late. I'm tired and rambling and in need of a shower.'

She made a move to go past him. Ethan couldn't stop himself. He grabbed her to his chest and pulled his lips to hers. He kissed her hard, thrusting his tongue inside her warm mouth.

He'd wanted her for what seemed like an eternity. His shaft was hard, nearly painfully erect. It had been most of the day. Then, to see her parading around all evening in her bikini, knowing he couldn't touch her, it had been too much. He had to touch her, needed to touch her.

Alexis moaned into his passionate kiss as she slowly lifted her arms around Ethan's neck. There had been something erotic in watching him work. His hands were so precise in what they did. Whereas she didn't completely understand his lifestyle and maybe never would, she could appreciate his dedication to it.

Ethan tugged the towel from her waist. It fell to the

floor and he instantly replaced it with the press of his cock. He touched her hips, running his fingers up her spine to her bikini top. Looking deep into her eyes, he slowly nodded his head. He didn't have to say a word. She knew what he was asking. Their harsh breath mingled between them. Slowly, she nodded. Yes, she wanted this. It seemed silly to deny their bodies any longer.

Ethan kissed her again, this time softer. Alexis found herself moaning as his tongue swept between her teeth. He untied her bathing suit behind her back and it fell forwards, draped about her neck. Warm hands cupped her breasts, massaging them in soft circles.

Her hair was damp from the swimming pool and she smelled like chlorine. Ethan didn't seem to care as his lips moved to her throat. He nibbled her neck, kissing down across her chest to the other side.

Alexis was pressed along the wall. The mirror behind his back reflected her face back to her. She watched his red-tipped head moving over her body, saw his tattoos. They only served to turn her on more when she thought she'd be repulsed. She'd never been with a man like him.

Ethan wasn't refined. He didn't open car doors or automatically guide her elbow when walking. But, when she talked, she felt he really listened. When he talked, she felt he spoke the truth. And when he looked at her, he really looked. He saw her – the good, the bad, the everything. She'd told him things about her life that she barely admitted to Susan and he was still here, kissing her as if her past didn't matter. As he touched her, she felt as if he was accepting who she was, faults and all.

His back flexed in the mirror, drawing her eyes to his butt. She watched her hands gliding over his muscles, kneading them. Ethan lowered himself, leaning to suck her nipples into his mouth. He bit lightly, causing a jolt of sensation to course through her. She lifted her leg, moving it along his waist, trying to entice him to press his erection back into her.

When he lifted his head, his lids were lowered over his eyes. 'Ah, you mentioned something about a shower?'

'Yes,' Alexis said, just as softly.

He glanced down her body. 'Don't go anywhere.'

Alexis nearly fell over as he left her. The shower turned on and soon steam was curling out of the bathroom. Ethan cussed softly and she heard him fumbling with the shower curtain. She stood against the wall, watching her reflection. Her skin was flushed, her nipples wet and hard from Ethan's kisses. Her top was pulled to the side, but still hung about her neck. She weakly pulled the tie at her nape, letting the bikini top drop to the floor. She tried to catch her breath, but her heart was racing fast and her body was tight with longing.

Alexis refused to touch herself. She was already heated to the point of urgency and seeing her half-naked body, her dishevelled hair, was arousal enough. She wiggled her hips, finally deciding to push the bottoms off as well. There was no point in wasting time with undressing.

Ethan stepped out of the bathroom followed by steam. He held his breath, his eyes automatically trailing down to her thighs. Alexis groaned, reaching to grab him. She pushed him to her place against the wall, taking the lead as she kissed his neck and chest. Her lips brushed past his pierced nipples. He felt good, warm. Pushing his hands away when he tried to touch her, she pinned them by his head only to trail her fingers down his arms to his waist.

The steam caressed her back as she drew her hands to his boxers. She kissed him, slowly freeing his arousal. His hands dropped to her arms and he moaned softly. The boxers fell around his ankles.

Stroking his hard length, she shivered. Her fingers ran over the piercings along the top of his shaft. She'd been curious about them since she'd first seen them. 'What are these for?'

'Most genital piercings are done with a woman's pleasure in mind,' he answered, grinning.

Alexis swore her thighs tightened and more cream came pouring out of her at the look he gave her. Awed, she asked, 'What's it feel like?'

Ethan chuckled. 'You'll have to tell me.'

'Condom,' Alexis said, stroking him.

'Ah.' Ethan looked worried for a moment and then confused. He glanced around. 'My bag.'

'Hurry. I can't wait much longer. I'll be in the shower.' Alexis kissed him and then turned to the bathroom. Ethan's hand brushed her backside as she walked away. Climbing into the warm water, she barely turned around when Ethan was right there beside her, box of condoms in hand.

Water glided over their bodies. Alexis grabbed soap and rubbed down her breasts, spending more time caressing herself than getting clean. Then, she ran her soapy hands over Ethan's body as he fumbled with the box. Finally getting a condom, he slipped it over his cock, pinching the tip.

Ethan grabbed her, lifting her soapy body up against the wall. Water hit his back, as he placed her butt near the handrail. Alexis tensed, waiting for the first thrust, needing him desperately. Any more foreplay and she was likely to go mad. His hips moved along her as he found entrance.

She held onto the rail with one hand and his shoulder with the other. He thrust, stretching her body to his. The way he moved bumped his firm stomach along her clit, stimulating the sensitive bud with each pass. He kept moving, gripping her thighs as he rocked his hips in deep strokes.

'Ah, this, good,' he managed, speeding his thrusts and making them harder.

'Mm, yeah, good,' she answered, breathing too hard to say much else. She never imagined being taken up against the shower wall in a cheap motel in Iowa City would be so enjoyable.

'Come for me, I can't hold back much longer,' he said.

Alexis rolled her hips. She reached between them, firmly rubbing herself to increase her own pleasure. All the tension of waiting for this moment exploded within her. Her climax came to her hard and she stiffened. Ethan's body jerked as soon as the first tremor hit her. He grunted, making animalistic noises as he came.

Slowly, he lowered her. He smiled and leaned in to kiss her. She turned her head. Breathing hard, his eyes closed as he said, 'Tell me you don't regret it.'

'No.' Alexis reached to touch his face. 'We just have to be clear about something. No one can know, especially Susan and Ted.'

'Ashamed of me?' His tone was light, but she saw the hurt look on his face.

'No, of course not,' Alexis said. 'It's just that Susan won't understand. She and Ted will stare at us, making us feel all uncomfortable. There'll be pressure to act like a couple, or like we're in some kind of serious relationship like they are. If they just think we're friends, then there will be no pressure.'

OK, it was partly the truth. The other part was the idea of her mother finding out that her daughter was having an affair with someone who was socially beneath her. Alexis didn't know how her mother would find out, but she wasn't one to take the chance. A one night fling her mother would understand. But, an extended affair? The woman would break out of prison just so she could commit Alexis to a home for the mentally insane.

'OK?' Alexis prompted when Ethan continued to stare at her, his face blank.

'Sure.' He pushed the hair back from his face. 'We should get some sleep.'

'I'm just going to wash my hair,' Alexis said. 'I shouldn't have let the chlorine stay in it so long.'

Ethan leaned over and gave her a light kiss, which turned slowly deeper. 'Mm, OK. See you in bed.'

'OK,' she said, her voice soft.

Ethan stepped out of the shower. Alexis smiled to herself, her body sated. Ethan was a great lover and this trip might end up being pretty darned good. The best part was that no one would ever have to know about them. She'd have her cake and eat it too.

Chapter Eleven

The next morning they got a late start. Alexis was exhausted and a little too aroused. Waking up, she'd been about to seduce Ethan when the phone rang. It was Susan telling them that they had twenty minutes until check-out.

Alexis sleepily pulled on the V-neck, green-apple-coloured mesh shirt with the built-in camisole, her Joie vintage denim jeans and black leather boots. For the first time in her life she didn't debate about what she wore. She just got dressed barely looking in the mirror before leaving. Susan and Ted were ready to go when Alexis came stumbling out of the hotel room.

Ethan took care of check-out. Ted said he'd drive since Ethan and Alexis had had a long night with the tattooing. Susan was amazed at how well they did, but even more so that Alexis had arranged it. Alexis told Ethan to hold onto her half of the money for her. He'd proven himself to be a fairly honest, generous person. She trusted him with her cash and it saved her the trouble of carrying it in a purse everywhere.

As they rode in the back seat, all Alexis wanted to do was curl up next to Ethan and sleep. Instead, she settled for curling up on the black leather seat. When she awoke, Ethan's fingers were absently stroking her hair. Embarrassed, she realised she'd drooled a little bit. Ethan just chuckled as she yawned, trying to sneakily wipe the evidence away.

'Mm.' Alexis blinked as her eyes adjusted to the light. Glancing out the window, the land looked the same, maybe a little browner.

'Morning sleepyhead,' Susan said.

'Are we almost to Missouri?' Alexis yawned again, this time loudly as she covered her mouth.

'We're almost out of Missouri,' Susan answered, smiling. 'Kansas City's coming up in a few miles. We thought we'd stop and get something to eat there.'

Alexis nodded, not answering as she tried to wake up. She glanced at Ethan and he gave her a secretive smile. He looked so adorable. Alexis stretched, twisting her back as she tried to lengthen her legs in the car. Looking out of the back window, she frowned. 'Ted, how long has that grey car been behind us?'

'What grey car?' Ted craned his neck. 'Huh, I don't know. I haven't been paying attention. Why?'

'I think it's following us,' Alexis said.

'What?' Susan asked, slightly alarmed. 'What makes you say that?'

'You remember that first night when I was standing outside? We thought Ethan . . .' Alexis stopped, giving a dirty look at the Ethan. 'A man was smoking a cigarette, watching me.'

'You thought Ethan what?' Ethan asked.

Alexis ignored him, pretending like she couldn't hear him though he was right there. 'He asked me if he could help me with my luggage. I told him no.'

'You thought Ethan what?' Ethan repeated.

'I don't remember,' Susan said to Alexis. She too refused to look at Ethan. Ted laughed.

'You thought Ethan what?' Ethan asked again.

'They thought you were having sex with that hotel clerk you were tattooing. They heard buzzing and thought you were using, you know, sex toys.' Ted laughed. Susan made a mortified sound and hit him playfully in the arm.

'Mm, so you guys were spying on me?' Ethan grinned. Alexis felt his eyes on her. She couldn't resist glancing at him. He gave her a wickedly handsome smile that made her thighs tighten. She shook her head to clear it.

'Anyway,' Alexis drawled to get the conversation back on track. 'I only remember it because he had really gross armpit stains and smelled a little like stale corn chips.

Anyway, I don't remember seeing him in Wisconsin, but he was definitely at a few of the same gas stations we were at.'

Susan frowned, getting worried. 'You don't think he could be following us, do you? I mean, what do you think he wants?'

'I don't know.' Alexis frowned, looking at Ethan.

'You're probably just paranoid,' Ted said. 'If it is the same man, he's probably just a traveller on vacation.'

'I don't know,' Alexis said. Voicing her fears out loud only made her more nervous about it. She was sure it was the same man.

'We all know what the car looks like now.' Ethan's fingers reached out and he secretly stroked the back of her hand. Alexis shivered at the contact. 'We'll all keep an eye out for him. OK?'

Susan and Alexis both nodded.

'In the meantime, don't stare at the guy,' Ted said. 'If he is following us, we don't want to alarm him by letting him know we suspect something.'

'Oh, listen to you. All of a sudden you're like a secret agent.' Susan laid her head on his shoulder. 'My big bad spy.'

Alexis glanced at Ethan and rolled her eyes. He smirked but didn't say a word. His hand stayed next to hers, his fingers lightly touching her as he stared out the window.

'You guys up to another three hours today? I got us a place to stay if you are,' Ethan said, walking outside the fast-food restaurant. He'd just gotten off the phone with one of his friends. Adam had been surprised to hear from him, but automatically offered him a place to crash for the night.

Ethan went to sit with the others, next to the busy interstate. The weather was warm, but it was nice to get out of the stuffy car. With the sun shining in the window all afternoon, the air felt stuffy and he was a little jet-lagged.

'Really, where?' Susan asked.

'With a friend of mine and his family,' Ethan said. 'He owns a tattoo shop about three hours west of here in Wichita and offered to let us crash for a couple days if we wanted.'

'We don't need to impose,' Alexis said.

'Believe me, we won't be. Besides, if I know Adam, he'll have every DVD known to man and he'll insist on cooking. I don't know about you guys but I'm getting a little tired of eating out all the time.' Ethan picked up his half-eaten hamburger and shook it for emphasis. The others readily agreed. 'In fact, he said he'd make lasagne if we were coming down tonight.'

'Mm,' Susan moaned. 'Real food. I think I love your friend.'

'Careful, don't let his wife hear you say that.' Ethan laughed.

'Is she mean?' Alexis asked.

'She's ... ah ... a writer. Basically, she's cool but a little strange.' Ethan shook his head, remembering the first time he'd met Adam's wife, Veronica. He'd been convinced for about a month that she didn't like him. Ended up, she was just preoccupied with a book she was working on. 'I'd be talking to her and she'd grab a notepad and start writing ideas down for her next book. Adam says she even keeps a notepad under her pillow at night and writes ideas down in the dark when she can't sleep.'

'She sounds weird,' Alexis said.

'Oh, I don't know.' Susan smiled. 'I think creative people are allowed to be a little eccentric.'

'Free room. Homemade meal. Eccentric writer.' Ted stood, stretching his arms over his head. 'I say let's do it.'

Driving along the Kansas highway, they got stuck behind a large green combine going twenty miles per hour for nearly ten minutes before the farmer could pull over to the side and wave them past. Alexis leaned against the window, looking up at him. He smiled and tipped his faded red baseball cap.

'Do you notice how everyone we drive past waves?'

Alexis asked. The sky was starting to get darker with the evening. 'You grew up here, Ethan. Is it always like this or is today some kind of special wave at the other cars day?'

'Yeah, it's pretty much always like that,' Ethan said. 'People are friendlier and more laid back in the Midwest. It took me a while to get used to New York when I first moved there. I said hi to a guy out of habit once and he screamed like I was about to mug him.'

'OK, smarty pants, I have another question,' Alexis said. She pointed out the window to where a row of trees stretched between two fields like a border. She wouldn't have found it odd, except for the fact they passed many such rows. 'Why are all the trees growing in straight lines?'

Ethan chuckled. 'My grandpa told me it was because of the Dust Bowl. They planted them like that to act like wind blockers so it wouldn't happen again.'

Alexis looked thoughtful. 'You think you're pretty smart, don't you.'

'I know, let's play a game,' Susan said.

'I haven't played car games since I was a kid.' Ethan laughed. 'What do you have in mind?'

'Um, twenty questions. If you get them right, ah –' Susan looked around the car '– Alexis has to give you a foot massage.'

'Ew, what? Why me?' Alexis instantly answered.

'Deal,' Ethan said at the same time. 'But they have to be about something I could possibly know.'

'Deal,' Susan said. 'Ted keep count.'

'Aye, aye, captain,' Ted said.

'Hey, no, no deal,' Alexis protested out of principle, but the truth was she wanted an excuse to touch Ethan again or to have him touch her. 'What happens if he doesn't get it? I want a foot massage.'

'Fine,' Ethan said. 'I answered about the waving and the trees. Any other Kansas trivia I can recite for you? Bring it on.'

'State bird?' Susan asked.

'Um, the meadowlark,' Ethan answered.

'State motto?' Ted asked.

'Ah, crap, it's . . .' Ethan started humming softly.

'Tick, tock, tick, tock, time's running out,' Susan said.

Alexis clapped her hands. 'Pressure's on!'

'*Ad Astra Per Aspera*,' Ethan said, nearly shouting.

'Which means?' Ted asked.

'To the stars through difficulties.'

'Is that right?' Susan asked Ted. Ted shrugged.

'Ah-ha. Yes, it is right,' Ethan said, grinning. 'Next question.'

'Great going, Susan, quit wasting questions,' Alexis said, pretending to pout, 'or I'll make you help me massage his feet.'

'State capital?' Susan asked.

'Too easy. Topeka.'

'Flower?' Alexis asked.

'Sunflower.' Ethan lowered his voice as he looked at her.

'Mother's maiden name?' Alexis continued.

'Smith.'

'Social security, bank account and pin numbers?' Ted said.

'Nice try, buddy.' Ethan laughed.

'First girl you ever slept with?' Susan asked, nodding slowly as if she'd stump him.

Ethan nearly choked. He looked guiltily at Alexis. 'Um, Mary Jo Smith.'

'Ew, a cousin?' Alexis recoiled from him.

Ethan quirked a brow. 'No. No relation whatsoever.'

'Did you love her?' Alexis didn't meet his eyes. She held her breath. Was that jealousy burning in her chest?

'Ooh, good one, Lexy,' Susan said. 'Put him on the spot.'

'No,' Ethan answered. His voice dipped slightly. Alexis stomach knotted.

'Have you ever been in love?' Alexis studied his face for the truth.

'No. Not that I know of.'

'Don't you think you would know?' Alexis asked.

'Not if I was blind to it,' he answered. 'Or if I didn't want to admit it to myself.'

'Oh, good try, Lexy. He's a hard nut to crack,' Susan said. Alexis nodded. She hadn't been trying to crack him. She wanted to know how he felt about her.

'That's fourteen,' Ted said. 'I'm counting the ones about the trees and the waving.'

'Thanks, buddy,' Ethan said, patting Ted's shoulder.

'Yeah, no problem. Lexy wore that T-shirt and made me lose ten bucks,' Ted said.

'Hey,' Alexis protested. 'Not fair.'

'Paybacks are hell.' Ted chuckled as Susan slugged his arm. 'Man, honey, you've gotten violent.'

'Oh, did I hurt my baby?' Susan said, talking baby talk. She instantly leaned over to sprinkle kisses on his arm.

'No, Ted's fine,' Ethan said quickly. 'That's fifteen.'

'Hey, now that one really doesn't count.' Alexis pushed his thigh. She'd moved closer to him in the course of the game. It took all her willpower not to touch him again.

'Ugh. What is that smell?' Susan asked, covering her mouth. 'Ted, did you fart? Gross.'

Ted laughed. 'No. It wasn't me.'

Ethan chuckled and pointed ahead as Ted sped the car to pass a large semi. 'Cattle truck.'

'Oh, if that's what beef smells like, I'm never eating a cheeseburger again,' Alexis said.

'You're such a diva,' Susan said, plugging her nose. 'Ugh, but this time I agree.'

'Hey, is that Mr Grey behind us again?' Ted asked, frowning. 'I thought we lost him.'

Alexis turned around to look out the back window. Indeed a grey car was following them. She stiffened. The car came closer and moved to pass. She relaxed, seeing it was a family of five and not the possible stalker.

'No. That's not Mr Grey.' Ethan laughed. 'And you should've seen the look on your face, Alexis.'

Alexis frowned. 'It's not funny.'

His gaze dipped to her mouth and he looked like he wanted to kiss her. She shivered, instantly forgetting the grey car.

'Seventeen,' Ted said, unintentionally breaking the spell. 'Ladies, you better stump him. You only have three questions left.'

'Oh, I know. How many names does Alexis have?' Susan asked.

'Four,' Ethan answered, smiling at Alexis. 'Alexis Samantha Wellington Grant.'

'Susan,' Alexis scolded.

'Well, how was I supposed to know you told him?' Susan demanded. 'I thought that would stump him for sure.'

'You weren't,' Ethan said, chuckling. 'And I believe I'm about to win this game. Two questions left. Bring it on.'

'When's the last time you had sex? And with who?' Susan said.

Ethan hesitated. Alexis held her breath. Oh, no, this was bad.

'Ah, if you don't answer, we win,' Susan said. She looked triumphantly at Alexis. Alexis gave her a weak smile.

'So, Lexy, how do you like your foot massages?' Ethan asked. Alexis let loose a long breath. 'Hard or soft?'

'We won,' Susan cried before going into her victory song. 'Oh, yeah, I got him. Oh, yeah. Oh, yeah.'

Ethan stared deep into her eyes. Alexis let the corner of her mouth pull up as she mouthed, 'Thank you.'

Ethan nodded once, but he didn't smile. 'Are we almost there yet, Ted? I'm starving for lasagne.'

Ethan's friend lived right outside of Wichita, Kansas in a small suburb. The town looked like many of the other small towns they'd driven through, except that it seemed to have a lot of trees. Ted let Ethan borrow his cell phone to call Adam for directions. Alexis was a little nervous to meet Ethan's friends, wondering what they would be like.

'Right on Broadway. Left on Staton Street,' Ethan said when he hung up. 'It'll be the tattoo shop on the right.'

'We're going to an actual tattoo shop?' Alexis bit her lip.

'Yeah, he got busy at work today. Looks like lasagne's cancelled until tomorrow,' Ethan said.

'Oh,' Susan groaned. 'His wife couldn't make it?'

Ethan laughed as Ted turned the corner. 'Veronica doesn't cook.'

'Tornado Tattoo.' Alexis read the giant heart with wings sign as Ted pulled into the long parking lot in front of a brick building. 'Hey, isn't that what's on your jacket?'

'Yeah, Adam sent me the jacket for Christmas.' Ethan opened the car door.

Alexis looked out the window. An airbrushed mask stared out from the front window of the shop. A big, scary-looking guy stood by an old-fashioned black motor-cycle. The man had short brown hair and giant holes in his ears as if he'd been shot in the lobe. Instantly, she assumed it was Adam by the black T-shirt he wore with the shop's name on it. Her fingers shook as she reached for the door handle. They couldn't possibly be staying with him. This had to be a mistake.

'Adam,' Ethan called to the big guy, confirming her fears. He held out his hand. 'Hey, man, great to see you.'

Alexis couldn't hear what was said, but watched the men banter back and forth. Ted and Susan opened their doors and got out. Alexis was slower to follow.

'This your bike?' Ethan asked the big, scary tattoo artist. He motioned to the black motorcycle.

'Yeah, just got it back from the mechanic last week,' Adam answered. His voice was deep and he spoke loud, as if used to talking to crowds of people.

'It's an old Triumph?' Ethan asked.

'Yep,' Adam said. 'Sure is. A seventy-eight. I traded a back piece for it. I just had it chopped, raked, stretched. Looks a lot better than when I got it, that's for sure. I see you still have the Lincoln. I remember when you hauled me down to Oklahoma to get that thing. It's looking good. A lot better than the pile of rust it was.'

'Ah, it wasn't that bad. Oh, hey, I want you to meet some friends of mine.' Ethan turned around and pointed at each person as he said their name. 'Ted, Susan, Alexis.'

'Hey, man, thanks for letting us crash,' Ted said, shaking Adam's hand.

'Not a problem. Glad to have ya. We just remodelled our attic and basement, so we have plenty of room,' Adam said.

Inside, the shop was huge. Adam informed them that it was the biggest in Kansas. It was nothing like Alexis expected. She'd imagined something dark, like an underground torture chamber.

The walls were covered with flash. Ethan told her that the sheets of artwork were to help people pick tattoos, much like the designs in his computer. Alexis could see four enormous fish tanks – one with bright saltwater fish, one with large piranhas and two with freshwater fish. Where there wasn't flash, the walls had been spray-painted with designs. A familiar buzzing sounded in the back, but she couldn't see who was tattooing.

'Is that your wife?' Alexis asked, wondering what sort of woman would marry a tattoo artist. She was probably just as big as he was and twice as frightening.

Adam laughed. 'No, that's my apprentice, Raulf. Veronica doesn't tattoo. She takes care of the boring paperwork stuff I don't want to do.'

'She works here then?' Alexis asked, still curious.

'Sometimes. That is if she's not home on the computer writing.' He laughed. 'Crap, that reminds me. I have to go find those receipts. If I misplaced them again she'll most likely threaten to divorce me. You know, behind every tattoo artist is a woman getting ready to hit him over the back of the head. Truth is, if she didn't keep up the paperwork this place would've closed the first year.'

The phone rang and Adam excused himself. Susan had wandered off with Ted to look at designs. Ethan motioned to a lime-green couch in the front waiting area. 'So, what you think?'

Alexis sat down by him. 'It's not what I pictured at all.'

'Let me guess. You pictured a small little rat's nest filled with cigarette smoke and guns and drugs and big, bad bikers in black leather?' Ethan laughed.

'Well, yeah,' Alexis said. 'That's how it is in the movies.'

Ethan's hand lifted briefly to touch her cheek, stroking her with his thumb. 'You really shouldn't believe everything you see in movies. This is a legitimate business. I can't tell you how frustrating it is to fight the constant stereotyping.'

'I know what you mean,' Alexis said. 'People look at me and see a spoiled little rich girl who's had everything handed to her.'

'People look at me and see an uneducated hack that's too lazy to get a real job,' Ethan said.

'But that's not who we are, is it?' Alexis's voice lowered to a whisper. She leaned closer. 'You're not a hack. You're a true artist.'

'And you're not a spoiled little rich girl,' Ethan said, leaning closer. He pressed his forehead to hers. The tips of their noses touched. She could feel his breath against her lips. 'At least, not any more.'

Alexis smiled. He was right. She had changed and she knew he was partly the reason for it.

Someone cleared their throat. Ethan instantly pulled away. Adam joined them, sitting across from them on a bright-orange couch. Alexis quickly looked around the shop to make sure Susan and Ted hadn't seen them. She'd been centimetres away from kissing Ethan. What had gotten into her?

'We were just talking about tattoo stereotypes,' Ethan said.

'Uh-huh, sure you were.' Adam laughed. Alexis started to relax around him. The man might look scary, but he didn't act it. He opened his mouth to say more but the door chime went off and a group of young teenage girls walked in. Instead, he called, 'Can I help ya?'

'Um, yeah,' one girl said after glancing at her three friends. She stepped forwards, the unofficial spokesperson for the group. Swallowing nervously, she said, 'We'd like our belly buttons pierced.'

'Everyone over eighteen?' Adam asked.

'Yes,' the girl answered, nodding.

'Not a problem. Right this way and we'll get started on the paperwork.' Adam stood back up, bantering good naturedly with the girls as he had them fill out release forms. Afterwards, he gave them care instructions. Alexis craned her neck, watching the whole process curiously. Susan and Ted joined them.

'Do you think we can watch?' Susan asked.

'Have to ask Adam, it's his shop,' Ethan said. Alexis looked at him. He was looking at her with a strange expression on his face. She wondered what he was thinking.

Alexis and Susan turned back to watch Adam work. The girls spoke ninety miles a minute and giggled in nervous excitement.

'Is this going to hurt?'

'Oh, look at this purple ring! I love purple.'

'How long did you say until we can change it?'

'Should we get matching rings?'

'Did you say this was going to hurt?'

Alexis had no idea how Adam kept up with their bombardment of questions, all the while maintaining a smile on his face. OK, so maybe the guy only looked big and scary. He was actually quite nice.

Susan waited until Adam finished helping the girls pick out rings from the long jewellery case. 'Do you mind if we watch?'

Adam glanced at the girls. 'Up to them.'

'Do you care if we watch?' Susan asked the girls, smiling hopefully.

They all shook their heads in denial, saying at once, 'No, that's fine.'

'Go ahead.'

'I don't care.'

'Do you have anything done?'

The girls started giggling before Susan could answer. Alexis stood, following them to the back. They stopped before the low partition, keeping back from the piercing area, but still able to see it. Adam pulled on his gloves. She couldn't see his station as he set up his area.

Alexis felt Ethan behind her. They were at the back of the group. His hand skimmed the back of her arm in a light caress. She turned to look at him and he gazed deep into her eyes.

'Ow!'

Alexis jumped in surprise, turning back around. The piercing was done.

'That was fast,' Susan said. 'Did you see that?'

'No,' Alexis said. 'I wasn't looking.'

The second girl lay down. Alexis felt another brush along the back of her arm. She turned to Ethan and mouthed, 'What?'

He smiled. Her stomach tightened. He looked so cute, and so very kissable.

'Mm,' the girl getting pierced moaned. 'Ah!'

Alexis frowned. She'd missed that one as well. She turned around to see, waiting while the third lay down. Adam was pulling on a fresh set of latex gloves. The two with piercings admired their stomachs in the mirror, swaying back and forth as they toyed with the gemstone barbells, all the while dotting at the piercings with a paper towel to stop the bleeding.

Waiting for Ethan to touch her again, Alexis turned her head to the side. He didn't reach for her. She turned around to look at him.

'What?' he mouthed, grinning.

This time Alexis ignored the girls as the third one received her piercing. Ethan looked at her mouth. Time seemed to stand still as she stared at him. Licking her lips, she wanted to kiss him.

'Last one,' Adam announced.

Alexis forced herself to turn back. This would probably be the only time she'd see something like this. She hated to think of what her mother would say if she found out she was even in a place like this, having impure thoughts about Ethan. Adam took a needle and pierced the girl's navel. Alexis cringed. Adam threaded a curved barbell into the hollow needle and ran it back through.

'It's in there like swimwear,' Adam announced, pulling off his gloves.

Susan turned around, her mouth agape. To Alexis, she whispered, 'Do you see that? He just made like two hundred and fifty dollars in ten minutes.'

After the girls left, they called in a pizza order to the shop. No one was in the mood for takeout, but that was all the town had for delivery. Once they'd eaten, Adam closed the shop and they went a block away to his house. It looked like a modest middle-class home from the outside, but Adam and Veronica had completely remodelled the inside. Veronica wasn't much for decorating beyond the basics, but there was a simplicity about the house that seemed to fit the couple nicely.

Veronica was pretty with long auburn hair and bright-green eyes. She was nothing that Alexis had expected. In fact, she couldn't see a single piercing or tattoo on the woman. By the looks of her pale skin, she never went out of the house. Adam laughingly said it was because she was lazy. Veronica claimed it was because she was a writer, to which he replied it was because she just didn't want to change out of her pyjama pants. Apparently, it was practically the only thing she wore. They bantered back and forth, but the couple were unmistakably in love.

Ethan wasn't lying when he said Adam had a lot of DVDs. Alexis had never seen so many movies in one place. The man also had the big-screen TVs to go with it. Not just one, but three. The dark wood furniture was understated and went well with the blue-grey walls and Impressionist paintings. They were by no means as rich as Alexis had once been, but it was clear they made a pretty good living in the tattoo business. It made Alexis continue to look at Ethan in a new light. Maybe there was something to his career choice after all. Adam and Veronica seemed to be doing all right with it.

'So, you and Ethan, huh?' Veronica said when she and Alexis were alone in the kitchen. Veronica wandered about aimlessly, looking for food. She opened a cupboard only to shut it, coming away empty handed. She then moved to the refrigerator, opened it and then closed it without taking anything out.

'What about us?' Alexis asked, feigning ignorance. She watched Veronica go back to the cupboard only to sigh heavily when she didn't see anything she wanted.

'OK, you're in denial yet,' Veronica said, shrugging.

Alexis furrowed her brow. Denial about what? OK, creative type or no, the woman was definitely a little weird.

'So.' Alexis searched her mind for conversation. 'How'd you and your husband meet?'

'In a bar. I was head waitress. He was the DJ. We both needed roommates so we moved in together,' Veronica said. 'I tried to deny liking him. I couldn't believe all the tattoos he had. I'd never seen anything like it. Mm, but they grew on me. I barely even notice them any more.'

'Do you have tattoos?' Alexis asked.

Veronica laughed. 'A couple, but it's his thing. I have mine.'

'And it doesn't bother you what people think?' Alexis lowered her voice and stepped further into the kitchen.

'Maybe a little at first, but I've never really been one to worry about what other people think. There are too many idiots out there with opinions. You can't please them all. Besides, what's to be embarrassed about? Adam's a good man. I love him. We have a wonderful life together. We have a beautiful family. The shop makes money. My bills are paid. And anytime I want something, I just have to mention it to him and he somehow manages to trade a tattoo for it.'

'Like what?' Alexis bit her lip. Veronica did seem happy.

'Well, I offhandedly mentioned I wanted to learn to

play guitar and by the end of the week he'd found one for me. Apparently, it's a very nice one, or so I'm told.' Veronica grinned. 'It's collecting dust in my bedroom. I never even took a lesson.'

'Is there a reason why you won't drive?' Ethan asked, crawling next to Alexis. She looked so beautiful lying on the sofa bed. The soft light from the bathroom caressed her skin. He'd just gotten out of the shower. They were sharing the basement guest room. Susan and Ted had the attic.

'I can't,' Alexis admitted. 'I haven't been behind the wheel since I was sixteen in Drivers Ed class.'

'Maybe I'll re-teach you sometime,' Ethan said. 'After we get to California.'

'You think we'll still be friends in California?'

'Don't you?'

'I hope so.'

'Then I think we will, definitely,' Ethan said.

'You know,' Alexis said, 'you owe me a foot massage.'

Ethan laughed. 'You're going to try and cash that in, are you?'

She nodded enthusiastically.

'How about I give you a full body massage instead?' Ethan didn't wait for her to answer. He ran his hand over her hip, slowly digging his fingers under her camisole. He slowly worked her shirt up, exposing her breasts. Her nipples were already hard.

Alexis lay back, parting her lips as he kissed her. He made love to her slowly, caressing her body as he undressed her. His hands went to her waist and he pushed the lacy shorts off her hips, revealing the narrow thatch of hair between her thighs.

'You're beautiful,' Ethan said.

'You enjoy looking?' Without waiting to hear his answer, Alexis pushed him onto his back. Ethan groaned softly, trying to stay quiet. Giggling, she stripped him of his boxer shorts. When he was naked, she straddled his hard stomach and reached for her breasts.

Backing her butt against his cock, she let the erection settle between her cheeks. She rocked her body against his hard stomach and let him feel how hot she was for him, how ready. Each gentle movement slid her wet sex along his firm muscles. She ran her palms over his chest, down his stomach and back up to his arms. As she leaned over, her nipples grazed him. He opened his mouth and made a move for her, stretching his tongue out to lick at her breast. She pulled back and he missed.

'Alexis,' he groaned. It was pure torment, but he liked the torture. He touched her wherever he could reach, enjoying the look of their hands on her body. Her fingers twined with his as she guided his palms to her breasts. 'I've thought about making love to you all day.'

'Me too,' she said. 'I didn't ever think the car ride would end.'

Before Ethan could answer, Alexis lifted her body up and impaled herself on his shaft. He moaned at the tight fit. Her fingers gripped into his shoulders, clawing him as she used his body for leverage. She wiggled her hips back and forth as she thrust up and down. He'd spent the day in the car dreaming of this very thing, of all the ways he wanted to make love to her. It was nice knowing she was as frantic as he.

Ethan watched as she rode him at her own hard pace, reaching between her thighs to stimulate the tender bud hidden there. He bit his tongue to keep from groaning, not wanting to wake the household. It was strikingly erotic the way her hair fell over her shoulders. The way the light danced on her breasts. He pushed his hips up into her, giving it his all. She was wild, beautiful.

She scratched his chest. Her mouth opened but no sound came out. He could feel she was close to coming. Ethan held back, forcing his eyes to stay open so he could watch her climax. Her movements became frantic, jerking wildly against his hand as she met with release. Ethan could hold back no longer, as he released himself. Alexis rubbed her hips in shallow circles riding out her climax.

Weakly, she fell against him, breathing heavily. Suddenly, Ethan tensed, pulling her body off of him. 'Oh, shit.'

Alexis pulled back. 'What?'

'Condom.' Ethan shook his head. 'We forgot to use a condom. Damn, I'm sorry, Alexis. I've never forgotten something that important before, I swear. It was just you were looking so cute and . . .'

Alexis took a deep breath. 'When's the last time you've been tested?'

'No, I'm good there. I'm worried more about getting you pregnant,' Ethan said.

'Don't be, I get the birth-control shot at my mother's insistence.' Alexis gave a short laugh, moving to cuddle into Ethan's arms.

Ethan had a few choice words for Alexis's mother. He kept them to himself.

'She says she's too young to be a grandmother,' Alexis said. 'And I just had my check-up so we're fine. I mean, we shouldn't slip up again, but it's a little too late to worry about it now.'

They lay in silence for a long time, just holding each other.

Chapter Twelve

Their time in Kansas was almost surreal and went by quickly. Adam took time off from his shop while they were there. Both he and Veronica were gracious hosts. They stayed for two days. Ethan made love to Alexis every chance he got. It had become a game of sorts, finding ways to kiss and touch without getting caught by the others. They made love each night several times and even once in his car when they were out running 'errands'.

The first day, they drove into downtown Wichita, visiting museums. One was outdoors. It was set up like an actual town from the Old West completely staffed with people in period-style clothing. Ethan secretively bought her a small rose made from iron right there at the museum by the blacksmith. That evening, Adam cooked lasagne for everyone and they spent the evening watching movies on his big screen.

The second day they spent relaxing and talking. That night Adam and Ethan barbecued. Alexis noted that Veronica didn't lift a finger in the kitchen, unless it was to hug her husband while he was trying to cook. He'd pretend to get annoyed. She'd laugh and do it again. The couple had a nice life together. Alexis was jealous to see it. Veronica was intelligent and didn't seem at all the type of person to marry a tattoo artist. Every time Veronica and Adam would lovingly fight, she'd think of Ethan and wish that it could've been them. Alexis would've traded lives with them in a second.

On the third morning, they left for Colorado just before dawn. Alexis was a little amazed to realise that she hadn't thought of her clothing once. She couldn't even remember what she'd worn the day before. That had never happened to her. She'd been too wrapped up in Ethan to care about superficial things like that.

Ethan bid Alexis to wear a dress. He joked that he'd be unable to wait until that evening to be with her again and he wanted easy assess up her skirt. As they drove, he'd shoot her a steamy look and she'd instantly melt. Unfortunately, the drive through western Kansas didn't provide many places for a quick tryst and they were forced to wait.

'Anticipation might make it all the sweeter,' he'd whispered when they stopped for gas. 'But it's also a living hell.'

Alexis had thought other parts of the country were flat, but western Kansas definitely won the award. Still, there was something majestic about the way the grasses rolled over the plains. The beauty was more subtle compared to the other places they'd been, but it was still there. When they crossed over into Colorado, the land was still flat. She'd been expecting mountains and was a little disappointed.

When they finally reached them, the Rocky Mountains were gorgeous to behold. The foothills almost seemed to pop up out of nowhere. They travelled through the mountains, driving the steep curving roads. Alexis's ears kept popping and she got a small headache. Ethan stopped, buying chewing gum to help them adjust to the pressure change. Alexis purchased Colorado T-shirts for everyone off a sales rack.

'I want you,' Ethan said, nipping her ear as he opened her car door for her. Alexis was amazed. It was the first time he'd opened a door for her. Maybe there was hope of teaching him gentlemanly manners after all.

Now that the trip was almost half over, Alexis didn't want the adventure to end. What would happen when they got to California? Would Ethan just walk out of her life? They had never talked commitment and she was too scared to broach the subject. She knew whatever they had couldn't last. Someday, their different worlds would come crumbling down on them, forcing them apart. Her mother would never understand or condone her relationship with a man so socially beneath her.

Alexis told herself that so long as they could stay on the road none of that mattered. No one would find out. She wanted to drive for ever. They made good time and were able to go to the summit of Pikes Peak just outside of Colorado Springs.

'Did you see that?' Susan gasped, pointing out the window. 'Slow down.'

'What?' Alexis asked, grabbing her camera and lifting it up.

'Over there,' Susan said. 'It's like a deer or something.'

Suddenly, a large animal came out to the clearing. It's huge rack spiked up high on its head.

'It's an elk,' Ted whispered. Alexis shook and lifted her camera to take a picture. 'Now that might actually charge us.'

'Yeah, not like your rabid cow mooing alongside the road in Wisconsin,' Ethan teased.

Alexis couldn't help but laugh. 'I'm telling you, that cow had a bloodthirsty look in his eyes.'

A car honked behind them and the elk ran off into the trees. Alexis frowned in disappointment as they continued up. She gave a shy glance at Ethan but he was too busy looking out the window.

'Hey, look, a bald eagle,' Ethan said, pointing up. 'Aren't they endangered?'

'Yeah, it's on the threatened species list. It's nearly repopulated and they were going to take it off, but no one was sure how they were going to handle all the laws when they did so. It's illegal to even have one,' said Susan.

'Thanks, Teach,' Alexis teased, her camera ready.

Susan laughed.

'Where? I can't see it.' Alexis looked up to the sky.

'It's already gone,' Ethan said.

Alexis sighed, disappointed to have missed it. They continued up and she wasn't sure she wanted to go any higher into the mountains. The peak was over fourteen thousand feet above sea level but when they reached the top it was worth it. She took pictures of everything. Low-growing vegetation sprinkled over the sides, becoming thicker and taller the further down the mountain she looked. The late afternoon cast shadows over the red and grey rock of the surrounding area beneath them, which contrasted with the little bit of snow still on the peak and the dark green of the evergreens. She bought another T-shirt at the little store on top of Pikes Peak.

'Anything you need to tell me?' Susan asked, when they had a moment alone on the mountain. Being so high up, the air was chilly. Alexis shivered in her dress, but Ethan's jacket kept her somewhat warm.

'Not yet,' Alexis said. It was clear by the look on her friend's face that she knew something was up with Ethan.

'OK, I'll just keep pretending like I don't notice any-thing until you're ready to talk,' Susan said, patting her shoulder.

Alexis nodded, grateful. 'Thanks.'

'But, I'm warning you now. My patience will only last until about Las Vegas.' Susan chuckled. 'So you better get ready to talk by then.'

'I hear you loud and clear,' Alexis said. 'I just need some time to sort my head out first.'

That night they stayed in a small hotel in Colorado Springs. The room was like many of the others. The soft pastel walls and insipid artwork was hardly noteworthy and Alexis didn't even pay attention to it. How could she when Ethan was close at hand, looking incredibly sexy in his loose blue jeans and bare feet.

Ethan managed to do a couple of tattoos for extra cash, but nothing like the rush they did in Iowa City. Alexis thought she'd go mad waiting for him to get done. Finally, she was forced to take a shower while she waited, then pampered her body with lotion before sliding into a slinky La Perla chemise. The burgundy mesh was trans-parent over her body. Only her breasts were covered with dark satin. It was one of her more risqué nighties and made her feel incredibly sexy. The chemise was short, reaching just to her thighs, with a deep slit along her hip. Only after making sure Ethan's customers had left, did she come out of the bathroom.

Frowning, she saw the room was empty. The door opened and she spun around. Ethan was carrying a bucket of ice, sodas and candy bars from the machine.

'Susan's offered to wash our clothes at the laundry mat across the parking lot. I took them over. She said not to worry. She knows how to take care of your dry-clean stuff. The machine was out of diet, so you're just going to have to settle for . . .' He looked up, his eyes instantly roaming over her. Slowly, he set the candy and soda down on the end table. '. . . regular. Are you wearing underwear?'

Alexis smiled. She wasn't.

Ethan sat the ice bucket on the floor next to the bed. 'So, ah, does this mean . . .?'

Her smile widened and she crawled onto the bed, tossing her damp hair over her shoulder as she posed.

'Yeah, I'm . . .' Ethan threw off his shirt and hopped on one foot as he tried to pull off his shoes.

'You're?' Alexis prompted, thinking it adorable how eager he sounded.

'Oh, I'm ready for bed.'

Alexis flipped over on her back and rubbed her arms and legs restlessly against the mattress. She purposefully let a pout come to her voice. 'Well, I don't know that I want to share a bed tonight. There doesn't seem to be enough room.'

'I'll bet I can convince you,' Ethan said, looking around. He went to his bags and began digging through them. Alexis sat up. What was he up to? When he stood before her, he was holding a cloth belt. A brow quirked up on his face. 'Want to play?'

Alexis wiggled on the bed. Her heartbeat kicked up a notch. She licked her lips. 'What did you have in mind?'

Ethan crawled up over her. 'Put your wrists together.'

Alexis hesitated.

Ethan moved until he was above her. 'Are you scared?'

She didn't move.

'You don't trust me?' he asked. He gave her a lopsided grin, sitting back on his legs without putting weight on her body. 'Still think I'm a drug dealer going to murder you off and bury you in the desert?'

Slowly, she put her wrists together. 'Did I really say that?'

Alexis knew full well she had. Ethan merely laughed. 'Yeah, you sure did. I almost left you in New York.'

'I almost stayed in New York.'

'I'm glad you didn't.' Ethan bound her wrists together and fastened them over her head.

Despite her actions, apprehension coursed through her at the restraints. 'I'm glad I didn't, too.'

'Did I tell you how beautiful you are today?'

Alexis shook her head in denial. 'No, I don't think you ever have.'

He grinned, not saying anything as he pulled back. Alexis frowned, struggling slightly as he moved away. Her wrists were secure. Ethan turned off the main lights, leaving only the soft glow from the bathroom on to illuminate the hotel room. She watched the outline of his body come back to the bed. Slowly, he undid his jeans and slid them off his hips, underwear and all. When he stood, he was naked.

Alexis tensed, already very aroused by her helpless position. She was a woman used to being in control of others, ordering them around. It was wild, almost freeing to be the one helplessly at the whim of another. He didn't even touch her and her nipples were hard. Her sex became moist. She licked her lips, breathing hard.

Ethan leaned over and set the ice bucket on the bed.

'What are you doing?' she asked, her voice soft.

'Mm, I'm going to torture you,' he answered. Alexis shivered. When he said it, torture didn't sound all that bad. His hand ran up her ankles to her knees. She gasped in surprise. One hand was wet and cold, the other was warm and dry. He came onto the bed, straddling her calves. He chuckled, tossing an ice cube back in the bucket.

'Oh, that was a nasty trick,' she said.

'That was nothing,' Ethan said. She could see him smile in the dim light. He drew the tips of his fingers lightly over her skin, pushing up her nightie. 'When you wear stuff like this it really turns me on.'

His hands became bolder, touching everywhere as he worked his way up her body. Slowly, he pulled the chemise up to expose her hips. He took a deep breath.

'You smell so good,' he said.

His fingers danced over her lower half, teasing, brushing, stroking, but never too hard. It was torturous pleasure. By the time he'd touched every inch of her legs and waist, avoiding her pussy, she was writhing against her binds.

'Untie me,' she urged him, ready to toss him down onto the floor.

'No,' he said simply, chuckling. Then, almost thoughtfully, he added, 'This is too much fun.'

Alexis was inclined to agree.

Ethan pulled her nightie higher, working it up over her head. He let it lie on her arms. Now that her chest was free, he gave it the same finger-brushing torture as he did her legs. Each time a hand grazed her nipples she nearly arched off the bed.

'Ethan,' she cried softly. 'I'm ready for you.'

'I know,' he said. 'But I want you burning for me.'

'Ethan,' she said, but couldn't form a coherent enough argument to get him to untie her.

Ethan again moved down to her feet. He took an ice cube, lightly gliding it over her heated flesh. She tensed at the shock of cold. Her mind followed the movements, so focused that nothing else penetrated her concentration. After he'd made the first past up her length, he started again on the other leg. This time, he followed the cube with his warm tongue. It was a strange contrast, one that made her mad with lust.

'Ethan,' she gasped, wiggling. The whiskers from his goatee tickled. Her skin was alive with sensations – cold ice, warm tongue, soft lips, coarse goatee. 'Please.'

'Not yet,' he answered. 'You're not there yet.'

'Oh, believe me, I'm there,' Alexis pleaded. He pretended like he couldn't hear her.

Ethan drew a pattern on her body with the cube. It was chilly torment the way he circled her nipples into hard peaks. He brought his hot mouth to warm her back up, breathing onto her skin until she was warm, but not sucking the nipples like she wanted him to.

'Ethan, please,' she begged. He licked her breast lightly. Alexis moaned, half in pleasure, half in frustration. 'Ethan.'

Ethan moaned softly. He took her nipple into his mouth, finally sucking it. Alexis was sure she felt the kiss all the way through her body. It shot through her like a spark. She arched her back, trying to press closer to him. He stayed up, just out of reach. He worked his way to the other breast, giving it the same wonderful treatment. Just when her nipples were warm, he shocked them with cold, only to heat them in his mouth, over and over. Alexis cried out, so close to orgasming just from his playing with her breasts.

His knees came between her thighs. The hairs on his legs tickled her. She tried to rub herself against him, but only succeeded in tormenting herself more as she couldn't press to him completely.

Alexis never knew foreplay could be so erotic. Her past lovers had never taken so much time before the grand finale. When the cube melted, she was sure he'd come to her. Instead, he grabbed another and drew it from her breast to her thighs. Alexis squirmed, unable to hold still as he circled the nub hidden within her folds. Her body tensed at the cold onslaught. Her orgasm was close, but the cold kept it at bay, just out of reach.

When his mouth finally closed over her sex, warming the chilly flesh, it was one of the most exquisite sensations she'd ever felt. She started her climax almost instantly against his lips. He drew back, grinning up at her.

'Not yet,' he said.

'Oh, yes, now,' she said, her words hoarse and demanding. He stood up from the bed. Alexis panicked. He couldn't leave her like this. 'Ethan? Ethan!'

'Shh,' he hushed, chuckling. 'I have to get a condom.'

By the time he finally moved on top of her, she was squirming for release. She tried to grab his hips with her legs, pulling him to her. 'Ethan, I need to feel you inside me.'

He obliged, thrusting into her. It felt wonderful the way his cock filled her. Alexis circled her hips, pulling and releasing her hold on his back. Her arms strained against the binds. The friction built. She loved watching his body over hers – the flexing of his muscles as he rode her, the way his mouth fell open in pleasure. His fingers danced along her clit, keeping a firm kneading pressure on her sex.

His claim on her felt so good, she fought her release, clamping her muscles to make it last a little longer, just a bit more. It was no use. When Ethan's hips rocked into her, thrusting deep, she let loose a groan. The climax hit hard, quaking her violently against him as she tensed and shook at the same time. He kept going, rocking into her, pulling and pushing himself until all she could do was ride out the pleasure he gave her.

When finally her body started to lose its rigid hold, he stopped rocking, coming with a shudder of his own. Almost instantly, her body let loose, falling weakly to the bed. Her legs slid off of his waist to the mattress, lying open as he finished. Weakly, he fell on her, still trembling as he kept his weight from crushing her.

'Ah,' Alexis said, unable to form a coherent word as she gasped for breath. She was sure she'd never come like that.

Ethan rolled to her side. He reached to untie her, but her arms stayed right where they were. She looked at his handsome face now that she could see him clearly in the soft light. 'So, did I earn my place in the bed tonight?'

Alexis laughed softly. She was exhausted, could barely move. 'I'd say so.'

'Good,' he said, kissing her mouth deeply. 'Because I want to make love to you again.'

No one was in a great hurry to leave the mountains the next morning so they decided to stay another day. Susan and Ted had brought back laundry the night before so there were clean clothes. They didn't keep the hotel rooms, not sure where they'd end up.

Susan found a bunch of brochures in the laundry mat and they ended up at the Royal Gorge Bridge. It was the world's highest suspension bridge, hanging over a thousand feet in the air. Just looking down at the churning water of the Arkansas River made Alexis queasy. The bridge was a quarter of a mile across and they walked every inch of it. She stayed close to Ethan as they crossed, for once not caring if Ted and Susan saw her holding his hand. She could barely get herself to lift her camera when standing by the edge. Susan did it for her, taking her and Ethan's picture together.

'Mm, I kind of like holding you like this,' Ethan said as they made their way back. He wrapped his arm around her waist as they followed Susan and Ted. Alexis lifted her camera and took a picture of them.

'I kind of like you holding me like this,' Alexis said. She pretended to adjust her camera as she secretly probed him to see how he felt about her. After last night, he had to have some sort of opinion on where they stood. Just thinking of ice cubes made her knees weak. 'I forgot to tell you. Yesterday Susan mentioned something to me about us. She wanted to know what was going on.'

'What did you tell her?' Ethan's face was blank.

Alexis felt as though her heart dropped in her chest. It wasn't the exact outpouring of emotion she'd been hoping for. Actually, she would've settled for a reaction of any kind. He remained calm, his features unreadable.

'That there was nothing to tell,' she said at last. Alexis felt him stiffen and his arms fell away, not hugging her as close as he walked beside her. 'Was that wrong?'

'Not if it's the truth.' Then, pointing into the distance

at a bird in flight, he changed the subject. 'Check that out. That'll make a great photograph.'

Alexis dutifully lifted her camera and took the picture. She stayed close to the middle of the bridge, not wanting to get too close to the edge. Ethan stayed by her side, making a few jokes and talking of non-important things as they walked back to the car.

They were surrounded by people wherever they went and so it was hard to soak up any of the local culture without fighting a crowd. Being a big tourism area, everything was expensive – food, gas, lodgings. By late afternoon, they changed their minds about staying in Colorado Springs for another night and headed south.

As they drove south, Susan leafed through the pile of brochures. 'I was looking at these maps. I'm not so sure it's wise to be driving down to New Mexico at night. A lady at the hotel told me the road heading south through the mountains is one of the most dangerous in the US.'

Alexis was tired and said nothing. She glanced at Ethan, feeling as if a rift had formed between them ever since she mentioned Susan suspecting them. Did he care? Was he embarrassed by her? She was always worried what everyone would think about her dating a tattoo man, but she never once considered that he'd be embarrassed to be seen with her. It hurt deeply.

'What do you have in mind?' Ted asked, slowing down to let a truck pass.

'We could stay in La Veta. Then, in the morning, we can take a scenic drive down to Trinidad on the Highway of Legends.'

'Whatever you decide is fine with me,' Ethan said. He crossed his arms over his chest and closed his eyes. 'I'm taking a nap.'

Susan reached along the edge of her seat and touched Alexis's knee. When Alexis looked up, Susan mouthed, 'What's going on?'

Alexis shrugged. How could she answer? She was wondering the exact same thing herself.

The car was quiet as they drove into the evening. She

was preoccupied and edgy and even the soft music Ted was playing on the stereo annoyed her. With Ethan seemingly displeased with her, the mountains lost some of their brilliance. Alexis wondered what had happened, but came to the only conclusion she could. He was upset that Susan and Ted had found out about them. Even the beautiful sunset, streaking its reds and purples along the distance couldn't rouse a bit of interest in her. It was the most beautiful act of nature she'd ever witnessed and yet she couldn't even bring herself to take out her camera.

The hotel at La Veta was the best one they'd stayed at so far and also looked to be the most expensive. Since they didn't have reservations anywhere, they didn't have much of a choice. It was either the resort or the car. The early evening was already chilly and no one felt like camping out in a car.

'We'll take whatever you have left,' Ethan said to the clerk. She was dressed in a quilted vest of Southwestern design. Glasses hung from a chain around her neck and she carefully unfolded them and slipped them on her face. Humming softly, she looked at her register. 'Yee, hmm, well let me just see what we have. Oh, well, hmm. Ah, yep. We only have one room.'

Ethan glanced at Ted. Alexis sat sideways on a wooden chair in the front lobby, watching him. She waited for a kind smile, a secretive wink, and got nothing.

'It has two beds,' the woman offered, smiling brightly.

Ted nodded at Ethan. He suppressed a yawn.

'We'll take it,' Ethan said to the woman. Humming again she wrote down Ethan's information as she filled out a little card. She pondered his driver's licence, taking great care as she transcribed the numbers. Alexis sighed, leaning her head down on the back of the chair as she waited for the woman to finish. Before she would hand over the keys, she went through a long list of local attractions as if she'd memorised them off a list. Ethan politely thanked her, but his lips were tight when he said the words.

The room was huge, completely decorated with the

same Southwestern influence the clerk had. The two queen-size beds had matching plaid comforters and mission-style headboards. Dried flowers in a plain glass vase sat between the beds on a nightstand.

'It's cute,' Susan said. Ted set her bag down next to a bed. She looked helplessly at Alexis. 'How do we want to handle the sleeping arrangements?'

'I'll take the floor,' Ethan said, coming in. He set Alexis's bag on the ground next to his. 'You guys split up the beds however.'

'You don't have to do that,' Alexis said.

'Are you going to take the floor?' he asked, smiling slightly. 'It's fine. I've slept in worse places.'

Even though Susan had been her roommate for many years, it was still awkward as they got ready for bed. Alexis borrowed Ethan's sweats and wore one of her T-shirts. She didn't feel comfortable in any of her nighties with Ted in the room. She knew Susan had the same problem because she wore a pair of workout pants and a tank.

'Ethan,' Susan said. Ethan sat on the bed next to Alexis watching television, not touching her. Alexis leaned forwards to study her friend. 'I want a tattoo.'

Alexis stiffened. Susan wanted what? Usually they'd have discussed something like this before making an announcement.

Ethan chuckled. 'I wondered if anyone on the trip was going to get some ink.'

'You don't mind?' Susan asked.

'Heck, no.' Ethan chuckled.

'Oh, then I want one too,' Ted said. Everyone turned to look at Alexis.

Alexis shivered. 'What?'

'What do you say, Lexy?' Susan asked.

Ethan's face searched hers. Alexis shivered. 'They're so ... permanent.'

'Afraid of a little commitment?' Ethan teased.

'No,' Alexis answered. 'But I won't be pressured into something I don't want.'

'You're right.' Ethan nodded. He moved to look at Susan. 'So, wh – ?'

'I want cherries on my hip,' Alexis said, taking a deep breath and holding it. All three pairs of eyes came instantly back to her. Alexis covered her mouth with her hand. Her voice weak, she said, 'Really small ones.'

Ethan got a funny look on his face. Slowly, he smiled at her. 'OK. I'll draw something up tomorrow. I want you all to think about it for a day before I do it.'

He said everyone, but Alexis was sure he meant mostly her. She nodded, feeling giddy. Susan and Ted launched into an instant discussion about designs. Ethan crawled onto the floor, lying down on the bed he'd made for himself out of extra blankets. Alexis automatically tossed him a pillow.

It felt strange being on the bed without Ethan next to her. Susan turned down the lights, but Alexis still heard them whispering for quite some time. She wished they'd go to sleep so she could crawl down to talk to Ethan.

Alexis fell into a fitful sleep, having a hard time getting comfortable.

'Hey,' she heard a whisper through her dreams. She fought to wake up, but it was too hard. She was too tired. 'I think I'm in love you.'

Alexis blinked, partially paralysed as she tried to wake up. When she finally opened her eyes, everyone was asleep. It had only been a dream.

Chapter Thirteen

'Dude, are you really a tattoo artist?'

Ethan looked up from the opened trunk. It was early morning and the air was crisp. But, despite the chill, the sun shone bright with the promise of a glorious day. He'd missed sleeping by Alexis the night before, had even been compelled to check on her a couple of times, though she'd been asleep. He'd nearly choked when she said she wanted a tattoo. It didn't matter to him if people were tattooed or not. It was personal expression. But to hear her say it had done something to him. It was like her acceptance of who he was. The Alexis he'd picked up in New York would never have gotten ink.

Seeing a kid holding a skateboard against his leg, Ethan smiled. The slender deck was pretty banged up along the edges, attesting to its miles of use. The boy had black hair that was cut short at the back and flopped down over one eye. His pants were three sizes too big and his large black T-shirt had small holes along the seams.

'Yeah, sure am,' Ethan said. He turned back to the truck, shoving his bag towards the back.

'Cool, dude, that's cool,' the kid said. He had to be around ten. Ethan smiled. He kicked around his feet for a while, saying nothing. 'I want a tattoo, but my mom said no.'

Ethan nodded. He agreed with the mom. 'Yeah, moms are tough.'

'She's all right. She let me dye my hair.' The boy stood a while longer, not saying too much.

'Cool deck, you do the graphics?' Ethan asked, nodding to the skateboard as he closed the trunk. The kid held out the bottom of the board for Ethan to see. It was spray-painted green with a black skull. The lines were a little wobbly, but not bad for a ten-year-old.

'It was orange but I didn't like it. You skate?'

'Used to. Only the boards were a lot fatter,' Ethan said.

The boy grinned and held out his board. A mischievous smile crossed over his face. 'Old school. Cool. Here. Try it.'

Ethan glanced around. It had been years since he'd been on a skateboard. He glanced towards the hotel, making sure no one was watching. If Alexis saw this he'd be sure to lose some cool points.

'Come on, dude,' the kid said, grinning wider. 'Let's see what you got.'

How could he pass up a challenge from a ten-year-old kid? Ethan took the board and set it down on the sidewalk. He rolled a few feet before trying to kick-flip the board into the air. The trick failed miserably and he fell on his back with a heavy thud.

'Oh, dude.' The boy laughed, half in amusement, half in sympathy. He rescued his board before leaning over Ethan. 'You all right?'

Ethan groaned, chuckling at his own foolishness. He should've known better. His body was sore, but nothing he couldn't handle. He pushed up. The kid grabbed his arm, helping him. 'Hey, how'd you know I was a tattoo artist?'

'Oh, I heard that old guy on the phone,' he said.

'Brandon!' a woman screamed.

'That's my mom. I got to go,' the kid said.

'Hey, wait,' Ethan yelled. 'What old guy?'

'The one with the camera,' the boy yelled as he skated off down the sidewalk. As Ethan watched, he did the kick-flip perfectly, waved and kept going.

Ethan frowned. Old guy with a camera? Well, the kid was ten and it was possible he'd consider anyone over the age of twenty old. But with a phone and a camera? Could he mean Ted? Ted made business calls all the time. Only, Ted didn't have a camera. Maybe the boy was mistaken about that. Maybe Ted had borrowed Alexis's camera. Then, thinking of how she guarded that bag with her life, he doubted Ted would take it without permission.

A shiver worked over his spine. Instantly, he thought of Alexis's man in the grey car. He looked around the parking lot. There were no grey cars. He was probably just being paranoid.

Stretching out his back, he grimaced at his sore muscles. Mumbling to himself, he said, 'That's what you get, old man, for taking challenges from a kid.'

'I see a camel,' Alexis said.

'You're supposed to see a train and a face,' Susan insisted.

'Oh, yeah, I see it, right there,' Ted said, pointing at the distant rock.

Ethan looked, but said nothing. He was still a little disturbed about the kid's comments. The Highway of Legends was definitely worth the side trip. They'd just started to travel, but already they'd seen so much beauty. Alexis was demanding they stop the car every five minutes to take pictures. At this rate, they'd be sleeping in the wilderness. Ethan didn't mind. He liked seeing her happy. For that reason alone, he didn't mention the kid to anyone.

'OK, I got the picture,' Alexis said. 'I'll blow it up really big later and we can all stare at it because I still see a camel.'

Ethan was in the driver's seat. She smiled at him, an almost shy smile, as he put the car into drive. They drove in silence, taking in the beauty of the area. Large stone jutted up from the land, almost like a thick white wall that blocked one side from the other. Brown and red valleys turned into dark-green peaks. Tall, skinny trees lined the roads and wildflowers seemed to cover every inch of the landscape.

'Check out this town,' Susan said as the highway led through a small mountain town. Some of the buildings were made out of logs. 'It's just like turn of the century Colorado.'

'Check out that man,' Alexis added, pointing to a bearded mountain man in a flannel shirt. 'I think he's from the turn of the century too. Let's not stop. I really don't want to make friends with Billy Bob over there.'

As they watched, the man spat tobacco on the ground and glanced at the car. He smiled at the women, staring hard, his teeth stained brown. Yellow tobacco streaks stained his whiskered mouth.

'Drive,' Alexis hissed. 'Just drive.'

As they passed a lake, Alexis's hand slid close to Ethan's thigh. She didn't caress him, just let her hand rest along his leg as she looked out the window. Just as he was about to take her hand in his, she pulled back, demanding he stop so she could take a picture of a bear.

'Don't unroll the windows,' Susan said, sounding panicked. Alexis ignored her. Ethan laughed. 'Lexy!'

'It's too far away to attack, sweetheart,' Ted assured her.

'But the brochure says not to bother the wildlife,' Susan insisted. 'And the lady at the hotel told me that bears have been known to attack people who bother them. Her cousin was camping and was mauled by one. And she said that one even attacked a car and smashed it to bits. That –'

'Sweetie, trust me,' Ted said, kissing the tip of her nose. 'We're fine.'

Alexis laughed. She winked at Ethan. His heart nearly stopped beating at the playful gesture. He drove down the highway again, not sure how much time passed. He felt like he couldn't breathe as he gripped the steering wheel. The urge to pull over was strong, but he fought it. If he pulled over now he'd jump out of the car and confess to Alexis and the whole world that he loved her.

Love?

Ethan forced a deep breath. He couldn't be in love. They'd only known each other a few weeks. So what if they spent every second of the day together in the car and that they slept together at night. Two weeks wasn't a long enough time to know something so important. He was just being foolish. Wasn't he? He turned to Alexis.

'Ethan?' she asked. 'Are you – oh my gawd, look out!'

Ethan looked at the road. A small furry creature darted in front of the car. Instinctively, he swerved to miss it. Alexis and Susan screamed as the car spun. When they stopped, no one said a word for several long moments.

'Is everyone all right?' Ethan asked, glancing at Alexis. She nodded.

'Yeah,' Ted said.

'Yes,' Susan said.

'What was that?' Alexis asked. As if to answer her question, they heard a dog bark. Ethan looked out the window. A small white dog sat on the pavement, looking at them as he made a horrendous racket. It looked like a little lion with long straight fur around its head and shorter fur on its body.

'It's a Pekingese,' Susan said.

'Where did it come from?' Alexis asked.

Ethan opened his car door to assess the damage. In the distance, several campers were stopped along the road. 'I think it came from there.'

'Ah, man, we have a flat,' Ted said.

Ethan came around the car. Everything looked fine, but for a punctured tyre. 'Damn it!'

'You have a spare?' Ted asked.

'Yeah, but I don't have a jack,' Ethan said.

'How could you travel without a jack?' Alexis asked him. A bit of the condescending diva was back in her voice as she looked at him.

'Because I don't own one and I figured if I ever needed one there'd be someone to ask.' Ethan pointed at the campers. 'So, let's go ask.'

Alexis grabbed her camera and Ethan locked up the car. The dog followed them, yipping the quarter of a mile it took to reach the cars. The animal held his head high with obvious self-importance. Ethan's mood had soured with the accident and he had the strangest urge to kick the annoying dog, launching it into the surrounding valley. But since he'd never hurt an animal in his life, he wasn't about to start now.

'Oh, great,' Ted said under his breath as they neared the parked caravan. The first small camper had a tie-dyed peace sign in the window surrounded by love beads. 'Hippies. Just great. They creep me out.'

Ethan laughed, his mood lightening some at the odd comment. It was the first time Ted had ever expressed even the slightest hint of negativity.

'His mother's a hippie,' Susan explained.

'Yeah,' Ted said. 'And she creeps me out. I grew up having to listen to her describe my aura and trying to read my future.'

'They're artists.' Alexis pointed down into the valley where several artists with their canvases and easels painted quietly. A long stretch of a flat green field with tall grasses stretched out. Dark-brown fence posts leaned sideways, their railing long collapsed. In the distance there were green hills dotted with evergreens, more of the curious white-stone wall jutting from the ground and finally snow-cap peaks. The sky was bright blue with white, fluffy clouds. It was breathtaking.

The little Pekingese yipped and took off into the taller grasses, disappearing in the field. They watched the grass move until the dog reached one of the nearby artists. The woman turned, looking down and then straight at them. Ethan waved. The artist set down her brush and left her canvas to walk towards them.

'Well, Emperor, what have you found?' the woman said to the dog. Her long black hair had touches of grey along the bangs and temples. She wore a dress of bright orange, the front of which was spattered and smeared with paint.

'We've come to borrow a jack,' Ethan called. 'We found your dog just up the road. He ran in front of our car and we had a slight accident.'

The woman almost looked offended. 'If my dog ran out in front of your car, it was no accident. Pekingese are known for bringing good luck. If you wrecked, it was lucky that you should do so.'

'Yep, hippies,' Ted mumbled under his breath so she couldn't hear him.

'And, it's equally lucky that I don't have a jack,' she said, continuing forwards. 'You must be meant to stay here.'

Ethan frowned. 'Actually, we're meant to go to New Mexico today.'

The woman reached them, glancing down the road to Ethan's car. She smelled of patchouli. 'No, I'd say you were meant to stay.'

'Maybe someone else has a jack,' Ted said.

The woman ignored him, looking down at Alexis's camera. 'You're a photographer?'

'No,' Alexis began modestly.

'Yes,' Ethan automatically supplied, 'she is.'

The woman grinned. 'Then welcome, child. This day is for artists. And the rest of you?'

When no one said anything, Alexis motioned at Ethan and said, 'Ethan's actually the artist of the bunch. He's the one with the talent.'

Ethan felt a moment of tremendous pride at her statement. He wanted nothing more than to pull her into his arms and stake claim to her with a kiss. He held back from the impulse. It wasn't like they were officially a couple. Susan might suspect something was going on, but Alexis had made it clear she didn't want to be seen publicly as his girlfriend, or lover, or whatever she was.

'And what do you do?' the woman asked.

'Tattooing,' Ethan said.

'But he draws as well,' Alexis supplied. 'He's very talented.'

The woman nodded. 'Ah, then you are in the right place. We're all artists here. We're travelling north along the Sangre de Cristo Mountains to capture them in all their beauty. Get your supplies and join us. It's a beautiful day for it. The lighting is perfect. Later tonight we will gather by a campfire and share stories. Tomorrow some-one can take you to town if no one has a jack. I'd ask them today, but today is a quiet day where we all concen-trate on the beauty of nature, breathing her in. We can't break their meditative trances. By the way, I'm Summer.'

'Ethan, Alexis, Susan and Ted,' Ethan introduced.

The woman nodded and walked back towards her canvas, her dog trailing behind her.

'Told you,' Ted said, shaking his head, 'hippies.'

'What do you want to do?' Ethan asked.

'I'm hungry,' Susan said.

'Want to go into the woods and pick berries?' Alexis asked, giggling. It was clear by the look on her face she wasn't going anywhere. Ethan eyed her designer denim jeans and her long-sleeve cashmere sweater. Yeah, she wasn't one to hike – at least not in that outfit. She wouldn't make it too far in her heeled boots.

'Well, Ted and I did get stuff for a picnic earlier,' Ethan said. Susan grinned. 'It was supposed to be a surprise.'

'Oh,' Susan instantly sighed. She wrapped her arms around Ted's neck. 'You did? How sweet.'

'I'd say here is as good a place as any.' Ted waved his hand towards the valley before hugging her close. Susan kissed him, moaning softly.

Ethan glanced at Alexis and teasingly wiggled his eye-brows, pursing his lips for a kiss. She laughed, but didn't come to him. He was slightly disappointed.

The picnic was hardly a grand affair, but no one com-plained about the sandwiches, sodas and potato chips. Ethan borrowed a blanket from one of the artists. Emperor kept them company. They tried to shoo him away, but the dog kept trying until they let him sit on the blanket. Ted tossed the animal a piece of sliced roast beef.

Ted and Susan went for a walk near the woods, leaving Alexis to her photographs and Ethan to his sketch pad. Alexis smiled at him, taking his picture. She wanted to remember this day always. Seeing that they were finally alone, she asked, 'Today really is wonderful, isn't it?'

'Mm, yeah, it is.' He glanced at her, grinning.

'I think I'm actually running out of space on my memory sticks,' Alexis said, studying her camera. 'Do you think I could load the software on your laptop and store the photos I've taken on there?'

'Sure,' Ethan answered. 'No problem. We'll do it at the next hotel.'

'Can I ask you something?' She sat down by him on the blanket. Emperor lifted his head up for a moment, yawned and then laid it back down to sleep.

'Sure,' Ethan said, concentrating on his drawing. 'But I don't have to answer.'

Alexis studied his drawing of the mountains. It was a rough sketch, but decent. 'When we first started this trip, you said that a girl like me wouldn't understand about the marking off the maps.'

Ethan lowered his sketch pad and turned to her. 'I shouldn't have been so hard on you.'

'No, you should have. I know it sounds crazy but I'm different now. I can feel that I am. I mean, nobody changes overnight, but –' She grew nervous, trying to backtrack her words.

'Alexis,' Ethan said, gently, 'you have changed.'

She smiled, feeling like he'd just given her the biggest compliment in the world. 'So, can I know now about the maps?'

Ethan threw back his head and laughed. 'It really isn't a big deal.'

'Still,' Alexis said, 'I'd like to know.'

Ethan flipped to the end of his sketch pad and took out an outline map of the United States. Some of the states were coloured in with bright-orange marker. Alexis didn't know if she should be insulted or not. He'd thought she wouldn't understand a coloured-in map?

'It's like a private game. I keep track of where I've been,' Ethan explained. 'I want to travel everywhere in the world before I die.'

Alexis handed the map back to him. Unable to stop herself, she reached to brush a strand of his red-tipped hair from his face. 'I think you will, Ethan. I think you'll see everything.'

'I have a question for you,' he said. 'In Wisconsin, why did you say those things about me?'

Alexis's hand dropped to her lap. Mortified, she didn't speak.

'You called me a dog to that girl, Tressa,' he prompted.

'Ah, mm, yeah,' she said, unable to look at him. 'You heard that, did you?'

'Yeah, I heard that,' he said. 'Why'd you say it?'

'I, ah, well,' she said. She couldn't force the words out.

'Alexis?' he insisted.

'Oh, all right, fine,' she said, her voice a little sharp. 'I was jealous that you might be sleeping with her that night and I didn't want you to. Are you happy now? It was me. The whole time we were there, it was me. I'm the reason you didn't land any tattooing jobs. I told the lady in the bar that you were diseased and that your male parts leaked green ooze. I told the lady at the grocery store you were married. I told someone else you were gay. Actually, I told that to several people. I told –'

Ethan pulled her face to his and kissed her, shutting her up. Alexis moaned weakly in surprise. It felt good confessing to him, but even better to have him kissing her. His tongue rolled gently against hers. She reached for him, touching his face. When he pulled back, he said, 'You were jealous.'

Alexis nodded.

'Over me.'

She nodded again.

'I was jealous of you and Mr Nasty as well,' Ethan said. 'It's why I ran him off.'

'You were?' Alexis laughed softly, filled with hope. 'I'm sorry for all of it. I'm sorry for being a royal bitch on this trip and for assuming you'd gone to prison just because you have tattoos.'

'I'm sorry, too.' Ethan kissed her again, rolling her down onto the blanket. A shadow fell over them.

'I said your stopping here was lucky, not that you were

supposed to *get* lucky,' Summer said from above them, laughing. Her easel was folded up under her arm and she carried a small art case. 'Come, Emperor. It's time to eat.'

The dog instantly hopped up. He jumped over Ethan and Alexis's legs to follow Summer to her camper. Ethan laughed, but didn't pull away.

'I'm glad you're here,' he said, when they were alone.

Alexis had hoped he'd say more. She forced a smile. It wasn't hard, seeing his handsome face so close to hers, his head outlined by the afternoon sun. There was something very magical about the valley. 'I'm glad you're here too.'

Susan took a deep breath, looking around the narrow nature trail. The sun shone through the tree limbs. They were surrounded by little dots of light, dancing on the dirt trail. Birds sang and insects hummed. Sighing wistfully, she said, 'I love it here.'

'I love you,' Ted said, wrapping his arm around her from behind.

'Mm,' Susan hummed in contentment.

'And I'd love to spend the rest of my life with you.'

Susan stiffened. What did he say?

'Susan –' Ted's arms left her and he took her hand '– will you marry me?'

Susan slowly turned, no longer seeing the trees. Ted knelt on one knee, looking earnestly up at her. He didn't have a ring, but that didn't matter to her. Her whole body shook. She hadn't expected this. Not now. Not here. He never let on, never hinted. She took a deep breath, looking into his soulful brown eyes.

'Oh, well, all right,' Ted said, when she didn't answer him. He stood up, looking as if she'd kicked him.

'Yes,' she whispered. Ted blinked in surprise. 'Yes!'

'Yes!'

Ethan and Alexis sat up in surprise. Birds took to flight over the trees where Susan and Ted had disappeared.

'You don't think they're . . .' Alexis looked at Ethan with wide eyes.

Ethan looked at Alexis. She was gorgeous. Her hair was dishevelled from where his fingers had thrust into it during their kiss. The taste of her was still on his mouth. He wanted to be able to make love to her right there in the afternoon sun, but he held back. Too many people were around.

'. . . having sex, do you?' Alexis finished after a long pause.

'Ah, I don't know.' Ethan laughed. 'If they are, I'm a little jealous.'

Alexis heated at his words. She nodded. 'Me too. Think we can sneak off anywhere for a little bit?'

'Like where?'

'We could break into a camper,' Alexis joked.

'I'd be too scared Summer would want to join us in the love fest,' Ethan said. Alexis laughed. He reached out, grabbing a strand of her hair and twirling it in his fingers. 'I want to draw you.'

Alexis blinked, stunned for a moment by the change of conversation. 'All right. Now?'

Ethan nodded. He flipped to a new page on his sketch pad. 'Well, I'd prefer to do a nude portrait, but here's good too.'

Ethan drew her portrait over the course of the afternoon, refusing to let her see it no matter how hard she begged. He claimed it wasn't finished yet. Susan and Ted came back after a few hours. Susan had a healthy flush to her features and couldn't quit grinning. Ted was just as bad. As late afternoon turned into evening, Summer invited them to join the others for dinner. Not everyone was as extreme as Summer. In fact, they were a blend of different personalities with one thing in common – art.

Sunset had been a beautiful affair of purples, reds, oranges and golds. An older couple sat in lawn chairs around the campfire, holding hands. Alexis smiled to see them. There was a man who was distracted beyond measure and would only complete about half of his sentence before drifting off to draw in his notebook. Several of the artists took turns showing their paintings to the group for critiques. It was a little dark trying to study the artwork by firelight, but no one seemed to mind. Alexis was amazed at all the different interpretations the artists had of the exact same view. Some painted close-ups, some landscapes, some with an uncanny almost photographic realism, some with bolder lines and brighter, almost unnatural colours.

'How about you?' Summer asked, looking expectantly at Ethan. She smiled.

When Ethan looked like he'd deny showing anything, Alexis said, 'Yes, he's done something.'

'Oh, let's see it,' a young man with glasses said.

'Come on,' the older woman in the lawn chair urged. 'We're all friends here.'

Ethan looked at Alexis and sighed. He reached behind him and pulled out his sketchbook. He opened it to a sloppy mountain scene and handed it to Summer.

'Mm, yes, yes,' she said.

'Strong beginning,' a man added, looking over her shoulder. 'Nice lines. Shade could use some work.'

Ethan didn't say anything as they passed his work around. Summer started flipping through the pages, stopping suddenly.

'Now this,' Summer said, 'this is beautiful.'

The artist huddled around the notepad. Alexis craned her neck, trying to see, but they were in her way. Suddenly, they all looked at her.

'What?' Alexis asked. Summer turned the sketch pad around. In the orange firelight, Alexis saw her face staring back at her. Her hair was tousled, her cheeks flushed, her lips parted ever so slightly. There was a look on her face, almost dreamy, yet shy. There was nothing of the elitist snob she'd been in New York in that picture. Is that how Ethan saw her? It that what she'd become? She swallowed, shaking terribly. It was the most beautiful thing she'd ever seen and Ethan had done it of her.

'He captured your soul,' Summer said, handing the sketchbook back to Ethan. Alexis couldn't look at him. He'd captured a lot more than just her soul. She'd suspected it for a while, but now she was sure of it. She was in love with Ethan James. Slowly, Alexis stood up, walking away from the campfire. She had to think.

Ethan watched Alexis walk away, wondering at the look on her face. She refused to look at him. Her silence stung him to the core. Was she that upset about the portrait? Or was it something more?

'I'll go,' Susan said quietly, standing up. Ethan nodded. He wasn't sure Alexis would want to see him right now anyway.

'Ah, you've moved her,' Summer said knowingly. 'Not everyone knows how to take it when they see themselves clearly for the first time.'

Ethan forced a polite smile. The artists began talking anew. He didn't say a word as he stared into the flames.

'Lexy, wait,' Susan said. 'What was that all about?'

Alexis dashed a tear from her face. 'My mother's going to kill me.'

'What? Why? What happened?' Susan demanded. She reached for Alexis's arm. 'What's going on?'

'I slept with Ethan,' Alexis whispered.

'You what?' Susan said, surprised. She shook her head in awe. 'I mean, I thought that you might, someday, if things kept going well between you, but . . .?'

'I think I have feelings for him,' Alexis said. 'And I don't think he feels the same way. And I'm scared that when I get to California I'm going to realise that I'm just being emotional right now because my life is so up in the air. I'm scared that in California I won't love him any more, or won't like him, or he won't like me. We are so removed from reality out here on this trip.'

Susan stayed quiet, just listening.

'It's like you said. We're different people from different worlds. When we get back to reality I might just find out this is a dream. I mean, the old Alexis would never fall in love with a tattoo artist, would she?'

'Then why not just wait and see how you feel once we get back to reality?' Susan asked. 'There's no rule saying you have to declare your feelings for him as soon as you think you have them. It's not fair to him and it's not fair to you. If you don't know how you feel, then you should maybe wait until you do. You don't want to profess feelings only to have to take them back later.'

Alexis actually relaxed. 'You're right. I've been so stressed out over nothing. I don't have to tell him anything. Not yet. There's no reason it can't wait for California. I mean it's stupid saying something like that when he might not feel the same way, right?'

Susan nodded, but the gesture was unconvincing.

Chapter Fourteen

Alexis stared up at the stars. They slept close to the fire in borrowed sleeping bags. Susan and Ted were on one side. She and Ethan were on the other. Turning over on her side, she looked at Ethan and said, 'Sorry about earlier. I wasn't feeling well, but I'm better now.'

Well, it was almost the truth. She did feel better after talking to Susan. Besides, the more she thought about it, the less she liked the idea of professing her love to a man who didn't even try to call her his girlfriend. In fact, he hadn't called her his anything.

'Don't worry about it, Alexis,' he said, flipping onto his back to look away from her. '*I'm* not.'

That hurt. Alexis tried not to take it personally, but it was hard. 'I really liked your drawing.'

'Hum,' he said. Was he angry? His body was stiff like he was angry. She reached out and touched him.

'Want to go somewhere private? Work the tension from your body?'

Ethan briefly closed his eyes, sighing. When he looked at her, she drew her hand away, sure he was going to say no.

'Is that all I am to you? A way to get off?' he asked.

'What?' she whispered, glancing over at Ted and Susan to make sure they couldn't hear him. 'What are you talking about?'

'Me. Us. Am I just your sex toy?' he demanded. 'Some guy you can sleep with so long as no one knows about it?'

'Ethan, please, be quiet. We don't want to wake everyone.' Alexis sat up. Glancing around, she said, 'If you want to talk, we'll talk. Come on, the moon's full enough to see by. Let's go for a walk.'

He stood up, not looking pleased. He started towards his car. When they'd gone away from the campsite, she said softly, 'Ethan, I don't understand. Where is this coming from?' Alexis reached for him, touching the side of his face. 'You're more to me than a sex toy, you know that. You're my friend.'

'You're ashamed of me,' Ethan said, jerking away. He walked faster in his irritation.

'Ah, wait, slow down. I don't have shoes on,' Alexis said. The highway was rough under her feet and a little cool. The evening was nice. The sweat pants she had borrowed from Ethan kept her legs warm, but the T-shirt left her arms a little chilly.

He didn't stop walking, but he did slow down. 'Admit it. That's what your little temper tantrum was about earlier, wasn't it? These people, these strangers, looked at us like we could be together and you didn't like it. You were ashamed that strangers might think you were my girlfriend.'

'But I'm not your girlfriend,' she said softly. Was she?

At that he laughed. Licking his lips, he studied the sky. He looked like he wanted to say so many things to her, but in the end he only mumbled, 'Right.'

'Are you saying you want more?' Alexis asked. Her breath caught. She prayed he'd say yes.

'What would it take, Alexis? What would it take for me to be acceptable to you? What changes would I have to make? Remove the tattoos? Dye my hair a normal colour? Wear khakis like Ted? Get a cell phone and a regular job with a briefcase?' Ethan didn't give her time to answer. He tried to walk away from her. She followed him.

'That's not fair and you know it. I never asked you to change.' Alexis tried to grab his arm. He shrugged her off. 'Hey, what about you? Like you haven't wanted to change me from the beginning?'

'I was never ashamed to be seen with you,' he said. 'I never judged you.'

'What?' She shook her head in disbelief. 'You judged me

that first day. One look at me and you pegged me as a spoiled rich girl.'

'You were a spoiled rich girl,' Ethan said.

Alexis took a deep breath. Tears came to her eyes. She stopped walking.

Ethan took several more steps, cursed and then turned around to face her. 'I'm sorry, I didn't mean that.'

'Yes, you did.' A tear trailed down her cheek. She hugged her arms around her waist. 'And you're right. I have had it easier than most. I've had everything money could buy. Growing up all I wanted was someone to tell me they cared for me, even a little. So I'm sorry if I'm shallow. I'm sorry if I don't get whatever it is everyone else seems to get. But I'm trying to change. And if I seem ashamed of you, well, then maybe on some level I am.'

Ethan looked away. Alexis wished she could say the words were a lie, but they weren't. On some level, a level bred into her since birth, she did wish he was different. But if he was different, would she care for him?

'I don't want to be ashamed of you. I like you. I like being with you. And I am trying, Ethan. If you even saw a glimpse of what it was like to grow up in my world then you would know. You would know how hard it is. You would understand that the only time my mother praised me was when I lived up to her expectations of what I should be. She didn't want an education for me. She didn't want me to excel. She wanted me to grow up to be a fashion plate, a vacuous shell who smiled and did what she was told and married well.'

He opened his mouth to speak, but she held up her hand to stop him.

'You want to know why I don't write my mother? Her last words to me were to marry a rich husband because I was now on my own. Not I love you. Not I'm sorry I messed up and your personal life is all over the papers. Just to get married to someone who could take me over for her.' Alexis swiped at her tears. 'I'd say, out of the two of us, you were the truly privileged one growing up. My

home wasn't like yours. My mother's love is not uncondi-
tional. There are many strings attached and one of those
strings is to never date beneath my social status, to never
embarrass the Grant family name with disgrace. That is
what I've been told since I could understand the concept
of dating. That is what I'm trying to change.'

'Alexis.' He reached for her, crossing the distance to get
to her. He hugged her to his chest. 'I'm sorry. I shouldn't
have been so touchy.'

Alexis soaked in his warmth, clinging to him. It felt so
good to just be held.

'What about your father?' he asked, stroking her hair.

'He was a rich man's son. My grandparents are just like
my mother in mentality. But I like to think he was like
me in some small way. I honestly think he married her
because he was supposed to. I don't remember there being
a lot of love between my parents. He died when I was
five so I never really knew him, but he had a camera he
gave me. He loved taking pictures. He told me that as
long as I could look at the world like a photograph, hold
it still and try to see it for what it is, I would be OK. I
didn't understand, but I think he was trying to tell me to
think for myself, judge for myself.' Alexis pulled back.
'Until now, I really thought those words to me were just
the medicine talking. He wasn't exactly lucid those last
days and then the years after whenever my mother talked
about him ... It just became all distorted.'

'Alexis.' Ethan cupped her cheek. His mouth opened
and he looked at her like he wanted to say many things.
She shook her head. There had been enough sharing for
one night. This was new emotional ground for her. She
needed time.

'Can you understand now? I need your patience. I don't
know how to act in a normal relationship. I don't know
how to show I care. The last serious relationship I remember my mother having ended with her buying the bed
and breakfast they stayed at and burning it down after
he broke up with her.' Alexis took a deep breath. 'And
before you, none of my boyfriends had more than ten

words to say to me at a time. We were together because it was socially acceptable for us to be together. There was nothing else between any of us. Before now, I didn't want to slow down and examine my life like a photograph because then I would've had to admit it was empty.'

'Are calling me your boyfriend?' he asked, pulling back enough to study her face. He swiped her tears with his thumb, trying to get her to smile with his look.

'I feel like I'm in seventh grade,' she said, rolling her eyes. Then, in a slightly self-deprecating tone she asked, 'Ethan James, will you be my boyfriend?'

'Yes,' he whispered.

Alexis gasped, instantly smiling through her self-pity. 'Really? You're not just trying to get me to shut up? I feel like I'm unloading all this personal junk on you.'

'If I wanted to get you to shut up, I'd just do this,' he said, right before he kissed her. Alexis moaned, pulling his body closer to hers. Slowly, he walked backwards, taking her with him as he neared his car. 'I know this isn't the most romantic spot, but are you still interested in . . . ah . . . relieving my tension?'

'What do you mean not romantic?' Alexis laughed lightly, feeling so much better. She looked up at the sky, so filled with stars. It was something she'd never see in New York City. The moon shone lightly on the snow caps of distant peaks. Then, she looked at Ethan's face. 'There is no place I'd rather be right now than here. With you.'

'I care for you, Alexis. If you need to take it slow, we'll take it slow. Take all the time you need.' Ethan kissed her. They reached the car. He pulled back, looking around.

'What?'

'I don't have the keys.' He patted his sweats. 'They're in my jeans.'

'Hum, well, you know, nobody can see us from the campsite.' Alexis pulled away from him and walked around to the trunk of his car. Slowly, she pulled on her waistband, pushing the sweats down over her legs to reveal her black thong panties. As she bent directly over, Ethan touched her hip. He groaned lightly, pushing his arousal against her body. Standing back up, she let her butt caress his erection.

Alexis walked away from him and tossed the sweats on the trunk. She pulled off her thong and dangled it in the air. Leaning against his car, she wiggled the finger holding the panties at him.

'Someone might drive by.' Ethan glanced down the empty highway.

'I'm willing to take that chance.' Alexis dropped the panties on the trunk and slipped a spaghetti strap off her shoulder. Looking him in the eyes, she pulled it down, freeing a breast. 'Come here.'

Alexis wrapped her arms around him. Sitting on his car, she pulled him close, kissing him passionately. The moonlight made their skin glow with a blue light. Insects hummed in the nearby woods. She was caressed by cool air, only to be warmed by his hands. The sensation brought back the memory of his delectable ice-cube torture.

She moaned softly, letting him hear what he did to her. Her legs wrapped around his waist. His hands ran over her hip, her waist, her exposed breasts. When he pulled back, a provocative smile lined his lips.

'You're so beautiful,' he said.

Alexis moaned again, pulling his lips back to hers. A great urgency welled inside her. She wanted him, needed to feel him inside her now. Even if she wanted to, she couldn't pull her lips away from him. His kisses were like a drug she couldn't get enough of. She wanted to drink of him, inject him into her veins until the euphoria she felt when he was near never left her. Her body was wet, hot, needy, and he stroked the fire between her thighs, dipping his fingers to find the buried pearl within the slick folds of her sex. Frantically, Alexis pulled at his clothes, not really succeeding in stripping him so much as relaying the urgency she felt to be with him.

The cool, hard metal of the car pressed against her butt, almost making her shiver as it contrasted with the heat of his flesh. Her legs were opened to him, her body ready. She couldn't stop now, not until he filled her.

Alexis angled her body, as she freed his arousal from his sweats. She wrapped her fingers around his heavy length, stroking along his shaft several times. Ethan gasped, pulling his lips from hers.

'Ah, stop,' he said, his words close to a groan.

Alexis's body jerked in protest. He couldn't stop now. She needed him too badly.

'The condoms are locked in the trunk. I need my keys,' he said, his voice hoarse. 'I'll have to sneak back to the camp and get them.'

'I need you.' She kissed him, light sprinkling presses to his lips and cheeks. She had her shots and they'd already had unprotected sex. Her fingers gripped his shoulders. 'I can't wait. I want you inside of me.'

Ethan's expression was torn between his desire and his logic. He glanced over her shoulder then down her wiggling body. He started to pull away. His hands gripped her hips, kneading her. His arousal was still out of his sweats where she'd left it.

Alexis knew she was being foolish, but didn't care. Nothing seemed to matter out here in this world. The passion inside her overwhelmed all reason. Staring at his shaft, she licked her lips with slow meaning. The potency of her look was not lost. She braced her feet on the bumper and spread her legs wide. Leaning back, she arched her back over his trunk. She massaged her breasts, jerking at her camisole to free the second breast. Pinching her nipples, she thrust her hips up and down as he watched. She slid her hand between her thighs. Her voice nearing a small, playful pout, she said, 'I'm so wet for you, Ethan, so hot. I want you to take me, right here, right now, just like this. I want to feel your flesh inside me with nothing between us. I want how it felt that time in Kansas. Your hard shaft, so hot, so stiff, so alive, taking me.'

'Alexis –'

'Don't you want to feel how wet I am for you? How hot?' She shot him her most coy look. Her thighs moved back and forth. The cool mountain air did nothing to dry the cream dampening her body for him. If anything, seducing him like this turned her on more. She sat up, bracing herself back with one arm and holding his shoulder with the other. Taking him in hand, she knew he was close to losing his sanity. His shaft was filled to the point of explosion. 'Don't you like the way my body feels when there's nothing between us?' She squeezed him firmly in her hand. 'Don't your nerves scream to feel every inch of my wet body clamping around you?'

Ethan groaned and she knew by the look on his face he couldn't refuse her offer. Hastily, as if coming to a great decision, he said, 'I'll pull out.'

Alexis nodded in agreement. Ethan stood before her. He had to pull her hips off the end of the trunk. The position wasn't the most comfortable, but the urgent need raging inside her was more important than comfort. Repositioning her legs, they managed to come together.

Ethan thrust, filling her up. The feel of flesh to flesh was definitely different than the condom. It was more intimate, more real.

'Ah, damn,' he whispered, holding himself deep. His body shuddered and he took a concentrated breath. 'You are hot.'

Alexis giggled at the awe in his voice. 'Take me, Ethan. You feel so good.'

Ethan moved, doing most of the work as he took her in heated thrusts. His body trapped her to the car. With each push of his hips, her fingers were jolted against her clit, building the pleasure within. She felt like she was falling off, but his strength kept her on.

'Damn,' he said, his whispers drawn out as he moved inside her. 'I just want to stay like this for ever.'

Alexis felt great pleasure at his words. At the awkward angle it was hard to reach up and kiss him, so she reached briefly to cup his cheek with her palm before bracing her weight once more. She let her head fall back on her shoulders. The starry night surrounded them with its breathtaking splendour. Ethan's hard breathing mingled with hers. She felt so free, as if telling Ethan about her problems had lifted a weight off her chest.

'Ah,' he said, 'I can't hold back much longer.'

He thrust a few more times before she climaxed. Her body tensed and her toes curled. Ethan bit his lip, thrusting a few more times, giving her a full release before he pulled himself out and spilled his seed on the ground.

Alexis closed her eyes, nearly slipping off the trunk of the car. Ethan caught her as her feet landed on the ground. She laughed softly. Then, seeing a bright light in the distance, growing bigger each passing second, she gasped, 'Car.'

Ethan glanced over his shoulder before looking around. They were dishevelled in the middle of the road. There was no place to hide. The trees were too far to run to and even if they chanced it, they'd most likely hurt themselves in the dark woods.

'Hide,' Ethan said, pushing her to the side of the car. He was still dressed, so all he had to do was pull up his sweats. She ducked along the side, pulling her clothes off the trunk with him. Alexis adjusted her shirt. 'I think they'll pass.'

Alexis peeked up, holding really still. The headlights grew bigger. Whoever it was, they weren't driving very fast.

'Shit,' Ethan cursed. 'They're slowing down. Don't move.'

He stood, smiling. Alexis tried to hide herself along the car, struggling in the dark to pull the sweatpants on her legs.

'You a'right?' some guy called from the car.

'Yeah, just a flat. No big deal,' Ethan said. Alexis got the pants on and stood, pushing back her hair. A woman propped her arm on the pickup's window and the man driving leaned over her to study them. The truck was new and she saw the faint impression of a rifle in the window.

'Not much around these here parts,' the man said. 'I give you a hand?'

'No jack,' Ethan said, motioning helplessly.

'We got a jack, don't we, Slim?' the woman said. 'Get on out there and help this nice couple out.'

Slim audibly sighed, but nodded his head. Alexis looked at Ethan in horror as the truck pulled up alongside the road.

'Ethan?' she said, frantic. 'They have a gun.'

He nodded. 'Hunting rifle. People hunt this area quite a bit.'

'It's still a gun,' Alexis insisted.

'Shh, don't worry. The campsite is nearby. I want you to run and get my car keys out of my jeans. Wake up Ted.'

'Ethan, no, I –'

'Shh.' He cupped her face. Then, holding up her panties, he said, 'Take these with you.'

Alexis gave a short laugh despite her fear and grabbed her panties from him. She balled them in her fist. 'I'll hurry.'

Alexis took off running, nodding only slightly to the woman as she got out of the car. She glanced at the truck. The gun was still on the rack. Her heart beat faster. Suddenly the beautiful mountain night seemed the thing of horror movies. By the time she got to the campsite, she was frantic with fear.

She shook Ted awake gently, motioning him to follow. He yawned, sleepily rubbing his eyes. Alexis dug Ethan's car keys out of his pocket. They left Susan asleep by the campfire. As they made their way the quarter-mile back up the road, Alexis said, 'Ethan and I were talking by the car. Some people stopped and they're going to help fix the flat.'

'Now?' Ted asked, yawning. 'It's the middle of the night.'

'They, ah, didn't really give us a choice,' Alexis said, wringing her hands as she walked faster to get back to Ethan. She heard a laugh. The sound cackled strangely and she knew it wasn't Ethan. Softly, she added, 'They have a rifle in their truck.'

At that news Ted seemed to wake up. He pushed Alexis behind him. 'Get back to the camp.'

'No,' Alexis protested. They were close to the car.

Before Ted could insist, Ethan said, 'There you are. Got the keys?'

Alexis relaxed to hear his voice. Ted assessed the situation and then turned to frown slightly at her. She bit her lip. Perhaps she had judged too quickly. The woman stood on the side of the road holding lug nuts in one hand and a flashlight in the other. Ethan and Slim loosened the flat. Alexis shot Ted an apologetic look as she gave Ethan the keys. He popped the trunk and pulled out their bags with Ted's help and got out the flat tyre.

'Which way ya'll headin'?' Slim asked.

'New Mexico next,' Ethan said. 'But ultimately California.'

'Ya'll stoppin' at the Grand Canyon?' Slim pulled the flat tyre off and set it aside.

'Sure are,' Ted said. He and Ethan put the spare on.

'You be sure to stay out of Las Vegas,' the woman said. 'That city is nothing but sin and trouble.'

'Yes, ma'am,' Ethan said. She seemed pleased with his answer.

'Ah, good.' Slim nodded, standing back to watch them. 'Glad to see ya'll didn't have one of those doughnut tyres. These roads are too rough to be drivin' on a doughnut. They're so small, I can't see how anyone rides around on them. Ya'll just make sure to get another spare real soon. California is a sight off from here.'

'Will do, sir,' Ethan said.

Slim nodded, obviously satisfied. Alexis moved closer to Ethan, lightly touching his back.

'Thank you.' Ethan lowered the car and handed the jack to Slim.

'Not a problem.' Slim swung the jack into the back of his pickup.

'You kids have a nice night,' the woman said, switching off the flashlight. The moon was adequate to see by and the trunk light was giving off a soft glow.

They said their goodbyes. The pickup took off. Ted and Ethan put the flat where the spare had been before reloading the trunk of the car.

Ted chuckled as they finished. 'I don't even want to know what you guys were doing out here "talking".'

'At least we got the car fixed,' Ethan said, winking at Alexis.

'Yeah, the way Alexis made it sound, you were about to be murdered,' Ted teased. They walked towards the campsite. Alexis couldn't help but laugh at herself. It did seem foolish now. Ethan wrapped his arm over her shoulder and lightly kissed her temple. Ted eyed them briefly before looking ahead. Alexis smiled and couldn't help but think that Ethan had just claimed her as his woman.

They woke up early the next morning just after sunrise to Summer giving herself a sponge bath outside her camper. The sight caused them to hurry as they packed up to go. Thanking everyone for their hospitality, they finished their drive down the Highway of Legends. Alexis just smiled at Susan before leaning over to cuddle by Ethan's side in the car. He kissed her temple. Driving with one hand, he draped his arm over her shoulders.

The mountain scenery was beautiful in the morning light, turning from green to dark browns to greys and bright blues. They passed by abandoned coal mines and a town full of beautiful old architecture. Stopping for gas along the Colorado border, Alexis waited as Susan followed her into the bathroom.

'Well?' Susan asked immediately. 'Ted told me what happened.'

'Oh, yeah?' Alexis asked.

'You seem pretty cosy.' Susan crossed her arms over her chest.

'Are you mad at me?'

Susan sighed, uncrossing her arms. 'No, of course not. Are you happy? You're sure you want to . . .'

Alexis smiled, unable to help it. She felt wonderful this morning. 'It's not like I'm getting married. Ethan and I had a good talk, that's all. We're taking things very slowly and we'll see what happens.'

'I am getting married,' Susan blurted, before gasping and covering her mouth. She hopped on her toes in excitement, waiting for Alexis's reaction.

'What?' Alexis stood for a moment, shocked. Then, suddenly, she started screaming in excitement. Susan joined her and they jumped up and down hugging like excited teenagers.

'I know, right?' Susan nodded.

'Oh my,' Alexis said.

'I know.'

'Wow, I can't . . .'

'Yeah.'

'Wow.'

'Uh-huh.'

'When?'

'Yesterday on our walk.' Susan quickly told Alexis everything, finishing with, 'I can't believe he just did it then and there. It was so beautiful. I nearly fainted.'

Alexis grinned. 'That stupid dog was good luck, wasn't it? That crazy lady was right.'

Susan laughed.

'I can't believe you waited to tell me in a bathroom,' Alexis scolded.

'Well –' Susan shrugged '– it's the first second we had alone and I couldn't keep the secret from you any longer.'

'Oh, congratulations, sweetie,' Alexis said, giving her friend a big hug. 'I know you two are going to be so happy together.'

Ethan felt Alexis's hand on his thigh. It was a big turn-on, just holding her next to him as he drove. The couples were quiet as they headed into New Mexico. He smiled to know Susan and Ted had gotten engaged. It was about time. The two were mad for each other, almost sickeningly so at times, though it was sweet and Ethan could well understand the tendency as he held Alexis.

'You know,' Ethan said. They were still in the mountains but the landscape looked more like a desert, with its red sands and high cliffs. Hot-air balloons floated overhead, contrasting the colours of the mountainous desert beauty. 'All and all, this trip has gone really well.'

Alexis looked up at him and just smiled. She looked a lot different than the prissy debutante he picked up on the sidewalks of New York City.

'I can't believe all we've seen,' Susan said, sighing.

The trip through New Mexico was uneventful. They stopped for food in Taos around noon. They went to the Taos Pueblos, an ancient community still inhabited by Taos Indians. The adobe homes and churches were gorgeous structures. Alexis took her camera and didn't want to leave. Ethan loved watching her when she was taking pictures.

The land became more like a desert as they headed into Arizona. They passed by the Petrified Forest National Park but didn't stop, as they drove through the Painted Desert towards the Grand Canyon. Gigantic dinosaur statues were alongside the road. The first time Alexis saw one in the distance, she stiffened and pointed. By the time they figured out what it was, Ethan couldn't help but tease her. She took it all in her stride, jolting him in the ribs with her elbow.

'Ow.' He winced. She had got him in a sore muscle. Falling off the skateboard hadn't been too bad when it happened, but after making love to Alexis on the trunk of his car and then spending the night on the hard ground, his back was a little sore.

'What's wrong?' she asked, looking mortified.

'Back in Colorado I was messing around with this kid and his skateboard. I had a little accident,' Ethan said, trying to act like it was no big deal.

'It looked like it hurt to me,' Ted said, laughing.

Ethan grinned. 'Saw that did you?'

'Yep.' Ted reached up and patted his shoulder. 'It's all right. I won't tell everyone you were showed up by a nine-year-old boy.'

Ethan laughed. 'I think he was at least ten.'

The terrain became rich with colours along the road-side. The plains seemed to go on for ever with only tumbleweeds and cactuses to break up the landscape. It was a vast contrast to the mountains. Alexis took pictures from the car window, letting the desert heat into the car.

'Let's just keep driving,' Alexis said when Ethan offered to pull over. 'I don't want to get stuck in the desert like we did in the mountains.'

Ethan stroked her cheek and nodded in agreement.

Chapter Fifteen

By the time they made it to Flagstaff for the night, it was dark. Alexis was tired of being in the car. They'd driven a long way, touching three states. She watched Ethan shift uncomfortably in his seat. She too felt stiff and longed for a shower. They hadn't been able to bathe the night before as they camped outside.

They found a hotel along the road. The air smelled of pine trees as they stepped outside. Ethan booked the hotel rooms while everyone waited in the car.

After her shower, Alexis loaded some of her photographs into Ethan's computer, freeing up a memory stick. It only took a few minutes once the software was installed. Yawning, she collapsed on the bed. She wore her navy-blue silk chemise. It felt good to be in pretty clothes again. Flipping through the channels, she waited for Ethan to get out of the shower.

When the water shut off, Alexis smiled, turned off the television and went to the bathroom door. Knocking softly, she said, 'Don't bother getting dressed. I'm going to give you a massage. Let me work those kinks out of your back.'

Ethan pulled the door open to look at her, grinning. Water dripped down his face from his hair. 'Really?'

'Mm.' Alexis looked him over. 'Dry off first. I'll get the lotion.'

His grin widened. Alexis went to her bags and pulled out her lotion. It was the expensive kind and she didn't have much left. Seeing Ethan crawling on the bed to lie naked on his stomach, she knew she didn't care.

Alexis started at his feet, taking her time as she massaged up one leg and then the other. The scent of cucumber and green tea wafted between them. She kneaded his butt until he groaned. The muscles tensed slightly under her palms and she felt his hips thrust subtly forwards, as if involuntarily. Next, she worked her hands up over his back and arms. He made soft groaning noises of appreciation, grunting a few times as she worked knots out of his back. She straddled his hips, becoming very aroused by the sensual feel of his body beneath hers.

'Turn over,' she said, her words sounding husky and low. She stood up on the bed. Ethan flipped over. He gave her a lopsided grin as he glanced down at his erection. He was at full mast. Alexis sat beside him this time, rubbing his chest. His hand lazily wandered along the back of her thigh as she bent over him, gliding up to her butt to play with her lacy thong.

'When we get to California, I'm going to buy you a bunch of lacy, silky, girly underwear,' he said. 'You look too damned hot in them.'

Alexis smiled, liking the sound of still being with him in California. She moved to sit between his thighs, forcing him to spread his legs. His body was open to her and he looked almost vulnerable on the bed. She massaged down his hips to his thighs, ignoring his centre.

He chuckled softly. 'Mm, you missed a spot.'

'Shh, who's giving this massage?' Alexis pretended to scold.

'But –'

She pulled her hands off him and he groaned, not saying another word. Slowly, she squirted lotion into her hands, rubbing them together, warming it between her palms. Ethan watched her from under heavy lids. She made a great show of working the lotion through her fingers. He bit his lip.

'Is this the spot?' she asked, her voice a sultry murmur. She cupped his balls, rolling them in her palm, reaching to the sensitive piece of flesh buried just beneath them.

'Ah, yes.' His hips jerked.

With her other hand, she grabbed his shaft lightly and ran her fingers up the length of him. His feet dug into the mattress as he thrust himself into her palms.

'Tighter,' he begged.

Alexis squeezed his cock harder. He groaned in approval. She began to wiggle, completely aroused by the sight of his pleasure and feeling very dominant by the way his legs were spread to her. She wanted to conquer him, show him how much he desired her, needed her in his bed. Her lotioned index finger slipped between the cheeks of his firm butt. His eyes opened in surprise, but she kept working her hands.

'Alexis,' he tried to speak. His cheeks clenched over her finger but didn't stop her progress. The lotion helped the digit to slide to the tight rosette. She didn't penetrate, merely rimmed the outside.

'Ah, shit!' he swore softly, suddenly jerking and thrusting around like a madman against her hands. 'Ah, shit. Shit.'

He exploded, spilling himself on his stomach. Alexis drew her hands away, watching him, suddenly shy as she awaited approval. Ethan looked at her, eyes wide. Alexis stood and went to wash her hands. Then, grabbing a warm towel, she handed it to him for his stomach.

'You're absolutely amazing, you know that?' he said, cleaning himself and tossing the towel on the floor.

She smiled, relaxing with his words of approval. 'I know.'

Laughing, he pulled her into his arms, and proceeded to make love to her until they both fell asleep, thoroughly exhausted.

The Arizona town was nothing like they'd expected. It had been too dark to see much of the landscape, but instead of desert, there were thick tree-covered hills backdropped by mountains.

'This country really is worth seeing, isn't it?' Alexis said, climbing back into the Lincoln. Ethan kissed her temple, starting the car. They were getting a late start for the Grand Canyon, but none of them had been in too big of a hurry to get back on the road.

'According to the hotel clerk,' Susan said, 'the South

Rim of the Grand Canyon is closest. We should come across some signs.'

Two hours later they were near the South Rim. The rocky terrain was covered with small cactuses. There was hardly any traffic. In fact, they'd only passed three cars during the last hour. The sky darkened to a blue-grey and it started to drizzle by the time they pulled up to see the canyon. They'd come this far and decided to hike through the unpleasant weather. Even huddled beneath Ethan's jacket, trying to take pictures in the rain, was worth the trip. The canyon spread out before them, deep and wide as far as the eye could see. It truly was one of the greatest sights they'd seen on the trip.

They would've stayed longer, but the rain only got worse. It was falling full force by the time they came to the Hoover Dam on the Nevada border, making it hard to see. Traffic was backed up due to the weather and it took them several hours longer than planned to reach Las Vegas.

'All right, guys,' Susan announced as they drove into the brightly lit streets of the city. 'I have coupons for hotels.'

Alexis chuckled. 'Do you spend all your time at the brochure racks?'

'What?' Susan asked, laughing. 'I'm cheap and living off my boyfriend right now. I spent my last dime in Colorado.'

Alexis frowned, sitting up to look at Ethan. She'd just been letting him carry her money and pay for things since they had that great run of tattooing luck in Iowa City. In fact, she really had no clear idea of what the trip was costing. There were the hotels, the cost to get into some of the roadside attractions they'd been to, road tolls, gas, food, souvenir T-shirts she'd started collecting along the way in each state. She just assumed Ethan would tell her when her money ran low, or tell her to get a job like in Wisconsin. Realising that she'd unintentionally let her life slip back into the old pattern of letting other people pay, she asked, 'How much money do I have left?'

'You're good,' he said. 'No gambling, though.'

Alexis glanced back at Susan. She was looking out the window at the bright lights. Now wasn't the time to talk to Ethan about money. She had a strange feeling he was lying to her. Had he been paying her way? Suddenly, she didn't feel so well.

As everyone debated on hotels, Alexis stared out the window. It was strange seeing the tall buildings. After driving through the middle of the country there was a surreal sense of coming back to civilisation. Sure, they'd been through cities, but places like New York and Las Vegas were in a league of their own. They pulsed with energy. Numerous stretched limos passed by. One had a couple standing up through the sunroof. The man wore what she guessed was an Armani, or at least very close to, and the woman was in an unmistakable Nicole Miller masterpiece. The stretched black gown was gorgeous.

Alexis caught her reflection in the window. Her dark hair was a little frizzed by their hike through the rain. Her skin was pale. She needed make-up. Looking down at her clothes, she suddenly became embarrassed by the Colorado T-shirt. And, though her blue jeans were designer, one would hardly glance twice at the package she presented. She looked hideous.

Alexis pulled down her hair and combed her fingers through the length, trying to smooth it. Ethan glanced at her, a curious look on his face. He reached for her, stroking her cheek. She tried to smile, but the look was weak.

The hotel Susan picked was nice. However, Alexis's embarrassment only grew as Susan presented her coupons at the front desk. She didn't say anything. Ethan put the room on his credit card, furthering her suspicions that she might have become a financial burden on him. She tried not to be shallow, but being surrounded by the glamour that was Las Vegas only made her realise how much she'd lost. Ethan had put a bag on a cart. Though they had free valet parking, they had to take their own luggage up to their rooms.

The blue and gold décor in their room was so much

better than the pastels they'd encountered at their other stops. The thick bedding and matching curtains were printed with a delicate leaf pattern. Ethan dropped off their bags and went to bring the luggage rack downstairs. From the window, Alexis could see the bright lights of the strip.

'Hey, is everything all right?' Ethan asked. Alexis jumped, not realising she had zoned out for so long on him. He wrapped his arms around her waist, pulling her back along his body.

'I'm not in the mood right now, OK.' She moved out of his arms.

'It's not like I expected us to just have sex,' he said, his words measured.

'I'm just tired,' she said, yawning for effect. 'I'm going to take a shower.'

Ethan stepped out of the hotel suite and took a deep breath. Something was definitely up with Alexis. He couldn't explain it, but he felt like he was losing her. Did he even really have her? He'd known what would most likely happen when they got to the end of the trip, only he hadn't expected it to happen so soon. California was still one state away.

Susan came out of her room. Seeing Ethan, she blinked in surprise. 'Oh, hey, what are you doing out here?'

'Taking a breather,' Ethan said. 'You?'

'Um, actually, I was just going to see if you guys wanted to go out to eat with us tonight,' Susan said.

'Alexis is in the shower,' he said. 'She says she's tired.'

'Oh.' Susan turned to go back into her suite.

'Wait, Susan,' Ethan said. He glanced at the hotel door. He opened his mouth, wanting to ask her so many questions and unsure where to start. They'd become friends over the course of the trip, not so close as she was with Alexis, but he'd like to think of them as friends.

'You want to know about Alexis?' Susan prompted. Ethan nodded. 'I'm afraid the fairy tale might be ending. I feared this, Ethan. I didn't want to see either of you hurt. In the middle of nowhere, it is so easy to forget who you are. That's the beauty of going on vacation. You can have fun, forget yourself. But, as the vacation ends, you realise you're the same person you were with the same problems. Alexis has been to this city many times with her mother. I imagine that reality is coming back a little bit.'

'I don't fit into that reality, do I?' Ethan felt as if he'd been beaten. His shoulders slumped and he was suddenly very tired.

'I don't know,' Susan said. She placed a hand on his shoulder, squeezing lightly. 'I'd like to think so, but the truth is I don't know. Maybe if you met her mother you'd understand. That woman is a piece of work and she really pulled a number on Alexis growing up.'

'So I've heard,' Ethan said.

'Well, I'll see you tomorrow.'

'Good night.'

'Night, Ethan.'

Ethan took a walk around the hotel to think. By the time he got back to the room, Alexis was already in bed. He took his shower and climbed quietly into bed next to her. Lying awake, he waited for her to come to him. She didn't. Taking a deep breath, he rolled over on his side, wrapped his body around her and held her as he went to sleep.

'My gawd, it's true!'

Alexis shot up in bed, disorientated. The room was light, the curtains drawn. She frowned, seeing the shapely silhouette of a woman in front of the window. Lifting her hand, she tried to block the light.

'What the . . .?' Ethan said. Alexis felt the bed move.

'Alexis Samantha!'

'Mother?' Alexis asked weakly. She shook violently. It couldn't be. 'What . . . ah?' Alexis grabbed her head, trying to make sense of what was happening. 'What are you doing here?'

'I should think to ask you the same thing,' Francine

Grant said, her voice clipped. 'Haven't you been watching the news? Haven't you cared what happens to me? I've been acquitted of those fictitious charges and I've come to take you home.'

'Acquitted?' Alexis repeated, as if in a daze. Wait. If her mother was acquitted that meant she had her life back – her clothes, her apartment, the money.

Francine stepped out of the harsh light, coming closer to Alexis on the bed. She was a slender woman, more so now after her time behind bars. She wore a grey and white pinstripe suit with curved lapels and two decorative buttons. The grey slacks were matching. The suit looked like it belonged in the boardroom. Alexis shivered. If her mother was dressed for business that meant she was in her barracuda mood. It was best not to start a fight. Her short dark hair was the same colour as Alexis's. It was cut up above the ears and only an inch and a half on top.

'I like your haircut,' Alexis said.

Her mother actually started to smile, moving to touch her shorn locks. Her face fell. 'Don't change the subject.'

'Alexis?' Ethan asked, touching her arm. Francine's eyes narrowed on Ethan.

Alexis turned to look at him. He was so handsome. She took in his face, his dishevelled hair. He'd cut the red off, leaving soft brown waves. Then she saw his tattoos, knowing what they'd look like to her mother.

'Alexis,' her mother said, 'I'm waiting.'

'Mother, I'll meet you downstairs.'

'No, you'll be joining me now,' Francine said.

Alexis knew that tone. She closed her eyes briefly. 'Ethan, I'm sorry. I have to go.'

'Wait, no, that's –' Ethan began.

'Alexis,' Francine interrupted, walking to the end of the bed. It didn't seem to faze her at all that her daughter was half-dressed, that Ethan's chest was bare and that he was potentially naked under the covers. She refused to speak to Ethan directly and Alexis knew her mother was purposefully slighting him. 'Tell this young man that it's over. You had your little fling. It's time to come home.'

'Ethan, I have to go,' Alexis said. 'I'll come find you later today.'

'You have no right breaking into my room,' Ethan said to Francine. He flung off his covers, standing up in his boxer shorts. 'I'm calling security.'

Francine gasped dramatically like he was going to attack her. She threw up her hands and called, 'Tony!'

Francine's seven-foot bodyguard came lumbering into the room. Tony folded his arms over his chest and looked down at Ethan. Alexis got out of bed. Tony was huge. If Ethan even tried to fight him, he'd lose.

'Mother, I know you don't care who sees you naked, but could you have Tony turn around?' Alexis asked.

Francine nodded at Tony. Tony backed away towards the door. Alexis slipped on a pair of jeans and a designer shirt. Her mother waited silently, eyeing Ethan.

'Alexis, you don't have to go. We need to talk,' Ethan said.

'Actually, we need to talk,' Francine said. 'Tony, escort my daughter outside.'

Alexis looked at Ethan, trying to relate with her eyes what she was feeling. He opened his mouth, but what could he say? Francine was standing right there. As Tony firmly escorted her out the door, Ethan yelled, 'Alexis!'

Once outside the suite, Alexis looked at Tony. 'How'd she find me?'

'She's had a private detective on your tail since you left New York. They've been following Mr James's credit-card purchases. She tried to meet up with you in Colorado, but you disappeared. When Mr James used his card in New Mexico, the detective deduced you were heading this way.' Tony didn't look at her as he spoke. It wasn't the first time he clued her in to her mother's doings and he knew she'd keep her mouth shut about it to Francine.

'Let me guess. Smelly, sweaty man in a grey car?' Alexis asked.

Tony's lip twitched. She had her answer. She hadn't

been crazy. That man was following them. She should've known her mother would do something like that.

'Let me say goodbye to Susan and Ted?'

Tony nodded. 'Make it fast.'

Alexis knocked on Susan's door. It didn't take long for Susan to answer. She smiled brightly. 'Hey, I was waiting for you to get up. Guess what? Ted and I have decided to get married here in Vegas. I want you to stand up for me ... Alexis? What's wrong?'

Alexis glanced at Tony.

'Hi, Tony,' Susan said.

'Ms Susan,' Tony answered.

'She's here?' Susan asked. 'How?'

'Acquitted,' Alexis whispered.

'Where?'

Alexis looked at her room.

'With Ethan?' Susan gasped. 'But ...? You know how she is, Lexy. You can't –'

'Tell Ethan I'm sorry. Tell him to take ...'

The door opened. Francine stepped out. 'Come, Alexis.'

'Ms Grant,' Susan said to the woman.

'Susan, you can see to Alexis's bags, can't you?' Francine asked.

Susan nodded.

'Bye,' Alexis said quietly, moving to follow her mother. Part of her wanted to rebel, but knew if she caused a scene right now then it would only make it worse for everyone. She needed to get her mother alone first and then she could reason with her.

Glancing at her mother, Alexis said, 'You're looking well, Mother.'

It was the truth. Francine looked great for her age. Her skin was smooth, thanks to the magical workings of her plastic surgeon's micro-lifts over the years. Her make-up was flawless, as was her hair.

'I can't say the same for you, Alexis.' Francine stepped into the elevator. 'And quit calling me Mother. It makes me sound old.'

* * *

Ethan stared at the envelope in disbelief. He thought stuff like this only happened in movies, but apparently not. Francine Grant was paying him to go away. Though by the way Alexis just left without a fight, it was obvious she was done with him.

A soft knock sounded on the door. His heart leapt, but he knew it wasn't her. Alexis had left him without a goodbye.

Ethan pulled on his jeans. The knock sounded again. Susan and Ted were at the door.

'Hey,' Susan said. 'We just saw Alexis.'

Ethan's jaw tightened. He didn't answer.

'She asked me to tell you she was sorry. She wanted to say more but there wasn't much time,' Susan offered.

'I wanted to know where I stood with Alexis and now I know,' Ethan said. He picked up the cheque and handed it to Susan.

'Oh my gawd, Ethan! This is for twenty thousand dollars,' Susan said, handing the cheque to Ted. Ted whistled softly in amazement.

Ethan gave a short, humourless laugh. 'Yep. Just enough to open my own shop in California.'

'You're going to take it?' Susan asked.

'Of course I'm going to take it,' Ethan said. 'Why shouldn't I take it?'

'Because, well, Alexis.' Susan handed the cheque back to him.

'What about her? She made her decision when she walked out that door without a fight. She didn't even try to stay with me.' Ethan shook his head. 'Her mother's right. To Alexis I'm just a dirty little fling, nothing more. I'll never be her social equal and to be honest, I wouldn't even want to try.'

'You should give her a chance to explain herself,' Ted said. 'If you care for her, you should at least do that much. Maybe her leaving peacefully was the right decision. Francine Grant is a powerful woman. She could've probably had you thrown in jail with one phone call.'

Ethan stared at Ted. He wanted to cling to the hope the

man gave him, but found it hard. Alexis didn't even try to fight for him, for them. She'd just stood up and walked out like he was nothing. She didn't stand up to her mother, didn't proclaim she ... She what? Loved him? Ethan sunk down on the bed. What was he thinking? Alexis never said once that she loved him. She said she cared. She said she liked him. But, love? No, she'd never said she loved him.

'What harm is there in giving her a chance to explain?' Ted asked. 'If you care for her ... Do you care for her?'

'Yes,' Ethan whispered. He studied his hands. 'I love her.'

Susan gasped. 'You didn't tell her, did you?'

Ethan shook his head in denial. No, he'd been too scared to tell her. He was still scared. All he knew was that watching her walk out of the hotel room had ripped out his heart until he couldn't see straight.

Ted looked him directly in the eye. 'Then you have to fight for her.'

Francine Grant had the penthouse suite. She always stayed in the nicest hotels in the nicest rooms. The suite had a classical allure, as did the entire hotel, from the subtle tans and reds of the décor to the wet bar and elegant furniture.

As soon as they reached the hotel room, Francine insisted Alexis take a steam shower to wash the stench of the lower classes from her. When she got out, her mother had a whole team of specialists waiting for her. They plucked her eyebrows, waxed her legs, and gave her a facial and a massage, a pedicure and manicure, even a haircut. Though she tried to, she couldn't hate the royal treatment.

Afterwards, she dressed in a brand new Helen Wang dress. The black accordion pleat skirt had a drop waist and, though it didn't conform to her figure, it was a stunning work of art. The sleeveless top and crocheted trim added a simplistically chic appeal. The T-strap black leather pumps were to die for. She topped the look off with a wide-brim hat and a string of her mother's pearls.

'Ah,' Francine said, standing. She held her arms out wide and smiled as if nothing had happened that morning. 'There's my girl. You look so much better. Come, I've got us reservations.'

Francine had also changed her clothes while her daughter was pampered. The black wool wrapped her body with a side-tie belt with a deep V-neckline. It complemented her overly slender form to perfection. It went perfectly with her Sergio Rossi round-toe ankle-strap pumps. Instead of classical white pearls, she chose faux steel-grey ones.

The restaurant was part of the luxurious hotel. The intimate lighting and private nooks lent itself well to the talk Alexis wanted to have with her mother. She wasn't unaware of the stares they received walking into the room. It had been that way her whole life. Her mother ordered for her as she always did when they were together, speaking in fluent French to the waiter. Alexis's French was poor at best and she could only make out some of what her mother said.

Alexis waited as the waiter came back with red wine. He showed the bottle to her mother. Her mother smiled and nodded regally at him. The waiter nodded back, very dignified, and poured two glasses. Alexis tried to smile at him out of habit and he actually looked like he was offended.

'I see you've picked up some vulgar manners as well. It's to be expected. If you slum for that long, you're bound to get a little dirty.' Francine closed her eyes as if she couldn't bear to look at her.

'It was only a smile, mother,' Alexis said.

'To the waiter,' Francine hissed as if it was the ultimate sin. 'He probably thinks you wish to sleep with him.'

'Like mother, like daughter,' Alexis mumbled.

'Sit up straight,' Francine ordered.

Alexis straightened automatically at the order.

'I have never slept with a waiter,' Francine said, her voice haughty.

'Bali,' Alexis reminded her.

'Foreign soil. It doesn't count.' Francine shot her a superior smile. 'How many times do I have to tell you, Alexis, an affair with such men is fine, but to be seen with that Ethan James in public? To share a room with him – several rooms with him all across the country? Ugh, and that car of his? Please. Are you trying to punish me? Isn't it bad enough that I was falsely accused of – ?'

'Save it for the press, Mother,' Alexis said. 'I've had time to think about things and I know better.'

'Fine.' Francine clenched her teeth before sipping the wine. 'We won't discuss it.'

'Mother, you might as well know that, after dinner, I'm going to go see Ethan.' Alexis put her linen napkin down on her lap.

'No, you're not,' Francine said. 'That little indiscretion has been taken care of.'

'What if I told you nothing happened?'

Francine tipped her head back and laughed. She pulled her black clutch off her lap and opened it. Taking out a packet, she placed it on the table.

Alexis swallowed. Her fingers shook as she lifted it up. 'What is this?'

'Your nothing,' Francine said.

Alexis pulled out a stack of photos from the envelope. The top one was of her by Ethan's car. They'd just left New York. It was that first gas station. She could still remember how mortified she'd been to have to urinate in the dirty restroom. Without leafing through the stack, she said, 'You had a detective following me.'

'Oh, they get better,' Francine said, sipping her wine. 'Go ahead, dear. I'm sure you'll not be nearly as shocked as I was.'

Alexis looked at the photographs. It was parts of her whole trip laid out. Ethan's car parked at hotels, all of them at gas stations, eating in a diner. She stopped. 'So we drove across country in an old car. It's vintage chic, a classic. Hardly the social suicide you're making it out to be.'

Francine took another sip, motioning her hand lightly for Alexis to continue. Alexis took a deep breath. Ethan looked so adorable, even with his red goatee. She missed him. She wanted to talk to him. Then she got to a photograph of them together in bed. Alexis was on her hands and knees and Ethan was behind her. She hurried past it, but the next ones were more of the same. The frames were hidden partially by curtains. There was one with Ethan kissing between her thighs, one with her on top, on bottom, hanging off the side of the bed. Getting to one where she was giving Ethan head, she blushed.

'I see you've found my favourite,' Francine said. 'Please tell me you used protection.'

'You're sick,' Alexis said. 'You're my mother. How could you look at these? Let alone comment? Do you know how twisted that is? Do you have any idea?'

'Oh, please, you know we've always been more like best friends than mother and daughter. I swear if it wasn't for my having to bail you out of messes like these, people would assume we were sisters.'

Alexis stuffed the pictures into her purse. 'I'm leaving.'

'If you walk away from me you'll never see another penny,' Francine said.

'I don't care,' Alexis said. Her whole body shook. She meant it. She might regret it tomorrow, but right at that moment, she meant it. 'I've done fine these last weeks without you.'

'You'll give up everything for him?' Francine demanded. Her face became tight with rage. 'For a man? You can't possibly be in love after two weeks. You're just trying to get back at me for this whole judicial misunderstanding.'

Judicial misunderstanding? Her mother gets arrested. It's all over the news. Alexis's life is raided, her belongings taken by the government and it's just a judicial mis-understanding?

Alexis couldn't answer. If Ethan asked her then yes, yes, she would give it up for him. For the first time in her life she felt like she was more than an empty shell, a fashion plate. 'Goodbye, Mother.'

'He doesn't love you.' Francine's words kept her from standing up and walking out. They were a blow to her heart. 'Alexis, he's from another world. He won't understand you, even if he continues to put up with you. I know men, darling. To men like Ethan James you're nothing more than a conquest. It's so he can tell people that he once dated Alexis Grant, the rich girl whose mother is on the news. He'll laugh about you. He isn't in love with you. I saw it in his eyes.'

'Would you recognise love if you were to see it?'

'What's going to happen when he discovers that I've cut you off? That you have no money, no prospects, no idea how to hold down a well-paying job? Do you think he'll want to support you? Even if he did, would you want to live in his one-room studio apartment having children like a breeder rabbit? Buying your clothes from a discount store? Forget the facials. Forget shopping and designer clothes. Forget the pedicures and manicures and spa treatments. Forget travelling. Forget everything you like to do.'

'It's not like that,' Alexis said softly. Was it? Ethan said he cared for her, but what of love? He never said he loved her. Was she a fool to throw everything away on him when he didn't care for her? Was she a conquest? Her heart said no, but her mind wasn't so sure. 'He knows me better than you do. I . . . I love him.'

Francine shook her head, giving her daughter a pitying look. 'If that's true, darling, then let him go. Face it. You're too much like me. I wasn't cut out for PTO meetings and play dates. Do you really want to be a soccer mom clipping coupons?'

'Who said anything about having children?' Alexis's mouth was dry. She lifted her glass to sip the red wine.

Francine laughed. 'You are so naive sometimes. Where do you think these things lead? That's what those people do. They get married, have children and die miserable. Now, I've worked too hard and too long moulding you into a lady to throw you away on some piece of trash who draws on people for a living. I've already compensated him for his trouble in driving you across country.'

'You paid him off?' Alexis shook her head in disbelief.

'Yes, quite nicely, too,' Francine said. 'It'll give him a pretty good start at opening his business. What? You look shocked. Yes, I know all about his plan to open a tattoo shop. Really, Alexis, sometimes I think you underestimate me.'

Alexis looked down at her lap.

'I didn't want to have to do this, but you leave me no choice.' Francine leaned forwards, catching her daughter's eye. She arched a brow and said, 'It would be really easy for me to make a few phone calls to make sure that man never works as an artist again. By the time I'm done with him, he'll be working in a mine shaft, digging coal.'

Alexis didn't move. Her mother was serious. The scary thing was that she could probably hold true to the threat. The waiter came back with dinner salads. Francine picked up her chilled salad fork and stabbed a piece of lettuce in obvious irritation.

'The vacation is over, Alexis,' Francine said, piercing her daughter with a pointed look. 'It's time to remember who you are. It's time to come home. A limo will take us to the airport in one hour. You're not to see him again.'

Ethan stared at his hands. Alexis had left. She'd really left. He'd searched everywhere for her, every swank hotel on the strip. In the end it was Susan who told him the news. Alexis had gotten on a private jet and flown out of his life. Just like that. It was like her mother had said to him. Alexis couldn't possibly care for a man so beneath her social standing. Grabbing his bag, he slung it over his shoulder. It was time for him to move on with his life. It was time for this cross-country trip to end.

Alexis stared out of the window of the jet. The ground grew smaller the higher they got. She watched the runway, waiting for Ethan to run onto the pavement, screaming her name like the ending of a movie. He didn't come.

Closing the plastic blind, she sat back in her seat. She told herself it was better for everyone that he didn't come. A tear slipped over her cheek and she gently swiped it away. She refused to cry, though the heartache stung so badly she could barely breathe.

'Drink this,' Francine said, thrusting a glass of wine at her. 'You'll feel better once we get to New York. We'll redecorate your apartment. You'll not think of what's his name ever again.'

Alexis automatically lifted the glass to her lips. At the last second she looked down at the glass, watching it fizz. Slowly, she lowered it and handed it back to her mother. 'You first.'

'Don't be silly. I don't feel like wine.'

'Drink the wine, Mother,' Alexis said. When Francine didn't move, she asked, 'What? Not in the mood for a little nap?'

'I would never.'

Alexis rolled her eyes. 'The flight to Scotland when I was seven. I was scared because I just watched a movie with a plane crash in it. I didn't wake up for two days.'

Francine actually paled. Alexis rolled her eyes and unbuckled her seat belt. 'Where are you going?'

Alexis didn't answer. She walked up to the cockpit, went inside with the pilot and locked the door behind her.

'Miss Alexis,' Captain Tom said, nodding.

'Captain,' Alexis said, taking the co-pilot seat. The man was back in the bathroom. 'I forgot something back in Vegas. We need to turn around.'

'Oh, yeah?'

Alexis nodded. 'Yeah. I forgot my heart. If you wouldn't mind, I'd like to get it back.'

Tom grinned. 'Happy to oblige, Miss Alexis.'

Chapter Sixteen

Bright lights shone over the busy strip. Ethan waited for his car. He'd tried one last casino where Francine Grant had been staying, hoping against hope that Alexis would be there waiting for him. She wasn't. What did he expect? Susan said she went with her mother back to New York. He'd been a fool to dream. Pulling out the twenty thousand dollar cheque, he sighed. He wouldn't keep it. How could he? He didn't need Francine Grant's money. He didn't need anything from her but her daughter and it looked like that was the one thing she wouldn't let him have.

Suddenly, his heart stopped as he looked up. He stopped walking. No, it couldn't be. He closed his eyes and didn't move. He tried to stay indifferent but it was hard. His body wanted to go to her, to hold her close, pull her into his arms and never let go. But, he was scared. She'd broken his heart when she left him. He didn't want to risk it again. He couldn't survive it a second time – not in the same day, not in the same life.

Alexis was standing before him, dressed like the princess she was. She looked prim and proper, like the Alexis he'd picked up in New York. It was like his best dream and worst nightmare rolled into one. The rich, pampered Alexis wasn't the woman he loved. He wanted the woman who showed herself to him – all of herself. He wanted the woman who kissed him and laughed at his jokes. By the looks of her, that woman no longer existed.

'Ethan?' Alexis fidgeted nervously as she waited for him to speak.

'What are you doing here, Alexis?'

'Well, you know, I was in the neighbourhood.' OK, bad

joke. She shook terribly. A day had passed, but it felt like an eternity.

'Yeah, some neighbourhood.' He glanced at the rich hotel. The valet pulled his car up and got out.

'Oh, are you leaving?'

'I've got a life to get on with.' Ethan started to go. Then, stopping, he reached into his pocket and pulled out an envelope. 'Tell your mother that I don't need her money.'

'Won't you look at me?' she asked, wanting to read his face, wanting a hint of what he was feeling, thinking. Nerves bunched in her stomach. 'Won't you talk to me, Ethan?'

'What do you want, Alexis?' he asked, still not moving to look at her. She slowly took the envelope, clutching it in her hands.

A few passers-by looked at her curiously as she stared at Ethan's back. A male couple stopped to watch, one of them dressed like a showgirl. Alexis ignored them, as she peeked inside the envelope. It was the cheque from her mother – a very generous cheque. Others stopped to watch them as well.

'I just want to talk to you,' she said, stepping closer. She didn't care who heard her, just so long as Ethan did. 'I want to tell you something.'

'Then tell me.'

'Here?' she asked.

'Tell him, honey,' the drag queen yelled, flicking her long nails, laughing. 'Don't be shy.'

'I . . .' Alexis looked around, feeling helpless. There was so much she needed to say. Every carefully planned word left her. She didn't know what to do. The crowd only seemed to grow. She didn't want to do this with an audience. The man who laughed nodded his head eagerly at her, motioning that she should speak.

'I see,' Ethan said, making a move to get into his car. 'Even now, you're ashamed.'

'Wait,' she demanded, taking a step towards him. She looked around the crowd – some rich, some poor, some glittering with feather boas. 'I was looking at my photographs the other day and most of them are of you, Ethan.'

That was so not how she wanted to say that. She held her breath, waiting.

'Photographs,' he repeated softly, giving a short, humourless chuckle. He finally turned to her. His eyes travelled over her face. She held still, watching as he stared at her face before moving down her clothing. 'You left me this morning without so much as a word. Now, you show up telling me you have pictures of me?'

'You tell her!' someone yelled.

Ethan frowned. 'What am I supposed to do with that, Alexis?'

She opened her mouth to speak, but nothing came out.

'Well?' a woman asked from the crowd. 'Why'd you leave him?'

'Yeah, what he do to you?' someone added.

'My father, he told me to look at life like a photograph and...' Alexis glanced at the crowd in annoyance. She fidgeted before the prying eyes, feeling like she was on trial. Maybe she was. Maybe she deserved this humiliation. 'I had to go. If I stayed it would've been bad.'

'Why?' a man's voice asked.

'Yeah, why?' a woman added.

'Did you leave him at the altar?' a third person cried. 'Tell us what happened.'

Alexis looked helplessly at Ethan. He frowned. He pulled open the door to the passenger seat. 'Come on. Let's go somewhere private.'

The onlookers sighed with a collective, 'Ahh!'

Alexis climbed in. Some of the crowd followed them and were looking in the car window. Ethan started the car and she was glad that they were finally in private. Maybe now she could concentrate. Ethan navigated the busy streets, driving aimlessly. She glanced in the back seat, seeing his suitcase.

'You're leaving Vegas?'

'Yep.'

'Oh.' Alexis frowned. He'd been on his way to leave. Only the fact that she'd found him outside her mother's hotel gave her hope. Maybe he'd been trying to see her. She'd only gone there to try and bribe the concierge into letting her use a limo under her mother's account to look for him.

'Well, you wanted to talk. So talk.'

He looked so angry. She didn't expect him to be angry. 'Maybe this was a bad idea. It's just, I thought . . .'

'What?' his voice softened, but not his expression.

'I wanted to explain about this morning. I had to go. You don't know my mother.' Alexis took a deep breath.

'You're a grown woman, Alexis. You don't have to do what your mother says.'

'She paid you off.'

'Don't change the subject.'

Alexis shook her head. She didn't want to start a fight. 'It's the same subject. You took the cheque she gave you this morning. What was I supposed to think?'

'That I'm not a fool. It's not like you asked me to stay with you, to give it back. In fact, I seem to recall you just walking out on me when she told you it was time to go. You didn't fight her. You didn't try. You let her treat me like dirt, like I was some family embarrassment you had to hide from the world. Do you know what it's like to be treated like you're not good enough? You didn't even say goodbye. I figured you wanted your mother to pay me off. You didn't lift a finger to stop her from doing it. Besides, I wasn't raised to throw a good thing away when it comes along, unlike some people. Such noble pursuits are a luxury of the rich.'

'Ethan, I didn't throw you away. My mother is a very influential, powerful person. With just a few phone calls she could . . . She still could . . .' Alexis stopped talking. She took a deep breath and tried to give him the envelope in her hand. 'I'm not mad about the money. I want you to have it. You deserve it and she could well afford to give it to you.'

'It doesn't matter,' Ethan said. 'I don't want it.'

She tried not to cry. 'I can see you don't want me here. I'll go. Just pull over.'

He took a deep breath, pulling the car into the hotel parking lot where they'd stayed the night before. Alexis glanced up, wondering if Susan and Ted were still inside. At least he dropped her off by friends. Slowly, she nodded and weakly moved to get out of the car.

'Wait.'

'I'm sorry,' she said at the same time. She looked at him, her eyes boring into his. 'Please, I'm babbling and not explaining this very well. I've never had to grovel before.'

Ethan didn't move.

'If I would've stayed, she would've caused a scene. She would've done something. I know her. She'd call the police and claim you tried to mug her. She'd have your car towed. In fact, she still might call in a few favours and make sure you didn't get a shop at all once you get to California.'

'I'm not afraid of her,' he said.

'Please, let me get this out. I know that you were paying my way on the last part of the trip and I didn't want to be some helpless girl that you had to take care of. I've been that helpless girl my whole life.' Alexis moved closer to him, so close he could touch her if he wanted to. He didn't. 'I shouldn't have left like that, but I was confused. I wanted to do the right thing. No, that's a lie. I wanted to do the safe thing. I was scared. I saw my old world and I saw what I had become with you and I got scared. I never felt for anyone the way I feel about you. And I'm not trying to blame my mother, because it's my fault for believing her when she told me you wouldn't want anything to do with me. You said you cared for me and I should've believed that. But I couldn't see why you would care for me. Before, the only thing I had to offer anyone was money and a good family name. You liked me without any of that. You're so ...' Alexis sniffed, tears coming to her eyes. '... and I'm so ...'

'You should've known better than listen to that woman,' Ethan said. She wanted to touch him so badly. Her body craved him, always craved him.

'I did, I do, it's just she said that you would never want a person like me and I believed her.' Alexis shrugged. A lone tear slipped down her cheek. 'I could understand why it would be true. I'm no prize. I'm bad with money. I'm judgemental and arrogant. I've never kept a job more than a few weeks. All I could think of was what would happen when we got to California and the vacation ended and you realised your girlfriend was just some spoiled rich girl. You're so perfect and I'm just not.'

She stared at his mouth, wanting the feel of her lips against his. It made it hard to concentrate. Her body was heating with his nearness, the virile smell of him.

'You could've talked to me last night about this,' he said. 'You could've trusted me.'

'What could I say?' Alexis sighed. 'I had to regroup. I had to make sure that I could change, that this new life I was living was what I wanted. You didn't need to be there while I worked out my neurotic childhood. But, most of all, I needed to have a plan to change myself into someone you not only cared for, but could maybe love. Someday.'

Ethan didn't move.

'I know you don't like me very much right now, Ethan.' Alexis lifted her hand, letting it hover near his cheek. The city lights added an odd contrast to his features. She didn't touch him. 'But I'm going to prove to you that I'm changing. I'll get an apartment in San Francisco. It might be horrible and small and even have a funny smell. I might really hate it, but that's all right, because it'll be mine.'

'Alexis,' he whispered with an incorrigible look on his handsome face, 'would you just say whatever it is you're getting at?'

'Haven't you been listening to me? I'm here to win you back. I'm here because I'm madly and completely, hopelessly in love with you.'

Ethan smiled.

'I've missed you. It was only one day and I missed you. I can't go back to that life. I don't want it. Things like these,' she motioned down her dress, 'designer dresses don't matter. They're not what's important.'

'So,' he said, sounding suddenly very rakish, 'just how far are you willing to go to get me back?'

Alexis smiled, hope unravelling inside her as she leaned closer to him. She touched his chest. 'Well, what exactly did you have in mind?'

'You grovelled really well,' he said, his voice dipping. 'But I think maybe there should be some begging.'

'Begging,' she repeated, the word husky. Her lids fell low over her eyes and he knew she'd missed him as he had her. He glanced at the hotel behind them.

'And screaming.' He leaned over, closing some of the distance between their lips.

'Screaming.'

'Yes, definitely screaming.' He leaned closer. 'And perhaps a little wrestling.'

'Nude wrestling?'

'Mm, I know how particular you are about your clothes.' Their lips brushed, but he didn't kiss her. 'Susan has your bags upstairs. We can get another room and pick this trip up where we left off. There's still one more state to go.'

'Does this mean you forgive me?' she asked. 'And that you'll maybe take me back?'

'Do you promise that from now on, if you're feeling scared or there's a problem, you'll come to me first and not run away?'

'I do.'

'Then I'd say this means you'll not be moving into your little, horrible, smelly apartment but into my big, horribly decorated apartment.' Ethan chuckled at the look of shock on her face. He tilted his head the other way, drawing back each time her lips dipped closer to his. 'And I think it's only fair that you be forced to help me run my shop. I mean, you've come this far.'

'A tattoo shop?' Alexis asked, grinning. 'I can work with that.'

Ethan laughed with pleasure. Happiness coursed through her at the sound. She couldn't resist any longer. Alexis had to touch him. Wrapping her arms around his waist, she drew her mouth to his, kissing him passionately.

Alexis moaned as he rolled his tongue into her mouth. She knew there was a lot that they still needed to talk about, but he was forgiving her and that was all that mattered. She squealed with happiness against his kiss, wrapping her arms around his neck. Ethan hugged her tight. She felt the press of his muscles and she needed him. Now. For ever.

Feeling aggressive, she pushed him back, tugging at his T-shirt. Ethan pulled back, breathing hard. 'We should get a room.'

'Mm, here's good,' she said.

'Ah, no. The last thing we need is to get arrested.' Ethan got out of the car. Alexis did the same and they hurried into the hotel. She couldn't keep her hands off him. The clerk didn't seem to notice as Ethan handed him a credit card. It was Las Vegas. He probably saw couples making out everyday. Thankfully, the room wasn't too far. Ethan led the way, pulling her behind him. Once they were in the room, he pulled her back into his arms and instantly tried to free her of her blue jeans. He got them as far as her hips.

'I want you,' Alexis said.

'I want you.'

'I love you.' She paused, pulling back. 'Do you think that maybe, someday, you'll feel the same?'

'Neither of us is perfect, but we're right for each other,' he said. 'I love you, too. Just don't run away again.'

'I promise.' She tugged at his pants, unzipping them. Reaching down the front, she stroked his arousal. She giggled as he shut the door. Alexis pushed him down so he was sitting on a large chair near the door. She pushed her blue jeans off her hips, taking her underwear with it.

Ethan closed his eyes, groaning. She straddled his legs, kissing him as her hands explored his chest. He reached between her thighs, pushing along her folds with his fingers, stroking her just how she liked it. Working her hips up and down, she kissed him, wiggling as he thrust two thick fingers up inside her.

It was too hard to come together with the arms of the chair blocking her legs. Ethan lifted her up and carted her the rest of the way to the bed. He flung her on her back and she instantly wrapped her legs around his waist. She dipped her fingers under the denim hanging on his hips and squeezed his butt. Lifting up on his arms, he entered her. Alexis arched, gasping at the wonderful feel of him inside her. He groaned loudly. 'Oh, man, I love doing this.'

Alexis squirmed, urging him to move. They became frantic as they thrust, erasing the pain of the long day. Her leg hooked over his hip. He took her hard and deep in his passion. Alexis reached between her thighs, feeling his body enter hers as she pleasured herself.

'Ethan,' she gasped, climaxing hard. His moan of pleasure answered hers as he stiffened and released himself inside her.

Alexis relaxed. 'I think moving in together is a really good idea.'

Ethan chuckled.

'That way, we can do this whenever and however we want.'

'Hey.' He tried to look hurt but she saw through it easily. 'I thought you were going to say because you love me and can't live without me.'

'That too.' She kissed him, knowing there was no other life she'd rather live than the one she was living with him. 'That too.'

Chapter Seventeen

San Francisco, California, three months later...

'Boss, you got a package!'

Ethan glanced up from the tattoo of a butterfly he was doing on a young woman's back. He'd honestly done that same design so much he could've drawn it in his sleep, but if that's the tattoo she wanted who was he to tell her no? They'd just opened up a month ago and couldn't afford to turn the business away. In Kansas, Adam had hooked him up with some suppliers so he was able to open his doors rather quickly. Things would've been so much easier if he'd let Alexis keep the twenty thousand like she wanted to. In the end, they burned the cheque.

'Just sign for it. It's probably those gloves I ordered last week,' Ethan said to his front man. Greg was a good kid with hopes of someday apprenticing. He had real talent, but it was still raw. With a little work, he'd have great potential.

'Ow.' The girl squirmed.

'We'll be done in five minutes,' Ethan said, grinning at her.

'Ugh, you said that ten minutes ago.' She laughed. Like with all his customers, he'd established a good repartee with her, telling jokes and chatting to keep her mind off of the discomfort. She smiled at him and Ethan knew the look of invitation.

Rock star without the music, he thought. Though the notion did little to amuse him as it once did. In fact, no woman drew his interest like Alexis. She was his everything.

Their shop was in downtown San Francisco, just like he'd planned. They'd hired a piercer. Joe didn't always show up to work on time and he sometimes flirted too heavily with the female customers, but he was good at his job and it was working out rather well.

The shop was small, but clean. Greg had airbrushed the walls with skulls, hearts, flames, alien heads, lotus flowers and coy fish, until almost the whole place was covered with artwork. There was some flash on the walls – not as much as he would've liked, but enough to get started with. Whatever he didn't have he could draw.

Fast-tempo music pumped over the speaker system. The system was hooked up to his laptop. He had files set to reflect whatever mood the shop was in – be it heavy metal, alternative, or hits from the 70s and 80s. Alexis always tried to turn the volume down when no one was looking.

Ethan pulled his tattoo machine back and examined the design. 'We're all done.'

'Oh, cool.' The girl jumped up and went to the mirror. He smiled, barely listening as she gushed over how perfect it was and how much she loved it. His answers were automatic and by the time she left the shop she seemed more than satisfied with her choice.

The phone rang and he heard Greg answer, 'Cross-Country Tattoo. This is Greg.'

Ethan cleaned up his station and washed his hands. He heard Greg talking to Joe. Apparently, Joe was going to be a little late again. He didn't have any piercing appointments, so Ethan merely nodded.

'Tell him he's fired.' Alexis grinned down at him from her ladder. She was hanging large black and white photographs from their cross-country trip along the top edge of the wall. Most of them were landscapes. There was one of him sitting in his car, one of Susan holding Ted in a headlock. She'd even hung the sketch he did of her in Colorado.

'Want to get lunch?' Ethan asked, his eyes drifting to her butt. She looked sexy in the faded blue jeans and the tight black shirt. She'd cut her hair. The short bangs made her look trendy and hip, almost like the girls in tattoo magazines. Well, only Alexis didn't have tattoos and piercings.

'Uh, yeah,' she answered, reaching to hook the frame on a nail.

Ethan went back to his station and grabbed his wallet from the drawer.

'Why don't you go get it?' Ethan said to Greg.

'Cool,' Greg answered. 'I made three appointments for tomorrow and that package is over by the phone. It doesn't look like gloves.'

'It's probably a supply catalogue or something,' Ethan said.

Greg reached behind him and tossed the envelope at Ethan. Ethan caught it and slipped it under his arm.

He handed the man a twenty-dollar bill and looked up at Alexis. 'Take your time.'

Greg winked, picked up the money and left. As the door closed, the man said, 'Don't do anything I wouldn't do.'

Ethan moved to lock the front door, flipping a sign that read, 'We'll be back in ten minutes.'

Alexis came up behind Ethan, grinning as he stared out at the hilly streets of downtown San Francisco. It was summertime and tourist season. A bright-red trolley came by, so packed full of people that some were hanging onto the outside.

'Hum, what do you think you're doing closing the door so early?' she asked, slipping her arms around his waist. An envelope was in her way. 'What's this?'

He turned around and handed it to her. As she flipped it around to read the address label, he backed her towards the privacy of the employee lounge. The walls were grey and unfinished. It looked like someone had started to paint a rose, but it had yet to be finished. There was a television and DVD player, an old coffee table that was painted green. It clashed with the long blue couch and yellow chair. The room wasn't as glamorous as the front, but it was cosy.

'It's from Susan and Ted,' Alexis said.

'Open it.' Ethan kissed her neck, moaning. 'I've been thinking about doing this all morning. I don't think I'll ever get enough of you.'

Alexis giggled, trying to see what was in the envelope as she held it up behind his head. Ethan ran his hands over her body. 'Stop, I can't see what it is.'

Ethan moaned, took the envelope and opened it up. He pulled out a fancy card first. It was a wedding invitation. After Alexis's mother interrupted their trip, the couple had decided not to get married in Vegas. He smiled and handed it to her. The wedding was in Colorado along the Highway of Legends where Ted had proposed. The package was also stuffed full of wedding-dress brochures with a note from Susan saying, 'Help! I need to pick a dress.'

'Good for them,' he said softly.

Putting the card back in the envelope, he reached to pull Alexis back into his arms. He was so cute, even with the orange in his hair and the newly added labret piercing in his chin. At least it was a ball and not a spike like Joe the piercer wore. 'Mm, and good for me. The publisher liked the cross-country book idea. They called while you were tattooing. They're going to publish my work.'

'I knew they would.' Ethan smiled.

Alexis grinned. Life was perfect. It had been hard at first, but she was happy – even without the designer clothing and the fancy apartments. She had Ethan and he was everything she could ever want.

Epilogue

The tattoo shop prospered and Ethan hired more full-time artists to help keep up with the booming business. Alexis's book is set to be released next year and she landed her first art show at a very fine San Francisco gallery.

Francine Grant disowned her daughter for about six months. However, after receiving an anonymous tip about Alexis's impending success with her new photographic collection, she paid Ethan and Alexis a visit in San Francisco to make amends. She tried to redecorate their apartment. Alexis said no. Ethan still denies that he sent the postcard to Francine telling her about the show in the first place. Suspiciously, though, it was in his handwriting.

Susan made a beautiful bride. Alexis helped pick out the gown. It wasn't the most expensive on the rack, but it was gorgeous with its box pleat silk organza skirt and strapless bodice. The faux diamond band around the waist was the only adornment.

Alexis's cognac taffeta halter gown with the rust sash was a great complement to her rounder frame. Living with Ethan, she didn't diet as much. She even learned to appreciate the many fine ways to dress a hot dog. Ted and Ethan wore tuxedos. Naturally, they both complained about it, but looked devilishly handsome all the same.

The wedding was simple, by the mountains near where Ted proposed. The weather couldn't have been more perfect. Susan and Ted said their vows at sunset. The gathering was small, made up of Susan and Ted's families and a few friends. Someone played music in a CD player as they danced over the grassy valley well into the night.

There, under the full moon and a sprinkling of stars, Ethan proposed on bended knee. Seeing how well everything had turned out for the four of them, he figured the Pekingese was right. The place was lucky. Alexis said yes. They are still madly in love.

THE
INVESTIGATION

By the same author

The Marat/Sade (a play)

Leavetaking and *Vanishing Point* (two novels)

The Conversation of the Three Walkers and *The Shadow of the Coachman's Body* (two novels)

Discourse on Vietnam (a play)

Notes on the Cultural Life of the Democratic Republic of Vietnam (essays)

THE INVESTIGATION

Peter Weiss

Oratorio in 11 Cantos

English Version by Alexander Gross

MARION BOYARS
LONDON • NEW YORK

Re-issued in Great Britain and the United States in 2012
by Marion Boyars Publishers Ltd
26 Parke Road, London SW13 9NG

www.marionboyars.co.uk

First published in Great Britain in 1966 by Calder and Boyars Ltd.
Reprinted 1982, 1996, 2005, 2012, 2015, 2020
10 9 8 7

© Suhrkamp Verlag, Berlin, Germany
© Translation Marion Boyars Publishers Ltd, 1966, 1982, 1996, 2005,
2012, 2015, 2020

10 digit ISBN 0-7145-0301-0
13 digit ISBN 978-0-7145-0301-1

A CIP catalogue record for this book is available from the British Library

Printed and bound in Great Britain by the CPI Group

AUSCHWITZ I

(Original Camp)

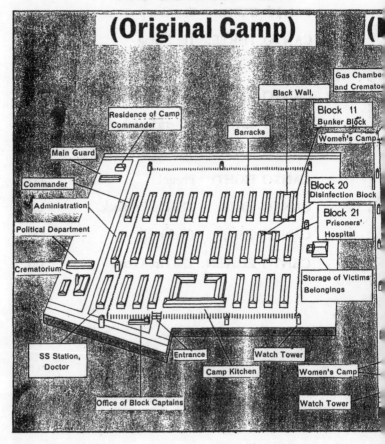

Gas Chamber and Crematorium

Black Wall,

Block 11 Bunker Block

Barracks

Women's Camp

Residence of Camp Commander

Main Guard

Block 20 Disinfection Block

Commander

Block 21 Prisoners' Hospital

Administration

Political Department

Crematorium

Storage of Victims' Belongings

SS Station, Doctor

Entrance

Watch Tower

Camp Kitchen

Women's Camp

Office of Block Captains

Watch Tower

AUSCHWITZ II
ermination Camp Birkenau)

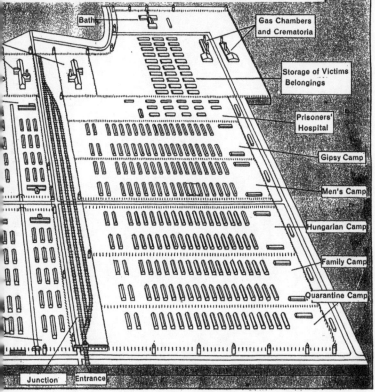

Bath

Gas Chambers and Crematoria

Storage of Victims Belongings

Prisoners' Hospital

Gipsy Camp

Men's Camp

Hungarian Camp

Family Camp

Quarantine Camp

Junction Entrance

The Investigation was first presented as a play simultaneously in thirteen theatres in both East and West Germany on October 19th 1965 and had a public midnight reading by the Royal Shakespeare Company under the direction of Peter Brook that same night at the Aldwych Theatre, London.

CHARACTERS

JUDGE

COUNSEL FOR THE PROSECUTION
representing the Public Prosecutor
and the Co-Plaintiff *

COUNSEL FOR THE DEFENCE

DEFENDANTS 1 - 18
representing actual people

WITNESSES 1 - 9
representing successively quite
diverse and anonymous witnesses

* One of the most interesting aspects of the Auschwitz trials in Frankfurt was the presence of
a legal emissary from East Germany, whom the author here refers to as the co-plaintiff.

Translator.

REMARKS

In presenting this play no attempt should be made to reconstruct the courtroom before which the deliberations over the camp actually took place. Such a representation seems just as impossible to the author as a representation of the camp on stage would be.

Hundreds of witnesses appeared before the Court of Justice. The confrontation of witnesses and defendants, like the speeches for and against, was loaded to the breaking point with emotional power.

From all this only the central core of the evidence can remain on stage.

This can contain nothing but the facts as they came to be expressed in words during the course of the trial. The personal experiences and confrontations must be softened into anonymity. Which means that the witnesses in the play lose their names and become little more than megaphones. The nine witnesses report only what hundreds expressed. The different experiences can be at most indicated by alterations in voice and posture.

Witnesses 1 and 2 are witnesses who sided with the camp authorities.

Witnesses 4 and 5 are female witnesses, the others being male, from among the ranks of the surviving prisoners.

Each of the 18 Defendants represents a definite person. They bear names that are taken over from the actual trial. That they have their own names is significant, for they also bore their names during the time that is the subject of this hearing, while the prisoners had lost their names.

But in the play it is not the bearers of the names who should once again be accused. They lend the author only their names, which here stand as symbols for a system which conferred guilt on those many others who never appeared before this court. For the purpose of stage production an interval can be inserted after the Sixth Canto.

Canto One: THE LOADING RAMP

I

JUDGE:	Herr Witness
	You were the head of the railway station
	where the shipments arrived
	How far was the station from the camp
WITNESS I:	A mile from the old barracks
	and about 3 miles from the main camp
JUDGE:	Did you work in the camps
WITNESS I:	No
	I was only supposed to make sure
	the train lines were in order
	and that trains came in and out
	according to time-table
JUDGE:	What condition were the lines in
WITNESS I:	They were in extremely good condition
	very well laid-out tracks
JUDGE:	Did you have anything to do
	with arranging the time-tables
WITNESS I:	No
	I was only supposed to take care
	of the technical details
	connected with the shuttle service
	between the station and the camp
JUDGE:	The court is in possession
	of time-table forms signed by you
WITNESS I:	Maybe once it happened I had
	to sign them on someone else's behalf
JUDGE:	Were you aware of the purpose
	of these shipments
WITNESS I:	That was outside of my field
JUDGE:	You knew the trains were loaded with people
WITNESS I:	We were told only

	that it had to do with resettling
	people who were under the protection
	of the State
JUDGE:	And the empty trains
	coming back so regularly
	you didn't think about that
WITNESS I:	They sent the people off to resettle there
PROSECUTOR:	Herr Witness
	you have today a leading position
	in the direction of the government railways
	We can assume therefore
	that you are familiar with questions
	of fitting out and loading trains
	How were the trains arriving at your station
	fitted out and loaded
WITNESS I:	These were freight trains
	That means the bills of lading
	were for about 60 people per car in transit
PROSECUTOR:	Were these freight cars
	or cattle cars
WITNESS I:	There were also cars
	used for shipping cattle
PROSECUTOR:	Were there sanitary arrangements
	in these cars
WITNESS I:	I couldn't tell you
PROSECUTOR:	How often did these trains arrive
WITNESS I:	I really can't say
PROSECUTOR:	Did they come frequently
WITNESS I:	Yes of course
	It was an important terminus
PROSECUTOR:	Didn't you notice
	that the shipments came
	from almost every country in Europe
WITNESS I:	We were so busy
	we couldn't bother
	with that sort of thing
PROSECUTOR:	Didn't you ask yourself
	what was going to happen
	to all those evacuees

WITNESS 1:	They were supposed to be sent on work assignments
PROSECUTOR:	But there weren't just workers there were whole families with old people and children
WITNESS 1:	I didn't have any time to check what was in the train
PROSECUTOR:	Where were you living
WITNESS 1:	In the village
PROSECUTOR:	Who else was living there
WITNESS 1:	The village was cleared of its original inhabitants Officers of the camp lived there and personnel from the factories
PROSECUTOR:	What kind of factories
WITNESS 1:	There were branches of IG Farben Company and Krupp and Siemens
PROSECUTOR:	Did you see any prisoners working there
WITNESS 1:	I saw them coming and going to work
PROSECUTOR:	What was their condition
WITNESS 1:	They marched in step and they sang
PROSECUTOR:	You learned nothing about conditions in the camp
WITNESS 1:	You heard a lot of nonsense but you never knew what to make of it
PROSECUTOR:	You heard nothing about people being exterminated
WITNESS 1:	How could anyone believe something like that
JUDGE:	Herr Witness You were responsible for the goods trains
WITNESS 2:	I was only supposed to hand over the trains to the people in the shunting yard
JUDGE:	And what were their duties
WITNESS 2:	They put on the switching engine and took the train to the camp

13

JUDGE:	According to your estimate how many people were in a goods wagon
WITNESS 2:	I can't tell you that It was strictly forbidden to examine the trains
JUDGE:	Who stopped you
WITNESS 2:	The guards
JUDGE:	Was there a bill of lading for each shipment
WITNESS 2:	There were rarely any documents Only chalk figures written on the cars
JUDGE:	What sort of figures
WITNESS 2:	60 or 80 sometimes depending
JUDGE:	When did the trains arrive
WITNESS 2:	Usually at night
PROSECUTOR:	What impression did you have of these carloads
WITNESS 2:	I don't understand the question
PROSECUTOR:	Herr Witness you are an Inspector for the railway and know something about travel conditions Did nothing you saw through the hatches or heard from the goods wagons tell you that something was amiss
WITNESS 2:	Once I saw a woman who held a little child near the air hatch and cried out incessantly for water I went for a can of water and wanted to give it to her As I held it up to her a guard came along and said If I didn't go away at once I would be shot
JUDGE:	Herr Witness How many trains do you estimate came to the station

14

WITNESS 2:	On an average I'd say one a day
	When things got rushed
	there might be two or three
JUDGE:	How long were the trains
WITNESS 2:	They could be 60 cars
JUDGE:	Herr Witness
	were you ever in the camp
WITNESS 2:	I went along once with the switching engine
	because there was something to discuss
	about a bill of lading
	Right behind the entrance tower
	I left the train and went into the office
	I almost didn't make it out again
	because I had no permit
JUDGE:	What did you see of the camp
WITNESS 2:	Nothing
	I was happy to get out again
JUDGE:	Did you see the chimneys
	at the end of the ramp
	and smoke and the glare of fire
WITNESS 2:	Yes
	I saw smoke
JUDGE:	What did you make of it
WITNESS 2:	I thought
	those were the bakeries
	They told me
	bread was baked by night and day
	It was a very big camp

CANTO ONE: THE LOADING RAMP

II

WITNESS 3:	We travelled for five days
	On the second day
	we went through our provisions
	There were 89 people in the car

15

along with suitcases and bundles
We performed our necessities
in the straw
Many of us were ill
8 were dead
At the stations we could watch
through the airholes
how the guards were being given
food and coffee
by girls in uniform
Our children had stopped crying
The last night we turned off
the main track onto a siding
We travelled through a flat area
that was lit up by searchlights
We came closer to a long building
shaped like a barn
There was a vaulted gate beneath a tower
Before we went through the gate
the engine gave a whistle
The train stopped
The car doors were pulled open
Prisoners in striped clothing appeared
and shouted
Come on hurry hurry
It was six feet down
to the gravel on the ground
The old and disabled fell together
on the sharp stones
The corpses and the baggage
were thrown out
Then we heard a command
Leave everything there
Women and children over here
Men on the other side
I lost my family before my eyes
Everywhere people were calling
to their families
They were driven along with sticks

Watchdogs were barking
From the towers searchlights
and machine guns were trained on us
At the end of the ramp the sky
was coloured red
The air was full of smoke
The air was singed and sickly sweet
We came to know this smoke

FEMALE WITNESS 4: I could still hear my husband
calling after me
They lined us up
and we were not allowed
to change places
There were a hundred of us
women and children
We stood in rows five abreast
Then we had to pass a group
of officers
One of them held out his hand
and pointed left and right
The old women and children
went off to the left
I went to the right
The others had to cross
the tracks to a road
For an instant I saw my mother
with the children
I was glad
and felt we would soon find
each other again
A woman next to me said
they would go to a camp of mercy
She pointed to the lorries
that were standing on the road
and to a Red Cross vehicle
We saw
them loaded onto the lorry
and were happy they could ride
We had to go on foot

                                    along the marshy roads
FEMALE WITNESS 5: I held my sister-in-law's child by the hand
                                    She had her smallest in her arms
                                    One of the prisoners came up to me
                                    and asked if the child was mine
                                    When I answered No
                                    he said give it to its mother
                                    I did so thinking
                                    she might receive better treatment
                                    They all went to the left
                                    I went to the right
                                    The officer who split us up
                                    was very friendly
                                    I asked where the other group was going
                                    and he replied
                                    They're just going to take a bath
                                    You'll see them again in an hour
JUDGE: Can you tell the court
                                    who this officer was
FEMALE WITNESS 5: I learned later
                                    that his name was Dr. Capesius
JUDGE: Could you point out
                                    Dr. Capesius
                                    among the Defendants
FEMALE WITNESS 5: It's difficult to tell
                                    from looking at their faces
                                    whether I recognise them
                                    But this gentleman
                                    looks very familiar
JUDGE: Who is he
FEMALE WITNESS 5: Doctor Capesius
DEFENDANT 3:   The witness must have me
                                    confused with someone else
                                    I never separated people
                                    on the ramp
WITNESS 6:   I knew Dr. Capesius
                                    from my home town
                                    I was a physician there
                                    and he often used

                                    18

	to visit me before the war
	as representative of the Bayer Company
	I said hello to him
	and asked what would happen to us
	He said
	everything would be alright
	I told him
	my wife wasn't feeling well
	Then she must stand over there
	he said
	She will be given care
	He pointed to the group
	of the old and infirm
	I said to my wife
	Go over there and stand in line
	She went with her niece
	and some other relatives
	to stand with the infirm
	They rode off in the van
JUDGE:	Are you sure
	It was Dr. Capesius
WITNESS 6:	Yes
	I was very happy
	to see him again
JUDGE:	Defendant Capesius
	Do you know this witness
DEFENDANT 3:	No
JUDGE:	Were you on the ramp
	when the shipments arrived
DEFENDANT 3:	I was only there
	to take medicine from the prisoners' baggage
	I kept it for them
	in the dispensary
JUDGE:	Herr Witness
	which of the other Defendants
	did you see on the ramp
WITNESS 6:	That one
	I know him
	His name is Hofmann

19

JUDGE:	Defendant Hofmann
	What were your duties on the ramp
DEFENDANT 8:	I had to keep law and order
JUDGE:	Precisely how did you do that
DEFENDANT 8:	We made the people wait in line
	Then the doctors decided
	who was fit to work
	and who could not
	Sometimes we needed more
	sometimes we needed less
	We got them
	There was a fixed quota
	It depended on our need
	for manpower
JUDGE:	What happened to those
	who weren't needed for work
DEFENDANT 8:	They were gassed
JUDGE:	What was the quota
	of those fit for work
DEFENDANT 8:	It averaged
	about a third of each shipment
	If the camp got overcrowded
	They were all despatched
JUDGE:	Did you yourself take charge
	of allocating people
DEFENDANT 8:	The only thing I can say
	is that I sometimes put
	the ones who couldn't work
	in with the others
	if they pressed and pestered me about it
JUDGE:	Were you allowed to do that
DEFENDANT 8:	No
	it was forbidden
	but people looked the other way
JUDGE:	Were extra rations given
	to workers on the ramp
DEFENDANT 8:	Yes
	there was bread
	a portion of sausage

	and half a pint of schnapps
JUDGE:	Did you ever have to use force
DEFENDANT 8:	There was always a great deal of confusion
	and naturally it was sometimes necessary
	to raise your voice
	or slap someone here and there
	I was only doing my duty
	Whatever my job is
	I only do my duty
JUDGE:	How did you come to the camp
DEFENDANT 8:	By accident
	That's how it happened
	My brother had a uniform left over
	that I could use myself
	That way I had no expenses
	It was more economical
	My father ran an inn
	and a lot of Party Members passed through
	When I was assigned to the camp
	I had no idea
	what I was getting into
	When I arrived I asked
	Am I in the right place
	And somebody said
	Here everybody's in the right place
PROSECUTOR:	Defendant Hofmann
	did you know what would happen
	to the people you separated
DEFENDANT 8:	Herr Prosecutor
	I personally had nothing
	against these people
	Why we even had them at home
	where I came from
	Before they were taken away
	I always said to my family
	Keep buying at the grocer's
	I mean they're people too
PROSECUTOR:	Did you still feel that way
	when you worked on the ramp

DEFENDANT 8: Well
apart from the minor abuses
you're sure to get
in that kind of life
when people are confined together
and apart from the gassings
which naturally were terrible
everyone still had the chance
to survive
I personally
always behaved decently
What was I supposed to do
Orders had to be obeyed
And now I have
this trial on my neck
Herr Prosecutor
I've lived a quiet life
just like everybody else
and then suddenly they grab me
and start yelling about Hofmann
There he is it's Hofmann
they shout
I just don't know
what they want from me

WITNESS 7: While we were waiting
One of the guards came and asked us
Is anybody ill
Some stepped forward
believing their duties would be lighter
and followed him to the left
As he led them away
there was a disturbance
and he shot into the crowd
5 or 6 were killed

JUDGE: Herr Witness
is the person you just mentioned
now in the courtroom

WITNESS 7: Your Honour
It's a long time

22

since I've been face to face with them
and I still find them
hard to look at
This one looks like him
it could be him
His name is Bischof

JUDGE: Are you sure
or are you in doubt

WITNESS 7: Your Honour
I didn't sleep last night

DEFENCE COUNSEL: We question the reliability
of the witness
It's obvious
that he merely recognises the man
from one of the widely circulated photographs
The witness is tired
How can we believe
what he says

JUDGE: Defendant Bischof
would you like to comment
on the accusation

DEFENDANT 15: It's a mystery to me
what the witness is talking about
I also don't understand
why the witness said
5 or 6
If he had said 5
or if he had said 6
that would be understandable

JUDGE: Did you have ramp duty

DEFENDANT 15: I was only supposed to regulate the batches
I never shot anyone
Your Honour
I really want to make
a clean breast of it
For years it's been gnawing at me
I am a sick man now
And now here's all this filthy mess
ruining the last days

	of my life
PROSECUTOR:	What does the Defendant
	mean by that
JUDGE:	The Defendant is excited
	He is certainly not referring
	to the proceedings
	instituted by the prosecutor
	The Defendants laugh
WITNESS 8:	When I was a prisoner
	I worked with the Quartermasters
	We had to take away their luggage
	when they arrived
	Defendant Baretzki
	worked on the ramp
	He took part in the selections
	and escorted the people
	to the crematorium
JUDGE:	Herr Witness
	do you recognise the Defendant
WITNESS 8:	He is Block Captain Baretzki
DEFENDANT 13:	I was only a guard
	No one of my rank
	ever did the separating
	A Block Captain never decided
	who was unfit for work
	Only a doctor could do that
JUDGE:	Did you know the purpose of the selection
DEFENDANT 13:	We found out about it
	I was disgusted
	Once on leave
	I told my mother
	She didn't want to believe it
	That isn't possible
	she said
	You can't burn human beings
	because flesh won't burn
WITNESS 8:	I saw
	how Baretzki pointed at people
	with his stick

You could never go fast enough for him
He always made them hurry
Once a train came in with 3,000 people
Most of them were ill
Baretzki shouted to us
You have 15 minutes time
to clear them out of the freight cars
While we were unloading
a child was born
I wrapped it in some pieces of clothing
and laid it by its mother
Baretzki came after me with the stick
and beat me and the woman as well
What are you doing with that shit
he shouted
and he kicked the baby
and sent it flying 30 feet
Then he ordered me
Bring that shit over here
And the child was dead

JUDGE: Herr Witness
Can you swear to this

WITNESS 8:   Yes I can swear to it
Baretzki had a special blow
He was known for it

JUDGE: What do you mean a special blow

WITNESS 8:   He hit people with the edge of his hand
Like this
Against the aorta
In most cases
this blow
caused death

DEFENDANT 13:   The witness just said
I had a stick
If I had a stick
then I wouldn't have needed
to hit people with my hand
And if I used my hand
then I wouldn't have needed a stick

Your Honour
this is slander
I never had any special blow
The Defendants laugh

CANTO ONE: THE LOADING RAMP

III

JUDGE: Herr Witness
who else did you see on the ramp

WITNESS 8: All the doctors were there
They were in charge
of the separating
Dr. Frank was there
Dr. Schatz and Dr. Lucas

DEFENCE COUNSEL: Herr Witness
where were you
during the separating

WITNESS 8: I was on various parts of the ramp
I was busy collecting baggage

DEFENCE COUNSEL: Can you describe
the ramp for us

WITNESS 8: The ramp was behind the entrance gate
the men's camp was to the right
the women's camp to the left
At the end of the ramp
were the new crematoria
numbers II and III
The trains came in from the switch
on the right hand side

DEFENCE COUNSEL: How long was the ramp

WITNESS 8: About 900 yards

DEFENCE COUNSEL: And the trains

WITNESS 8: They often took up
two-thirds of the length

DEFENCE COUNSEL: Where were the people separated

WITNESS 8:	In the middle of the ramp
DEFENCE COUNSEL:	Where did they stand
WITNESS 8:	Either on the upper section
	or else on the lower
DEFENCE COUNSEL:	How wide was the ramp
WITNESS 8:	About 30 feet
DEFENCE COUNSEL:	And the people stood there
	in two groups facing each other
	in rows of five abreast
	If this is so
	we doubt that it was possible
	to stand near the selecting officers
	with people working on the baggage all around
JUDGE:	Defendant Frank
	Did you take part in the separating
DEFENDANT 4:	I worked on the ramp
	but only as a substitute
	My job was to take dental equipment
	from incoming dentists
	for the camp clinic
	Then I had to register the dentists
	and nurses and issue clothing to them
	If anyone happened to come in
	and pretended he was a dentist
	I didn't let him be sent on
	We also needed
	cleaners
JUDGE:	Did you never apply
	to be relieved of ramp duty
DEFENDANT 4:	I once lodged a complaint
	with the chief physician Dr. Wirth
	The only answer I got was
	Camp Service is Front Service
	Refusal to serve
	will be punished as desertion
JUDGE:	Did you escort the people
	to the gas chambers
DEFENDANT 4:	No
	that was

	undertaken by the guards
	I personally did everything
	I could to be of assistance
	to the prisoners
	In my position
	I tried to make their stay
	as pleasant as possible
	They had special clean clothing
	and they didn't have
	their heads shaved
JUDGE:	Please tell the court Dr. Schatz
	Did you take part in the separating
DEFENDANT 5:	I never had anything to do with it
	When they ordered me to take
	medicine and doctors' equipment
	from the prisoners
	I did everything I could
	to get out of it
	I only came to the camp
	under compulsion
	I was detached
	from an army dental station
	I want to make it very clear
	that I was on extremely friendly terms
	with the prisoners
JUDGE:	Dr. Lucas
	What were your duties on the ramp
DEFENDANT 6:	I played no part in it whatsoever
	I told them again and again
	I am a doctor in order to save human life
	not to destroy it
	My Catholic faith would not allow it
	When they tried to force me
	I said I simply couldn't do it
	I pretended to be ill
	and tried to get back to the troops
	I went to my old Commander
	who told me
	I should do everything I could

to avoid attracting attention
On leave I even spoke
with an archbishop
and an important judge
Both said to me
immoral orders should not be carried out
but that I shouldn't go so far
as to put my own life in danger
after all it was wartime
and lots of things happened

PROSECUTOR: Dr. Lucas
What kind of illness
did you simulate
when you were ordered to serve

DEFENDANT 6: I pretended I had gallstones
or some kind of stomach trouble

PROSECUTOR: Did no one wonder
why you got your gallstones
whenever you came near the ramp

DEFENDANT 6: There was never any trouble
My passive resistance
was the only possible way
to have as little to do with these things
as I could
Even today I don't see
how I could have done
otherwise

PROSECUTOR: And when you had to serve
what did you do then

DEFENDANT 6: Only in three or four cases
my resistance didn't work
I was ordered to go out
on the ramp under threats
of immediate arrest
if I didn't obey the order
It was clear what that meant

PROSECUTOR: And so you took part in the separating

DEFENDANT 6: I was only supposed
to look for people

29

	who were able to work
	and I did it in such a way
	that many who couldn't work
	went with them just the same
PROSECUTOR:	And the others
DEFENDANT 6:	They were taken elsewhere
DEFENCE COUNSEL:	In no way can it be charged
	that this was managed in a criminal fashion
	if doctors on duty
	selected the prisoners for the camp
	All they did was to reduce
	the number of the victims
	by the number of those
	they considered able to work
PROSECUTOR:	What happened
	To the prisoners' baggage
	After the separations were carried out
WITNESS 8:	It was taken to the baggage depot
	where it was sorted and stored away
PROSECUTOR:	How large was the baggage depot
WITNESS 8:	At least 35 barracks
PROSECUTOR:	Can you give us some idea
	of the quantity and value
	of the goods collected there
WITNESS 8:	It so happened
	that the prisoners were advised
	before deportation to bring
	as many useful items as possible
	underwear clothing money and tools
	on the pretext
	that nothing would be available
	where they were being resettled
	They all brought as much as they could carry
	Much of this was taken away immediately
	during the sorting on the ramp
	The doctors who did the separating
	took not only necessary items
	but also money and pieces of jewellery
	which they put away for themselves

30

in great quantity
Then the guards
and the people from the train
took theirs also
There was even something left over for us
that we could trade among ourselves later on
The total value
of the baggage depot
amounted to many millions

PROSECUTOR: Herr Witness
can you give the court a notion
of the precise value
of the goods taken from the prisoners

WITNESS 8: According to a final report
based on the time
from April 1, 1942 to December 15, 1943
the total value of confiscated money
foreign currency precious metals
and jewellery
amounted to 132 million marks
not counting 1900 car loads of clothing
valued at 46 million
And this was a year
before the largest shipments

PROSECUTOR: Who received these valuables

WITNESS 8: The goods were sent
to the National Bank
or rather to the National Finance Ministry
The jewellery was melted down
The watches were distributed
among the troops

JUDGE: Was there never any resistance
on the ramp
In terms of numbers the prisoners
had a considerable advantage over the guards
They were separated from their families
Their possessions were taken from them
Did they never struggle

WITNESS 9: They never struggled

JUDGE:	Why didn't they
WITNESS 9:	The prisoners were hungry
	and exhausted
	They only hoped
	that they were coming at last
	to a resting place
JUDGE:	Had they any idea
	of what was before them
WITNESS 9:	How were they to imagine
	that for all practical purposes
	they no longer existed
	Everyone of them believed
	that he could survive

Canto Two: THE CAMP

I

FEMALE WITNESS 4: When we had crossed the tracks
and were waiting
at the entrance to the camp
I heard
a prisoner say to a woman
The Red Cross van is only used
to carry gas to the crematoria
Your family will be killed
The woman began to scream
A guard who had overheard her
came up and said
But my dear lady
how can you believe a prisoner
They're nothing but criminals
and lunatics
Don't you see his prominent ears
his shaven head
How can you listen to such people

JUDGE: Please tell the court
can you remember
who the officer was

FEMALE WITNESS 4: I saw him again later
I worked as a clerk under him
in the Political Department
His name is Broad

JUDGE: Can you point out Defendant Broad to us

FEMALE WITNESS 4: This is Herr Broad
Defendant 16 gives the witness a
friendly nod

JUDGE: What happened to the prisoner

FEMALE WITNESS 4: I heard he was sentenced

	to be flogged
	150 blows
	for spreading rumours
	He died from it
JUDGE:	Defendant Broad
	have you anything to say about that
DEFENDANT 16:	I remember no such case
	No one ever hit a prisoner
	that many times
WITNESS 3:	Even though our baggage had been left behind
	and we had been separated
	from our families
	we still went through the gate
	and barbed wire without distrust
	We believed
	that our wives and children
	were being given something to eat
	and that we would soon see them again
	But then we saw hundreds
	of ragged forms
	thin as skeletons
	Our confidence fled
WITNESS 6:	One came up to us
	shouting
	Prisoners
	Do you see the smoke behind the barracks
	those are your wives and children
	Even for you
	who have entered the camp
	there is only one way out
	Through the gratings of the chimney
WITNESS 3:	We were driven into a washroom barracks
	Guards and prisoners came
	with bundles of papers
	We had to undress
	And everything we still had
	was taken from us
	Our rings identity cards and photos
	were listed on registration forms

34

Next we had a number
tattooed on the left forearm

JUDGE: How was the tattooing done

WITNESS 3: They stuck the numbers in the flesh
with the point of a needle
then ink was rubbed in
Our hair was shaved off
and they put us under cold showers
Finally we were provided with clothes

JUDGE: What kind of clothing was it

WITNESS 3: We had underpants that were full of holes
an undershirt
a tattered jacket
patchwork trousers
a cap
and a pair of wooden shoes
Then they ran us
to our block

JUDGE: What did the block look like

WITNESS 3: A wooden barracks without windows
A door in front and behind
A skylight beneath the slanting roof
Right and left bunks arranged in three tiers
The lowest bunk was on the naked ground
The bunks were mounted
between brick partitions
The barracks were roughly 120 feet long

JUDGE: How many prisoners were kept there

WITNESS 3: It was built for 500 men
There were a thousand of us

JUDGE: Were there many such barracks

WITNESS 3: Over 200

JUDGE: How wide were the wooden beds

WITNESS 3: About 6 feet wide
There were 6 men to a bunk
They had to alternate sleeping
on their right and left sides

JUDGE: Was there straw or blankets

WITNESS 3: Many beds had straw

35

The straw was rotten
The straw from the upper bunk
trickled down to the lower bunk
For each bed there was one blanket
Everyone pulled at it
first the one on the outside
and then the next
The strongest slept in the middle

JUDGE: Were the barracks heated

WITNESS 3: There were 2 iron stoves
From the stoves pipes ran out
to the chimney in the middle
The pipes were boxed in
to form a table
The stoves were seldom warm

JUDGE: What were the sanitary conditions like

WITNESS 3: In the barracks there was a wooden vat
for washing
with a perforated iron pipe above
Water trickled from the pipe
In the latrine were long concrete basins
There were boards on top with round openings
200 people could sit down at once
The latrine guard made sure
that no one sat too long
They beat the prisoners
with sticks
to chase them away
Many couldn't make it quick enough
and left the seats exhausted
with their intestines hanging down
If they were driven off
they had to sit down again
and wait their turn
There was no paper
Many ripped off shreds of their clothing
in order to wipe themselves
or stole pieces
from each other's uniforms at night

to have a supply
You had to settle your needs
in the morning
There was no possibility during the day
Anyone caught at it
was thrown into the cellar
The dirty water from the barracks
ran through the latrines
to flush the excrement away
Very often there were blockages
because the water pressure was insufficient
Then the Shit Commandos would come
to suck the rubbish out
The stink of the latrines
mingled with the stench
of smoke

FEMALE WITNESS 4: We were given bowls
which served a threefold purpose
To wash
To take our soup
And to perform our nightly needs
In the women's camp
the only source of water
was right next to the latrines
By the thin stream
that ran amidst the excrement
the women stood and drank
and tried
to run some water into their bowls
Those who gave up washing
gave up life as well

FEMALE WITNESS 5: As soon as I jumped out of the freight car
into the milling crowd on the ramp
I knew
that here it was everyone for himself
you had to resign yourself to your superiors
and make a favourable impression
you had to hold yourself apart from everything
that could pull you down

When we were left by the desk
in the reception room
and they hunted for hidden valuables
in our rectums and sexual organs
the last remains of our usual lives
were left behind us
Families homes professions and possessions
these were concepts
that were obliterated by the tattooed number
And we already began to live
for new concepts
and to find our places in a new world
which for those of us
who wanted to exist in it
became the normal world
The most important law
was to remain healthy
and to show bodily strength
I kept close to those
who were too weak to eat their rations
so as to take them
at the first opportunity
I waited in ambush
when someone with a better sleeping place
was about to die
Our advancement in the new society
began in the barracks
that were now our home
From a sleeping place on the cold ground
we fought our way upwards
to the warm places in the upper bunks
When two had to eat from the same bowl
they stared at each other's gullets
to make sure
the other swallowed not a single spoonful more
Our ambitions
were directed towards a single goal
to win the slightest bit of anything
It was perfectly normal

that everything was stolen from us
It was perfectly normal
that we stole the same things back
Dirt wounds and pestilence all around
this was perfectly normal
It was normal
that the dead were on every side
and the immediate prospect
of one's own death
was normal
The dying away of our feelings
was normal as was our indifference
to finding corpses
It was normal
that there were those among us
who helped our overseers
to use the stick
Whoever became the servant
of the Block Warden
no longer belonged to the lowest
and she went even higher
who could insinuate herself
among the Block Leaders
Only the cunning could survive
those who could conquer their foothold
of ground anew each day
with unceasing vigilance
The unfit
the dull-spirited
the gentle
the bewildered and the impractical
the grief-stricken and the self-pitiful
were crushed underfoot

WITNESS 6:   On the first morning
we were standing for roll call
It was raining
We stood for several hours
and saw
behind the barbed wire

39

on the other side of the ramp
women were being beaten into the vans
They were naked
and were screaming to us men
They expected help from us
but we just stood there and trembled
and couldn't help them

FEMALE WITNESS 4: I came into a barracks
that was full of bodies
Suddenly I saw
something moving among the dead
It was a young girl
I took her out onto the street
and asked her
Who are you
How long have you been here
I don't know
she said
Why are you lying here among the dead
I asked
And she said
I can no longer be among the living
In the evening she was dead

FEMALE WITNESS 5: We had to dig graves
Many women collapsed
beneath their shovels filled with clay
We stood in the water up to our waists
The guards watched us
They were very young
A woman went up to the leader
Herr Captain
she cried
I can't work this way
I'm pregnant
The people laughed
and one of them held her
under the water with his shovel
until she drowned

WITNESS 7: I heard

a guard amusing himself
through the barbed wire
with a nine-year old boy
You already know a great deal for your age
said the man
The boy replied
I know that I already know a lot
and I also know
that I shall never learn anything else
He was together with a group
of about 90 children
who were loaded into the vans
As the children were struggling
the boy shouted
Just get into the car
don't scream like that
haven't you seen how
your parents and grandparents
went away
Just get in
then you'll see them again
And as they drove off
I heard
the boy cry out to the guard again
You're not going to get away with this

CANTO TWO: THE CAMP

II

WITNESS 8: Every morning each prisoner received
a pint of broth
containing a coffee substitute
We each got a fifth of an ounce of sugar
Many still had a piece of dry bread
left from the night before
At noon they ladled out

a bowl of camp soup
made from potato peels
turnips and cabbage
with the smallest shred
of meat or fat
and the starchy things in it
that gave the soup the taste
of camp soup
There were also rags and strips of paper
in the soup
When they ladled it out
we all fought
not to be the first with our bowls
but to be last
The first third of the soup
was nothing but water
Underneath you might find something
nourishing floating around
In the evenings after roll call
each prisoner was given
from ten to twelve ounces of bread
and various extras
less than an ounce of sausage
one ounce of margarine
or a tablespoon of turnip marmalade
On some Fridays
we got five or six potatoes
in their skins
Often we only got half of the extras
or they ran out of them altogether
because the officers
from the guards on up to the commanders
freely took supplies
from the camp store room

PROSECUTOR: Herr Witness
how many calories
did an average day's food contain

WITNESS 8:   From 1,000 to 1,300 calories
In a state of rest

the human body can function
with 1,700 calories
A heavy labourer needs about 4,800
Everyone was a heavy labourer there
so the last reserves of strength
were soon used up
With each new stage of hunger
the movements became slower
No more strength was left
even to carry one's own body
Apathy and drowsiness
were typical symptoms
of weakness
The wasting away of the body
was accompanied by mental exhaustion
which led to a complete loss
of interest in events
Such a prisoner could no longer
concentrate his thoughts
His memory faded so far
that he often could no longer
tell you his own name
On the average a prisoner
could live no longer than 3 or 4 months

DEFENCE COUNSEL: Herr Witness
how is it possible
that you yourself survived

WITNESS 8: The only ones who could survive
were those who during the first week
asked for some kind of internal duties
because of some skill they possessed
or those who were appointed
to one job or another
For a prisoner
who knew how to use
his abilities
it was possible to obtain
almost everything in the camp

DEFENCE COUNSEL: What kind of special position

43

	did you have
WITNESS 8:	I was a doctor
	at first in the quarantine station
	later in the hospital
JUDGE:	What were conditions like
WITNESS 8:	In the quarantine station there were rats
	they nibbled away not only at the corpses
	but at those who were gravely ill as well
	The feet of those who lay in agony
	were often bitten by morning
	At night the animals would go after bread
	in the pockets of the prisoners
	Often people accused each other
	You stole my bread from me
	But it was the rats
	Millions of fleas
	infested the camp
	Anyone who had boots gave them away
	because the vermin spoiled the pleasure
	of owning such a luxury
	People who had only socks and rags
	could at least scratch themselves
	In the prisoners' hospital it was better
	There we had bandages of crepe paper
	some cotton-wool
	a barrel of ointment
	and a barrel of chalk
	All wounds were painted with ointment
	and for barber's rash we put on chalk
	so you couldn't see it any more
	We even had a couple of aspirin tablets
	hung on a thread
	Patients with fever under a hundred
	got to lick them once
	Patients with fever over a hundred
	were allowed to lick them twice
JUDGE:	What were the most frequent diseases
WITNESS 8:	Aside from general weakness
	and damage to bodies through mistreatment

44

we had spotted fever and paratyphus
Stomach typhus erysipelas and tuberculosis
as well as the usual camp illness
an incurable form of diarrhoea
Boils really bloomed in the camp
Often the guards beat the sores
with their sticks
until the flesh peeled down to the bone
I saw illnesses in the camp
that I never believed
I would ever have to see
Diseases
that one only reads about in textbooks
There was Noma
a disease that only appears
among completely debilitated beings
It eats holes in the cheeks
and you can look through and see the teeth
Or Phemphicus
a rarely encountered disease
in which the skin peels off
in blisters
ending in death after a few days

WITNESS 9: After the evening roll call
the head of the block
selected some of us to amuse him
We had to leap like frogs
Leap faster leap faster
he cried
and when one of us couldn't keep up
he beat him to a pulp with a footstool

JUDGE: What was the name of this official

WITNESS 9: His name was Bednarek
and I can point him out to you

DEFENDANT 18: I know absolutely nothing
about anyone being beaten
during the exercise session

JUDGE: Can you describe these exercises

DEFENDANT 18: Prisoners who felt like it

45

	had to carry out simple body movements
	first to the left
	then to the right
	That's all
WITNESS 9:	In winter Bednarek
	made prisoners stand under the cold shower
	for half an hour
	until they were cold all over and freezing
	Then they were thrown out into the yard
	where they died
DEFENDANT 18:	These accusations are wild inventions
	I couldn't do anything like that
	I myself was only a prisoner in charge
	I was an underling
	The Chief Inspector
	the Labour Service Leader
	and the presiding officers of the camp
	were all above me
	I myself
	and I can say this today with pride
	I let fellow prisoners in my block
	catch up on their sleep
	In our block in the evenings
	we always had a lot of fun
WITNESS 9:	If Bednarek
	had beaten a prisoner
	he went inside his cubby hole
	and prayed
DEFENDANT 18:	Yes I'm a god-fearing man
	That's what I am
	But I never dared to pray
	There were too many informers
	And I never beat anyone to death
	At the most I would slap someone
	occasionally
	when I had to settle a quarrel
WITNESS 3:	Of all the people in the camp there was one
	who was always to the fore
	whenever people were beaten and killed

46

	His name was Kaduk
	Kaduk was a byword
JUDGE:	Herr Witness
	Can you point out
	Defendant Kaduk for us
WITNESS 3:	This is Herr Kaduk
	Defendant 7 grins at the witness
	Kaduk was called the Professor
	by the prisoners
	or
	The Holy Doctor Kaduk
	because he independently took charge
	of separating people
	With the handle of his cane
	he would pull a victim out
	by the neck or the leg
DEFENDANT 7:	Your Honour
	This statement is untrue
WITNESS 3:	I was there
	when Kaduk brought hundreds
	of prisoners from the infirmary
	They had to take off their clothes
	in the washroom
	and run past Kaduk in a row
	He held his cane before him
	about a yard above the ground
	The prisoners had to jump over it
	Whoever touched the stick
	was sent to be gassed
	Whoever made it over the stick
	was beaten until he collapsed
	Now jump again
	cried Kaduk
	and the second time
	the man could no longer make it
DEFENDANT 7:	I never separated prisoners
	I never decided anything
	I wasn't responsible for it
JUDGE:	What were you responsible for

47

DEFENDANT 7:	I was only supposed to keep guard
	During the separations
	I had to watch them like a fox
	to make sure that none of those
	who had been separated
	changed over to the other group again
JUDGE:	Did you also do work on the ramp
DEFENDANT 7:	Yes
	I was supposed
	to regulate traffic
JUDGE:	How did you do that
DEFENDANT 7:	Everybody out
	Baggage on the ground
	Form ranks of five
	Forward march
WITNESS 3:	Kaduk shot at random
	into the people
DEFENDANT 7:	To shoot at random
	would never have occurred to me
	If I'd wanted to shoot
	I would have hit
	anyone I aimed at
	I was a pretty good shot
	I can tell you that
	But I only did
	what I had to
JUDGE:	And what did you have to do
DEFENDANT 7:	Make sure things were running smoothly
	Children were sent out right away
	as a matter of principle
	also mothers who refused to be separated
	from their children
	Everything went smoothly
	The shipments moved along
	like bread out of the oven
	There was no need to use force
	They accepted everything quietly
	They didn't struggle
	because they realised

48

	that all resistance
	had become senseless
WITNESS 6:	Once Kaduk was beating someone up
	in our work battalion
	He hooked the cane around his neck
	held on to both ends
	and rocked him back and forth
	until the man was strangled
DEFENDANT 7:	Lies lies
JUDGE:	Sit back Kaduk
	Don't shout at the witness
DEFENDANT 7:	Your Honour

what has been said
simply isn't true
I'm only concerned with the truth
We never killed prisoners
in this manner
We had orders
to deal gently
with the skilled workers
But I remember one of them
he would topple over
if I just raised my hand to him
He was only pretending
   The Defendants laugh
Your Honour
We had absolutely no interest
in beating people
We were on our feet from 5.30 in the morning
and in the evening we still
had to serve ramp duty
That was more than enough
Your Honour
all I want to do is live in peace
That's what I've done these past years
I've been working as a male nurse
and I am loved by all my patients
They can bear witness to it
Papa Kaduk they call me

Doesn't that say everything
Am I now supposed to suffer
for what I had to do then
Everybody else did the same
Why are you picking on me

CANTO TWO: THE CAMP

III

FEMALE WITNESS 4: The more successful you were
in pushing down your inferiors
the more secure your own position became
I saw how the Block Captain's face
would change if she spoke
with a superior officer
then she was gay and friendly
but you knew she was really frightened
Sometimes she was treated by the overseer
as the best of friends
and enjoyed many privileges
But if her superior slept badly
then the privileges
could go tumbling down
from one moment to the next
She had already endured everything
her family shot down before her eyes
they made her watch
while they murdered her children
She was worn blunt like the rest of us
she knew
that if she went under even once
no one would help her
and another in her place
would continue to beat us
So she beat us
because she wanted to stay on top

at any price

FEMALE WITNESS 5: The question
of what was right and what was wrong
no longer existed
For us the only thing that mattered
was what could be useful for the moment
Only our overlords were entitled
to have moods
and even show emotion
or pity
or plan for the future
The Camp Physician Dr. Rohde
let me work in his department
He found out
that we had studied in the same city
and he asked me
if we hadn't met at an inn
where he had drunk many glasses of wine
and I thought
if that's what you want
then why not
and I helped him to remember his youth
and he said
After the war we will go there
and sit down together
Dr. Mengele sent flowers to a pregnant woman
and the wife of the Commander
knitted a baby's jumper
and sent it to the children's barracks
where someone else had the idea
to paint pictures of dwarfs on the walls
and to bring in a sandbox
They would rake the roads
to the crematorium smooth
in between the batches
There were well-tended hedges
and flower beds laid out amidst the grass
above the subterranean chambers
Mengele came along in his dashing manner

hooking his thumbs
into his braces
Giving a friendly nod to the children
who used to call him Uncle
before they were cut to pieces
in his laboratory
There was also someone
named Flacke
In his department no one died of hunger
and the prisoners went around
in clean clothes
Herr Sanitary Inspector
I said to him
why are you doing what you're doing
we're all going to disappear anyway
there may not be a single witness left
And he said
there would be enough of us left
in order to prevent this

PROSECUTOR: You mean to tell the court
that it lay within the power
of every single guard to fight
against the conditions and to alter them

FEMALE WITNESS 5: That is precisely what I mean

WITNESS 1: You could only react normally
during your first hours in the camp
When you had been there any length of time
it was no longer possible
You were absorbed into the routine
you were in prison
and you had to make do

PROSECUTOR: Herr Witness
As a doctor you were in charge
of fighting against epidemics

WITNESS 1: Cases of spotted fever
and typhus had broken out
among the camp personnel and their families
I was assigned to the camp
on the orders

	of the Health Ministry
PROSECUTOR:	Then you weren't concerned
	with treating the prisoners
WITNESS 1:	No
PROSECUTOR:	Did you have a glimpse
	of conditions in the camp
WITNESS 1:	Directly after my arrival
	the Laboratory Chief said to me
	This is all new to you
	it isn't so bad
	We have nothing to do
	with the liquidation of men
	and it's none of our business anyway
	If after two weeks
	you no longer want to stay
	you can go away
	With the intention
	of leaving the camp after two weeks
	I went about my work
	After a few days the Head Physician
	Doctor Wirth ordered me to take part
	in the separations on the ramp
	When I explained
	that I wanted nothing to do with it
	he said
	there's not much to do there
	But I refused
PROSECUTOR:	What happened after your refusal
WITNESS 1:	Nothing happened
	I didn't have to do it
PROSECUTOR:	Did you leave the camp after two weeks
WITNESS 1:	I decided to stay on
	anyway
	to do something about the epidemics
	I saw that it was possible to do
	at least a little something here and there
	without exposing myself
	My profession made it necessary
	to overcome the danger of contagion

PROSECUTOR:	Among the camp personnel
	Not among the prisoners
WITNESS 1:	Yes
	That was my duty
JUDGE:	Herr Witness
	You were at that time responsible
	for the inner and outer sentry lines
	and also for the guards
	on the labour battalions
	What did you actually do
WITNESS 2:	My job was to make sure
	the soldiers stayed alert
	and kept their eyes open
JUDGE:	Did you have any rules to guide you
WITNESS 2:	If a prisoner tried to escape
	the soldier had to shout
	three times to him
	and then give a warning shot
	if the prisoner still didn't stop
	he had to shoot him until he did
JUDGE:	Were the prisoners shot dead
WITNESS 2:	Not in my section
JUDGE:	Did prisoners
	run into the high-tension wire
	surrounding the camp
WITNESS 2:	Not in my section
JUDGE:	But did it ever happen
WITNESS 2:	I heard about it sometimes
JUDGE:	Did the guards follow
	these instructions
WITNESS 2:	As far as I'm aware
	yes
	My word of honour
JUDGE:	Do you know anything
	about the cap-shootings
WITNESS 2:	About what
JUDGE:	About the cap-shootings
WITNESS 2:	I've heard about it
JUDGE:	What have you heard

54

WITNESS 2:	They used to tell about
	throwing their caps away
	and then they shot them
JUDGE:	Who threw the caps away
	What caps
	And who did the shooting
WITNESS 2:	I don't know
JUDGE:	Then what did they tell you
WITNESS 2:	Yes
	they would order a prisoner
	to take his cap off his head
	and throw it away
	and then they shouted
	alright
	run and get your cap
	and if he ran
	he was shot down
JUDGE:	And if he didn't run
WITNESS 2:	He was shot down anyway
	because that was disobedience to orders
PROSECUTOR:	Is it true that additional leave
	and extra rations
	were given as rewards
	for shooting down escaping prisoners
WITNESS 2:	I know of no such case
	I don't believe it either
	It would be contrary to a soldier's honour
	if he were rewarded for that sort of thing
PROSECUTOR:	The court is in possession of documents
	according to which in various cases
	guards were commended
	for shooting escaping prisoners
	Routine lists were displayed
	showing the names of prisoners
	who had been shot trying to escape
WITNESS 2:	I've never heard that before
PROSECUTOR:	According to our information
	you are now the director
	of an insurance company

DEFENCE COUNSEL:	We object
	to these irrelevant statements
	by the prosecution
PROSECUTOR:	We presume
	that you understand the significance
	of a personal signature
WITNESS 2:	Certainly
PROSECUTOR:	One of these lists
	was signed by you
WITNESS 2:	It is possible
	that I was obliged to do that sometimes
	as a matter of routine
	I can no longer
	recall it

Canto Three: THE SWING

I

JUDGE:	As a prisoner you worked in the Political Department What were your duties there
FEMALE WITNESS 5:	At first I was a shorthand-typist in the typing room then because of my knowledge of languages I became an interpreter
JUDGE:	Who did you work with
FEMALE WITNESS 5:	Herr Boger
JUDGE:	Tell the court do you recognise Defendant Boger
FEMALE WITNESS 5:	This is Herr Boger *Defendant 2 greets the witness* *in a friendly manner*
DEFENCE COUNSEL:	Where was the Political Department located
FEMALE WITNESS 5:	It was a wooden barracks behind the entrance
DEFENCE COUNSEL:	Behind which entrance
FEMALE WITNESS 5:	Straight to the left behind the entrance to the old barracks camp
DEFENCE COUNSEL:	How far was the old camp from the outer camp
FEMALE WITNESS 5:	About a mile and a half
DEFENCE COUNSEL:	Where did you live
FEMALE WITNESS 5:	In the women's camp
DEFENCE COUNSEL:	Can you give us a description of the road to your place of work
FEMALE WITNESS 5:	We had to leave the camp every morning and march along by the fields The road led over the railway embankment

The freight trains were being switched there
We often had to wait by the barrier
On the other side of the tracks
were more fields
and a couple of abandoned farms
Then we went through an iron gate
There were trees
and you passed by the old crematorium
The Political Department stood facing it

DEFENCE COUNSEL: Was the Political Department
inside the camp itself

FEMALE WITNESS 5: It was outside the concentration camp
First came the administration buildings
then the double barbed wire
and the watch towers
Beyond them were the blocks of prisoners

DEFENCE COUNSEL: What did the Political Department
building look like

FEMALE WITNESS 5: It was a one-storey barracks
painted green

DEFENCE COUNSEL: What was the typing room like

FEMALE WITNESS 5: There were flower pots on the window sill
and there were curtains
On the walls there were pictures and proverbs

JUDGE: What kind of pictures and proverbs

FEMALE WITNESS 5: I no longer remember

DEFENCE COUNSEL: Who was in charge of the office

FEMALE WITNESS 5: Herr Broad was
we typists always had
to look our best
we were allowed to let our hair grow
we wore scarves on our heads
and we had real clothing and shoes
In the morning we spat on our shoes
and polished them with our hands

DEFENCE COUNSEL: How did Herr Boger treat you

FEMALE WITNESS 5: Herr Boger always treated me
in a very gentlemanly fashion
He would often give me his messkit

	with what was left of his food
	Once he saved my life
	when I was sentenced to go with the others
	because I had been negligent
	in dusting things
	one of the captains assigned me to go
	Herr Boger annulled the assignment
JUDGE:	How many clerks were in the department
FEMALE WITNESS 5:	There were 16 girls
JUDGE:	What did you have to do
FEMALE WITNESS 5:	We had to make out the lists of the dead
	We called it marking off
	We had to enter the names
	the date of death and the cause
	The entries had to be made
	with absolute precision
	If anyone made a typing error
	Herr Broad got terribly angry
JUDGE:	How were the files arranged
FEMALE WITNESS 5:	There were two tables
	On the one table were the boxes
	with the numbers of the living
	On the other the boxes
	with the numbers of the dead
	We could see how many
	were still alive from each shipment
	Out of every hundred after a week
	only a couple of dozen were left
JUDGE:	Were all the deaths
	that took place in the camp
	registered here
FEMALE WITNESS 5:	Only prisoners who had
	received a number
	were entered in the books
	Those who were shipped
	direct from the ramp to the gas chambers
	never appeared in any list
JUDGE:	What did you list
	as causes of death

FEMALE WITNESS 5: Most of the causes we listed
were fictitious
For example we couldn't write
Shot while trying to escape
but heart attack
And instead of malnutrition we wrote
dysentery
We had to be careful
that no two prisoners died in the same minute
and that the causes of death
corresponded with their ages
This meant that a twenty-year-old
wasn't allowed to die of heart failure
In the beginning we even wrote
letters to their relatives

PROSECUTOR: Can you remember
how these letters ran

FEMALE WITNESS 5: In spite of all medical care
It has unfortunately not been possible
to save the life of the prisoner
We express to you our sincerest condolence
over this great loss
If you wish we can send you
the urn for fifteen marks
C.O.D.

PROSECUTOR: And did these urns contain
the ashes of the deceased

FEMALE WITNESS 5: Such an urn had the ashes
of many deceased
From the window we could see
the piles of corpses in front
of the old crematorium
They dumped them from the motor vans

PROSECUTOR: Can you give us some figures
in connection with the cases of death
that you registered

FEMALE WITNESS 5: We worked 12 to 15 hours a day
over the official death rolls
They went as high as 300 a day

PROSECUTOR:	Did these include cases of death through the direct operation of the Political Department
FEMALE WITNESS 5:	Prisoners died daily in that department from mistreatment and being shot
DEFENCE COUNSEL:	Would the witness please tell us where the prisoners were shot
FEMALE WITNESS 5:	In Block Eleven of the camp
DEFENCE COUNSEL:	Were you allowed to visit the camp
FEMALE WITNESS 5:	No but we found out everything All communications passed through our hands Boger said to us What you see here and what you hear you have not seen or heard
JUDGE:	How were the interrogations carried out in the Political Department
FEMALE WITNESS 5:	Boger always began the proceedings very quietly He approached the prisoner and asked questions which I then had to translate If the prisoner didn't answer he shook a bunch of keys in his face If the prisoner still wouldn't speak he hit him in the face with the keys Finally he went even closer to him and said I have a machine that will make you speak
JUDGE:	What kind of machine was it
FEMALE WITNESS 5:	Boger called it the Speech Machine
JUDGE:	Where was it located
FEMALE WITNESS 5:	In the room next door
JUDGE:	Did you see the machine
FEMALE WITNESS 5:	Yes
JUDGE:	What did it look like

FEMALE WITNESS 5:	There were poles
DEFENCE COUNSEL:	Is the witness certain her memory
	is not deceiving her
FEMALE WITNESS 5:	It was a bar
	They were hung on it
	We heard the blows and cries
	After an hour
	or even after several hours
	they were dragged out
	You could no longer recognise them
JUDGE:	Were they still alive
FEMALE WITNESS 5:	Anyone who wasn't dead
	rarely survived the next few hours
	Once Boger saw that I was crying
	He said
	Here your personal feelings must be
	excluded
JUDGE:	For what reason were the prisoners
	subjected to these punishments
FEMALE WITNESS 5:	Sometimes it was for stealing
	a piece of bread
	or because you didn't obey the order
	to work more quickly right away
	Sometimes it was enough if the person
	was accused by a stool pigeon
	There was a letter box for informers
	You just had to drop a note in it
DEFENDANT 2:	I never had anything to do
	with trifling matters like these
	In the Political Department
	we were exclusively concerned
	with problems of resistance
JUDGE:	How often did the witness
	see prisoners die
	after they had been taken down
	from the machine
FEMALE WITNESS 5:	At least 20 times
JUDGE:	In at least 20 cases you can swear
	that death took place

	in your presence
FEMALE WITNESS 5:	Yes
JUDGE:	Please tell the court
	did you see the sentence carried out
FEMALE WITNESS 5:	Yes
	Once I saw a man hanging
	upside down
	Another time a woman
	was tied to the pole
	Boger made us
	come in and look
DEFENDANT 2:	It is perfectly true
	that the witness was an interpreter for us
	Nevertheless she never took part
	in the more intense interviews
	Ladies were not allowed
	on such occasions
FEMALE WITNESS 5:	Ladies
DEFENDANT 2:	I can say that perfectly well today
	The Defendants laugh
JUDGE:	Please tell the court
	If you saw any of the defendants
	beating prisoners
FEMALE WITNESS 5:	I saw Boger in his shirt sleeves
	holding a bludgeon in his hand
	and I often saw him come out
	covered with blood
	Once I heard Broad say to Lachmann
	a member of the Political Department
	You know Gerhard
	it really squirted out didn't it
	Then he gave me his jacket
	to clean for him
	The men were always very concerned
	about cleanliness
	Broad liked to look at himself in the mirror
	especially after he was promoted to Sturmmann
	and I sewed on his stripe for him
	I had to polish Boger's boots

	on one occasion
JUDGE:	And then what happened
FEMALE WITNESS 5:	A motor van drove up outside
	with a load of children
	I saw it through the window of the office
	A young boy jumped down
	He held an apple in his hand
	Out came Boger through the door
	The boy stood there with his apple
	Boger went to the child
	and picked him up by the feet
	and dashed his head against the barracks wall
	Then he picked up the apple
	and called me out and said
	Wipe this off the wall
	And later as I sat at an interrogation
	I saw
	him eating the apple
DEFENCE COUNSEL:	The witness never mentioned
	this incident in previous
	examinations
FEMALE WITNESS 5:	I couldn't speak about it
DEFENCE COUNSEL:	Why not
FEMALE WITNESS 5:	For personal reasons
DEFENCE COUNSEL:	Can you explain them to us
FEMALE WITNESS 5:	Since that time
	I have never wanted a child of my own
DEFENCE COUNSEL:	Why can you talk about it today
FEMALE WITNESS 5:	Now
	that I see him again
	I have to tell about it
JUDGE:	Defendant Boger
	have you any reply
	to this accusation
DEFENDANT 2:	This is an invention
	I see now that the witness
	scarcely deserves the trust
	I placed in her at the time

CANTO THREE: THE SWING

II

WITNESS 7:	Together with some other prisoners
	I was brought
	To the interrogation room
	of the Political Department
JUDGE:	Can you describe this room
WITNESS 7:	On the floor there were precious carpets
	that had been part of a shipment from France
	Boger's desk
	was opposite the door
	He was seated at the desk when I came in
	The interpreter sat behind the desk
JUDGE:	Who else was in the room
WITNESS 7:	The head of the Political Department
	Grabner
	and Defendants Dylewski and Broad
JUDGE:	What did they say to you
WITNESS 7:	Boger said
	This is the Political Department
	We don't ask we just listen
	You yourself should know what you have to say
JUDGE:	Why were you sent there
WITNESS 7:	I didn't know
	I didn't know what I was supposed to say
	and I begged them to tell me
	Then I was beaten unconscious
	When I came to I was lying in the hall
	Boger was standing near me
	Get up he said
	But I couldn't get up
	Boger came nearer
	Then I raised myself to the wall
	I saw blood flowing under me
	The floor and my clothes
	were covered with blood
	My head was shattered

	my nose broken
	The whole afternoon until late at night
	I had to stand with my face to the wall
	There were others standing there
	Whoever turned around
	had his head beaten against the wall
	On the next day I was interrogated again
	I was led into the room
	with the other prisoners
JUDGE:	What did they want to find out
WITNESS 7:	The whole time I had no idea
	what it was about
	They hit me on the head with something
	a few times
	I think it was a metal coil
	then I had to go out in the corridor again
	and the man next to me
	was led off by Boger
	into the next room
	His name was Walter Windmüller
JUDGE:	Do you know what happened to him
WITNESS 7:	I would say
	he was in there 2 or 3 hours
	I stood in the corridor
	with my face to the wall
	Then Windmüller came out
	They made him stand next to me again
	He was bleeding from his trouser legs
	and fell over a couple of times
	We had learned to speak
	Without moving our lips
	When I asked him about the interrogation
	he said
	They crushed my balls in there
	He died that very day
JUDGE:	Was Boger responsible
	for the death of this prisoner
WITNESS 7:	I am certain
	that Boger assisted

66

	if Boger
	did not do it himself
JUDGE:	Defendant Boger
	have you anything to say
DEFENDANT 2:	Your Honour
	May I explain
	The incident did not occur in this manner
JUDGE:	How did it occur
DEFENDANT 2:	Your Honour
	I never killed anyone
	I was only carrying out interrogations
JUDGE:	What kind of interrogations
DEFENDANT 2:	Often they were heated interrogations
	they were carried out
	according to the prevailing regulations
JUDGE:	How were these regulations determined
DEFENDANT 2:	In the interests of camp security
	strong measures had to be taken
	against traitors and other vermin
JUDGE:	Defendant Boger
	as a criminal investigator
	you must have known
	that a man
	who is brought before such a hearing
	will say anything you want to hear
DEFENDANT 2:	I am of a completely different opinion
	particularly with reference
	to our office
	With stubborn prisoners
	force was the only way
	to obtain confessions
WITNESS 8:	When I was called into the interrogation room
	I saw a bowl of herring
	on Boger's desk
	Grabner asked me if I was hungry
	I said no
	But Grabner said
	I know when you last had a decent lunch
	Today you will learn about my good heart

67

I'm giving you this to eat
Boger has made a salad for you
Then he ordered me to eat
I couldn't
because I was in handcuffs
Then Boger pushed my face into the bowl
I had to gulp it down
The herring was so salty that I vomited
I had to lick up the vomit
and the rest of the herring
When at last I still had a piece in my mouth
Boger cried out
See that he doesn't spit
the rest out in the corridor
Then I was taken to Block Eleven
and hung in the loft
with my hands tied behind me
This was called hanging from a pillory
You hung so high
that the tips of your feet
barely touched the ground
Boger pushed me back and forth
and kicked me in the stomach
There was a pail of water in front of me
Boger asked me if I wanted a drink
He laughed and pushed me up and down
When I was unconscious
they poured water over me
My arms were numb
My wrists were bursting
Boger asked me questions
but my tongue was so swollen
that I couldn't answer
Then Boger said
We have another swing for you to ride on
I was
brought back to the Political Department

DEFENCE COUNSEL: Would the witness tell us
if he underwent treatment

	on the machine
WITNESS 8:	Yes
DEFENCE COUNSEL:	Then it was possible after all
	to survive this treatment

CANTO THREE: THE SWING

III

WITNESS 8:	I remember a morning
	in the spring of 1942
	A row of prisoners was marching out
	to the barracks
	which had housed the Post Office
	but which now contained
	the Political Department
	The prisoners went ahead
	and they carried two pieces of wood
	like the side bars of a hurdle
	Sentries followed them carrying machine guns
	and also the department chiefs
	with briefcases and bullskins
	which had been dried and specially prepared
	as whips
	for the purposes of corporal punishment
	These hurdle bars
	formed the foundation of the swing
JUDGE:	Was that the first time
	the machine was used
WITNESS 8:	It existed earlier
	in a simpler form
	At first it was only an iron pipe
	placed on two tables
	with the prisoners strapped tightly to it
	Because the pipe
	rolled back and forth
	they prepared a foundation

69

	to stabilise it
DEFENCE COUNSEL:	Would the witness tell us
	his source of information
WITNESS 8:	There was no occurrence in our section
	of the camp that went unknown
	In the old camp everything was
	confined to the smallest space
	The camp measured no more
	than 200 by 300 yards
	You could see all of the camp
	from every one of the 28 blocks
JUDGE:	Why were you summoned
	for questioning
WITNESS 8:	I was assigned
	to help build a drainage ditch
	that stretched around the outer camp
	During this I had helped
	one of my fellow prisoners
	to meet his mother
	who was imprisoned in the women's camp
	The prisoner's name was Janicki
	He was led
	into the interrogation room first
	Soon he was thrown out into the corridor
	He was still alive
	He opened his mouth
	and stretched out his tongue
	He licked the floor in his thirst
	Boger came up
	and pushed his head to the other side
	with his boot
	then he said to me
	Now it's your turn
	If you don't tell the truth
	the same will happen to you
	Then they stretched me on the swing
JUDGE:	Would the witness
	describe the proceeding
WITNESS 8:	The prisoner had

	to sit on the ground with his knees bent
	his hands were tied in front of him
	and pushed down over his knees
	The pole was shoved
	between his underarms
	and his bended knees
	Then the pole was raised up
	and placed on the mounting
JUDGE:	Who was responsible for these preparations
WITNESS 8:	Two prisoners in charge
JUDGE:	Who else was in the room
WITNESS 8:	I saw Boger there
	Broad and Dylewski
	Boger asked questions
	but I couldn't answer
	I hung with my head down
	and two prisoners in charge
	rocked me back and forth
DEFENCE COUNSEL:	What kind of questions did they ask you
WITNESS 8:	They wanted me to name names
JUDGE:	Were you beaten during this interrogation
WITNESS 8:	Boger and Dylewski took turns
	beating me with the bullwhip
DEFENCE COUNSEL:	Wasn't it the prisoners in charge
	who did the beating
WITNESS 8:	I saw Boger and Dylewski
	with the whip in their hands
JUDGE:	Where did they beat you
WITNESS 8:	On the buttocks
	the back the thighs
	the hands the feet
	and the back of the head
	But most of all my sexual organs
	were the object of their violence
	They aimed for them specially
	Three times I became unconscious
	and they poured water over me
JUDGE:	Defendant Boger
	Do you admit

	to having mistreated this prisoner
DEFENDANT 2:	I can only answer this question
	with a clear and distinct No
WITNESS 8:	I have the marks on me until this day
DEFENDANT 2:	But not from me
JUDGE:	Defendant Boger
	Did you administer treatment
	with the instrument
	we have heard described
DEFENDANT 2:	In certain cases
	I had to give the orders
	The punishment was administered
	by prisoners in charge
	under my supervision
JUDGE:	Defendant Boger
	do you maintain
	that the testimony of the witness
	is untrue
DEFENDANT 2:	The testimony is fragmentary
	and does not correspond
	to the truth in every detail
JUDGE:	What was the truth
DEFENDANT 2:	If the prisoner confessed
	the punishment was suspended
JUDGE:	And if the prisoner didn't confess
DEFENDANT 2:	Then he was beaten until the blood came
	That was the end
JUDGE:	Was a doctor present
DEFENDANT 2:	I never saw any order
	that mentioned consulting a doctor
	It was also unnecessary
	in the very moment
	that the blood started flowing
	I stopped
	The goal of intensive interrogation
	had been reached
	if the blood ran through the trousers
JUDGE:	You felt yourself justified
	in carrying out intensive interrogation

DEFENDANT 2:   According to orders
                I had this responsibility
                moreover I am of the opinion
                that even today
                if flogging were brought in
                for example in cases of juvenile delinquency
                you might be able to control
                all these outbreaks of violence

DEFENCE COUNSEL: The witness
                has reported that no one
                could withstand
                treatment on the swing
                To all appearances
                this statement would seem exaggerated

WITNESS 8:   When I was taken down from the swing
                Boger said to me
                Now we've made you ready
                for a happy trip to heaven
                I was brought to a cell in Block Eleven
                There I waited from hour to hour
                to be shot
                I don't know
                how many days I spent there
                My buttocks were festering
                My testicles were black and blue
                and swollen to gigantic size
                Most of the time I lay unconscious
                Then I was led
                along with a large group of others
                into the washroom
                We had to undress
                and our numbers were written
                on our breasts
                in blue pencil
                I knew that this
                was the death sentence
                As we stood there naked in a row
                The Liaison Chief came and asked
                how many prisoners he should register

as shot
After he left we were counted
once again
It turned out there was one too many
I had learned
to always place myself last
so I received a kick
and got my clothing back
I was supposed to be taken to my cell
to wait for the next batch
but a male nurse
who was also a prisoner
took me with him to the hospital
It just happened
that one or two were supposed to live
and I was
one of them

Canto Four: THE POSSIBILITY OF SURVIVAL

I

WITNESS 3 : The atmosphere in the camp changed
from day to day
It depended on the Camp Commander
the Liaison Chief
the Block Leader and their moods
and these were dependant
on the stages of the war
At first while there were still victories
they still had a certain arrogance about them
and often made jokes as they flogged us
In rhythm with the losses and retreats
their treatment of the prisoners
gathered momentum
But you had no way of telling
what would happen next
Falling in could mean anything
waiting for nothing
or drudgery
In our hospital prisoners
could be well cared for
and even receive good food
only to be sent up the chimney
as soon as they recovered
A prisoner working as a nurse
could be beaten by a camp doctor
because he had forgotten a detail
in a patient's medical record
and there was that same patient killed
I myself
only escaped gassing
by accident

	because on that evening
	the ovens were clogged up
	On the way back from the crematorium
	the physician in attendance learned
	that I was a doctor
	and he accepted me in his department
JUDGE:	What was the doctor's name
WITNESS 3:	His name was Dr. Vetter
	He was a man with perfect manners
	Dr. Schatz and Dr. Frank also
	were always friendly with the prisoners
	they delivered over to death
	They killed not from hate or conviction
	they killed because they had to
	and it wasn't worth talking about
	Only a few were passionate in their killing
	Among that number was Boger
	I saw prisoners
	when they were called to Boger
	and I saw them
	when they came back again
	As the prisoners were taken away to be shot
	I heard Boger say with pride
	These people are mine
	Once a prisoner who had been shot
	was delivered to the infirmary
	on Boger's orders
	He had to be saved
	so that he could be hanged
	But the prisoner died too soon
JUDGE:	Defendant Boger
	Do you know about this case
DEFENDANT 2:	Prisoners shot while escaping
	were brought to the hospital
	as a matter of principle
	so that they could be interrogated
	after their recovery
	Up to this point the declaration
	of the witness might be entirely correct

	In this case I gave the further order
	that the prisoner should be kept alive
	I said
	He had to be saved
	so that he could be interrogated
JUDGE:	Was he then to be hanged
DEFENDANT 2:	Possibly
	That lay outside my responsibility
WITNESS 6:	Boger and Kaduk
	used to hang people with their own hands
	Once 12 prisoners
	were executed as reprisal
	after an escape
	Boger and Kaduk
	put the noose around their necks
DEFENCE COUNSEL:	How does the witness know this
WITNESS 6:	We stood in the yard
	and had to watch
	The prisoners screamed a bit
	Boger and Kaduk were beside themselves
	with fury
	They kicked them with their boots
	and slapped their faces
	then they hung on to them by their feet
	and pulled them down in short jerks
DEFENDANT 2:	I remember this incident
	one of the criminals
	escaped from his fetters
	He was being led to execution
	under strong security precautions
	according to the rules
	The person in question assaulted me
	and broke one of my ribs
	The man was then overpowered
	The chairs were refastened
	and I read the sentence
JUDGE:	Did the witness
	hear the reading of the sentence
WITNESS 6:	No sentence was read

DEFENDANT 2:	It was rather difficult to hear because of the shouting
PROSECUTOR:	What were they shouting
DEFENDANT 2:	The prisoners were shouting political slogans
PROSECUTOR:	Of what sort
DEFENDANT 2:	They were stirring up the prisoners against us
DEFENCE COUNSEL:	How did the other prisoners behave
DEFENDANT 2:	There were no unforeseen incidents The sentence was carried out as all sentences were carried out I myself did not perform the execution This was done by prisoners in charge
DEFENCE COUNSEL:	Is it possible that the witness may have failed to hear the reading of the sentence
WITNESS 6:	The execution took place immediately after the escape The time was too short for the case to be analysed by a central authority and a sentence to be pronounced
JUDGE:	Was the Camp Commander present or his Chief Officer
WITNESS 6:	At public executions higher officers were always present They wore white gloves for the occasion Whether the Chief Officer was present on this occasion I cannot say with certainty In any case it can be assumed that he was responsible for the carrying out of all orders within the area of the Command Post
JUDGE:	Herr Witness Do you recognise the Chief Officer among the Defendants

WITNESS 6:	That's him
	Mulka
JUDGE:	Defendant Mulka
	Did you attend this hanging
	or any other hangings
DEFENDANT I:	I had absolutely nothing to do
	with any killing
	at any time whatever
JUDGE:	Did you receive orders about them
	and did you pass them on
DEFENDANT I:	I heard a good deal about such orders
	But I myself never passed them on
JUDGE:	How did you deal with them
DEFENDANT I:	I was careful
	to ask questions
	in higher quarters
	to determine the legality
	of the executions
	I had heard about
	In the long run I had to bear
	the responsibility for myself
	and for my family
PROSECUTOR:	Defendant Mulka
	did you see the gallows
DEFENDANT I:	Did I see what please
PROSECUTOR:	I want to know
	if you saw the gallows
DEFENDANT I:	No
	I never set foot in the camp
PROSECUTOR:	You want to tell us
	that you as second in command
	were never in the camp
DEFENDANT I:	That's the absolute truth
	My work was exclusively
	administrative in nature
	I lived entirely in the executive offices
PROSECUTOR:	Where were these offices
DEFENDANT I:	In the buildings
	outside the camp limits

PROSECUTOR: Was there no view
of the camp from there
DEFENDANT 1: Not that I would know about
PROSECUTOR: Could the witness describe for us
the location of the outer buildings
in relation to the concentration camp
WITNESS 6: From all the back windows
of the office buildings
the camp could easily be seen
Immediately behind them
the cement piles rose into the air
with their electrically charged
barbed wire
The first block was 30 feet away
The other blocks were immediately
behind in 3 rows
no more than 30 feet from each other
The view onto the cross-streets
of the camp was unobstructed
PROSECUTOR: Where was the gallows located
WITNESS 6: In the square in front of the camp kitchen
Straight to the right
if you were going from the gate
to the main road
PROSECUTOR: What did the gallows look like
WITNESS 6: Three poles
with an iron track on top
PROSECUTOR: Defendant Mulka
you were living in the immediate vicinity
of the camp
According to regulations
you were supposed to report
to the Commander about all incidents
and to deal with secret code messages
you were also responsible
for the ideological indoctrination
of the guards
In your position
weren't the punishments

80

	being carried out in the camp
	made known to you
DEFENDANT I:	Only once I saw some kind of excerpt
	from an out-of-date document
	on the authorisation of corporal punishment
PROSECUTOR:	Did you never have
	to investigate the reasons
	for the hangings and shootings
DEFENDANT I:	It wasn't my duty
	to worry about that
PROSECUTOR:	Then what were your duties
	as Chief Officer
DEFENDANT I:	I worked out prices
	set up work assignments
	and dealt with personnel
	Furthermore I had to accompany
	the Commander to receptions
	and lead the Corps of Honour
PROSECUTOR:	When did that happen
DEFENDANT I:	On festive occasions
	or for funerals
	Then we organised a mourning procession
PROSECUTOR:	What funerals were these
DEFENDANT I:	For the death of one of our officers
PROSECUTOR:	Who was informed of cases of death
	among the prisoners
DEFENDANT I:	I don't know
	Perhaps the Political Department
PROSECUTOR:	Did you never learn anything
	about the 100 or 200 prisoners
	who died each day
DEFENDANT I:	I cannot remember
	having seen regular statistics
	There were 10 or 15 deaths each day
	but at the time I had not heard
	figures of the size
	you have mentioned
PROSECUTOR:	Defendant Mulka
	didn't you know about the mass murders

	in the gas chambers
DEFENDANT I:	This was not known to me
PROSECUTOR:	Didn't the smoke
	from the crematorium chimneys
	attract your attention
	After all
	you could see it for miles around
DEFENDANT I:	Well it was a big camp
	with many deaths from natural causes
	That's why they had to cremate the dead
PROSECUTOR:	Didn't you notice
	the condition of the prisoners
DEFENDANT I:	It was a concentration camp
	People weren't there on a rest cure
PROSECUTOR:	Had you no interest
	as Chief Officer
	to find out how the prisoners lived
DEFENDANT I:	I never heard any complaints
PROSECUTOR:	Did you never talk with the Commander
	about incidents in the camp
DEFENDANT I:	No
	There were no unusual incidents
PROSECUTOR:	What was the purpose of the camp
DEFENDANT I:	In a detention camp
	enemies of the state
	should be brought around
	to another way of thinking
	It was not my concern
	to question this
PROSECUTOR:	Did you know
	what the term Special Treatment
	meant
DEFENDANT I:	That was a state secret
	I could know nothing about it
	Whoever mentioned it
	was threatened with death
PROSECUTOR:	But you still knew about it
DEFENDANT I:	I can't answer that
PROSECUTOR:	In what way

	did you look after the troops
DEFENDANT 1:	There were plays and film shows
	and gala evenings
	We had a Herr Knittel who looked after them
	He also took care of evening classes
	for the officers
PROSECUTOR:	How did he come to do this
DEFENDANT 1:	He was a schoolmaster
	and if I am correctly informed
	he is at present a headmaster
	somewhere
	and is obviously well qualified to teach
PROSECUTOR:	And you gave ideological instruction
	to the enlisted men
DEFENCE COUNSEL:	We wish to advise our client
	that he is not obliged to answer
	the questions of the co-plaintiff
PROSECUTOR:	The decision concerning this
	rests solely and entirely
	on the Defendant
	By this action
	the Defence far oversteps its authority
	as established by law
	It is obvious
	that the Defence is attempting
	through these tactics to prevent
	the discovery of the truth
DEFENCE COUNSEL:	We must completely disassociate ourselves
	from this astonishing performance
	It is clear to see
	that the prosecutor has no command
	of criminal procedure
	and knows nothing about the law
	The plaintiffs have come to this trial
	with preconceived opinions

The Defendants laugh in agreement

CANTO FOUR: THE POSSIBILITY OF SURVIVAL

II

WITNESS 3:   The power of anyone
               among the camp personnel
               was unlimited
               Everyone was free to kill
               or to grant clemency
               I saw the physician Dr. Flage
               standing by the fence with tears in his eyes
               as a file of children
               was being led to the crematorium
               He let me take
               the medical records
               of individual prisoners
               who had been picked out
               so I could save them from death
               Camp Physician Flage showed me
               that it was still possible
               to think of one life
               among the thousands
               he showed me
               that it would have been possible
               to influence the machinery
               if there had been enough
               of his kind

DEFENCE COUNSEL: Herr Witness
               did you have any influence
               on the life and death
               of prisoners in your care

WITNESS 3:   I could save
               a life here and there

DEFENCE COUNSEL: Were you on the other hand
               obliged to pick out patients for execution

WITNESS 3:   I had no influence
               on the total number assigned
               This was determined
               by the Camp Administration

                        I still had the possibility
                        of influencing the lists
DEFENCE COUNSEL: What standards did you apply
                        when you had to choose
                        between two patients
WITNESS 3:   We had to ask ourselves
                        who had the better chance
                        of survival according to the medical prognosis
                        And then the much more difficult question
                        Who was likelier to be more valuable
                        and more useful in taking care
                        of the prisoners
DEFENCE COUNSEL: Was there any special consideration shown
WITNESS 3:   Naturally the ones
                        who were politically active
                        stuck together and helped each other
                        as much as they could
                        As I belonged
                        to the Camp Resistance Movement
                        it was understandable
                        that I did everything
                        I could to save above all
                        the lives
                        of my comrades
DEFENCE COUNSEL: What could the Resistance Movement
                        accomplish in the camp
WITNESS 3:   The main duty of the Resistance
                        was to maintain
                        solidarity
                        To do this we documented
                        events in the camp
                        and buried our documents
                        in metal boxes
DEFENCE COUNSEL: Did you have any contact
                        with the outside world or with partisan groups
WITNESS 3:   The prisoners working in the factories
                        were now and again able
                        to make connection with partisan groups
                        and they received news

	of war operations
DEFENCE COUNSEL:	Were preparations made
	for an armed uprising
WITNESS 3:	Later on we succeeded
	in smuggling in explosives
DEFENCE COUNSEL:	Was the camp ever attacked
	either from within or without
WITNESS 3:	Except for an unsuccessful uprising
	by the Special Corps
	in the crematorium during the last winter
	there was no active resistance
	Nor were any attempts
	made from outside
DEFENCE COUNSEL:	Did you ask for outside help
	through your contacts
WITNESS 3:	We gave out continual reports
	on conditions in the camp
DEFENCE COUNSEL:	What kind of results did you expect
	from these reports
WITNESS 3:	We were hoping for an air attack
	on the gas chambers
	or the tracks leading to the camp
DEFENCE COUNSEL:	Would the witness tell us
	How he maintained his will to resist
	when he saw that he had been
	left in the lurch
	by all possible military authorities
WITNESS 3:	In the conditions of the camp
	it was sufficient resistance
	to remain vigilant
	and never forget
	that a time would come
	when we would be able
	to relate our experiences
DEFENCE COUNSEL:	Would the witness tell us
	how he kept the oath
	he swore as a doctor
PROSECUTOR:	We object to this question
	which the Defence is using in an attempt

	to associate the witness with the Defendants
	The Defendants killed out of free will
	The witnesses were forced to be present
	when death was administered
WITNESS 3:	I would like to answer as follows
	Those among the prisoners
	who through their special positions
	had managed a postponement
	of their own death
	had at least taken a step
	against the rulers of the camp
	In order to achieve
	the possibility of survival
	they were forced to show
	a semblance of co-operation
	I saw this clearly in my department
	Soon I was bound to the Camp Physician
	not only by our common profession
	but also by my co-operation
	in making the system work
	Even we ourselves
	the prisoners
	from the important ones
	down to the ones who were dying
	belonged to the system
	The distinction between us
	and the camp personnel
	was slighter than the difference
	between us and outsiders
DEFENCE COUNSEL:	Does the witness
	mean to say
	that there was an understanding
	between the administration
	and the prisoners
WITNESS 3:	If we speak today about our experiences
	with people who were not in the camps
	these people always regard them
	as something unimaginable
	And yet it was the same men there

who were both prisoners and guards
We came to the camp
in such great numbers
and there were so many who brought us there
that what happened ought to be
comprehensible even today
Many of those who had been chosen
to play the role of prisoners
were brought up with the same values
as those
who played the role of guards
They had worked hard for the same nation
and for the same incentives and rewards
and if they hadn't been called prisoners
they might just as easily have been guards
We must get rid of our exalted attitude
that this camp world
is beyond our comprehension
We all knew the society
which had produced the regime
that could bring about such a camp
we were familiar with this order
from its very beginnings
and so we could still find our way
even in its final consequences
which allowed the exploiter
to develop his power
to a hitherto unknown degree
and the exploited
had to deliver up his own guts

DEFENCE COUNSEL: We absolutely refuse to accept
this kind of theory
which presents a totally
distorted view of society

WITNESS 3: Most of those who arrived on the ramp
could no longer find the time
to orient themselves
Bewildered and struck dumb
they went their final way

and let themselves be killed
because they could not understand
We call them heroes
but their death was senseless
We see these millions
before us
in the glaring light
of abuse and barking dogs
and the outside world still asks today
how it was possible
that they let themselves be destroyed
We
who still live with these images
know
that once again millions may be
waiting in full view of their destruction
and that this destruction
exceeds the old arrangements
many times in its effectiveness

DEFENCE COUNSEL: Was the witness
politically active
before his internment
in the camp

WITNESS 3: Yes
It was our strength
that we knew
why we were there
That helped us
to keep our identity
But even this strength
helped only a few
to die
Even these could be broken

WITNESS 7: There were 1200 of us
who had been led to the crematorium
We had to wait a long time
because there was another batch before us
I stayed a little to one side
Then a prisoner came along

	he was very young
	He whispered to me
	Get away from here
	So I took my wooden shoes and went away
	I came to a corner
	Another stood there
	who asked me
	Where do you want to go
	I said
	They sent me away
	Then come with me he said
	That's how I came back to the camp
DEFENCE COUNSEL:	Was it so easy
	Could one just go away
WITNESS 7:	I don't know how it was for others
	I went away
	and came to the hospital
	And the prison doctor asked me
	Do you want to live
	I said Yes
	He looked at me a while
	and let me come with him
DEFENCE COUNSEL:	Then you survived your time
	in the camp
WITNESS 7:	I got out of the camp
	but the camp is still there

CANTO FOUR: THE POSSIBILITY OF SURVIVAL

III

JUDGE:	You spent several months
	in Women's Block Number Ten
	where medical experiments
	were carried out
	What can you tell us about them
FEMALE WITNESS 4:	*She is quiet*

90

JUDGE:	We can understand
	that the witness
	may find it difficult to speak
	and that she would rather remain silent
	But we ask her
	to explore all those parts
	of her memory
	which might shed light on the circumstances
	being considered
FEMALE WITNESS 4:	There were 600 of us there
	in the Women's Block
	Professor Clauberg directed the research
	The other camp doctors
	supplied the human material
JUDGE:	How were the experiments carried out
FEMALE WITNESS 4:	*She is quiet*
DEFENCE COUNSEL:	Is the witness suffering
	from loss of memory
FEMALE WITNESS 4:	Ever since my time in the camp
	I have been ill
DEFENCE COUNSEL:	How does your illness manifest itself
FEMALE WITNESS 4:	Fits of dizziness and nausea
	Just now I had to vomit in the toilet
	because it smelled of chlorine
	They spilled chlorine over the corpses
	I can't stay
	in closed rooms
DEFENCE COUNSEL:	No failure of memory
FEMALE WITNESS 4:	I would like to forget
	but I still see it before me
	I would like to remove the number
	on my arm
	In summer
	when I wear sleeveless dresses
	people stare at me
	and there is always the same expression
	in their eyes
DEFENCE COUNSEL:	What kind of expression
FEMALE WITNESS 4:	Scorn

DEFENCE COUNSEL: Does the witness
still feel herself persecuted

FEMALE WITNESS 4: *She is quiet*

JUDGE: Please tell us
what kind of experiments do you remember

FEMALE WITNESS 4: There were girls
17 to 18 years old
They were selected
from among the healthiest prisoners
They carried out X-ray
experiments on them

JUDGE: Can you describe them

FEMALE WITNESS 4: The girls were placed
before the X-ray machine
A plate was fastened to their stomachs
and to their buttocks
The rays were directed into their ovaries
to burn them out
Severe burns and abscesses
developed on their flesh

JUDGE: What happened to the girls

FEMALE WITNESS 4: Within 3 months
they were subjected
to further operations

JUDGE: What kind of operations

FEMALE WITNESS 4: Their ovaries and sex glands
were taken out

JUDGE: Did the patients die

FEMALE WITNESS 4: If they did not die during the operation
they died soon afterwards
After a few weeks the girls
had completely changed
They took on the appearance
of aged crones

JUDGE: Does the witness recall
if any of the Defendants
was involved in the operations

FEMALE WITNESS 4: All doctors met each other daily
in their quarters

	It can be assumed
	that they were at least
	informed of the proceedings
DEFENCE COUNSEL:	We vigorously object
	to statements of this kind
	The fact that our clients
	happened to be in the vicinity
	of the proceedings described
	in no way makes them accessories
JUDGE:	Would the witness tell us
	what other operations were performed
FEMALE WITNESS 4:	*She is quiet*
DEFENCE COUNSEL:	We are of the opinion
	that the witness
	due to her state of health
	is in no condition to give
	reliable answers to the court
PROSECUTOR:	Can you describe to the court
	other experiments you attended
FEMALE WITNESS 4:	With a spray tube lengthened by a hose
	that was fitted
	along the vagina
	a fluid was pressed
	into the womb
JUDGE:	What kind of fluid
FEMALE WITNESS 4:	It was a kind of batter
	as thick as cement
	that produced a burning ache
	like labour pains
	and a feeling
	that the stomach might explode
	The women could only walk
	doubled over to the X-ray table
	where a picture was made
JUDGE:	What was the purpose of this experiment
FEMALE WITNESS 4:	The Fallopian Tubes were
	supposed to be plastered over
	to prevent conception
JUDGE:	Were these experiments

	repeated on the same patient
FEMALE WITNESS 4:	After the spray tube
	another liquid was introduced
	for the purposes of X-ray observation
	After this the batter
	was often pumped in again
	In a period of 3 or 4 weeks
	the process might be repeated several times
	Most cases of death were caused
	by inflammation of the womb or peritoneum
	I never noticed
	that the medical instruments
	were sterilised
	between operations
JUDGE:	How many of these operations
	would you estimate were carried out
FEMALE WITNESS 4:	During the 6 months
	that I spent in Block Ten
	400 operations of this type were performed
	At this time
	artificial insemination was also undertaken
	If a pregnancy resulted
	an abortion was performed
JUDGE:	In what month of the pregnancy
	did this occur
FEMALE WITNESS 4:	In the seventh month
	During the pregnancy
	numerous X-ray experiments were performed
	After the premature birth the child
	if it actually came into the world alive
	was killed and an autopsy was performed
DEFENCE COUNSEL:	Is the witness
	speaking from her own knowledge
	or giving a second-hand report
FEMALE WITNESS 4:	I speak from personal experience
DEFENCE COUNSEL:	What protected you from contracting
	a fatal disease
FEMALE WITNESS 4:	The evacuation of the camp

Canto Five: THE END OF LILI TOFLER

I

JUDGE: Does the name Lili Tofler
mean anything to you

FEMALE WITNESS 5: Yes
Lili Tofler was a very
pretty girl
She was taken into custody
because she wrote a letter
to a prisoner
The letter was found
while it was being smuggled
to the prisoner
Lili Tofler was interrogated
she was asked to name the prisoner
Boger presided at the interview
On his order
She was brought into the Bunkerblock
There they made her stand naked
several times before the wall
and they pretended
that they were going to shoot her
They played at giving the orders
Finally she beseeched them
On her knees to shoot her

JUDGE: Was she shot

FEMALE WITNESS 5: Yes

WITNESS 6: I was confined to my bunker
when Lili Tofler
together with 2 other prisoners
who had taken part in smuggling the letter
were confined there
During those days I was allowed only once

95

through the intercession of Jakob
the prisoner in charge
to use the washroom
But on the way there
Jakob dragged me suddenly into another room
Through the crack in the door
I saw Lili Tofler
being led into the washroom by Boger
I heard two shots
and saw the girl lying dead
on the floor after Boger left
The two other prisoners were later
liquidated by Boger in the yard

JUDGE: Defendant Boger
Do you know anything about this case

DEFENDANT 2: The shooting of Lili Tofler
coincides with the truth
As a typist in the Political Department
she was in possession of state secrets
and was not allowed under any circumstances
to have contact with the prisoners
I had nothing to do
with her being shot
I was just as shattered by her death
as Jakob was
whose tears ran down his cheeks

JUDGE: Can you tell us
what was in the letter

DEFENDANT 2: No

JUDGE: Can you tell us
what was in the letter

FEMALE WITNESS 5: Lili Tofler asked in her letter
if it was still possible for them
to go on living
after the things they had heard
and the things they knew about
I remember that she next asked her friend
if he had received her previous message
she also wrote him

	whatever encouraging news she had
DEFENCE COUNSEL:	Where has the witness
	obtained this information
FEMALE WITNESS 5:	I was friendly with Lili Tofler
	we lived in the same Block
	She told me about this letter
	I saw it afterwards
	I worked in the camp office
	The death certificate
	for Lili Tofler ended up there
	The letter was attached
JUDGE:	Did you know the prisoner
	to whom the letter was sent
FEMALE WITNESS 5:	Yes
JUDGE:	Did Lili Tofler betray his name
FEMALE WITNESS 5:	No
	The prisoners were summoned to the yard
	and Lili was supposed to accuse her friend
	I remember precisely
	how she stood before him
	and looked him straight in the eye
	and immediately went on
	without saying a word
DEFENCE COUNSEL:	Were you required to appear at roll call
FEMALE WITNESS 5:	Yes
DEFENCE COUNSEL:	Where was the roll call yard
FEMALE WITNESS 5:	It was the street and the empty square
	in front of the kitchen barracks
DEFENCE COUNSEL:	How did the square look
FEMALE WITNESS 5:	On the right across from the gallows
	stood the little watch-tower
	belonging to the Liaison Chief
	It was made of wood
	and painted to look like stone
	A weather-vane stood on the pointed roof
	The tower looked as though
	it had been made from building blocks
	The prisoners stood on the street
	and on all the roads between the blocks

	Lili Tofler was led along by them
	On that day I also happened to read
	what was written in large letters
	on the kitchen roof
	THERE IS ONLY ONE ROAD TO FREEDOM
	ITS MILESTONES ARE CALLED
	OBEDIENCE INDUSTRY CLEANLINESS
	HONESTY TRUTHFULNESS
	AND LOVE FOR THE FATHERLAND
JUDGE:	Was the prisoner
	to whom the letter was sent
	ever discovered
FEMALE WITNESS 5:	No

CANTO FIVE: THE END OF LILI TOFLER

II

JUDGE:	Herr Witness
	At that time you were in charge
	of the agricultural management of the camp
	At the time of her imprisonment
	Lili Tofler worked
	at one of the plant stations
	that were under your jurisdiction
	What did Lili Tofler do there
WITNESS 1:	As far as I can remember
	she was a clerk or secretary
JUDGE:	Had she come to you
	from the Political Department
WITNESS 1:	Today I can no longer tell you
	Our business had nothing
	to do with the camp directly
	it was under the head economic bureau
	The cultivation of rubber plants
	made it an important war industry
	My duties were principally

scientific

JUDGE:	Do you know about the arrest of Lili Tofler
WITNESS I:	I remember that it had something to do with a letter
JUDGE:	Do you know that Lili Tofler was arrested because of this letter
WITNESS I:	I believe the letter was found in a shipment of carrots
JUDGE:	What were the carrots for
WITNESS I:	They were planted for the medical department
JUDGE:	For what purpose
WITNESS I:	As food for the patients presumably Professor Clauberg ordered them
JUDGE:	What did you know about Professor Clauberg's work
WITNESS I:	He undertook research for the pharmaceutical industries
JUDGE:	What kind of research
WITNESS I:	I don't know All I knew of the camp was that it was connected with a vast complex of industries whose various branches provided the prisoners with work
PROSECUTOR:	Which of these industries was in charge of your department
WITNESS I:	We belonged to the Buna factory of I-G Farben we were all working on war production
PROSECUTOR:	Did you know that in the very establishment of these factories the prisoners formed an integral part of the plan
WITNESS I:	Yes naturally

PROSECUTOR: Did the factories pay wages
                 to the prisoners who worked there
WITNESS I: Certainly
                 According to fixed rates
PROSECUTOR: What kind of rates
WITNESS I: A skilled worker
                 was paid 4 marks a day
                 an unskilled worker 3 marks
PROSECUTOR: How long was the work day
WITNESS I: Eleven hours
PROSECUTOR: To whom were the wages paid
WITNESS I: To the camp administration
                 It was their job to look after
                 the prisoners
PROSECUTOR: How were the prisoners fed
WITNESS I: In my factory they were well-fed
PROSECUTOR: Didn't you know
                 that the prisoners were worked to the limit
                 and then killed
WITNESS I: I always tried
                 to do more for the prisoners
                 than I was supposed to
                 I suffered terribly
                 when I saw
                 how every day
                 the prisoners in our care
                 had to walk for miles on foot
                 along the road from the barracks
                 to the work camp and back again
                 I devoted the highest priority
                 to making sure
                 that the workers
                 who were employed in our department
                 were better cared for
                 and got better shoes
PROSECUTOR: How many prisoners
                 worked in your factory
WITNESS I: 500 to 600
PROSECUTOR: Didn't you notice

	a heavy turnover in the workers
WITNESS 1:	I was very concerned
	to hold on to my people
PROSECUTOR:	Were there cases of illness
WITNESS 1:	Naturally there were
	I also knew about the epidemics
	the prisoners had suffered
	in the camp
PROSECUTOR:	Didn't it attract your notice
	that those who went on sick call
	failed to return
WITNESS 1:	No
	Actually they often came back
	from the camp
PROSECUTOR:	Did you hear about mistreatment
WITNESS 1:	Hear yes
PROSECUTOR:	What did you hear
WITNESS 1:	I heard
	they were beaten
JUDGE:	By whom
WITNESS 1:	I don't know
	I never saw it
	I only heard about it
PROSECUTOR:	Did you know about the liquidations
WITNESS 1:	If you were there 3 years
	naturally one thing and another
	trickled through
	Yes we knew what was going on
	But later on
	when I heard the first figures
	I simply wasn't able to grasp them
PROSECUTOR:	Did you ever see any of these shipments
WITNESS 1:	Once or twice at most
PROSECUTOR:	Do you know the Defendants in this room
WITNESS 1:	I know some of them
	Mainly the executives
	We met together in the executive club
	in a purely social atmosphere
PROSECUTOR:	You are today a Government Counsellor

	Haven't you met these people again
	after the war also
	now that most of you are back
	in civilian life
WITNESS I:	I may run across
	the one or the other
PROSECUTOR:	Did you happen on these occasions
	to comment on events of that time
WITNESS I:	Herr Prosecutor
	we were all primarily concerned
	with winning the war
PROSECUTOR:	The court has summoned as witnesses
	three former executives
	from the factories
	dependant on co-operation with the camp
	One witness has sent the court
	an affidavit that he is blind
	and therefore unable to come
	the other witness is suffering
	from a broken spine
	Only one former chairman
	of the administrative staff
	has appeared
	Now you Herr Witness
	you are still employed
	by the firm
	which supplied the prisoners
	with work at that time
DEFENCE COUNSEL:	We protest against this question
	which has no other purpose
	than to undermine confidence
	in our industries
WITNESS 2:	I am no longer
	actively engaged in business
PROSECUTOR:	Do you receive an honorary pension
	from this concern
WITNESS 2:	Yes
PROSECUTOR:	Does this pension amount to 300,000
	marks a year

DEFENCE COUNSEL:	We object to this question
PROSECUTOR:	If you live in your castle
	and are no longer concerned
	with the business matters of your firm
	which today has changed nothing but its name
	what do you do to keep yourself busy
WITNESS 2:	I collect porcelain paintings and engravings
	as well as items of peasant folklore
DEFENCE COUNSEL:	Questions of this sort
	have not the slightest relevance
	to the proceedings of this trial
PROSECUTOR:	In your business you were
	directly responsible for the employment
	of prisoners as workers
	What do you know about the agreement
	between your firm and the camp administration
	concerning those prisoners
	who were no longer fit to work
WITNESS 2:	I know nothing about it
PROSECUTOR:	This court has in its possession
	weekly reports
	telling about prisoners
	found too weak to work by the company
WITNESS 2:	I know nothing about it
PROSECUTOR:	Didn't the physical condition
	of the prisoners attract your notice
WITNESS 2:	I personally always fought
	against the employment of these workers
	who were composed for the most part
	of a social or politically unreliable elements
PROSECUTOR:	The court is in possession of documents
	which mentions the beneficial friendship
	between the camp administration
	and your company
	One of these reports says
	On the occasion of a dinner
	we have furthermore determined to ratify
	all the measures
	incorporating the excellent camp arrangements

	in the running of the Buna works
	What were these measures
	Herr Witness
WITNESS 2:	I was only supposed to do my duty
	and to make sure
	that the demands of the state agency
	were fulfilled
PROSECUTOR:	Herr Witness
	Why don't you allow yourself
	to speak out clearly
	and verify the statements
	made by an earlier witness
	concerning the system of exploitation
	by which the camp operated
	You Herr Witness
	and the other directors
	of your great company
	achieved through unlimited human sacrifices
	yearly turnovers of unprecedented sums
DEFENCE COUNSEL:	Objection
PROSECUTOR:	Let us consider once again
	that the successors of this company
	amassed glittering fortunes
	and that they are now about to enter
	what is called a period of expansion
DEFENCE COUNSEL:	We ask the court
	to make a record
	of these slanders

CANTO FIVE: THE END OF LILI TOFLER

III

JUDGE:	And what do you know
	about the detainment
	of Lili Tofler
WITNESS I:	I don't really know

104

	any details
	I just remember
	that she was taken off
	I asked what was happening
	and heard
	that the investigation was still going on
	Later I heard
	that they had killed her
JUDGE:	Who killed her
WITNESS 1:	I don't know
	I wasn't there
JUDGE:	The witness was at that time a Chief Officer
	which is higher than a colonel
	and lower than a Brigadier General
	Had you no right to intervene
	when a fellow worker was taken away
WITNESS 1:	I was not sufficiently acquainted
	with the case
JUDGE:	Didn't you inquire after the reason
	for her detainment
WITNESS 1:	That was outside my jurisdiction
JUDGE:	But it was a rather massive attack
	on your personal staff
	They simply took away from you
	someone whom you needed
	for your important war production
WITNESS 1:	Lili Tofler had no particular ability
JUDGE:	Herr Witness
	A man in the Political Department
	was far below you in rank
	Why did you allow this attack
	on your own personal position
WITNESS 1:	Your Honour
	There was one rule at that time
	that was equally valid for everyone
	This was
	Be careful about helping prisoners
	You could go up to a certain point
	but no further

JUDGE: We summon as witness
the prisoner
to whom Lili Tofler
sent her letter
Herr Witness
how did you manage
to survive

WITNESS 9: A few days after her arrival in the bunker
I too was led out
I believed
Lili had betrayed me
but I had only been taken into custody
as a hostage along with others
I heard there
that Lili had to stand in the washroom
for an hour every morning
and afternoon
During that time Boger pressed
a pistol against her temple
This lasted 4 days
Then I was taken out to be shot
with 50 other prisoners
The whole time I believed
they knew
that the letter was meant for me
We had to undress
and stand in the corridor
I saw how the typist
had made a cross next to my number
on the list
On paper I was already dead
The prisoners were taken into the yard
and shot
Only two were held back
for some reason or other
One of them was me
I was loitering in the corridor
when suddenly Jakob came
and took me into the yard

I believed
then that I too was to be shot
But Jakob only showed me the pile
of dead prisoners
The two who had smuggled the letter
into the camp lay on top
A bit further to the side Lili lay
with two shots in her heart
I asked Jakob
who shot her
He said
Boger

JUDGE: Defendant Boger
Do you want to say anything

DEFENDANT 2: No thank you

JUDGE: Can anyone tell us
where Lili Tofler came from

FEMALE WITNESS 5: I don't know

JUDGE: What was her character

FEMALE WITNESS 5: Every time I met Lili
and asked her
How are you Lili
she said
Life is always good to me

Canto Six: UNTERSCHARFÜHRER STARK

I

WITNESS 8:   Defendant Stark
was our superior in the reception department
I worked there as a clerk
At that time Stark was 20 years old
In his free hours he prepared himself
for his higher school exam
He was very glad to have the graduates
among the prisoners test his knowledge
and he came to them with questions
In the evening
when a Polish woman with 2 children
was brought in
he was engaged in a discussion with us
on the humanism of Goethe

JUDGE: What happened
on this occasion

WITNESS 8:   We later found out the following
The eight-year-old boy
that the woman led by the hand
had taken a little rabbit away
from the camp office
to give it to his two-year-old sister
to play with
Because of this
all three were to be shot
Stark
performed the shooting

JUDGE: Were you able to see this

WITNESS 8:   At the time the shootings
were carried out at the old crematorium
located directly behind the reception barracks

Through the window we could see
Stark going into the crematorium
with the mother and her children
He had his rifle around his shoulder
We heard a series of shots
Then Stark came out alone

JUDGE: Defendant Stark
Does this description represent the truth

DEFENDANT 12: I absolutely deny it

JUDGE: What was your position in the camp

DEFENDANT 12: I was a Block Captain

JUDGE: How did you come to the camp

DEFENDANT 12: I was sent
along with a group
of other non-commissioned officers

JUDGE: Did you act as Block Captain from that time

DEFENDANT 12: That's what we were supposed to do
that's what we were appointed for

JUDGE: Were you prepared
for this vocation

DEFENDANT 12: We had finished the leadership course

JUDGE: Were there any practical rules
which you were supposed to follow

DEFENDANT 12: Only a short briefing session

JUDGE: What happened on your arrival in camp

DEFENDANT 12: There was a reception committee

JUDGE: Who took part in it

DEFENDANT 12: The Commander the Chief Officer
the Camp Security Officer
the Liaison Chief

JUDGE: What kind of duties were you given

DEFENDANT 12: At first I was attached
to a Prisoner's Block
There were mainly young people
schoolboys and students

JUDGE: Why were the prisoners there

DEFENDANT 12: I believe
because of their contact
with the resistance movement

109

	It was a group of suspects
	They were transferred to the camp
	by the Command Post of the Security Police
JUDGE:	Did you see assignment papers
	for these people
DEFENDANT 12:	No
	I had nothing to do with that
JUDGE:	What were your precise duties
DEFENDANT 12:	I had to see
	that the prisoners were all there
	and that they came
	to work on time
JUDGE:	Did anyone try to escape
DEFENDANT 12:	Not while I was there
JUDGE:	Did the prisoners have sufficient food
DEFENDANT 12:	Everyone had his quart of soup
JUDGE:	What happened
	if the people couldn't work
	or didn't want to
DEFENDANT 12:	That never happened
JUDGE:	Weren't you sometimes provoked to action
	if the prisoner did something forbidden
DEFENDANT 12:	That never happened
	I never filed a complaint
JUDGE:	Did you never beat anyone
DEFENDANT 12:	I had no need to
JUDGE:	When did you come
	to the Reception Block
	of the Political Department
DEFENDANT 12:	In May 1941
JUDGE:	What was the reason for your transfer
DEFENDANT 12:	Once when I was riding
	I met Major Grabner
	the chief of the Political Department
	He asked me what my profession was
	and I said I was a student
	and was about to take my exams
	he answered
	that such people were needed

	After a few days I was detached
	by an order from the Commander's Office
JUDGE:	What did you do in the Reception Department
DEFENDANT 12:	My next job
	Was to become familiar with registration
	Incoming prisoners
	were provided with a number
	Then their personal files were filled in
	and their record cards were put away
JUDGE:	How did the prisoners arrive
DEFENDANT 12:	Either on foot
	or in the vans
	or by train
	The trains came regularly
	on Tuesday Thursday and Friday
JUDGE:	How did these receptions take place
DEFENDANT 12:	I had to be ready
	when the shipments were announced
	First the prisoners were put
	in front of the camp gate
	and then the shipment leader
	handed over the papers
	The prisoners came in to be counted
	and to be given a number
	In those days
	they didn't tattoo the number
	Every prisoner received his number
	on cardboard in triplicate
	One number was kept by him
	one went with his clothing
	one with his valuables
	The prisoner had to hold on
	to his cardboard number
	until he was given one on cloth
JUDGE:	What did you have to do with this
DEFENDANT 12:	I had to give out the numbers
	and take the people to the clothing room
	There the prisoners were undressed
	bathed and put into uniforms

	and their hair was cut
	then they were taken
	through the reception procedures
JUDGE:	How was that done
DEFENDANT 12:	Their record forms were filled out
	their completed questionnaires
	were filed in the reception room
	Then an entry list was prepared
	Here it was listed if the person
	was a political prisoner
	a criminal prisoner
	or a racial prisoner
	The list then went to the various departments
JUDGE:	Which departments
DEFENDANT 12:	To the Security Officer
	the Command Post
	the Political Department
	the physician
	Eleven or twelve copies
	were distributed in the mail each day
JUDGE:	Did you have anything further
	to do with the prisoners
DEFENDANT 12:	Once reception was over
	I was finished with them
PROSECUTOR:	Defendant Stark
	were you present at all incoming
	shipments
DEFENDANT 12:	Those were my orders
	I had to be there
PROSECUTOR:	What were your duties
	when the shipments came in
DEFENDANT 12:	I was only responsible
	for the written work
PROSECUTOR:	What does that mean
DEFENDANT 12:	Some of the prisoners were transferred
	I had to register them
PROSECUTOR:	And the others
DEFENDANT 12:	The others were removed
PROSECUTOR:	Could you explain the difference

112

DEFENDANT 12:	The prisoners who were transferred
	entered the camp
	The prisoners who were removed
	were not taken and not held
	That is the difference
	between transferral and removal
PROSECUTOR:	What happened to those who were removed
DEFENDANT 12:	They were taken to the small crematorium
	for immediate liquidation
PROSECUTOR:	Was this still before the construction
	of the large crematorium
DEFENDANT 12:	The large crematorium of the outer camp
	first went into use
	in the summer of 1942
	Until that time the crematorium
	in the old camp was used
PROSECUTOR:	How did the removal
	of the prisoners take place
DEFENDANT 12:	The lists were compared
	and the names checked off
	Then we had to march with the people
	who had not been picked out
	during the reception
	to the small crematorium
PROSECUTOR:	What did you tell the prisoners
DEFENDANT 12:	We told them
	they were going to be deloused
PROSECUTOR:	Weren't they uneasy
DEFENDANT 12:	No
	They went along quietly

CANTO SIX: UNTERSCHARFUHRER STARK

II

WITNESS 8:	We could always tell if Stark
	had come from a killing

by his behaviour
He always had to have things
clean and orderly in his office
and we had to chase away the flies
with handkerchiefs
All hell broke loose
if he happened to discover a fly
He was absolutely beside himself with rage
Even before he took off his fieldcap
he would wash his hands in a bowl
that the caretaker had put on a stool
right next to the doorway
When he had washed his hands
he pointed to the dirty water
and the caretaker had to run
and bring fresh water
Then he gave us his jacket to clean
and washed his hands and face again

WITNESS 7: My whole life long I hear Stark
always Stark
Come on get in you bastards
and then we had to go into the chamber

JUDGE: Into what chamber

WITNESS 7: The corpse chamber of the old crematorium
Many hundreds of men lay there
women and children
like packages
There were even prisoners of war
Come on
Undress the corpses
shouted Stark
I was 18 years old
and had never seen the dead before
I just stood there
and Stark came up and hit me

JUDGE: Did the dead have wounds

WITNESS 7: Yes

JUDGE: Were they gun wounds

WITNESS 7: No

	The men were gassed
	They lay stiff against each other
	Often we ripped their clothing
	And then we were beaten again
JUDGE:	Didn't they undress them first
WITNESS 7:	That was later
	in the new crematorium
	there were rooms to undress in
JUDGE:	Was Stark there also
WITNESS 7:	Stark was always there
	I hear him shouting
	Come on
	Pick up that junk
	Once a small man was hidden
	underneath a hill of clothes
	Stark discovered him
	Come here he shouted
	and placed him against the wall
	He shot him first in one leg
	then in the other
	finally
	the man had to sit down on a bench
	and Stark shot him dead
	He liked to shoot people in the leg first
	I heard a woman screaming
	I haven't done anything
	He shouted
	Get up to the wall Sarah
	The woman begged him for her life
	as he began to shoot
JUDGE:	Can the witness say
	when he first saw Defendant Stark
	perform these killings
WITNESS 7:	In the autumn of 1941
JUDGE:	Was this the first time
	gas was used
WITNESS 7:	Yes
JUDGE:	What did the old crematorium look like
WITNESS 7:	It was a cement building

with a heavy square chimney
The walls were buttressed
by earthworks
The corpse room was about 60 feet long
and 15 feet wide
It was reached through a small anteroom
From the corpse chamber a door led
to the first crematorium oven
and another door to the hall
with the other two ovens

JUDGE: Defendant Stark
How large were the groups
you were given to lead to the crematorium

DEFENDANT 12: They averaged between 150 and 200 units

JUDGE: Were there women and children among them

DEFENDANT 12: Yes

JUDGE: Did you think it right
that women and children
should be part of these shipments

DEFENDANT 12: Yes
At that time it was a question
of family liability

JUDGE: You did not question
the guilt
of the women and children

DEFENDANT 12: We were told
they were involved
in poisoning the water supply
blowing up bridges
and other acts of sabotage

JUDGE: Did you also see prisoners of war
among these people

DEFENDANT 12: Yes
According to orders these people
had lost all claim to honourable treatment

PROSECUTOR: Defendant Stark
In the autumn of 1941 great hordes
of Soviet prisoners
were brought into the camp

116

	According to our records
	you were in charge of the treatment
	of these troops
DEFENDANT 12:	I only acted according to orders
	with this shipment
PROSECUTOR:	What do you mean
	according to orders
DEFENDANT 12:	I simply had to lead them off
	and take their record cards
	with the notice that they had been ordered
	to be shot
	Then I had to destroy
	their identity discs
	and keep their numbers on file
PROSECUTOR:	What reason was given
	for the slaughter
	of these prisoners
DEFENDANT 12:	It was a question of annihilating
	a philosophy
	With their fanatical outlook on politics
	these prisoners endangered
	the security of the camp
PROSECUTOR:	Where did the shooting take place
DEFENDANT 12:	In the yard of Block Eleven
PROSECUTOR:	Did you take part in the shooting
DEFENDANT 12:	In one case
	yes
PROSECUTOR:	How did it happen
DEFENDANT 12:	The people's names were read out
	and the formalities were observed
	They were led into the yard
	one after another
	It was almost over
	Then Grabner said
	It's Stark's turn now
	Until then the other Block Captains
	had taken turns shooting
PROSECUTOR:	How many did you shoot
DEFENDANT 12:	I no longer know

PROSECUTOR:	Was it more than one
DEFENDANT 12:	Yes
PROSECUTOR:	More than two
DEFENDANT 12:	It might have been four or five
PROSECUTOR:	You couldn't have refused to take part in the shooting
DEFENDANT 12:	It was an order I had to act as a soldier
PROSECUTOR:	Did you have any connection with other shootings
DEFENDANT 12:	No I came home on leave to finish my studies
PROSECUTOR:	When did you go on leave
DEFENDANT 12:	In December 1941
PROSECUTOR:	When did you bring your studies to a close
DEFENDANT 12:	I passed my examination in the spring of 1942
PROSECUTOR:	Did you come back to the camp then
DEFENDANT 12:	Yes for a short period
DEFENCE COUNSEL:	The court would do well to consider that our client was 20 years old when he was transferred to camp service As the witnesses have stated he had lively intellectual interests which as his entire character shows did not make him suitable for the duties he was assigned We should also like to point out that our client a year after he finished his studies received a further leave of absence in order to study law after which he was wounded during action on the front in the last year of the war

Right after the war
when he was able to return
to normal life he continued
his educational development
He now took up agriculture
passed the university exams
was a specialist for the Economic Ministry
and until his arrest
served as a teacher
in an agricultural school

PROSECUTOR: Defendant Stark
Did you take part in the first gassings
which were carried out as a test
on Soviet prisoners in 1941

DEFENDANT 12: No

PROSECUTOR: Defendant Stark
The mass annihilation
of Soviet prisoners
began in the autumn and winter of 1941
These annihilations claimed a sacrifice
of 25,000 lives
You were involved in the registration
of these prisoners
You knew of their execution
You agreed to their death
and permitted the necessary preparations

DEFENCE COUNSEL: We most urgently protest
against these attacks on our client
All-inclusive accusations
have no legal significance
We are only concerned with known cases
of dereliction and complicity
in connection with the history of the crime
Every possible doubt however slight
must be allowed to count in the favour
of the Defendants
The Defendants laugh in agreement

CANTO SIX: UNTERSCHARFUHRER STARK

III

JUDGE:	Defendant Stark Did you never help with the gassings themselves
DEFENDANT 12:	I had to once
JUDGE:	How many people were involved
DEFENDANT 12:	It could have been 150 At least 4 vans full
JUDGE:	What kind of prisoners were they
DEFENDANT 12:	It was a mixed shipment
JUDGE:	What did you have to do
DEFENDANT 12:	I stood outside in front of the stairs after I had led the people into the crematorium the first aid people who were responsible for the gassing had closed the door and were making their preparations
JUDGE:	What did these preparations consist of
DEFENDANT 12:	They got the containers ready and put on gas masks and they went up the slope to the flat roof Usually 4 people were necessary This time one was missing and they shouted that they needed someone Because I was the only one around Grabner said Come on give a hand But I didn't go right away Then a security guard came and said Get a move on If you don't go up there you'll be sent inside

	So I had to go up
	and help pour it in
JUDGE:	Where was the gas introduced
DEFENDANT 12:	Through hatches in the roof
JUDGE:	And what did the people do
	in the room below
DEFENDANT 12:	I don't know
JUDGE:	Did you hear nothing
	of what happened below
DEFENDANT 12:	They screamed
JUDGE:	How long
DEFENDANT 12:	Perhaps 10 or 15 minutes
JUDGE:	Who opened the room
DEFENDANT 12:	A first aid man
JUDGE:	What did you see there
DEFENDANT 12:	I didn't look closely
JUDGE:	Did you consider what you saw
	to be wrong
DEFENDANT 12:	No not at all
	Only in the manner
JUDGE:	What do you mean the manner
DEFENDANT 12:	If someone was shot
	that was something else
	But the use of gas
	was unmanly and cowardly
JUDGE:	Defendant Stark
	During your studies for a university degree
	did you never have occasion
	to doubt your actions
DEFENDANT 12:	Your Honour
	I should like to explain for once
	Every third word in our schooling
	was concerned with those
	who were guilty of everything
	and who must be rooted out
	It was hammered into us
	that this could only be
	in the best interests of our own people
	In the officers' schools we learned

above all to maintain silence
If anyone asked any further
he was told
Everything that is done
happens according to law
It matters little
that today the laws are different
We were told
You must learn
Your education is more important than bread
Your Honour
Our thinking was taken away from us
Others did it for us
Approving laughter of the Defendants

Canto Seven: THE BLACK WALL

I

WITNESS 3:	The shootings were carried out in the yard of Block Eleven in front of the Black Wall
JUDGE:	Where was Block Eleven
WITNESS 3:	To the right just outside of the old camp
JUDGE:	Can the witness describe the yard
WITNESS 3:	The yard was between Blocks Ten and Eleven and occupied the entire block area of 120 feet It was closed off front and back by a brick wall
JUDGE:	How was the yard reached
WITNESS 3:	Through a side door in Block Eleven and through a gate in the front wall
JUDGE:	Could anyone see into the yard
WITNESS 3:	Only from the front windows on the ground floor of Block Eleven When the yard gate was opened for carrying away the bodies curfew was proclaimed throughout the camp The remaining windows in Block Eleven had been walled up except for a tiny aperture at the top The windows of the Women's Block nearby were covered with boards
JUDGE:	How high was the wall
WITNESS 3:	About 12 feet
JUDGE:	Where was the Black Wall itself
WITNESS 3:	Opposite the gate

	along the rear wall
JUDGE:	What did the Black Wall look like
WITNESS 3:	It was constructed from thick wooden planks
	and had projecting wings
	on either side to intercept stray bullets
	The wood was covered with tarred sackcloth
JUDGE:	How large was the Black Wall
WITNESS 3:	About 10 feet high
	and 12 feet wide
JUDGE:	From what point were the condemned
	led to the Black Wall
WITNESS 3:	They came from the side door of Block Eleven
JUDGE:	Describe this process
WITNESS 3:	Jakob appeared in each case
	with two prisoners at a time
	They were undressed
JUDGE:	Who was this Jakob
WITNESS 3:	Jakob was the prisoner
	in charge of Block Eleven
	He was a big powerful man
	an ex-boxer
JUDGE:	How were the prisoners led out
WITNESS 3:	Jakob was between them
	and held them tightly by the arm
JUDGE:	Were the prisoners' hands tied
WITNESS 3:	Until 1943 they were tied together
	behind their backs with wire
	Later they did without it
	for experience had shown
	that almost all prisoners
	behaved quietly
JUDGE:	How far was it to the Black Wall
	from the side door
WITNESS 3:	First down the 6 steps from the door
	then the 20 paces to the wall
	It was all done in double time
	After Jakob had brought
	the prisoners to the wall
	he ran back

	to fetch the next ones
JUDGE:	How were the executions carried out
WITNESS 3:	The prisoners were turned
	with their faces to the wall
	3 to 6 feet away from one another
	Then the executioner stepped
	up to the first one
	raised his carbine to the neck
	and shot from a distance
	of about 4 inches
	The one next to him saw it happen
	As soon as the first had fallen
	his turn came next
JUDGE:	What kind of weapon was used
	at the executions
WITNESS 3:	A small calibre weapon with a silencer
JUDGE:	Whom did you see at these executions
WITNESS 3:	The Camp Commander
	the Chief Officer
	the Chief of the Political Department Grabner
	as well as their colleagues
	Among others I saw
	Broad Stark Boger and Schlage
	Kaduk was also often there
DEFENCE COUNSEL:	Are you certain
	that the Chief Officer was there
WITNESS 3:	He was a well-known personality
	One knew the Chief Officer
	just as one knew the Commander
DEFENCE COUNSEL:	What were you doing at these executions
WITNESS 3:	As a medical student I was assigned
	to the Corpse Bearers Battalion
JUDGE:	Which of the defendants
	actually did the shooting
WITNESS 3:	I saw Boger Broad Stark Schlage
	and Kaduk shoot with their own hands
JUDGE:	Defendant Boger
	did you take part in these executions
	at the Black Wall

DEFENDANT 2:	I never fired a shot
	all the time I was in the camp
JUDGE:	Defendant Broad
	did you take part in these executions
	at the Black Wall
DEFENDANT 16:	I was never obliged to perform such duties
JUDGE:	Defendant Schlage
	did you as the overseer for Block Eleven
	take part in these executions
	at the Black Wall
DEFENDANT 14:	I had no power to do so
JUDGE:	Defendant Kaduk
	did you take part in these executions
	at the Black Wall
DEFENDANT 7:	I never set foot
	in Block Eleven
	What has been said about me here
	is an absolute lie
JUDGE:	Can the witness tell us
	if death sentences were read
	before the executions
WITNESS 3:	At most executions no
	If a death sentence was pronounced
	a special battalion was present
	but I can only remember such a thing
	happening in a few cases
	Usually the prisoners
	were just brought in from the cells
	of Block Eleven
JUDGE:	What condition were the prisoners in
WITNESS 3:	Most of them were in rather poor condition
	after their interrogation
	and their stay in the bunker
	There were some who were carried out
	to the wall on a stretcher
JUDGE:	We call as witness
	the superior officer
	who was in charge of the Defendants
	at that time

	You were Chief of the Central Agency
	of the Security Police
	and presiding officer of the military court
	In your capacity what did you have to do
	with the executions
	which were carried out
	by the Political Department
WITNESS 1:	My office had not the slightest connection
	with the Political Department
	The only cases which came before me
	were ones which dealt with partisans
	These were led into the camp
	and sentence was passed in a hearing room
JUDGE:	Where was this hearing room
WITNESS 1:	In one of the barracks
JUDGE:	Wasn't the hearing room in Block Eleven
WITNESS 1:	Now you're asking too much
WITNESS 6:	I was a clerk in Block Eleven
	in this capacity I had a glimpse
	of the work of the military court
	The hearing room was off
	the corridor in Block Eleven
JUDGE:	What did this room look like
WITNESS 6:	There were 4 windows on the yard
	A large table stood in the middle
JUDGE:	Does the witness begin to remember
WITNESS 1:	No
JUDGE:	Have you never been
	in the inner section of the old camp
WITNESS 1:	You're asking me too much
JUDGE:	Did you never go through the camp gate
WITNESS 1:	It's possible
	I remember there was a band
	that used to play there
JUDGE:	Were you never in the yard of Block Eleven
WITNESS 1:	Once perhaps
	There may have been a wall there
	I can no longer see it in my memory
JUDGE:	Surely you must have noticed

127

	a wall painted black
WITNESS 1:	I have no memory
JUDGE:	Herr Witness
	You were the presiding judge
	of the military court
	Was there a Defence Counsel for the prisoners
WITNESS 1:	If one was desired
JUDGE:	Was one ever desired
WITNESS 1:	It rarely happened
JUDGE:	And if it did happen
WITNESS 1:	Then one was provided
JUDGE:	Who was the Defence Counsel
WITNESS 1:	An officer of the Department
JUDGE:	Was there heated questioning
WITNESS 1:	There was no occasion for it
	In any case I have never heard
	of any heated questioning
	The facts of the case were so clear
	that there was no need for heated questioning
JUDGE:	What were the facts of the case
WITNESS 1:	The cases were exclusively concerned
	with enemies of the state
JUDGE:	Did the prisoners confess to this
WITNESS 1:	There was no way they could deny it
JUDGE:	How were they brought to confess
WITNESS 1:	By interrogations
JUDGE:	Who led the interrogations
WITNESS 1:	The Political Department
JUDGE:	As a judge did you not reflect
	on the manner in which confessions
	were brought about
WITNESS 1:	What could I do about it
	if one or another of my people
	overstepped his authority
	I constantly admonished my colleagues
	that they should deal fairly with all cases
JUDGE:	Were witnesses present at questionings
WITNESS 1:	As a rule no
	we asked if everything was in order

	and they all said yes
JUDGE:	You pronounced only death sentences
WITNESS 1:	Yes
	There were very few acquittals
	Proceedings were only opened
	if everything was clear
JUDGE:	Did you never see signs
	that the accused
	had been convicted
	on inadmissible grounds
WITNESS 1:	No
JUDGE:	Were women and children
	also executed at the Black Wall
WITNESS 1:	I know nothing about that
WITNESS 6:	Among the prisoners
	who were brought to judgment
	at the military court in Block Eleven
	were numerous women and children
	The charges referred to smuggling
	or contact with partisan groups
	In contrast with the camp prisoners
	who were locked in the cellar
	the criminal prisoners were held
	on the ground floor of the block
	They were led one by one
	into the hearing room
	The judge read the sentence
	he merely recited the name and then said
	you are sentenced to death
	Most of the sentenced
	didn't understand the language
	and had no idea
	why they had been imprisoned
	From the courtyard they were immediately
	led to be undressed in the washroom
	and brought from there into the yard
PROSECUTOR:	Would the witness tell us
	how many sentences he read
	as presiding officer of the military court

WITNESS 1:	I can't remember
PROSECUTOR:	How often were you summoned
	to pronounce sentence
WITNESS 1:	I no longer know
PROSECUTOR:	How long did a court session last
WITNESS 1:	I really can't say
PROSECUTOR:	You are today an executive
	of a great mercantile enterprise
	As such you must be accustomed
	to dealing with figures
	and with units of time
	How many men
	were sentenced by you
WITNESS 1:	I don't know
WITNESS 6:	In one session of the military court
	an average of 100 to 150 sentences
	was read
	The session lasted from 1½ to 2 hours
	and took place every 2 weeks
PROSECUTOR:	Herr Witness
	how many men in all
	would you estimate were shot
	before the Black Wall
WITNESS 6:	According to the death registers
	and our records
	it is clear
	that in connection with the routine
	clearing out of the bunkers
	approximately 20,000 men
	were shot before the Black Wall

CANTO SEVEN: THE BLACK WALL

II

| WITNESS 7: | In the autumn of 1943 |
| | I saw a little girl |

quite early in the morning
in the yard of Block Eleven
She had a red dress on
and a pigtail
She stood alone and held her hands
at her side
like a soldier
Once she bent down
and wiped the dust from her shoes
then she stood still again
Then I saw Boger enter the yard
He held the gun hidden
behind his back
He took the child by the hand
and she went with him like a good girl
he made her stand
with her face to the Black Wall
The child turned around once more
and Boger turned her head
against the wall again
raised the gun
and shot the child dead

DEFENCE COUNSEL: How can the witness have seen that

WITNESS 7: I was cleaning myself in the washroom
right opposite the entrance to the yard

JUDGE: How old was the child

WITNESS 7: 6 or 7 years
The Corpse Bearers later said
the parents of the child
had also been shot there
a few days earlier

DEFENDANT 2: Your Honour
I never shot a child
I absolutely never shot anyone

WITNESS 3: I often saw Boger before the Black Wall
I can still hear him calling to his prisoner
Head up
and then he'd shoot him in the neck

JUDGE: Are you sure you haven't deceived yourself

131

	and confused Boger with someone else
WITNESS 3:	We all knew Boger
	and his clumsy way of walking
	We often saw him with his rifle
	over his shoulder
	riding on his bicycle to Block Eleven
	Sometimes he dragged his prisoner
	on a leash behind him
	like a little dog
JUDGE:	Defendant Boger
	wouldn't you like to reconsider
	your declaration that you never
	shot anyone in the camp
DEFENDANT 2:	I stand by my statement
	today and a thousand years from now
	I wouldn't have been afraid to shoot
	for that would merely have been
	performing my duty in the service
WITNESS 3:	There were shootings
	every Wednesday and Friday
	I saw Boger kill
	17 prisoners
	on the 14th of May 1943
	I made a note of the date
	because my friend Berger was in it
	Before that he was beaten
	to pieces on the swing
	Berger screamed
	You murderers you criminals
	as Boger shot him
	Another lay beside him on his knees
	Boger shot him in the face
	Whenever it was known
	that Boger was in the house
	We knew what was in store
	Among ourselves we called the man
	The Black Death
DEFENDANT 2:	I had many other nicknames
	We all had nicknames

	It means nothing
JUDGE:	Defendant Boger
	During this trial
	it has been repeatedly
	stated by witnesses
	that you killed prisoners
	in the camp
	Are you of the opinion
	that all these statements are inventions
DEFENDANT 2:	I was the one most often present
	at shootings
	It is obvious
	that the prisoners
	are confusing me with someone else
	They caught Boger
	so it is quite clear
	that they've unloaded
	all their hate on me
JUDGE:	Did you in no single instance
	shoot anyone
DEFENDANT 2:	I did
	once
JUDGE:	You shot
	once
DEFENDANT 2:	This was an individual case
	in which I obeyed orders
	and took part in a shooting
JUDGE:	How did it happen
DEFENDANT 2:	Grabner once ordered me to do it
	when we were clearing out a bunker
	Captain Boger
	will carry on the shooting
JUDGE:	How often did you shoot
DEFENDANT 2:	Twice
	in only one case
	Later I refused
	to take part in such things
	I said
	Either I work here

	or I work in the identification department
	I can't manage
	both together
JUDGE:	What kind of people
	did you have to shoot at that time
DEFENDANT 2:	They belonged to a shipment
	which had not been processed
	by the identification department
JUDGE:	That means
	that no one probably thought
	that they were going to live
DEFENDANT 2:	That is my opinion also
JUDGE:	Defendant Boger
	Why have you always maintained
	until now that you didn't shoot
	anyone in the camp
DEFENDANT 2:	Your Honour
	There are so many accusations
	against me that it is impossible
	to pin them down
JUDGE:	And you still maintain
	that you shot in only two cases
	and that no one died
	during the intensive interrogations
DEFENDANT 2:	Yes
	I absolutely swear it
JUDGE:	Herr Witness
	Would you tell us when you
	had to be present in Block Eleven
	as a member of the Corpse Bearers Battalion
WITNESS 3:	We were required to be there
	about an hour before the execution
JUDGE:	Where were you stationed
WITNESS 3:	In the ambulance block
JUDGE:	Where was the ambulance block
WITNESS 3:	Opposite the Bunkerblock
	on the far right side of the camp
JUDGE:	How were you summoned
WITNESS 3:	A clerk from Block Eleven

134

	came running in
	He shouted
	Corpse Bearers
	One stretcher
	Two stretchers
	If he shouted one stretcher
	we knew it had been a small execution
	if more were required
	it was a big execution
JUDGE:	Where was the clerk
WITNESS 3:	He stood in the door
	and we ran to him from our station
	Our chief decided
	how many Bearers to send
	according to what the clerk said
JUDGE:	Where did you go after that
WITNESS 3:	When the sirens
	had announced a curfew throughout the camp
	we went through the door
	into the yard of Block Eleven
	We had to station ourselves
	opposite the gates and stand ready
	with the stretchers
JUDGE:	What kind of stretchers were they
WITNESS 3:	Canvas with wooden poles
	and metal supports
JUDGE:	Was a doctor there
WITNESS 3:	Only at the big executions
	were there doctors present
	Otherwise the only people there
	were from the Political Department
JUDGE:	Where did the prisoners wait
WITNESS 3:	They waited in the washroom
	and in the passageway
JUDGE:	What kind of preparations were usual
WITNESS 3:	When the prisoners came out of the cellar
	they had to leave their clothing
	in the washroom or at the entrance
	They had their numbers written

	on their chests
	with a moist aniline pencil
	The clerk checked the numbers
	and crossed them off his list
	for the ones who were led
	into the yard
JUDGE:	What order was shouted
	to bring in the condemned men
WITNESS 3:	The order was
	Out
	Then Jakob ran out with the first pair
	As soon as they were at the wall
	we too heard the order
	Out
	and we ran out with our stretchers
JUDGE:	Who gave you this order
WITNESS 3:	Either the doctor
	or one of the officers
JUDGE:	Were the prisoners shot
	as soon as you arrived
WITNESS 3:	Usually the first one went down
	and the second went down right afterwards
	Sometimes it lasted longer
	then we waited
	behind
	the executioners
JUDGE:	Why did it sometimes last longer
WITNESS 3:	It happened
	that they had trouble loading
	so we waited while they fumbled
	with their guns
JUDGE:	The prisoners who were about to die
	How did they behave
WITNESS 3:	Some prayed
	I heard others singing
	national or religious songs
	Only once
	when a woman started screaming
	someone ordered

Let that lunatic have it first
JUDGE: How did you carry away the dead
WITNESS 3: As soon as they had fallen in the sand
that was strewn before the wall
we picked them up by the arms and legs
and laid them back-down on the stretchers
Then we put the other one on upside down
so that his head
lay between the legs of the first one
Then we ran to the discharge gutter
and dumped the bodies
JUDGE: Where was this gutter
WITNESS 3: On the outskirts of the yard
JUDGE: What happened then
WITNESS 3: While we ran with the stretcher
to the unloading place
Jakob ran to the wall
with the next two
and the two other stretcher bearers
stood ready behind
We placed the bodies on top of each other
in layers so that the heads lay
over the gutter to discharge the blood
JUDGE: Did the prisoners die immediately
WITNESS 3: It could happen that the shot
only went in the ear or chin
and they were still alive
when they were carried away
Then we had to set the stretchers down
and the wounded ones were shot
again in the head
Criminal Officer Schlage
supervised the unloading
from time to time
and if someone was still moving
he had him taken from the pile
and gave him a finishing shot
Once Schlage said
to one of those still living

```
                        Get up
                        I saw the prisoner trying to
                        then Schlage said
                        Stay there
                        and he shot him in the heart
                        and in both temples
                        But the man was still alive
                        I don't know how much more he got
                        first a shot in the neck
                        so that black blood came out
                        Schlage said
                        he has the lives of a cat
JUDGE:                  Defendant Schlage
                        What do you have to say
DEFENDANT 14:           To me it's a mystery
                        I can say absolutely nothing about it
```

CANTO SEVEN: THE BLACK WALL

III

```
WITNESS 7:              I once saw Schlage in the washroom
                        with a family of new arrivals
                        The man had to squat down
                        and Schlage shot him in the head
                        Next it was the child's turn
                        and then the wife
                        He had to shoot the child several times
                        It screamed and was not killed right away
DEFENCE COUNSEL:        Why did he do the shooting
                        in the washroom if the execution wall
                        was right next door
WITNESS 7:              Lesser shootings
                        were often performed in the washroom
                        for the sake of convenience
                        Then the shower was turned on
                        and they washed away the blood
```

DEFENCE COUNSEL:	What did the washroom look like
WITNESS 7:	It was a small room
	with a window covered by a blanket
	The lower half of the wall was tarred over
	the upper half painted white
	There were large black pipes in the corners
	A perforated shower pipe
	ran down the middle of the room
	about 6 feet off the ground
JUDGE:	Defendant Schlage
	do you still maintain
	that you shot no one
DEFENDANT 14:	I absolutely deny the charges
	levelled against me
	In no case did I take part
	in the executions
WITNESS 7:	They also brought to the washroom
	the bodies whose flesh had been carved away
JUDGE:	What do you mean by that
WITNESS 7:	In the summer of 1944 I saw
	the first of these mutilated bodies
	A man was unloaded
	who had attracted my notice
	while he undressed for the execution
	He was a giant
	Then I saw him lying in the washroom
	There were men dressed in white
	they had surgeon's instruments
	Flesh was cut
	from his stomach
	At first we believed
	he had swallowed something
	and they were pulling it out again
	but then it happened more often
	that flesh was taken from the bodies
	Later it happened mainly
	to the stronger women
WITNESS 3:	Once we had to carry away
	the bodies of 70 women

Their breasts had been removed
and deep cuts had been made
from their abdomens and thighs
First aid men were loading
containers of human flesh
onto a motorcycle with side-car
We had to hide the bodies
on the cart with boards

FEMALE WITNESS 4: In Experimental Block Ten
I saw the bodies below in the yard
through a gap in the window covering
We heard a drone
It was a swarm of flies
The ground in the yard was full of blood
And then I saw
the hangmen smoking and laughing
as they walked across the yard
She points to the Defendants

DEFENCE COUNSEL: We cannot let this gross insult
to our clients go unchallenged
Please enter this on the record
*The Defendants utter their
indignation*

Canto Eight: PHENOL

I

WITNESS 8:	I accuse Sanitary Inspector Klehr
	of the unauthorised murder
	of thousands of prisoners
	by injecting phenol into the heart
DEFENDANT 9:	This is slander
	Only in one case
	did I supervise any such operation
	and even then I did it
	entirely against my will
WITNESS 8:	Every day at least 30 prisoners
	were killed in the hospital
	Sometimes it was as many as 200
JUDGE:	Where were the injections given
WITNESS 8:	In the Injection Block
	That was Block Twenty
JUDGE:	Where was Block Twenty
WITNESS 8:	On the right in the middle row of blocks
	opposite the prisoners' infirmary
	in Block Twenty-One
	As the prisoner in charge
	I had to lead selected cases
	across the yard
	to the Injection Block
JUDGE:	Was the yard shut off
WITNESS 8:	Only by three low iron gates
JUDGE:	What was the condition
	of the prisoners who were taken
WITNESS 8:	Those who could walk
	went in their shirts or half naked
	across the yard
	They held their blankets

141

	and wooden shoes over their heads
	Many of them had to be helped or carried
	They entered Block Twenty
	by the side door
JUDGE:	In what room
	were the injections given
WITNESS 8:	In Room One
	That was the doctor's room
	at the end of the passage
JUDGE:	Where did the prisoners wait
WITNESS 8:	They had to wait in the corridor
	The severely ill lay on the ground
	They went into the doctor's room in pairs
	Doctor Entress
	gave Klehr a third of the patients
	This wasn't enough for him
	When the doctor was gone
	Klehr undertook additional separations
JUDGE:	Did you see this yourself
WITNESS 8:	Yes I saw it myself
	Klehr loved round numbers
	If the number of victims didn't satisfy him
	he went collecting the missing victims
	in the sickrooms
	He looked at the fever charts
	which on his orders had to be filled out
	with absolute precision
	and then made his choice
JUDGE:	What kind of round numbers
	did Klehr like
WITNESS 8:	He would change 23 to 30
	and 36 to 40
	and so on
	He ordered the ones
	he had selected
	to follow him
JUDGE:	How did he order them
WITNESS 8:	You
	you

142

	you
	and you
DEFENDANT 9:	Your Honour
	This statement is untrue
	I had no authority to select them
JUDGE:	What did you do then
DEFENDANT 9:	I only had to make sure
	the right prisoners came over
JUDGE:	And what did you have to do
	with giving the injections
DEFENDANT 9:	I'd like to know that myself
	I just stood around
	The treatments were administered
	by the prisoners in charge
	I stayed away from it
	they were contaminated
	I didn't even want them to breathe on me
JUDGE:	What were your duties
	as Sanitary Officer
DEFENDANT 9:	I was responsible
	a) for order and cleanliness
	b) for registration
	c) for the prisoners' food
JUDGE:	What kind of food
DEFENDANT 9:	Milk soup was prepared
	in the dietary kitchen
	for post-operative patients
JUDGE:	How many patients
	were there in the infirmary
DEFENDANT 9:	It ran from 500 to 600
JUDGE:	How were they lodged
DEFENDANT 9:	They lay on three-tiered bunks
JUDGE:	How did you register the patients
DEFENDANT 9:	Every case of illness
	was filed on a card
	Furthermore we also registered
	and separated
	those who were on sick parade
JUDGE:	What do you mean sick parade

DEFENDANT 9:	Prisoners
	whose state of health was critical
JUDGE:	How was the separation performed
DEFENDANT 9:	The camp physician looked at the prisoner
	and the diagnosis on the record card
	If he did not return the card
	but gave it to the clerk
	it meant that this patient had been chosen
	for the injections
JUDGE:	What happened then
DEFENDANT 9:	The cards were piled on the table
	and processed
JUDGE:	What do you mean processed
DEFENDANT 9:	The clerk had to prepare a list
	from the record cards
	The list was delivered to the Sanitary Officer
	We had to lead the patients off
	according to this list
WITNESS 8:	On Christmas Eve of 1942
	Klehr came into the sickroom
	and said
	Today I am the Camp Doctor
	I'm taking sick parade
	With the end of his pipe
	he pointed to 40 of them
	and sent them to the Injection Block
	After Christmas
	extra rations were supplied
	to Sanitary Officer Klehr
	I saw the orders
	They read
	For the special detail
	carried out on 24.12.1942
	you are hereby supplied
	with a half-pint of liquor
	5 cigarettes and 4 ounces of sausage
DEFENDANT 9:	But that's ridiculous
	I was on home leave over Christmas
	My wife can testify to that

144

JUDGE:	Defendant Klehr Do you wish to maintain that you selected no prisoners and took no part in the phenol killings
DEFENDANT 9:	I had only been given instructions to supervise
JUDGE:	Did you find these instructions reasonable
DEFENDANT 9:	I found it astonishing when I first heard that patients were being injected by the prisoners in charge But then I understood that they were incurable and a danger to the entire camp
JUDGE:	How were the injections given
DEFENDANT 9:	The prisoner in charge Peter Werl and someone named Felix from the ambulance block administered the injections At first they were given in the veins of the arm But the veins were hard to hit because of malnutrition That is why the phenol was later injected directly into the heart Before the syringe was even empty the man was dead
JUDGE:	Did you never refuse to take part in this treatment
DEFENDANT :	I would have been put against the wall
JUDGE:	Did you never express your objections to the physician
DEFENDANT 9:	I did so many times But I was only told that I must do my duty
JUDGE:	Couldn't you have been transferred to other duties
DEFENDANT 9:	Your Honour

F

	We were all in a straitjacket
	We were just as much numbers
	as the prisoners
	You weren't really human
	unless you were highly educated
	How could we dare
	to question anything
JUDGE:	Were you yourself never forced
	to give an injection
DEFENDANT 9:	Once when I was complaining
	the physician said to me
	In the future you will do this yourself
JUDGE:	And you then took charge
	of separating and killing
DEFENDANT 9:	In a few cases yes
	when I was compelled
JUDGE:	How often did you have to give the injections
DEFENDANT 9:	Usually twice a week
	to about 12 or 15 patients
	But I was only there 2 or 3 months
JUDGE:	That means at least 200 dead
DEFENDANT 9:	It could have been 250 or 300
	I don't know exactly
	It was an order
	I couldn't do anything about it
WITNESS 8:	Sanitary Officer Klehr
	was involved in the killing
	of at least 16,000 prisoners
DEFENDANT 9:	That's too much
	everyone has a breaking point
	I'm supposed to have killed 16,000 people
	There were only 16,000 in the entire camp
	No one would have been left
	but the military band
	The Defendants laugh

CANTO EIGHT: PHENOL

II

JUDGE:	Defendant Klehr
	How did you kill the prisoners
DEFENDANT 9:	Just as has been described
	with an injection of phenol
	in the heart muscle
	But I didn't do it alone
JUDGE:	Who was with you
DEFENDANT 9:	I can't remember that
WITNESS 9:	Scherpe and Hantl also
	took part in the killings
	with phenol
	They treated us differently than Klehr did
	They were polite to us
	and said Good Morning
	when they entered the block
	and when they left they said
	Good-bye
	We often saw Klehr become angry
	But Scherpe was quiet and obliging
	He had a pleasant way
	of treating the men
	I never saw Scherpe
	beating or kicking people
	Those who came to him
	often trusted him and believed
	they would only be treated
	for their illness
JUDGE:	You were one of the doctors
	among the prisoners
	Can you tell us
	how the phenol injections began
WITNESS 9:	It was the Camp Physician Dr. Entress
	who began the use of injections
	At first he did it with benzine
	but this soon became impractical

	because it turned out that death
	would not take place
	for three quarters of an hour
	They looked for a quicker means
	The second substance used was hydrogen
	Then came phenol
JUDGE:	Who did you see present
	at these injections
WITNESS 9:	At first Dr. Entress himself
	Then Scherpe and Hantl
	Hantl rarely performed the killing
	We considered him a decent man
JUDGE:	Did you see Klehr
	do the killing
WITNESS 9:	I didn't see it myself
	The two prisoners Schwarz and Gebhard
	who had to hold the patients fast
	during the injections
	told me about it
	But we didn't waste
	much time on it
	It was such an everyday occurrence
DEFENCE COUNSEL:	The witness has given other names
	for the prisoners in charge
	Weren't they named Werl and Felix
WITNESS 9:	There were many prisoners
	who had to perform this duty
DEFENCE COUNSEL:	Didn't the prisoners
	also do the killing
WITNESS 9:	At first yes
	they were forced to
DEFENCE COUNSEL:	Then the prisoners
	were killed by their own people
PROSECUTOR:	We protest
	against this stratagem of the Defence
	to reproach the prisoners for actions
	they had to carry out
	under threat of life or death
DEFENCE COUNSEL:	The personnel of the camp

148

	worked under the same threat
PROSECUTOR:	In no case is it known
	that anything ever happened
	to those who refused
	to co-operate with the killing
DEFENCE COUNSEL:	According to penal law
	an inferior is only responsible
	if it has been made known to him
	that the order of his superior
	concerns an action
	which constitutes a civil or military crime
	Our clients acted in the best of faith
	basing their actions on their unconditional
	duty of obedience
	With their oath of allegiance
	even unto death
	they all bowed down
	before the goals determined
	by the then existing national government
	just as the administration
	the law courts and the army had done
PROSECUTOR:	We repeat that every one
	of the Defendants
	who was acquainted
	with the criminal aim of the order
	had the possibility
	of obtaining a transfer
	We know the reasons
	why they did not do so
	On the front
	they might have found
	their own lives in danger
	so they remained in the camp
	where they had only unarmed opponents
	to deal with
JUDGE:	We summon as witness
	one of the camp doctors
	who issued the orders
	at that time

	Did the witness have any contact
	in his duties with Defendants
	Klehr Scherpe and Hantl
WITNESS 2:	I did not come into contact
	with these gentlemen
JUDGE:	Weren't you their superior
WITNESS 2:	The superior was actually
	the Camp Physician
	I was only in charge of office work
JUDGE:	What was your position
	when you were summoned to the camp
WITNESS 2:	I was a university professor
JUDGE:	And with your high degree
	of specialised training
	you had only office work
	to perform
WITNESS 2:	For a time
	I was also active
	in pathology
JUDGE:	Weren't you also required
	to choose prisoners for Defendant Klehr
WITNESS 2:	I refused to do that
JUDGE:	Were you never present at the separations
WITNESS 2:	Only as assistant to the Camp Physician
PROSECUTOR:	Is the witness aware
	that extra rations
	were awarded to those
	who were involved in certain actions
WITNESS 2:	I find it humanly comprehensible
	that rations of liquor and cigarettes
	should be granted
	for extra labour
	It was wartime
	and liquor and cigarettes were scarce
	everyone was after them
	You saved up your coupons
	and then you went along
	with your bottle to get some
PROSECUTOR:	You did this also

WITNESS 2:	Yes
	Everyone did
PROSECUTOR:	How were you connected
	with the separations
DEFENCE COUNSEL:	We object to this question
	The witness has already
	atoned for his crime
	and this trial can not
	hold him in double jeopardy
WITNESS 2:	Even today I still consider myself
	as innocent
	Only the sick were chosen
	who in any case could not live much longer
PROSECUTOR:	Herr Witness
	Did you with your medical education
	see no other solution
WITNESS 2:	Not in the conditions that then existed
	Thousands of our own soldiers
	were dying on the front
	and men were suffering
	in the bombed-out cities
PROSECUTOR:	But this was a case of people
	with no guilt of their own
	who had been imprisoned
	and slaughtered
	You must have been
	aware of this
WITNESS 2:	I could do nothing about it
	Right after my arrival
	the troop physician said to me
	We are situated here
	on the arsehole of the world
	and we must minister to it
PROSECUTOR:	Were you present at the injections
WITNESS 2:	Yes
	I had to go sometimes
PROSECUTOR:	What did you see there
WITNESS 2:	Klehr put on a doctor's smock
	and said to a girl

	you have heart trouble
	you must have an injection
	Then came the blow
	and I ran away
PROSECUTOR:	Was Klehr alone
WITNESS 2:	Yes
PROSECUTOR:	Wasn't the woman held down
WITNESS 2:	No
PROSECUTOR:	Is the witness aware
	that the court is in possession
	of the diary you kept while in camp
	I am now reading
	Today there was roast rabbit for lunch
	a big thick joint
	with meal dumplings and red cabbage
	Then it says
	6 women finished off by Klehr
WITNESS 2:	I must have heard that
PROSECUTOR:	I'm still reading
	Beautiful weather
	Took a bicycle ride
	Then
	Attended 11 executions
	3 women who begged for their lives
	Living flesh
	removed
	from the liver spleen and pancreas
	What does that mean
WITNESS 2:	I was under orders
	to carry out autopsies
	This work was performed
	only in the interest of science
	I had nothing to do with the killings
PROSECUTOR:	The men whose flesh you removed
	Did you designate them
	before you killed them
DEFENCE COUNSEL:	We object
	and once again call the court's attention
	to the fact that the witness

152

	has already served his sentence
PROSECUTOR:	Would the witness
	tell us why human flesh
	was used in these experiments
WITNESS 2:	Because the guards
	ate up the beef and horseflesh
	that we had been given
	for this purpose
JUDGE:	Where did you keep
	the phenol which was used
	for these injections
WITNESS 3:	The phenol was kept in the pharmacy
JUDGE:	Where was the pharmacy
WITNESS 3:	In the service buildings outside the camp
JUDGE:	Who was in charge of the pharmacy
WITNESS 3:	Dr. Capesius
JUDGE:	Who picked up the phenol
WITNESS 3:	The order form
	which had been filled out by Klehr
	was delivered by a messenger
	from the hospital department
	to Dr. Capesius in the pharmacy
	This messenger received the phenol
JUDGE:	Defendant Capesius
	what can you tell us about this
DEFENDANT 3:	I know nothing
	about any such orders
JUDGE:	Did you know
	that prisoners
	were being killed with phenol
DEFENDANT 3:	This is the first I have heard about it
JUDGE:	Did you keep phenol in the pharmacy
DEFENDANT 3:	I saw no great quantity of it
WITNESS 3:	The phenol was kept in a yellow chest
	in the corner of the consignment room
	Later there were great wicker bottles of it
	in the cellar
DEFENCE COUNSEL:	How do you know this
WITNESS 3:	I worked in the pharmacy

I saw the order forms
for the incoming supplies
They were filled out and signed
by Dr. Capesius
They were for clarified phenol
I can no longer remember
if the words PRO INJECTIONE
were written on them

JUDGE: What quantities were required
WITNESS 3: Small amounts at first
Later from 5 to 12 pounds a month
JUDGE: What medical uses
does phenol normally have
WITNESS 3: It is mixed with glycerine
to make eardrops
DEFENDANT 3: That is precisely how the phenol
in my care was used
JUDGE: 5 to 12 pounds of phenol a month
With that many eardrops
you could have treated the ears
of the entire German Army
The Defendants laugh
JUDGE: Defendant Capesius
do you still wish to maintain
that you saw no phenol in your pharmacy
DEFENDANT 3: I neither saw great quantities
of phenol
nor did I know that men
were being killed with it
JUDGE: To whom was the phenol delivered
WITNESS 3: To the doctor on duty
who then gave it to the first aid attendants
in the doctors' room

154

CANTO EIGHT: PHENOL

III

JUDGE:	What did the doctors' room look like
WITNESS 6:	The room was painted white
	The windows facing the yard
	were smeared over
JUDGE:	How was the room furnished
WITNESS 6:	There were one or two lockers and chests
	and then there was the curtain
	which divided the room in two
JUDGE:	What kind of curtain
WITNESS 6:	It was six feet high
	and reached almost to the ceiling
	The material was grey-green in colour
	Sitting in front of it was the clerk
	who had to cross off the names
	of the patients as they were led in
JUDGE:	What was behind the curtain
WITNESS 6:	A small table
	and a couple of stools
	There were hangers on the wall
	holding rubber aprons
	and pink rubber gloves
DEFENCE COUNSEL:	Herr Witness
	What is the source of your knowledge
WITNESS 6:	I belonged to the Corpse Bearers
	We were in the adjoining room
	The door was open
	and we could see everything
JUDGE:	What happened to the prisoners
	who had been selected for the injections
WITNESS 6:	They were led in pairs from the corridor
	into the doctors' room
	One of the two prisoners in charge
	who was standing behind the curtain
	brought the first prisoner in
	for his injection

	The other had to wait in front of the curtain
	In the meantime the second prisoner in charge
	had filled the syringe
JUDGE:	What kind of syringes were used
WITNESS 6:	At first for the intravenous injections
	they used 5 cubic centimetres
	Later
	when it was stuck directly into the heart
	they only needed
	2 centimetres
	The syringes were provided with needles
	that were used for lumbar punctures
	The needles were kept in a bag
JUDGE:	What kind of container was the phenol kept in
WITNESS 6:	It was a bottle
	that looked like a thermos
	The phenol came out
	in a small bowl
	The syringe was filled from this
	The liquid had a reddish tint
	because the needle was rarely changed
	and was bloody from the injections
JUDGE:	Did the patients know
	what was about to happen to them
WITNESS 6:	Most of them did not know
	They had been told
	they would receive a vaccination
JUDGE:	Did all the patients
	let it happen
WITNESS 6:	Most of them allowed it
	Many of them were extremely weak
JUDGE:	Who did you see
	giving the injections
WITNESS 6:	Klehr took the full syringe
	He had tied a rubber apron around him
	wore rubber gloves and high rubber boots
	The sleeves of his white smock
	were rolled up
JUDGE:	What happened to the prisoner next

WITNESS 6:	If he still had a shirt on
	he had to take it off
	and sit down on the footstool
	with his upper body uncovered
	He had to lift his left arm to the side
	and place his hand before his mouth
	This way his cry was smothered
	and the heart lay free
	The two prisoners in charge
	held him fast
JUDGE:	Who were the prisoners in charge
WITNESS 6:	Their names were Schwarz and Weiss
	Schwarz held the prisoners
	by the shoulders
	Weiss pressed his hand
	on his mouth
	and Klehr stuck the needle
	into the heart
JUDGE:	Was death immediate
WITNESS 6:	Most of them gave off a weak murmur
	as if they were breathing out
	Usually they were then dead
	But sometimes one would give off a rattle
	and end up on the washroom floor
	Some walked along with us
	in their last agony
	The others were carried off
	with a leather snare
	which we wrapped around their wrists
	It went quite quickly
	We often finished off
	2 or 3 patients a minute
JUDGE:	What happened to those
	who were still alive
WITNESS 6:	I remember a man
	who was big and strongly built
	He got up in the washroom
	with the injection in his heart
	I remember quite clearly how it was

There was a washtub
Opposite the washtub a bench
The man supported himself
on the washtub and the bench
and raised himself high
Then Klehr went to him
and gave him a second injection
Many others were only unconscious
because the injection
had not entered their heart
and the phenol had gone into the lungs
Klehr always came
into the washroom afterwards
and looked at the bodies piled up in layers
If anyone was still alive
he gave them a shot in the neck
For others he would say
he'll breathe it out in the crematorium

JUDGE: Did it happen that the living
                were sent off with the dead
WITNESS 6:   It happened
JUDGE: And they were burned alive
WITNESS 6:   Yes
                Or beaten to death with a shovel
                in front of the ovens
JUDGE: Did it never happen
                that prisoners struggled
WITNESS 6:   Once there was a scream
                and I saw two prisoners
                sitting on a half-naked man smeared with blood
                The head of the man was beaten in
                A poker lay on the ground
                Klehr stood opposite
                the needle in his hand
                Klehr kneeled on the man
                who was still kicking violently
                and stuck the needle in
JUDGE: Defendant Klehr
                What do you have to say

	to these accusations
DEFENDANT 9:	I know nothing about the case
	you have mentioned
JUDGE:	Do you know the witness
DEFENDANT 9:	Your Honour
	you must understand
	that I do not know this witness at all
	I know all the other prisoners
	who served as Corpse Bearers
JUDGE:	Were there also children
	among those murdered
WITNESS 7:	On one occasion
	In the beginning of 1943
	over 100 children were killed at once
JUDGE:	Who performed the executions
WITNESS 7:	The executions were performed
	by Hantl and Scherpe
JUDGE:	Herr Witness
	Can you tell us
	the precise number of murdered children
WITNESS 7:	There were 119
JUDGE:	Do you know the precise date
WITNESS 7:	It was the 23rd of February
DEFENCE COUNSEL:	How do you know that
WITNESS 7:	I was the clerk in charge
	and had to cross the children
	off the list
	They were between 13 and 17 years old
	Their parents had been shot previously
JUDGE:	Where did the children come from
WITNESS 7:	They came from the region of Zamosc
	which had been cleared of people
	to make room for German settlers
JUDGE:	Defendant Scherpe
	did you take part
	in this killing
DEFENDANT 10:	Your Honour
	I want to stress emphatically
	that I never killed a man

JUDGE:	Defendant Hantl What have you to say
DEFENDANT 11:	That we also accepted children is completely outside my experience Please Scherpe Have you or I ever had anything to do with children
JUDGE:	You are not allowed to ask questions of the Co-defendant We want to know from you if you took part in the injections
DEFENDANT 11:	I can only say that these accusations are invented
JUDGE:	Were you present at the injections
DEFENDANT 11:	At first I refused I said Is it absolutely necessary that I should bear this load of shit Then I was only there 8 or 10 times
JUDGE:	How many were killed each time
DEFENDANT 11:	It wasn't more than from 5 to 8 men Then it was over
WITNESS 7:	Hantl also helped to select the prisoners and to kill them There were injections given almost every day Only Sundays were excluded
DEFENDANT 11:	I have to laugh at that I have never heard such nonsense I can't possibly imagine why this witness should be pointing at me why I even helped him once when he committed sabotage
JUDGE:	What kind of sabotage
DEFENDANT 11:	He had stolen bed linen

160

	Anyway I did everything
	I could for the prisoners
	I smuggled them heaters
	and radishes
JUDGE:	And you weren't involved
	in the killing
DEFENDANT II:	No and no once again
JUDGE:	Herr Witness
	would you continue the story
	of the children
WITNESS 7:	The children were brought
	into the hospital yard
	They played there the entire morning
	They even had a ball
	The prisoners around knew
	what was going to happen to them
	They gave them the best of what they had
	The children were hungry and nervous
	They said that they would be beaten
	They asked us again and again
	Will they kill us
	In the afternoon Scherpe and Hantl came
	During the hours
	when the thing took place
	there was a deadly silence over Block Twenty
JUDGE:	Did the children realise
	what was in store for them
WITNESS 7:	The first ones screamed
	Then they were told
	they were going to be vaccinated
	So they went in quietly
	Only the last ones cried out again
	because their friends
	had not come back
	Two by two
	they were led into me
	and then they went behind the curtain
	one by one
	I heard only the blows

	when the heads and bodies
	of the children fell
	on the washroom floor
	Suddenly Scherpe ran out
	I heard him say
	I can't take any more
	He ran out somewhere
	and Hantl took care of the rest
	In the camp it was said
	that Scherpe had broken down
JUDGE:	Defendant Scherpe
	Have you anything to say
DEFENDANT 10:	The witness's report
	seems to me quite exaggerated
	I can in any case
	remember none
	of these events
PROSECUTOR:	Herr Witness
	How many people
	do you estimate
	were victims of the phenol injections
WITNESS 7:	According to camp documents
	and our personal reckoning
	it must have been about 30,000 men

162

Canto Nine: THE BUNKERBLOCK

I

WITNESS 8:	I was sentenced
	30 times to a cell so small
	that you couldn't lie down in it
	That meant
	hard labour all day
	and at night the cell
JUDGE:	What was the reason for this sentence
WITNESS 8:	I queued up twice at mess call
JUDGE:	Where were these cells located
WITNESS 8:	At the end of the cellar passageway
	in Block Eleven
	There were four such cells
JUDGE:	How large was a cell
WITNESS 8:	It was three feet square
	and slightly over six feet high
JUDGE:	Did it have a window
WITNESS 8:	No
	There was only an airhole high up in the corner.
	This was an inch and a half square
	It ran through the wall and was covered
	with a perforated metal disc
	on the outside
JUDGE:	And the door
WITNESS 8:	You had to creep in
	through a 2 foot hatch in the floor
	It was made of hard wood
	Behind it was an iron gate
	which was bolted
JUDGE:	Were you alone in the cell
WITNESS 8:	At first I was alone
	During the last week

	there were 4 of us
JUDGE:	Were there prisoners
	who stayed day and night
	in these cells
WITNESS 8:	That was the most frequent kind of sentence
	The system varied
	Some received something to eat
	every 2 or 3 days
	others received no food
	these were sentenced to death by hunger
	My friend Kurt Pachala
	died in the cell opposite me
	after 15 days
	eventually he ate his shoes
	He died on the 14th of January 1943
	I remember
	because it was my birthday
	Whoever was sentenced without food
	to these cells
	could shout and curse
	as much as he wanted
	The door was never opened
	In the first 5 nights
	he would shout loudly
	Then the hunger left off
	and the thirst took over
	He groaned
	prayed and beseeched
	He drank his urine
	and licked the walls
	The period of thirst
	lasted 13 days
	Then there was nothing more
	to be heard from his cell
	It was over 2 weeks
	before he was dead
	The bodies from these cells
	had to be prodded out with poles
JUDGE:	For what reason

	was this man sentenced
WITNESS 8:	He had attempted to escape
	Before he was taken to the cell
	he had to march before the prisoners
	at evening roll call
	He had a sign tied around him
	with the notice
	HURRAH I'VE COME HOME AGAIN
	He had to shout these words loudly
	and beat in time with a stick
	on a drum
	The prisoner Bruno Graf spent
	the longest time in one of these cells
	that I know about
	Criminal Officer Schlage
	sometimes stood before his door
	when he was shouting
	and I heard
	him call back
	why don't you die
	Graf died only after a month
JUDGE:	Defendant Schlage
	Did you let prisoners
	go hungry in the cells
DEFENDANT 14:	Your Honour
	I want to bring this to your attention
	I was only the jailer in Block Eleven
	I received my orders from my superiors
	and I had to obey them
	I am not the one
	who was responsible
	for what happened in the bunker
	it was the Criminal Officer
JUDGE:	Who gave the prisoners food
DEFENDANT 14:	The prisoners in charge did this
JUDGE:	Who opened the cells
DEFENDANT 14:	That was also the duty
	of the prisoners in charge
	We overseers

	were only supposed
	to open the outer gates
	when the Political Department came
JUDGE:	Did prisoners
	die in these cells
DEFENDANT 14:	Quite possibly
	I can't remember
JUDGE:	Who filled out the death register
	and listed the cause of death
DEFENDANT 14:	It was all done
	by the prisoners in charge
JUDGE:	And you had nothing to do with it
DEFENDANT 14:	I had my own people to look after
	in the cells upstairs
	Sometimes there were as many as 18 people
	I had to pay attention
	that they didn't commit suicide
	or some other foolery
JUDGE:	You mean to say
	that members of the camp guards
	were also imprisoned
DEFENDANT 14:	Naturally
	Justice
	was extended to all
	Every source of weakness
	had to be resisted

CANTO NINE: THE BUNKERBLOCK

II

JUDGE:	How large were the other cells
	in the Bunker
WITNESS 9:	These cells were
	about 9 by 8 feet in size
	Some of them were without light
	Others had window hatches above

	surrounded by a concrete frame
	Air came through only one opening
	high up in the wall
	This opening was not bigger
	than the palm of one's hand
JUDGE:	How many cells of this kind were there
WITNESS 9:	28 cells
JUDGE:	How many prisoners might be
	lodged in one cell
WITNESS 9:	In such a chamber
	there were sometimes
	as many as 40 prisoners
JUDGE:	How long did they have to stay there
WITNESS 9:	Often several weeks
	The prisoner Bogdan Glinski
	was there 17 weeks
	from November 13, 1942
	to March 9, 1943
JUDGE:	What furnishings did the cell have
WITNESS 9:	There was only a wooden chest
	and a tub
JUDGE:	For what reason
	were the prisoners confined there
WITNESS 9:	Here also the punishment
	could be for one night
	or for a longer time
	And here too imprisonment
	with denial of food was practised
JUDGE:	What sentence
	did you serve
WITNESS 9:	I spent two nights there
JUDGE:	Would you describe
	what happened during your sentence
WITNESS 9:	At 9 o'clock in the evening
	I had to sign in at Block Eleven
	along with 38 other prisoners
	The prisoner in charge gave the numbers
	to the Block Leader
	Then he led us to the cellar

where he locked us in Cell Twenty
At 10 o'clock the air
had already become thick
We stood closely pressed against each other
We could neither lie nor sit
Soon the temperature went so high
that we began to remove
our jackets and trousers
Towards midnight we could no longer stand up
Some sank down together
the others hung against each other
Most were agitated
and hit and cursed their companions
The smell given off
by the suffocating men
mingled with the stink from the tub
The weaker were crushed underfoot
the stronger battled
for a place at the door
where a trifle of air was coming through
We screamed and beat on the door
we forced ourselves against it
but it wouldn't give
The peephole outside was opened and shut
and the gaoler on duty
looked in at us
At 2 o'clock most of us
had lost consciousness
In the morning
after they opened the cells at 5 o'clock
they pulled us out
and lay us in the corridor
We were all naked
Of the 39 only 19 were still alive
and of these 19
6 were taken to the infirmary
where 4 died later

WITNESS 3:   I belonged to the Corpse Bearers Battalion
              which had to clear out the hunger cells

168

There were sometimes corpses
who had been bitten
on their thighs and buttocks
Those
who had been kept there longest
were sometimes without fingers
I asked Jakob
How can you stand this
And he said
Thank God
for what makes us hard
I'm alright
I eat the rations
of those inside
Their death doesn't touch me
any more than it touches
a stone in the wall

CANTO NINE: THE BUNKERBLOCK

III

WITNESS 6:
On the 3rd of September 1941
the first experiments
in mass slaughter
using Cyclone B gas
were carried out
in the Bunkerblock
First aid assistants and guards
led some 850 Soviet prisoners of war
as well as 220 sick patients
into Block Eleven
As soon as they had been locked
in the cells
the windows were filled over with earth
Then the gas was introduced
through the airholes
On the next day it was determined

that a few were still alive
After that they poured in
a larger dose of Cyclone B
On September 5 I was ordered
along with 20 prisoners
of the Bunker Company and a number
of nurses
into Block Eleven
We were told
that we were to take charge
of special work
and under pain of death
were not to report to anyone
what we saw there
We were promised larger rations
after the work
We received gas masks
and had to bring
the bodies from the cells
When we opened the doors
the tightly packed mass of bodies
fell against us
Although they were dead
they were still standing
Their faces had a bluish tinge
Many held tufts of hair
in their hands
It took all day long
to disentangle
the bodies from each other
and arrange them in layers
outside in the yard
In the evening the Commander
came with his staff
I heard the Commander say
Now I feel calmer
Now we have the gas
and all these blood baths
will be spared us

And even the victims
can be treated well
up to the last moment

Canto Ten: CYCLONE B

I

WITNESS 3: During the summer and autumn of 1941
I worked in the clothing chamber
There the dirty laundry
was disinfected of Cyclone B
Our superior was
Disinfektor Breitwieser

JUDGE: Herr Witness
Is the man you have named
present in this court

WITNESS 3: This is Breitwieser
*Defendant 17 nods benevolently
to the witness*

WITNESS 3: On the 3rd of September
I saw Breitwieser
in the company of Stark and other gentlemen
from the Political Department
go with gas masks and tins
to Block Eleven
Curfew was ordered right afterwards
The next morning Breitwieser
was in a bad mood
because something hadn't worked out
They hadn't got the insulation right
and the gassing
had to be done again
Two days later
the motor vans left the yard
full of corpses

JUDGE: What time did you see Breitwieser
going to Block Eleven
on the 3rd of September

WITNESS 3:	Around 9 in the evening
DEFENDANT 17:	That's impossible
	First I was never in the camp evenings
	and second no one could have
	recognised me at that time of year
	The whole countryside was covered over
	with fog from the river
JUDGE:	Did you know
	that on this evening
	prisoners in Block Eleven
	were to be gassed
DEFENDANT 17:	Yes
	It had filtered through
JUDGE:	Didn't you see
	the prisoners being driven
	into the Block
DEFENDANT 17:	Your Honour
	Our duties were over at 6 o'clock
	I was never in the camp after 6
JUDGE:	Didn't you have
	to distribute clothing after 6
	if new shipments arrived
DEFENDANT 17:	If new shipments came in after 6
	the prisoners in charge took the key
	to the clothing room
	and distributed garments
JUDGE:	What was your job
	as Disinfektor
DEFENDANT 17:	If I may be permitted to say this
	It was my job to give the instructions
JUDGE:	Were you trained
	for this position
DEFENDANT 17:	I was assigned in the summer of 1941
	along with 10 or 15 others
	to the battle against vermin
	There were two gentlemen
	from the Degesch Company
	who delivered the gas
	They instructed us

173

	in the handling of the gas
	and of the gas masks
	which were equipped
	with special attachments
JUDGE:	How was the gas packed
DEFENDANT 17:	It was in one pound tins
	They looked like coffee tins
	At first they had cardboard lids
	they were always light and moist and grey
	Later they had metal stoppers
JUDGE:	What did the contents look like
DEFENDANT 17:	It was a grainlike crumbling mass
	It's hard to say
	Like starch
	Bluish white
JUDGE:	Did you know
	its composition
DEFENDANT 17:	It was a stable compound
	of cyanide and hydrogen
	As soon as the crumbs were exposed
	to the air
	prussic acid gas escaped
JUDGE:	Tell us about your work with the gas
DEFENDANT 17:	Prisoners had to leave their clothing
	hanging in the chamber
	Then I together with another Disinfektor
	introduced the gas
	After 24 hours we brought
	the stuff out again
	and new ones took their place
	and so on
	We also had to disinfect
	the quarters
	After the windows had been plastered over
	the tins were opened with hammers and chisels
	and a rubber covering
	was placed over the contents
	because the gas was already escaping
	and at first we had to open

	several tins
	When everything was ready
	the gas was scattered
JUDGE:	Was an irritant mixed in with the gas
	as a warning to the workers
DEFENDANT 17:	No
	Cyclone B worked very quickly
	I remember
	how Unterscharfuhrer Theurer
	once entered a house
	that had already been disinfected
	In the evening the ground floor
	had been aired out
	and the next morning Theurer wanted
	to open the windows on the first floor
	He must have inhaled a whiff
	of what was left
	he fell right over and rolled
	unconscious down the stairs
	until he reached the fresh air again
	If he had fallen the other way
	he wouldn't have come out of it
PROSECUTOR:	Weren't you
	with your specialised knowledge
	consulted
	when they began the killings
	with Cyclone B
DEFENDANT 17:	I am telling you
	nothing but the truth
	I couldn't stand the gas
	I got stomach ulcers
	and I begged to be transferred
PROSECUTOR:	Were you transferred
DEFENDANT 17:	Not immediately
PROSECUTOR:	When was it
DEFENDANT 17:	I can no longer remember
PROSECUTOR:	You were transferred in April 1944
	Until then you continued to be promoted
	First you were made a Squad Leader

and then you were promoted
to Unterscharfuhrer

DEFENCE COUNSEL: We object
to this imputation
That members of the camp staff
rose in the ranks
is solely and entirely an official matter
and in no way indicates their complicity
*Agreement from the side of the
Defendants*

CANTO TEN: CYCLONE B

II

JUDGE: Herr Witness
Where was the gas kept

WITNESS 6: It was packed in crates
in the cellar of the pharmacy

JUDGE: Defendant Capesius
Did you as Head Pharmacist know
that Cyclone B was being stored there

DEFENDANT 3: The witness
has surely fallen victim to some confusion
those crates in the cellar
contained
Ovaltine
It was a shipment
from the Swiss Red Cross

WITNESS 6: I saw the crates with Ovaltine
and I saw the crates with Cyclone B
and I also saw the trunks
in which Dr. Capesius kept
jewellery and the gold from dental work

DEFENDANT 6: These are inventions

WITNESS 6: Where did the money come from
that Defendant Capesius used

	right after the war
	to set up his own pharmacy
	and a beauty salon
	Let Capesius keep you beautiful
	that's how the advertisements went
DEFENDANT 3:	I got the money on loan
WITNESS 6:	And where did the money come from
	that was offered to me
	and the other witnesses
	if only we would swear
	that Capesius was solely
	in charge of the camp pharmacy
	and had no responsibility
	for the phenol and the Cyclone B
DEFENDANT 3:	I know nothing about this
PROSECUTOR:	Who offered you this bribe
WITNESS 6:	It came anonymously
PROSECUTOR:	Do you know
	if one of the legal protection groups
	for the ex-guards
	was behind it
WITNESS 6:	I know nothing about it
	But I would like to acquaint
	the court with the following letter
	which I received
	The stationery is headed
	Workers' Society for Justice and Freedom
	It reads
	Soon you will drop out of the picture
	You will die an excruciating death
	Our members are watching you constantly
	You can choose now
	Life or death
JUDGE:	The court will investigate
	the source of this letter
DEFENCE COUNSEL:	Herr Witness
	can you tell us
	what was written on the crates
WITNESS 6:	It said

	Danger poison gas
	and then there was the warning sign
	of the death's head
DEFENCE COUNSEL:	Did you see the contents
	of these crates
WITNESS 6:	I saw opened crates
	with the tins inside
DEFENCE COUNSEL:	What was on the labels
WITNESS 6:	Poison gas Cyclone B
DEFENCE COUNSEL:	Did it say anything else
WITNESS 6:	It said
	Caution odourless gas
	Only to be opened by experienced personnel
JUDGE:	Did you see
	these tins
	transported to the gas chambers
WITNESS 6:	We had to load such crates
	into the first aid van
	which came to fetch them
JUDGE:	Who was in the van
WITNESS 6:	I saw Dr. Frank and Dr. Schatz there
	and also Dr. Capesius
	They had their gas masks with them
	Dr. Schatz even had a steel helmet on
	I remember that
	because one of his colleagues said
	you look like a little mushroom
DEFENCE COUNSEL:	We should like to remind the court
	that during a certain period of the war
	the wearing of gas masks was compulsory
	Neither the departure
	nor the return of our clients
	with gas masks
	indicates their actual destination
JUDGE:	Did the witness
	see delivery forms
	for the gas
WITNESS 6:	I often had to bring these forms
	to the administrative offices

	They were for continually greater quantities
	which then had to be stored
	in the old theatre building
	outside the camp
	The sender was given as
	The German Pest Control Company
JUDGE:	How were the shipments delivered
WITNESS 6:	Sometimes they came
	directly from the factory in motor vans
	sometimes by railway
	on army bills of lading
JUDGE:	Can you remember
	the quantities
WITNESS 6:	There were from 14 to 20 crates
	in a delivery
JUDGE:	How often do you estimate
	these shipments arrived
WITNESS 6:	At least once a week
	In 1944 more often
	Then they even used the cars
	from the camp motor pool
JUDGE:	How many tins
	were contained in a crate
WITNESS 6:	Every crate contained
	30 one pound tins
JUDGE:	Did you see price tags
WITNESS 6:	The price was 2½ Reichmarks a pound
JUDGE:	How many tins were necessary
	for a gassing
WITNESS 6:	For 2,000 men in a chamber
	16 tins were needed
JUDGE:	At 2½ marks a pound
	that makes 40 marks

CANTO TEN: CYCLONE B

III

JUDGE:	Defendant Mulka
	As Chief Officer you were in charge
	of the motor pool
	Did you have to write out orders for this
DEFENDANT I:	I wrote no such orders
	I had nothing to do with it
JUDGE:	Defendant Mulka
	Did you know the meaning of
	Material Requirements for Evacuees
DEFENDANT I:	No
JUDGE:	Defendant Mulka
	the court is in possession
	of transfer orders for shipments
	of material for evacuees
	these documents were signed by you
DEFENDANT I:	It could be
	that I had to initial
	one order or another from time to time
JUDGE:	Didn't you discover
	that the material for evacuees
	consisted of Cyclone B gas
DEFENDANT I:	As I have already stated
	I did not know this
JUDGE:	Who was in charge
	of specifying the requirements
	for this material
DEFENDANT I:	They came in by teletype
	and were transmitted
	to the Commander or the Security Officer
	From there they reached
	the head of the motor pool
JUDGE:	Wasn't he subordinate to you
DEFENDANT I:	Only formally
JUDGE:	Wasn't it in your interest
	to learn what use was being made

	of the motor pool vehicles
DEFENDANT I:	I already knew
	that they were necessary
	for loading goods
JUDGE:	Were prisoners also transported
	in the vans
DEFENDANT I:	I know nothing about it
	In my time the prisoners
	went on foot
JUDGE:	Defendant Mulka
	we have in our hands a document
	which states
	that for the pressing necessity
	of completing the new crematoria
	it would be necessary
	for the prisoners charged with the labour
	to work on Sundays also
	This document is signed by yourself
DEFENDANT I:	Yes
	I may well have dictated that
JUDGE:	Do you still wish to state
	that you knew nothing
	about the mass murders
DEFENDANT I:	All of my statements
	coincide with the truth
JUDGE:	We have summoned as witness
	the workshop foreman in charge
	of the camp motor pool at that time
	Herr Witness
	how many vans were there
WITNESS I:	The van squadron
	consisted of 10 heavy vehicles
JUDGE:	From whom did you receive duty orders
WITNESS I:	From the chief of the motor pool
JUDGE:	Who signed the orders
WITNESS I:	I don't know
JUDGE:	Would the witness tell us
	why the cars were supplied
WITNESS I:	For carrying freight

	and the transport of prisoners
JUDGE:	Where were the prisoners transported
WITNESS 1:	I can't tell you this with any certainty
JUDGE:	Were you present on these trips
WITNESS 1:	I just had to go along sometimes as a substitute
JUDGE:	Where did you normally drive to
WITNESS 1:	Just into the camp whenever anyone wanted something or whatever it was
JUDGE:	And where did you drive with the prisoners
WITNESS 1:	To the end of the camp where a birchwood stood There the people were unloaded
JUDGE:	Where did the people go
WITNESS 1:	Inside a house Then I saw nothing more
JUDGE:	What happened to the prisoners
WITNESS 1:	I don't know I wasn't there
JUDGE:	Didn't you find out what happened to them
WITNESS 1:	They were burnt to cinders then and there

Canto Eleven: THE FIRE-OVENS

I

JUDGE:	Herr Witness You were one of the drivers of the first aid vans which were used to transport the prussic acid compound Cyclone B to the gas chambers
WITNESS 2:	I was assigned to the camp as a tractor driver and later I also had to serve as a van driver
JUDGE:	What were your duties
WITNESS 2:	I had to pick up the first aid assistants and doctors
JUDGE:	Who were the doctors
WITNESS 2:	I can't remember that
JUDGE:	Where did you have to take the doctors and first aid assistants
WITNESS 2:	From the old camp to the ramp of the barracks camp
JUDGE:	When did you drive
WITNESS 2:	When shipments came in
JUDGE:	How were the shipments announced
WITNESS 2:	By a siren
JUDGE:	Where did you drive from the ramp
WITNESS 2:	To the crematoria
JUDGE:	Did the doctors come with you
WITNESS 2:	Yes
JUDGE:	What did the doctors do there
WITNESS 2:	The doctors just sat in the vans or stood outside The first aid assistants

	had to take care of things
JUDGE:	What things
WITNESS 2:	The gassings
JUDGE:	On your arrival
	were the men already
	in the gas chambers
WITNESS 2:	They were still undressing
JUDGE:	Were there no disturbances
WITNESS 2:	While I was there
	everything always went very peacefully
JUDGE:	What could you see
	of the actual gassing
WITNESS 2:	When the prisoners had been led
	into the chambers
	the first aid officers went
	to the hatches
	put on their gas masks
	and emptied the tins
JUDGE:	Where were the hatches
WITNESS 2:	There was an oblique projection
	over the underground room
	with four hatches
JUDGE:	How many tins were emptied
WITNESS 2:	3 or 4 in each hatch
JUDGE:	How long did it last
WITNESS 2:	About a minute
JUDGE:	Didn't the people scream
WITNESS 2:	If someone noticed
	what was going on
	you might well hear a scream
PROSECUTOR:	Herr Witness
	How far away did your van
	stand from the gas chamber
WITNESS 2:	It was on the road
	about 60 feet away
PROSECUTOR:	And could you hear
	what was going on
	in the chamber below
WITNESS 2:	Sometimes I got out to wait

PROSECUTOR:	What did you do there
WITNESS 2:	Nothing I smoked a cigarette
PROSECUTOR:	Did you go up to the hatches above the gas chamber
WITNESS 2:	Sometimes I went up and down to stretch my legs
PROSECUTOR:	What did you hear
WITNESS 2:	If the hatch lid was lifted up I could hear a drone from below as though many people were underneath the ground
PROSECUTOR:	And what did you do then
WITNESS 2:	The hatch was shut again and I had to drive back
JUDGE:	Herr Witness You were physician to the prisoners in the Special Corps that was assigned to crematorium service How many prisoners were there in this corps
WITNESS 7:	860 men in all Every few months the Special Corps was eliminated and substituted with new personnel
JUDGE:	Whom did you work under
WITNESS 7:	Dr. Mengele
JUDGE:	Can the witness tell us how the delivery to the gas chambers took place
WITNESS 7:	The locomotive whistle before the entrance gate was the signal that a new shipment was coming in This meant that in about one hour the ovens had to be fully usable The electric motors were switched on

	These drove the ventilators
	which brought the fire in the ovens
	to the necessary temperature
JUDGE:	Could you see the groups
	coming from the ramp
WITNESS 7:	From the window of my workroom
	I could look out over
	the upper part of the ramp
	and the road to the crematorium
	The people came in rows of five
	The vans were bringing in the ill
	The crematorium grounds
	were closed off by iron bars
	There were warning signs on the gate
	The Reception Corps had to remain behind
	and the Special Corps took over
	Only doctors and first aid assistants
	came inside
	as well as members of the Political Department
JUDGE:	Which of the defendants
	did you see there
WITNESS 7:	I saw Stark there and Hofmann
	also Kaduk and Baretzki
DEFENCE COUNSEL:	We call attention to the fact
	that our clients deny
	taking part in these proceedings
JUDGE:	Would the witness continue his report
WITNESS 7:	The men were tired and came
	slowly through the door
	The children held on to their mother's skirts
	Older men carried babes in arms
	or pushed baby carriages
	The road was strewn with black ashes
	At right and left there were a pair
	of water taps on the plots of grass
	The people often crowded around them
	and the Corps let them drink a little
	but soon drove them quickly on
	They had another 50 yards to go

186

	until they came to the stairway
	that led below to the undressing rooms
JUDGE:	What could be seen from the crematorium
WITNESS 7:	Only the building itself
	with its huge four-cornered chimney
	Beneath the ground one entered
	the gas chambers
	branching to the sides
	and parallel to them
	the undressing rooms
JUDGE:	Was the crematorium in open view
WITNESS 7:	It was surrounded by trees and hedges
	and lay about a hundred yards away
	from the edge of the camp
	Directly opposite was the outer fence
	with watchtowers
	There were open fields spread out beyond
JUDGE:	How large was the undressing room
WITNESS 7:	About 40 yards long
	12 or 15 steps led downwards
	It was almost 7 feet high
	In the middle stood a row of pillars
JUDGE:	How many people were led down
	at once
WITNESS 7:	Between 1,000 and 2,000
JUDGE:	Did the people know
	what was waiting for them
WITNESS 7:	Above the little stairway
	signs were mounted
	saying in several languages
	BATH AND DISINFECTION ROOM
	That sounded soothing
	and brought peace to many
	who were still distrustful
	I often saw men going happily below
	and women joking with their children
JUDGE:	Did panic never break out
	among so many people
	in so small a space

WITNESS 7:	Everything was quick and efficient
	The order to undress was given
	and while the people
	were still looking around helplessly
	the Special Corps helped them
	to take off their clothing
	On the sides were rows
	of numbered hooks
	and the people were repeatedly told
	that shoes and clothing
	should be tied together and hung up
	and that everyone should notice
	the number of his hook
	so that there would be
	no misunderstanding when they came
	back from the bath
	In the piercing light
	the people took their clothing off
	Men and women
	Old and young
	Children
JUDGE:	Did none of these people
	hurl themselves at their keepers
WITNESS 7:	Only once I heard
	one screaming
	They want to kill us
	But another immediately answered him
	That is unthinkable
	Something like that could never happen
	Hold your peace
	And if children cried
	they were comforted by their parents
	and they joked and played with them
	as they carried them
	into the room next door
JUDGE:	Where was the entrance to this room
WITNESS 7:	At the end of the undresssing room
	It was a thick oaken door
	with a wheel

	for a handle
	to screw it shut
JUDGE:	How long did the undressing take
WITNESS 7:	About 10 minutes
	Then everyone
	was pushed into the other room
JUDGE:	Did you never have to use force
WITNESS 7:	The people from the Special Corps shouted
	Hurry hurry
	the water's getting cold
	And it could also easily happen
	that some of the people
	were threatened and beaten
	or one of the guards fired a shot
JUDGE:	Was the other room
	disguised as a shower room
WITNESS 7:	No
	There was nothing
JUDGE:	How large was this room
WITNESS 7:	Smaller than the undressing room
	Something more than 30 yards long
JUDGE:	When 1,000 or more people
	were pushed into such a room
	surely there must have been an uprising
WITNESS 7:	By then it was too late
	The last one had been pushed in
	and the door was screwed shut
JUDGE:	Herr Witness
	How do you explain
	that these people let this
	happen to themselves
	When they saw this room
	surely they must have known
	that their end was at hand
WITNESS 7:	Not a single one came out
	who could have told them about it
JUDGE:	What did the people see in this room
WITNESS 7:	There were cement walls
	with a few ventilation flaps

	In the middle there were pillars
	and to the right and left of every pillar
	were two columns of perforated sheet-iron
	On the floor were exhaust gratings
	Here too strong light was burning
JUDGE:	Was there anything to be heard
	from these people
WITNESS 7:	They were screaming now
	and beating on the door
	but you couldn't hear very much
	There was such a buzzing
	from the oven chambers
JUDGE:	Could you see anything
	through the hatches in the door
WITNESS 7:	The people pushed against the door
	and climbed up on the columns
	Then came the suffocation
	as the gas was thrown in

CANTO ELEVEN: THE FIRE-OVENS

II

WITNESS 7:	The gas was thrown
	into the iron columns from above
	Inside the columns
	was a spiral channel
	in which the mass spread out
	In the damp hot air
	the gas expanded quickly
	and pressed through the openings
JUDGE:	How long did it take
	for the gas to work
WITNESS 7:	That depended on the quantity of gas
	Most often for reasons of economy
	enough was not thrown in
	so that it could take as long

	as 5 minutes to die
JUDGE:	What was the immediate effect of the gas
WITNESS 7:	It caused dizziness and severe vomiting
	and paralysed the breathing
JUDGE:	How long was the room full of gas
WITNESS 7:	20 minutes

                      Then the ventilation was turned on
and the gas pumped out
After half an hour the doors were opened
The gas was still present in small quantitites
Only among the corpses
This caused coughing and irritation
so that the people of the Removal Corps
had to wear gas masks

JUDGE: Did you see the room after it was opened

WITNESS 7:   Yes

                      The bodies lay pressed against each other
by the door and the columns
and of course there were infants
and children and sick people underneath
women above them
and on the very top the strongest men
It can be explained in this way
that the men trampled the others down
and climbed on top of each other
because at the beginning the gas
was always strongest at floor level
The people were tied in knots
clutching one another
Their skin was scratched
Many bled from the nose and mouth
Their faces were swollen
and blotched
The piles of people were slimy
with vomit
with dung urine and menstrual blood
The Removal Corps came with rubber hoses
and sprayed the bodies off
Then they were pulled into the goods lift

	and hauled to the crematorium
JUDGE:	How large was the lift
WITNESS 7:	There were 2 lifts

each holding 25 corpses
As soon as one was packed full
someone rang a bell
Above by the lifts
the Corpse Bearers Battalion
stood ready
They carried snares in their hands
which they fitted around the wrists
of the corpses
On a specially constructed track
the bodies were slid along to the ovens
The blood was washed away
with constantly flowing water
Before they were burnt
they were evaluated by the Special Corps
Every kind of jewellery
that was still on their persons
such as necklaces bracelets
rings and earrings
it all was taken
and their hair was cut
immediately gathered into bundles
and packed away in sacks
and finally they called in
the corps of teeth extractors
which had been assembled
from first class specialists
on Dr. Mengele's express orders
In their work with pliers and handspikes
they also wrenched out
along with the gold teeth and bridges
entire pieces of jawbone
And the pieces of bone with its clinging flesh
were melted away in an acid solution
100 men worked continually
before the ovens

in 2 shifts

JUDGE: How many ovens were there
in each crematorium

WITNESS 7: In both the large crematoria
Numbers II and III
there were 5 ovens each
Every oven had 3 cremation chambers
Besides crematoria II and III
there were also crematoria IV and V
at the end of the ramp
each of these contained 2 four-chambered ovens
These crematoria were about 800 yards away
behind the birchwood
At full output
there were 46 cremation chambers
going at once

JUDGE: How many bodies
did an oven chamber contain

WITNESS 7: The capacity of a chamber
was from 3 to 5 bodies
It very rarely happened
that all ovens were working at once
as they were often damaged
from overheating
The manufacturer of these ovens
the firm of Topf and Sons
as they have stated
in their patent specifications
filed after the war
improved their equipment
on the basis of the experience
they had gained

JUDGE: How long did cremation take
in one of these chambers

WITNESS 7: Approximately one hour
Then a new batch could be handled
In crematoria II and III
over 3,000 people were burnt
within a 24 hour period

If things overflowed
they also burned bodies in pits
which were dug
opposite the crematoria
These pits were about 30 yards long
and 6 yards deep
At the end of the pits
were overflow channels
for the fat
This was scooped out with cans
and poured over the bodies
to make them burn better
In the summer of 1944
when the cremations reached their height
as many as 20,000 men
were liquidated daily
Their ashes were carried away in vans
they were taken to the river a mile away
and dumped into the water there

JUDGE: How were the valuables
and the gold teeth dealt with

WITNESS I: When the clothing was collected
the money and jewellery were thrown
into a locked chest
The guards filled
their own pockets first
The shoes and clothing
which were still neatly laid out
where the prisoners themselves had left them
went to the State
where they were given
to those who had been bombed out
The gold teeth were melted down
I was called in as an investigating magistrate
because outgoing packages
which contained many pounds of gold
had been appropriated
I determined that this gold
had been taken from prisoners' teeth

194

	After I measured the weight
	of a single filling
	I came to the conclusion
	that thousands of men were necessary
	to yield a single lump

JUDGE: Then you mean a judge from outside
was called in at that time
to investigate events in the camp

WITNESS I: Here and there the concept
of a state based on justice
continued to survive
The Commander wanted to fight
the corruption in the camp
On my visit he complained to me
that his people were often not morally
suited to hard work
Then he led me through the crematoria
where he explained to me all the details
Inside the furnace rooms
everything was polished spic and span
There was no indication
that men were being cremated here
There was not a speck of dust
on the oven mountings
In the control room the guards
were seated half-drunk on benches
and in the washrooms were pretty girls
carefully chosen from among the prisoners
Over a cooking stove
they were baking potato pancakes for the men
who kept the girls as servants
When I examined the wardrobes of the men
it became clear
that these were laden with riches
As a judge I filed a charge for larceny
and some of them were arrested
and brought to trial

JUDGE: How was such a trial handled

WITNESS I: It was a show trial

	No arrests could be made
	among the higher-ups
	and no charge for multiple murder
	was possible in this case
JUDGE:	Did you as an investigating magistrate
	see no other possibility
	to make known your findings
WITNESS I:	Before what court of justice
	could I have filed a charge
	for the numberless dead
	and for the valuables confiscated
	by the highest authorities
	I could certainly initiate no proceedings
	against the highest government leadership
JUDGE:	Couldn't you intervene
	in some other way
WITNESS I:	I knew
	that no one would have believed me
	I might have been put to death
	or in the best of cases
	locked up as mentally disturbed
	I also thought of fleeing across the border
	but I doubted
	if people would believe me there
	and I asked myself what would happen
	if they did believe me
	and if I were obliged to testify
	against my own people
	and I could only think to myself
	that they would annihilate this people
	for its deeds
	So I stayed

CANTO ELEVEN: THE FIRE-OVENS

III

JUDGE:	There are reports of a rebellion by the Special Corps Would the witness tell us when this took place
WITNESS 3:	On October 6 1944 The Special Corps was to have been liquidated by the guards on this day
JUDGE:	Was this known to the Corps beforehand
WITNESS 3:	They all knew that they were supposed to be killed Long before they had already obtained boxes of explosives from prisoners who worked in the armament factory The plan was to disarm the guards to blow up the crematoria and to escape But the crematorium where the explosives were hidden was raided sooner than they had expected and they blew themselves up into the air There was still a battle but everyone was overpowered Many hundreds were made to lie down behind the birchwood They lay on their stomachs and the men from the Political Department shot them in the head
JUDGE:	Which of the Defendants took part
WITNESS 3:	Boger was the leader
JUDGE:	Was the crematorium

197

	destroyed by the explosion
WITNESS 3:	The detonation of 4 powder kegs
	caused the entire building to explode
	and burn down
JUDGE:	What happened to the other crematoria
WITNESS 3:	After a short time
	they were blown up
	by the camp personnel themselves
	as the front line was drawing closer
PROSECUTOR:	Does the witness believe
	it is possible that the Chief Officer
	was not informed of the proceedings
	in the crematoria
WITNESS 3:	I believe it is impossible
	These proceedings were known
	to every one of the 6,000 members
	of the camp personnel
	and everyone carried out in his own job
	what had to be carried out
	for the functioning of the whole
	Furthermore every train engineer
	every linesman
	every railway employee
	who had dealt with the transport of men
	knew what was happening in the camp
	Every telegraph girl and every stenographer
	who passed on the deportation orders
	knew about it
	Every single one
	of the hundreds of thousands
	of office workers
	who were concerned with the actions
	knew
	what they were about
DEFENCE COUNSEL:	We protest against these assertions
	which are directed from hatred
	No one can use hatred
	as a basis
	for pronouncing judgment

	on the particulars
	we have discussed
WITNESS 3:	I speak purged of hatred
	I have no wish for revenge
	against anyone
	I am indifferent
	to the individual defendants
	and offer only the consideration
	that they could not have
	performed their handiwork
	without the support
	of millions of others
DEFENCE COUNSEL:	Our discussion is only concerned
	with what can be attributed to our clients
	on the basis of evidence
	This kind of general reproach
	is trivial
	particularly reproaches
	against an entire nation
	which during the time under discussion
	was engaged
	in a hard and dedicated
	struggle
WITNESS 3:	I should like to be allowed
	to call attention
	to how thick the streets once were
	with spectators when we were driven
	out of our homes and loaded
	into the cattle cars
	In the last analysis
	the Defendants in this trial
	are here only as underlings
	Others more important
	than those
	standing before this court
	have never had to justify themselves
	Some we have met here
	as witnesses
	They live without shame

	They enjoy high office
	They multiply their possessions
	and continue those works
	for which the prisoners were formerly employed
PROSECUTOR:	Herr Witness
	What is your estimate
	of the number of those
	who were killed in the camps
WITNESS 3:	Of the 9 million 600 thousand people
	who lived in the regions
	their persecutors ruled over
	6 million have vanished
	and it may be presumed
	that the majority of them
	were deliberately annihilated
	Those who were not shot beaten
	tortured to death
	and gassed
	died from overwork
	hunger pestilence and misery
	In this camp alone
	over 3 million people
	were slaughtered
	But to calculate the overall total
	of unarmed victims
	in this war of extermination
	we must also include the 3 million
	Soviet prisoners of war
	who were shot and starved to death
	as well as the 10 million civilians
	who died in occupied lands.
DEFENCE COUNSEL:	Even if every one of us
	most deeply laments these victims
	it is nonetheless our duty here
	to counter the exaggerations
	and the muck-tossing
	we have been exposed to
	from a certain quarter
	Not even the total of 2 million dead

can be confirmed
in connection with this camp
Only the killing of a few hundred thousand
can be proved conclusively
The majority of the groups mentioned
migrated eastwards
and we can not count among the murdered
those who were seized and liquidated
as guerillas nor can we count
the deserters who fell in the enemy army
It has become only too clear
to us during this trial
what political purposes
have been furthered by the statements
which the witnesses
have had ample opportunity to devise
The Defendants laugh in agreement

PROSECUTOR: That represents a conscious
and deliberate disregard and offence
against those who died in the camp
and also against those who have survived
and have been ready to give testimony here
Such behaviour on the part of the Defence
obviously demonstrates the persistence
of that very sentiment
which inspired those actions
for which the Defendants
are here arraigned
This must be stated here
with all possible emphasis and clarity

DEFENCE COUNSEL: Who is this co-plaintiff
with his unsuitable clothing*
It is typical of Middle European manners
to appear in court in a closed gown

JUDGE: We must have order
Defendant Mulka
Don't you now want to tell us
what you knew and arranged

* The reference is to the gown worn by the attorney sent to the Auschwitz trials in Frankfurt from East Germany

	in connection with the annihilations
DEFENDANT I:	In connection with this I arranged nothing
JUDGE:	Have you learned nothing
	from these actions
DEFENDANT I:	Only towards the end of my service
	Today I can say
	that I was filled with abhorrence
JUDGE:	If you were filled with abhorrence
	why didn't you refuse
	to take part in it
DEFENDANT I:	I was an officer
	and I knew military law
PROSECUTOR:	You were no officer
DEFENDANT I:	Excuse me
	I was an officer
PROSECUTOR:	You were no officer
	You belonged
	to a uniformed murder battalion
DEFENDANT I:	My honour is being questioned
JUDGE:	Defendant Mulka
	We are dealing with murder
DEFENDANT I:	We were convinced
	that by obeying these orders
	we were working towards the attainment
	of a secret war objective
	Your Honour
	I was almost
	torn apart emotionally
	I became so ill from it
	that I had to be sent to the infirmary
	But I must emphasise
	that I saw everything only from outside
	and I held my hand free
	from the thing itself
	Your Honour
	I was opposed to the entire concern
	I was myself
	one of those persecuted by the system
JUDGE:	What happened to you then

202

DEFENDANT I: I was imprisoned
                because I made defeatist remarks
                For 3 months I sat in prison
                After my release
                I was caught in the enemy bombings
                At that time I could still save many
                when I did what an old soldier could
                to help with clearing out the bombsites
                My own son died
                Your Honour
                In this trial we should also
                not forget the millions
                who gave their lives for our country
                we should not forget
                what happened after the war
                and what is still being
                instigated against us
                We all
                I should like to emphasise again
                we did nothing but our duty
                even if it was often hard to do so
                even when we wanted to despair of it
                Today
                now that our nation
                has once again worked its way up
                to a leading position
                we should be concerned with other things
                than with recriminations
                These should long ago
                have been banished from the lawbooks
                by the Statute of Limitations
                    *Loud agreement from the side of the
                    Defendants*

203

APPENDIX

For the convenience of readers and repertory companies we list the names of the Defendants appearing in this play.

DEFENDANT 1:	Mulka
DEFENDANT 2:	Boger
DEFENDANT 3:	Dr. Capesius
DEFENDANT 4:	Dr. Frank
DEFENDANT 5:	Dr. Schatz
DEFENDANT 6:	Dr. Lucas
DEFENDANT 7:	Kaduk
DEFENDANT 8:	Hofmann
DEFENDANT 9:	Klehr
DEFENDANT 10:	Scherpe
DEFENDANT 11:	Hantl
DEFENDANT 12:	Stark
DEFENDANT 13:	Baretzki
DEFENDANT 14:	Schlage
DEFENDANT 15:	Bischof
DEFENDANT 16:	Broad
DEFENDANT 17:	Breitwieser
DEFENDANT 18:	Bednarek

FINAL REMARKS

For the completion and verification of my notes from the Frankfurt Auschwitz trial I have used articles published in a great many newspapers and magazines. Above all Bernd Naumann's reports in the *Frankfurter Allgemeine Zeitung* were of great service to me.

Of the voluminous literature which I studied I should like to emphasise the following titles:

Gerhard Schoenberner, *Der Gelbe Stern*. Berlin 1961.

Gerhard Schoenberner, *Wir haben es gesehen*, Hamburg, 1962.

Adler, Langbein, Lingens-Reiner, *Auschwitz, Zeugnisse und Berichte*, Frankfurt/M, 1962.

Gerald Reitlinger, *Die Endlösung*, Berlin, 1956.

Rudolf Höss, *Kommandant in Auschwitz*. Stuttgart 1958.

Jüdisches Historisches Institut Warschau, *Faschismus - Getto - Massenmord*, Dokumentation, Berlin 1961.

Muzeum w Oswiecimiu, *Hefte von Auschwitz*, 1959-62.

Elie A. Cohen, *Människor i Koncentrationsläger*, Stockholm 1957.

Peter Weiss, July 1965